"Get out of the car."

I stared at her.

"I said get out of the car!"

When I closed the door, she slid over into the driver's seat and cranked down the window. Rattlesnake venom would've been friendlier than the way she looked at me. The only thing I could think of to say was "How am I supposed to find Mrs. Haskell?"

"You're the one with all the ideas about how I should run my business," Ginny snapped while she revved the engine. "You figure it out."

The Olds squealed its tires as she headed out of the lot.

I suddenly felt light-headed, and the pain in my stomach eased back a couple of notches. Ginny Fistoulari, I thought. By damn. I know that woman.

Also by Reed Stephens
Published by Ballantine Books:

THE MAN WHO KILLED HIS BROTHER

THE MAN WHO RISKED HIS PARTNER

REED STEPHENS

BALLANTINE BOOKS • NEW YORK

Library of Congress Catalog Card Number: 84-90815

ISBN 0-345-33474-4

Manufactured in the United States of America

First Ballantine Books Trade Edition: October 1984
First Ballantine Books Mass Market Edition: October 1986

Chapter One

Six months after that bomb took Ginny's left hand off, she still hadn't gotten over it.

I didn't need a degree in psychology or a direct message from God to figure out what was going on. I was living with her—I could see it. And I was living with her for all the wrong reasons. Not because she liked having me around. Not because she thought I was a particularly nice person to share a bed with. And certainly not because I was so all-fired tidy I made the mess in her apartment stand up and salute. I was living with her because she couldn't live by herself anymore. She only had one hand. She needed somebody to take care of her.

If I'd said that to people who knew her, they would've laughed out loud. Sure, Axbrewder. She needs you. Tell us another one. She was Ginny Fistoulari, the backbone and brains of Fistoulari Investigations. With her keen gray eyes and her attractive face and blond hair and the way her tall, lean body moved in her clothes, she could've been a society doll, the wife of some big snort who owned a country club or two, or maybe just half the firstborn children in Puerta del Sol. But her nose had been broken once when some clown had clipped her with a crowbar—and she'd replied to that indignity by shooting the sucker three times in the face. When things got

1

tough, she had a way of looking like her features were molded over iron instead of bone. And she'd lost her hand by holding a bomb out the window of a hospital so it wouldn't blow up in the building or on the people below.

As for me—at six foot five and 260 (with all the cooking I was doing, I'd gained some weight), I was big enough so most people wouldn't ordinarily laugh at the idea I was needed. But I was only temporarily sober. I was known to be totally fubar ("fucked up beyond all repair"), even before that wonderful day—the highlight of my life—when in a fit of civic righteousness and alcohol I tried to help apprehend a purse-snatcher and ended up shooting my brother instead. (Like they say, anybody who can't aim a .45 better than that ought to have his brains recalled for production defects.) And I was never going to get my license back. Ginny was watched like a hawk by the commission because she insisted on hiring me when I didn't have a license.

Sure, Axbrewder. She needs you. Tell us another one.

Well, in this particular case, "temporarily sober" had been going on for six months. Almost every night, I dreamed about the special amber peace you can only find somewhere near the bottom of a bottle and woke up grinding my teeth. Almost every day, when I wasn't braced for it, my throat ached for the lovely burning of whiskey. I still had withdrawal flashes that made me sweat and tremble and hold my head like a junkie. The simple smell of scotch was enough to turn my guts inside out. And almost every morning, when I got out of bed, I said to myself, Maybe today's the day. The day I get to take a drink. Just one. Or maybe two. Two drinks can't hurt me. I've earned two drinks. But I didn't do it.

For a drunk like me, sobriety is like trying to push a brick wall down with your nose. Six months of it gets to be pretty painful. But I hadn't had a drink yesterday, or last week, or last month, and I wasn't going to have one today.

Because Ginny really did need me.

She wasn't actually helpless. In practice, she could've done just about anything she wanted. With her purse on a strap over her right shoulder, she could get what she needed out of it almost as fast as usual. And the doctors had fitted her with a prosthetic device—"the claw," she called it—that looked pretty handy to me. Sure, it was made of stainless steel, which isn't exactly one of the primary flesh tones. But it strapped over her stump and worked off the muscles of her forearm, so she could open and close the pair of hooks just by acting like she still had a fist. Down at the base, they had sharp edges that came together like scissors—which I thought was a nice touch. And they were strong enough to punch in the tops of beer cans.

She refused to wear the damn thing.

It made her feel worse.

The problem was simple. She was Ginny Fistoulari, hotshot private investigator, smart, tough, give-me-a-running-start-and-I-can-do-anything. And she was maimed. Without her hand, she felt like a cripple—ugly, undesirable, and bitter. The claw made her hate herself.

I knew exactly how she felt. I was Mick Axbrewder, the drunk who killed his own brother. She never would've lost her hand if I'd had the brains God gave a spaniel—if I'd thought of using my belt to hold that bomb.

So I took care of her.

Yessir, we were quite a pair. Leaning on each other because neither one of us had the bare guts to stand up alone. Me, I was used to it. But I hadn't expected it to happen to her. If I hadn't been so busy being dogged and useful, I would've gone out and become a drunk again just to forget the constant misery burning like a low-grade fever in her eyes. Those eyes used to be as sharp and alive as a hunter's. Now they just hurt.

Somebody should've locked the two of us away in a nursing home somewhere so we wouldn't get into any more trouble. But maybe that wouldn't've solved the problem. And maybe trouble comes to those who need it. We sure as hell needed something.

Monday morning we slept in later than usual because we were between cases and didn't have anything better to do. I got out of bed first, used the bathroom, and went to make the coffee. While the pot was perking, I cleaned up the mess she'd made in the apartment the night before.

Her apartment was in Turtleshell, a complex near what used to be the business center of town, before the banks moved. The building was at least middle-aged, but it was designed and furnished in the American Impersonal absence of style—she could've been living in Indianapolis. She stood it the same way she stood the clutter.

Which wasn't all that bad—her coat on the floor, clothes dropped wherever she happened to be when she took them off, coffee cups everywhere, case and tax records tossed down on the table so hard a lot of them had splashed onto the carpet. And anyway, I couldn't really object to it. I knew why she did it. It was as close as she could come to expressing her resentment.

Before she lost her hand, of course, she'd been messy out of ordinary absentmindedness. Too many other things to think about. But now she cluttered the apartment because she knew I was going to clean it up. She resented being dependent—so she resented me for helping her, for being the one she was dependent on—so she did little things to make my job harder.

We had a lot in common that way. I kept cleaning up after her for exactly the same reason.

In fact, we were spending more and more time playing that kind of game. When the coffee was ready, I took her a cup. But instead of drinking it, she let it get cold while she was in the shower. Then she had me pour her a fresh cup. Meanwhile, I fixed her a breakfast she didn't want and could hardly choke down. If I'd been anybody else, I couldn't have made her eat breakfast by holding a gun to her head. By preference, she lived on vitamin pills and coffee until at least noon.

It was a rotten way to live. If something didn't change soon, one of us was going to go off the deep end.

So after we slogged our way through another breakfast, I helped her get dressed. I buttoned her blouse (which should've been a whole lot more fun than it was), buckled her shoes, got her coat over her shoulders. I stuffed the papers she wanted into her briefcase. Then I held the door open for her, and we went out into Puerta del Sol's winter.

We hadn't had anything to say to each other for going on sixteen hours.

Puerta del Sol is far enough south so we only get snow in alternate years. But the terrain around the city is high desert. The mountains east of us go up to 10,000 feet, but that's only 5,000 higher than the Flat Valley, where Puerta del Sol sprawls on either side of the river. So the winters are about as cold as I can stand—at least when the sun isn't shining. And the sun today had a bleached-out look, like it was overworked. But Ginny and I still could've talked to each other while we walked to her office. We just didn't. Instead, I huddled into my jacket, looking ridiculous the way somebody my size always does when he feels sorry for himself. And Ginny puffed at the cold while her broken nose turned red.

Her office was in the Murchison Building, on Paseo Grande. It's one of the three structures in Puerta del Sol that stand more than five stories tall—but that turned out to be misplaced optimism on the part of the developers when all the banks moved three miles farther down Paseo Grande, away from what the real estate speculators call "Chicano creep." As a result, space in the Murchison Building isn't as expensive as you'd expect. That suited me—it helped Ginny stay in business. But I wouldn't go to any doctor or insurance agent who had an office there.

Unfortunately, the heat wasn't working, and Fistoulari Investigations was on the wrong side for the morning sun. You could've stored cadavers in there. I picked up the mail and newspapers from the empty waiting room

and carried them into the actual office. I put the mail on
Ginny's desk and dropped the newspapers on the sofa I
used for a chair. Then I started up the electric coffeepot.
We had to have something warm to keep us going until
the sun reached the picture window looking out toward
the Flat Valley.

Booze would've been warmer, but I tried not to think
about that.

While Ginny scanned the mail and threw it into the
wastebasket, I glanced around at the only things she had
hanging on her walls—her diplomas and the display copy
of her license. In this state, the commission wants private
investigators to be "professional," like doctors and law-
yers. So Ginny has a waiting room for all the people who
never come to see her. (As a rule, the clients who come
to see a private investigator are the ones you don't
want—divorce cases and loonies. Good clients call. They
expect you to go see them.) And she decorates her walls
with the sort of stuff that makes the commission feel
good.

After the mail, she pulled one of the phones closer to
her and started dialing. To keep myself from watching
her, I picked up the papers. When I heard her ask for the
manager of the Murchison Building—she was calling to
complain about the heat—I stopped listening.

Amazing what you can learn from newspapers. Monday morning's edition was on top, and the headline said:

GANGSTER SLAIN
Body Found In River

Under that:

Murder Mob Related, Police Say

Do tell, I said. My, my.

At 11:09 last night, according to the story, the body of
Roscoe Chavez was fished out of the Flat River, down in

the south part of town where the warehouses and *barrios* are. He'd been shot six times in the chest. His pockets had been filled with rolls of pennies for weight, but the body bloated up enough to float.

Somewhere in the fourth paragraph, the Puerta del Sol *Herald*'s keen-eyed and incisive reporter finally got around to using the word "alleged." Roscoe "Bambino" Chavez was "alleged" to have ties to organized crime. He was "alleged" to be responsible for illegal "numbers" gambling in our fair city. The cops didn't have any particular theory about why he was killed. They were just glad he was gone.

I gave this flash the respect it deserved. Actually, until this minute I hadn't believed our fine and upstanding guardians of the law were even aware of the connection between the Bambino and Puerta del Sol's thriving numbers racket. As for why he was killed—I could've answered that with my eyes closed. He'd been killed for doing something el Señor didn't like.

Being a good citizen myself, I applauded the demise of brother Chavez. But I still wished he'd gotten away with it—whatever it was he was doing el Señor didn't like. (Actually, "el Señor" is an Anglo name. In Spanish, it doesn't make sense. But by now he's stuck with it. If he wanted a more self-respecting Chicano title, he should've stuck to ripping off his own people. Anglos are famous for renaming everything and everybody to suit themselves.) I had a small grudge against the man the *Herald*'s reporter would've called Puerta del Sol's "crime czar"— if the cops'd ever admitted such a man existed, or if the reporter'd been smart enough to figure it out—and I was glad to hear somebody'd had the guts to cross him.

On the other hand, there was nothing I could do to el Señor myself. He was too strong for me to mess with. And I'd never had anything to do with the Bambino. Ginny'd finished complaining about the heat. Now she was talking to her answering service. I looked to see what else was in the paper.

Near the back of the city section, an item caught my eye. I don't know why—I could just as easily have missed it. But when I started reading it, it didn't have any trouble holding my attention.

Ginny went on using the phone. Part of my mind heard her explaining we didn't do that kind of work, but I wasn't really listening. I was concentrating on this news item about Pablo Santiago.

He wasn't anybody special—not like Roscoe Chavez. Just a ten-year-old kid I happened to know. Ginny and I worked for his family a couple of years ago on a protection-racket case. The Santiagos ran a grungy little grocery store down in the old part of town—one of those places where toothless grandmothers bought beans and tortillas at prices that were actually reasonable, and kids stocked up on Coke and licorice—until some of the local *muchachos* decided to finance their hobbies by extorting "insurance" from small businesses. Since the *muchachos* were freelance, the Santiagos could've turned to el Señor for help. But then they would've ended up paying *him* protection money. That they didn't want, partly because they were honest, and partly because they valued their independence. So they hired Fistoulari Investigations.

Anyway, that was how I met Pablo Santiago.

According to the paper, he'd been missing since Saturday night.

I opened my mouth to say something to Ginny, but she was already in the middle of another phone call. I don't know what hit me hardest, the fact a kid I knew was missing—another kid!—or the fact a Chicano kid who'd been gone for less than forty-eight hours was suddenly considered news (which wasn't exactly normal behavior for the Puerta del Sol *Herald*)—or the sheer coincidence of it.

The combination felt like a gutful of rubbing alcohol. The last time I saw Pablo, he was running numbers. He was one of the errand boys who collected people's bets and distributed winnings.

I didn't bother telling myself it wasn't any of my business. I have a thing about kids in trouble. And I didn't have to guess very hard to figure out why somebody as insignificant—or at least Chicano—as Pablo made the news. Because the cops were looking for him and wanted help. Because of Roscoe Chavez. On top of that, the Santiagos were good people. They deserved better than they were going to get.

I dropped the papers back on the sofa, hauled myself to my feet, and started for the door.

Before I got there, Ginny hung up the phone and demanded, "Where do you think you're going?"

"Grocery shopping," I muttered. Reflex counterpunch. I didn't like her tone. When I looked at her, I saw her resentment had moved right up to the front of her face. Not very nicely, I added, "I'm getting tired of sitting on my hands."

A masterstroke of tact—she loved it when I reminded her about her hand—but this time there was something more complicated going on. She resented me for the same reason she didn't snap back. Almost politely, she said, "That can wait. This is more important."

Always fast on my feet, I stared at her and wondered how she knew about Pablo.

But she didn't know about Pablo. "There's a man up in the Heights," she said. "A Mr. Haskell. I just talked to him. He wants to hire us. We need to go see him."

If he hadn't been Ginny Fistoulari—and if I hadn't understood why she resented me—I would've said, Tell him to stuff it. I can't stand it when kids get into trouble and nobody helps them. But she was, and I did, so I didn't. Instead, I stood there and waited for her to finish.

Her eyes wandered away while she tried to get a handle on something that looked suspiciously like panic. "He says he needs protection. He says somebody's trying to kill him."

Well, at least we were talking to each other.

Chapter Two

Just for practice, I took the .45 out of its shoulder holster under my left arm and checked it over. I wasn't serious—I'm not very good with a gun, and most of the time I'm too big to need one. I was just trying to get into the spirit of the occasion. Console myself for having to postpone my visit to Pablo's parents. But Ginny wasn't playing. Her nice .357 Smith & Wesson was gathering lint in the bottom of her purse, and she was frowning at me in a way that said she didn't want any case that might be dangerous.

Like two people who really were going grocery shopping, we got ready. I helped her put on her coat. (I was still wearing my old raincoat over my jacket because of the temperature in the office.) She turned off the coffeepot. I locked the doors. Then we took the elevator down to the basement garage, where she kept her Olds.

On the way, I asked, "Did this whatsisname—Haskell— did he happen to say who's trying to kill him?"

She shook her head. Her broken nose was pale in the cold.

"Did he tell you why he thinks somebody's trying to kill him?"

She shook her head again.

"And you didn't ask? Whatever happened to the famous Fistoulari curiosity?"

That got a little rise out of her. "I thought he'd give me better answers if he had to look me in the eye."

"You know," I said, "you're beautiful when you're angry."

I thought she was going to express her appreciation by ramming her elbow into my stomach. Hell, I wanted her to ram her elbow into my stomach. I wanted her to at least try to act like the Ginny Fistoulari I used to know. But she didn't. She just walked out of the elevator and went to her car.

I had the keys. I opened the passenger side for her and held the door while she slid into the seat. Then I walked around the car, let myself in, and fitted my bulk behind the wheel. I ground the starter until the engine caught. Then I asked, "So where're we going?"

She stared out at the gloom of the garage. "First Puerta del Sol National Bank," she said distantly. "He works at the Heights branch. Corner of Acequia and Glover."

More to keep her going than because I was surprised, I said, "He thinks somebody's trying to kill him—and he went in to work?"

But she'd already figured that part out. "Makes sense. He's a whole lot safer in his office in a bank than he would be at home."

I chewed the situation over for a few minutes while I swung the Olds out of the garage and headed up Paseo Grande toward the beltway. She was right—it made sense. But sense isn't generally one of the main characteristics of people who think other people are trying to kill them. Most people don't get themselves into that kind of trouble. And when they do, they tend to panic.

Maybe Haskell wasn't surprised by what was happening to him? Or was he just that much more levelheaded than the rest of the human race?

The beltway wasn't direct, but it was quicker than plodding through umpteen dozen stoplights. Except during rush hour—and this was already the middle of the morning. In a few minutes, we were pulling up the long grade out of the Flat Valley.

Puerta del Sol sprawls. This is the Great American Southwest—us rugged frontier-stock types don't like to live by piling ourselves on top of each other. So the city spreads out. Mostly it spreads up and down the Flat Valley, where water is a little easier to come by. But it goes east, too, toward the mountains. In that direction, it falls into roughly three sections—the Valley, the Heights (this long, eight-mile grade where the city expanded when there wasn't any more room along the river), and the solid-gold real estate in the foothills of the mountains.

Overall, the Heights is the newest part of the city. It's full of people like doctors and plumbers working for the day when they can move up into the foothills—or down into the old-money regions of the North Valley. I took the Olds off the beltway on Hacienda, steered my way past a strip of hamburger joints, pizza parlors, and stereo warehouses on both sides of the street, then finally got out into easier driving among the residential developments. The pale sunlight made the houses look like places where people never dreamed of trying to kill each other.

During the whole drive, Ginny didn't say a word. She didn't even comment, never mind open her mouth to give me directions, when I missed the turn onto Glover and had to go the long way around a golf course to reach Acequia. She just kept staring through the windshield with a small frown nailed between her eyebrows. It wasn't like her to pass up a chance to give me directions.

I couldn't say I was starting to worry about her—I'd been worried about her for a long time—but something in the way I worried about her was starting to crystalize.

I was going to have to do something about it.

For a minute there, I thought what I ought to do was go out and get drunk. I was in that kind of mood. If I got drunk, she'd be forced to dig her way out of the pit she was in—or pull the top in after her. I felt positively noble. Axbrewder bravely sacrifices his soul to booze in order to save his partner. But there wasn't anything noble about the way every cell in my body jumped up and danced at the bare suggestion of alcohol. I pushed the idea away.

When I wheeled the Olds into the parking lot, I saw that the Heights branch of the First Puerta del Sol National Bank embodied one of the new concepts in modern banking. It tried to look like a place where nothing intimidating happens (a place where your money is safe and the people are your buddies and nobody ever says no and it's all just as wholesome and American as motherhood) by disguising itself as an ice cream parlor. It had a red, pitched roof, actual peppermint stripes on the walls, frilly white curtains in the windows, wrought-iron railings for the porch, and candy cane lights on either side of the front door.

A risky way for a bank to do business. I didn't think it was going to succeed. Me, I'd rather bury my money in the ground. I could picture people walking up to the tellers and ordering a dish of tutti-frutti—right after they made their deposits and cashed their checks somewhere else. But Puerta del Sol has a bank for about every eight people, and I suppose they have to do something to compete with each other.

Still, I had a hard time imagining that anybody who worked in an ice cream parlor could be in danger for his life.

"Quite a place," I commented, hoping Ginny would respond.

She got out of the Olds without saying anything and slammed the door. But when I sighed and followed her, she gave me a vaguely apologetic look. "Whoever thought that up," she said, pretending more sarcasm than she felt, "ought to have his brains overhauled."

"Shame on you," I said. "Didn't your mommie teach you not to say anything at all if you can't say something nice?"

She wasn't amused. But I guess she didn't like it either when we weren't talking to each other. Glaring at the bank, she said, "My mommie taught me not to trust people who don't have better sense than this."

Well, at least she was making an effort. I happened to know her mother died when she was four. Feeling a little better, I took a couple of quick steps to get ahead of her, then held the door open for her and ushered her into the bank.

Inside, the chairs where people had to sit while waiting for their loans to be approved or their mortgages to be foreclosed were upholstered with candy stripes, and the wallpaper had a peppermint stick pattern. Other than that, the place looked like an ordinary bank. Ginny spotted a desk with an "Information" sign, and we headed in that direction. She had her left forearm stuffed into the pocket of her coat so nobody would know about her hand.

The woman at the Information desk wore a name tag that said "Eunice Wint." She was young and pretty in a soft, imprecise way, the kind of pretty that goes with baby fat. But the only thing really wrong with her was her hair. It had an indecisive style and color that made her look like she didn't know how to make up her mind. I couldn't help noticing her engagement ring. If she'd tried to go swimming with that rock, it would've dragged her to the bottom.

She welcomed us to the Heights branch of the First Puerta del Sol National Bank and started into a bright spiel about how much she wanted to help us with our banking needs. But Ginny was in no mood for bright spiels. Without actually being rude, she cut in firmly, "Thank you, Ms. Wint. We have an appointment with Mr. Haskell."

"Oh." Ms. Wint blushed—which made her look about twelve years old. "I'm sorry. How silly of me." New at her job, I said to myself. To reassure her, I put on my Kindly Uncle Axbrewder smile. She gestured toward the offices at one end of the lobby. "Won't you come this way?"

"Thank you," Ginny said again.

We were both as solemn as brokers as we followed Ms. Wint between the desks.

All the offices along that wall had large windows aimed at the lobby—either so the customers could see the executives hard at work, or to let the executives keep an eye on the tellers and receptionists. The door in the corner had a neat, brass plaque:

REG HASKELL
Chief Accountant

Ms. Wint didn't need to knock. The man in the office saw us coming, jumped up from behind his desk, and waved us in. But she opened the door and held it for us anyway. She was blushing again. Or still—I couldn't tell which.

"Thank you, Eunice," he said in an easy, naturally rich voice you might expect from an actor or a preacher. As he came around the desk, he extended his hand to Ginny. "You must be Ms. Fistoulari." Then he looked at me. "And you?"

"Axbrewder." I took my turn shaking his hand. He had a good grip, and his hand was dry and steady. He was wearing a light blue Southwest-casual banker's doubleknit. "I work for Fistoulari Investigations." In a fit of perversity—directed at Ginny, not at him—I added, "I do the fetch-and-carry stuff."

Ginny gave me a glare that would've withered chickweed, but Haskell didn't seem to be noticing the details. "Thanks for coming so promptly," he said. "I'm glad you're here." Then he turned his smile on Ms. Wint. "If we need anything, Eunice, I'll let you know."

She smiled back as if he'd made her day. But he was already on his way to the business side of his desk. Pointing out chairs for us, he said, "Please sit down."

He sounded perfectly natural and comfortable. In fact, he looked perfectly natural and comfortable. He had a healthy tan and a solid, medium frame that looked like he took good care of it. Smile lines creased his cheeks. His reddish-brown hair ran back from his forehead in waves molded to his skull. There wasn't any gray in his hair, but he was still probably about my age—around forty. But his eyes were younger. They sparkled like a kid's. At a guess, I would've said he wasn't in any danger at all. He was just excited about something.

On the other hand, his desk seemed too tidy for a man with a kid's excitement in his eyes. He kept all the papers in front of him as straight as numbers. Over to the left sat this morning's *Herald*, with its headlines displayed at the ceiling:

GANGSTER SLAIN
Body Found In River

As we all sat down, I gestured toward the lobby and said, "So, Mr. Haskell, you're responsible for all this." Trying the oblique approach.

"Reg," he said. "Call me Reg." He pronounced it like *reg*ular instead of like *reg*iment. "I wish you were right. But I'm just the chief accountant." He was doing wry diffidence—and he was good at it. "Accountants don't run banks until they stop being accountants. We're like computers—we just churn out numbers. Other people make the decisions."

"Mr. Haskell," Ginny put in with all the subtlety of a ballpeen, "over the phone you said somebody's trying to kill you."

This was our Mutt-and-Jeff routine. I come on all soft and friendly, Ginny goes for the bone. It's supposed to make people more honest by keeping them off balance. But Haskell didn't look particularly disconcerted.

On the other hand, he acted disconcerted. "I'm sorry," he said. "This is embarrassing. I don't know why I did it." He avoided Ginny's stare like a boy caught raiding the cookie jar. "I guess I was just trying to make sure you would take me seriously."

"I don't like being lied to," she snapped. "What makes you think we wouldn't take you seriously?"

Haskell spread his hands in a rather theatrical shrug. After a quick glance at both of us, he admitted, "You aren't the first private investigators I've called about this."

That surprised me. There weren't that many private investigators in this town who could afford to turn down work. But I wanted a different answer first—and Ginny looked like she was about to say, Why did they turn you down? Did you lie to them, too? So I asked, "Mr. Haskell—Reg—what makes you think you need a private investigator?"

He gave me an encouraging smile. "I'm sure they don't want to kill me. That would be an overreaction. But they would be very happy to break my legs."

Ginny scowled formaldehyde and thumbtacks at him. "This is fun," she said. "Just to keep us entertained, why don't you tell us why anybody would want to break your legs?"

He grimaced and tried to look miserable, but I got the impression he was glowing inside. In fact, I would've taken my oath on a brand-new case of tequila that he somehow got handsomer every time Ginny poked at him.

"I was stupid," he said, "more stupid than usual. A week or so ago, a friend talked me into going down to El Machismo. Have you ever been there?"

I had, Ginny hadn't. We both stared at him. I didn't know what she was thinking, but my heart was suddenly jumping like I'd been hit with a cattle prod.

"It's a nightclub down near the old part of town," he explained. "They converted an old movie theater. But being a nightclub is just a front." He was watching us closely now—probably looking for signs we wanted to walk out on him. "It's really a casino."

"I've heard that," Ginny said drily. "It's also illegal in this state."

"I know. That's why I can't go to the police." For a minute, he seemed to lose the thread of what he was saying. Then he went on, "But after adding numbers all day, I sometimes want a little excitement. And this friend twisted my arm.

"God, I was stupid!" His eyes were wide with amazement, like he still couldn't believe it. "I'm not usually like that. But somehow I got"—he fumbled for the right words—"caught up in it. You know?" He was making an unabashed appeal for our sympathy. "It was like magic. It was new and exciting and dangerous, and if you got lucky—or if you understood the odds well enough—if you were good enough—you could win." He didn't look much like he regretted his folly. "I lost my head.

"Also my money." He grinned sheepishly. "I wasn't as good as I thought. Before I realized what I was doing, I lost more money than I had with me. A lot more than I could afford."

"Then what?" I asked. But I wasn't listening very hard. My heart was still thudding around inside my chest, and I was remembering the one time I'd been to El Machismo.

"They were polite about it," he said, "which surprised me." It didn't surprise me. That was how they hooked new Anglo suckers. "They gave me a loan to cover my losses—and forty-eight hours to pay it back."

There he stopped. He didn't need to explain the rest. Ginny said stiffly, "The people who run El Machismo don't like welshers." She had a tight grip on her temper. "Why didn't you pay them back?"

Now at least he managed to look serious. "I told you," he said. "I'd lost a lot more money than I could afford." Then he shrugged again. "And I was stupid. I underestimated them. They didn't know who I was. I thought they wouldn't be able to find me. If I never went back there, I thought I'd be safe.

"But they called me last night. I don't know how they did it, but they found me. They told me what they were going to do to me."

"Two broken legs for one welshed bet," I commented. "That sounds like the going rate these days."

Something in the back of his eyes seemed to share my sense of humor. But the rest of his face went on looking serious. "Since then," he concluded, "I've been trying to hire some protection for myself."

Sure, I thought. Anybody would feel the same way. Only he was in more trouble than he realized. None of the other private investigators he called would take the job because they didn't want any part of the trouble he was in.

Ginny didn't want any part of it either. I could see that in the way she held her head, the way her eyes seemed to have slipped slightly out of focus on Haskell. She was looking for the right kind of anger to turn him down. If the man who wanted Haskell's legs broken didn't get what he wanted, he'd just keep raising the ante until he did. Sooner or later, somebody was going to end up dead. Why should she risk it? She was a cripple, wasn't she?

She sure was. I could remember the Ginny Fistoulari who never would've considered refusing a case just because it might get messy. I didn't exactly trust Haskell. Either he had a screw loose somewhere, or he wasn't telling us the whole truth. Normal, honest folks get a little more upset when you threaten to break their legs. But I had my own ideas about what we needed to do. And why we had to do it.

Before Ginny could figure out how to dump him, I gave Haskell one of my smiles and said, "You got it. Nothing's guaranteed in this business, but we'll give it our best shot."

Chapter Three

"That's a relief." Haskell's smile made mine look like the grin of a gargoyle. But I wasn't really watching him. Most of my attention was on Ginny.

She didn't react with any obvious outrage. The muscles at the corners of her eyes were clenched white—that was all. "Mr. Haskell," she said, as smooth as a drill bit, "I need a moment alone with Mr. Axbrewder."

My guts gave a sympathetic little twist, like she'd already started chewing into them.

"Of course," Haskell replied. "I understand." With that boyish gleam, he seemed more charming than he had any legal right to be. "Use my office."

Before he got out of his chair, he reached for the phone. He dialed three digits, listened for a second, then said, "Eunice, Ms. Fistoulari and Mr. Axbrewder are going to conference in my office for a few minutes. Would you bring them some coffee?" He covered the mouthpiece and asked us, "Cream and sugar?" We shook our heads. "Just black," he said to Eunice Wint. "Thanks."

Still smiling, he made his way around the desk and out of the room. But we didn't say anything. Through the window, we could see Ms. Wint coming in our direction with a Styrofoam cup in each hand.

Haskell was headed toward one of the tellers, and Ms. Wint seemed to be watching him more than where she was going. She nearly ran into a tall, thin man in a classy gray pinstripe. He talked softly—I couldn't hear what he was saying. But he sounded angry, and her blush looked hot enough to set her hair on fire. When he let her go and she brought us our coffee, she couldn't quite swallow all the misery in her face.

"Thank you, Ms. Wint." Ginny wasn't paying any attention—she just wanted to get rid of the girl. As soon as Ms. Wint left, Ginny got up and closed the door.

I followed the receptionist with my eyes, sidetracked by her unhappiness. Ginny had to say my name to make me look at her. The way she said it, it sounded like she had a mouthful of broken glass.

I looked at her. If I'd been drowning, I would've forgotten everything and looked at her when she said my name like that.

She didn't say, I'm Fistoulari Investigations. You're just the hired help. Don't try to make my decisions for me. As soft and fierce as whip leather, she said, "Are you out of your mind? Have you forgotten who owns El Machismo?"

Faced with that glare of hers, I crossed my hands over my stomach. "Maybe it's the Divine Sisters of the Paraclete. What do you care? This guy's in trouble."

"Bastard," she lashed at me. "It's el Señor."

Which was why nobody else wanted Haskell's business.

Well, I remembered. But I remembered other things, too. I remembered when Ginny was in the hospital with her hand blown off I'd gone to el Señor because my niece was missing and I needed to know who was responsible. Instead of telling me, he had some of his muscle force-feed me a bottle of tequila. Then he let his main body-guard, Muy Estobal, give me one of the best beatings I'd ever had. By the time he was done with me, I was in such terrific shape I almost got both me and Ginny killed.

Slowly and carefully, I said, "That's exactly why I want this case."

She understood. She knew me well enough. But the fierceness in her face didn't change. "Brew." She took her stump out of the pocket of her coat and scowled hate at it. "It's too dangerous. I'm not equipped to handle it."

If this went on much longer, I was going to be sick. I wanted to shout at her, but I didn't. Instead, I said, "Is that a fact? Poor little Ginny Fistoulari. Why don't you retire? Then you can spend all day every day feeling sorry for yourself."

She was going to hit me. I knew it. Sure as hell, she was going to haul off and beat my skull open. And I was almost looking forward to it. I deserved it. Some days I was such a nice man I wanted to puke all over myself.

But she didn't hit me. She didn't even call me names. While I waited for her to tell me to get out of her life, her anger slowly changed from hot to hard, like melted iron cooling. In a voice I could've shaved with, she said, "Mick Axbrewder, I'm going to get even with you for this." Then she put her stump back in her coat pocket and stood up. Through the window, she signaled for Haskell.

Nobody calls me Mick. Not since my brother died. But this time I decided I'd better let it pass.

Haskell rejoined us with just the wrong hint of eagerness. Maybe he was still a kid at heart. Maybe being threatened by the bad guys was his idea of a game. That was going to make him hard to protect. But I didn't comment. I knew better than to interrupt Ginny now.

As soon as Haskell closed the door and sat down again, she said to him sharply, "First things first, Mr. Haskell. Are you married? Do you have a family?"

His mouth twitched, trying to grin and stay serious at the same time. "Does that mean you're really going to take the job? I didn't know whether Mr. Axbrewder spoke for you or not."

Well, he wasn't stupid, even if he did make stupid mistakes. But Ginny didn't blink. "Are you married?" she repeated. "Do you have children? Do you live with a girlfriend"—she must've noticed he wasn't wearing a wedding ring— "or your parents?"

People usually answer her when she uses that tone. "Actually," he said, "I thought of that." He was proud enough of himself to show it. "I'm married—no children. After that phone call last night, the first thing I did was to send Sara away, out of danger. She shouldn't be hurt for my mistakes. I told her to go to a hotel—any hotel. I didn't want to know which one. If I knew where she was, I might give her away accidentally. Maybe those thugs are listening to my phone. Or I might go to see her and be followed. I told her to call me every morning at work, and not to come home until I said so. She should be safe."

I was mildly impressed. Sara Haskell was an obedient woman. Or else Reg Haskell had more iron in him than I could see. For no particular reason, I suddenly wanted to talk to Mrs. Haskell about her husband.

But Ginny just nodded and didn't pursue the question. "Good enough," she said. "We'll do what we can for you. As Mr. Axbrewder said, there are no guarantees. For one thing, we're human—we might screw up." At the moment, she didn't especially look like a woman who screwed up. I was feeling better all the time. "For another, the people you cheated don't like interference. They might try to bury us, just as a matter of principle."

He shrugged. "If it's too dangerous—"

She cut him off. "For this kind of work, we get seven hundred fifty dollars a day plus expenses. Fifteen hundred dollars in advance."

I was beginning to think nothing ever flustered Mr. Reg Haskell, Chief Accountant. He glanced up at the ceiling like he was doing math in his head, then met Ginny's gaze. "I can afford that. For a while, anyway."

"Good. This may take a while."

As understatements go, that was no slouch. I thought about it while Haskell wrote out a check and handed it to Ginny. Actually, there was only one way to protect someone like Reg Haskell from someone like el Señor. El Señor couldn't afford to let welshers get away without being punished—most of his power depended on fear, so he didn't give up easy. You had to make the punishment more trouble than it was worth. In practice, that meant you had to catch the muscle he sent out to do the job and get the law to lock them away—unless you got lucky and happened to shoot one or two of those bastards in self-defense. And even then you had to hope el Señor kept a sense of perspective and didn't keep sending men out to get locked up or shot over a relatively minor bet.

I had exactly one idea about how to get started on the problem.

Ginny had the same idea. But she took a minute to get to it. She was busy covering all the bases. "You'll be safe enough here," she said. "Plenty of witnesses. So we'll pick you up after work. What time do you get off?"

"Four-thirty," he said.

"In the meantime, we'll try to figure out how they found you. That might give us something to go on." Almost casually, she said, "You went to El Machismo with a friend. What was his name?"

At that, the lines of Haskell's face shifted, and his eyes narrowed. For the first time, he looked his age. Slowly, he said, "This doesn't have anything to do with him. It isn't his fault. I'd rather not involve him."

I sat up straighter in my chair.

"I appreciate that," Ginny said acidly. "You want to be loyal to your friends. But you'll just have to trust us to be discreet. Right now, this friend looks like the only link between you and El Machismo. If he's any kind of regular there, they might have some hold on him. He might have told them how to find you. We have to check him out."

Haskell studied her hard for a minute, then dropped his gaze. "The fact is," he said, "he's in even more vulnerable a position than I am. If just a hint of this gets out"—he glanced toward the window and the lobby—"it would ruin me. People who work for banks aren't allowed to be in this kind of trouble. But for him it's worse. He wouldn't be that dumb."

Ginny snorted. She smelled the same rat I did. "He's already been that dumb. He talked you into going down there in the first place. We have to check him out."

Haskell didn't like her tone. "I don't want you to do that."

"In that case"—she rose smoothly to her feet—"hire somebody else." His check dropped from her hand and fluttered to the desk.

Right on cue, I followed her example. I wanted this case so bad it made my back teeth hurt, but it wasn't important enough to keep me from backing her up.

He surprised me by not getting angry. His eyes were gleaming again. "All right," he said with a stagy sigh. "All right. His name is Reston Cole. He's an executive vice president of the bank. He works downtown in the main office." Frowning, he muttered, "If he gets in trouble for this, I'll shoot myself."

Ginny didn't try to reassure him. While she had him where she wanted him, she took advantage of it. "One more question," she said. "Who referred you to us?"

I was glad she asked that. Somehow, I didn't think he was going to say he got Fistoulari Investigations out of the phone book.

"I told you you weren't the first people I called," he said candidly. He looked like he had a secret bit of spite hidden away in what he was saying. "One of them gave me your name. An outfit called Lawrence Smithsonian and Associates."

I almost whistled out loud. Lawrence Smithsonian—Ginny calls him "fatass Smithsonian"—ran one of the few agencies in Puerta del Sol that was too successful for its own good. He was what you might call a laundryman—he specialized in money. How dirty money gets changed into clean money. Who does it and why. And in his spare time he hobnobbed with half the bank presidents in town.

He and Ginny hated each other. Natural antipathy—she didn't like people who got successful without keeping their hands clean, he didn't like people who were more honest than he was.

Upon mature reflection, as they say, it made sense that Haskell had called Smithsonian. A few polite questions anywhere in Puerta del Sol banking would turn up Smithsonian's name. But for Smithsonian to refer Haskell to us made no sense at all.

It wasn't for love, I was sure of that.

I probably had a blank, stupid look on my face. I've never been good at poker. But Ginny didn't skip a beat. She thanked Haskell unnecessarily, reminded him we'd pick him up at four-thirty, retrieved his check, and pulled open the office door without offering to shake his hand. Not to ruin the effect of her exit, I followed as well as I could.

As we left the lobby, I glanced at Eunice Wint and waved. Sweet old Axbrewder feels sorry for everybody whose feelings get hurt. But she wasn't looking at me. She was watching Haskell's office like a woman who knew she shouldn't hope and couldn't help it.

Ginny and I walked back to the Olds without saying anything. I unlocked the passenger door for her and went around to the driver's side. But she didn't get in. Her face was aimed in my direction, but she wasn't looking at me.

I thought it wouldn't be very good for our image if we just stood there with our brains in neutral—and anyway, the sun wasn't putting out a whole lot of heat—so I asked, "What're you thinking?"

Like her eyes, her voice was aimed somewhere else. "He doesn't wear a wedding ring."

"So what? A lot of men don't. You know the old line—'My wife's married. I'm not.' Or maybe he just doesn't like rings."

So much for my wit and wisdom. In the same tone, she said, "Did you notice anything else?"

I leaned my elbows on the roof of the car and studied her hard. "You mean besides the fact he's just terrified in his little booties? You tell me."

She made an effort to pull herself into focus. "He's got that gleam. It's bound to be trouble. He's the kind of man women have trouble resisting."

In my usual clever way, I listened to what she said instead of what she meant. "Is that how you're going to get even with me?" I asked nicely. "You're going to hop in the sack with him while his wife's safely hidden away in some hotel?"

"Oh, shut up." She wasn't paying enough attention to me to get mad. "That's not the point."

Well, I knew that. And I probably should've said so. But right then something small and maybe insignificant clicked into place in the back of my head. Pushing my weight off the car, I said, "I'll be right back," and headed into the bank again.

Eunice Wint was sitting behind the information desk. There was nobody near her. I didn't see Haskell anywhere. As unobtrusively as I could, I went and sat down in the chair beside her desk.

She'd locked most of her unhappiness away somewhere, but she still looked a little lost. "Why, hello again, Mr.—," she began with the brightness demanded by her job, then fumbled slightly because she'd forgotten my name.

"Axbrewder," I supplied helpfully. I was concentrating on looking like an inordinately large teddy bear—kind and warm, no threat to anybody.

"Mr. Axbrewder. What can I do for you?"

"It's none of my business, of course," I began—it's never any of my business—"but who was that you were talking to—outside Mr. Haskell's office, when you were bringing us coffee?"

Somehow, the question hit too close to home. She

didn't do anything loud or messy, she just lost whatever capacity she may've had to tell somebody as big as me to drop dead. No matter how old she was, she was too young for her own circumstances. "You mean Mr. Canthorpe?" she asked. "Jordan Canthorpe?"

I nodded. "I couldn't help overhearing the way he snapped at you. What was he so upset about?"

"He doesn't like me to do things for Mr. Haskell," she said simply. She was too unhappy to look me in the eye. "He says it isn't part of my job."

"Is he your boss?" Axbrewder the teddy bear, kindly and treacherous.

She shook her head. "He's Mr. Haskell's boss. I'm in a different department."

I acted appropriately huffy. "Then what business is it of his who you bring coffee for?"

She was so helpless to keep her mouth shut, it made me ashamed of myself. In a soft, demure, miserable voice, she said, "He's my fiancé."

Click. And double click. Maybe it wasn't so insignificant after all. And maybe I should've paid better attention to what Ginny was trying to tell me. "Thank you, Ms. Wint," I said. "Don't worry—it'll all work out." Before she could think to ask me what I thought I was doing, I heaved myself off the chair and strode away.

When I got out to the parking lot, Ginny was still standing by the Olds, waiting for me. I felt like I owed her an apology—after what I'd just done, I wanted to apologize to somebody—but she didn't give me a chance. Her gray gaze was pointed straight at me.

"What the hell was that all about?"

I did the best I could. "You called it," I said. "He's irresistible. If you put a gun to my head, I'd be willing to bet he's having an affair with Eunice Wint. Even though she's engaged to his boss."

That made her raise her eyebrows. "Axbrewder," she said while she thought about it, "you do have your uses." Then she changed gears. "You weren't paying much attention back in the office this morning." She was only being a little sarcastic. "There were two calls with the answering service. The second was from Haskell." She paused to set me up. "The first was from Mrs. Haskell."

I stared at her. All I could remember about that call was hearing her turn somebody down.

"She wanted us to find out if her husband's being unfaithful to her."

My, my, I thought. What a coincidence. "Do you suppose," I asked, "Mrs. Haskell—or maybe somebody else—hired a couple of goons to lean on good old Reg for sleeping around?"

Ginny got into the Olds. I fitted myself behind the steering wheel. She said, "I think we'd better find out."

On a whim, I commented, "It does sound like our client likes to live dangerously."

Chapter Four

But when I rolled the Olds onto the beltway again and pointed it in the direction of the new downtown, where nothing but concrete grows and all the banks have their main offices, Ginny told me we weren't going to see Haskell's partner in crime, Reston Cole. Not yet. First she wanted to have a talk with Lawrence Smithsonian.

That suited me. It would've suited me in any case—I was as curious and maybe even as worried as she was about Smithsonian's motives—but now I had a particular reason for liking the idea. It would take time. It was already after eleven, and what with Reston Cole and Mrs. Haskell and some of our basic homework—like finding out whether our client had a criminal record—we had a lot to do before four-thirty. We were going to have to split up.

I had things I wanted to get done on my own.

So instead of driving all the way downtown I took the Olds off the beltway on Archuleta and started up into the North Valley.

By rights, Puerta del Sol ought to be easy to get around in. For one thing, you can't get lost—the mountains are right over there, and it's just a question of wandering in the right direction until you hit something familiar. For another, too much of the city is new, which means it was laid out by city planners and developers. But in practice it's more complicated.

The North Valley is complicated because the new developments and roads grew up around enclaves of old money—orchards where you least expect them, stud farms surrounded by riding trails and irrigation ditches, clusters of adobe houses and haciendas the Spanish built any way they liked three hundred years ago. The result is a city planner's nightmare. I knew where I was going, but it still took me more than half an hour to reach the neighborhood where Lawrence Smithsonian and Associates lived.

If I hadn't known better, I would've thought the place was a bank. Smithsonian had his own building, for God's sake, and it looked a whole lot more like a place to deposit checks than the ice cream parlor where Haskell worked. Naturally—at least I thought it was natural, knowing Smithsonian—the structure bore no resemblance to the rest of the area. The neighborhood was huge old cottonwoods, stark in the pale sunlight without their leaves, and flat-roofed houses that looked like dumps outside and mansions inside, and dogs that chased happily after everything they were sure they couldn't catch. Even the gas stations tried to fit in. Smithsonian's building looked mostly like a cinder block with a thyroid condition.

Still, it was a fancy cinder block. And Smithsonian knew his business well enough to put his parking lot and his entrance and even his name around back, so people felt less exposed going to see him. Even when their hearts are pure vanilla, most people don't want it known they're talking to a private investigator.

After I parked the Olds, Ginny looked at me and asked, "What do you suppose he's going to tell us?"

Whatever it was, I felt sure I wasn't going to like it. "Probably not the truth."

She considered the building morosely. "Actually, he

may tell us the exact truth. That's what worries me."
More vehemently than necessary, she unlatched the door
and shoved it open. "I always trust him more when he
lies."

Like I say, she didn't much care for Lawrence Smithsonian.

But now she was at least thinking about this case instead of trying to come up with reasons why we couldn't
handle it. That was enough for me. I was feeling feisty
enough to deal with Smithsonian as we left the car and
went into his domain.

No doubt about it—he was too successful for his own
good. Inside the heavy glass doors—everything in the
place that wasn't concrete was made out of glass—the
heat worked, and the carpet was so thick it seemed to
squish underfoot, and a receptionist sat at a desk in front
of a phone covered with buttons. A by-God receptionist!
Half the private investigators I know have trouble meeting the payments on their answering services. But
Smithsonian didn't have just any receptionist. He had
one who looked like the soul of discretion. In other
words, she was old enough to be everybody's grandmother—and she was bored straight out of her skull.

She looked up at us discreetly as we walked in. Ginny
had the pinched, white look around her crooked nose of
a woman who was either too cold or trying to put too
much Novocaine on her emotions, but she didn't hesitate. "Is Smithsonian in?" she asked the receptionist. "I
want to talk to him."

The woman blinked at us. Whatever she had left between her ears was calcifying fast. "Mr. Smithsonian is in
conference," she said primly. "I can tell him you're here,
but I'm afraid he won't be free for quite some time."
With an air of distaste, she added, "You could speak with
one of his associates."

"Never mind," I said. I'm probably too big to have an
engaging smile, but I always try. "We know the way."
After all, we'd been here before. One reason Smithso-

nian's so successful is that even people like Ginny who hate his guts have to do business with him every once in a while. With his contacts, he knows things you can't learn anywhere else.

Together, we headed for the hallway that led to Smithsonian's office. Behind us, the receptionist sounded vaguely apoplectic as she tried to protest. She probably had some kind of buzzer she could push to bring the associates running, but she didn't think of it in time.

When we reached the right door (of course it was the right door—it wasn't glass, and nobody else here was likely to rate mahogany), we didn't bother to knock. We just opened it and went in.

Ah, the advantages of surprise. Smithsonian wasn't in conference. He was in the chair behind his desk with his feet up on the blotter. His jacket was off, his tie was loose, sleeves rolled up, and his hands were propped behind his head, showing sweat stains on what should've been an immaculate shirt. He really should've considered turning the heat down. His mouth was open, and he was asleep.

He woke up when I closed the door. A jerk pulled his feet off the desk, swung him upright in his chair. He gaped at us blearily, as if he didn't have one idea in the world who we were.

"Lawrence," Ginny said, "you look tired." For a minute there, she was enjoying herself. "You've been working too hard. You've got to learn to delegate. Let somebody younger do the hard jobs."

He didn't answer right away. Slowly, he got to his feet. He rolled down his sleeves and buttoned the cuffs. He straightened his tie. He put on his jacket. I had to give him credit. By the time he was done, about eight layers of film were gone from his piggy little eyes, and he looked ready.

As he buttoned his jacket over his belly, he started to smile. He wasn't really fat, he just seemed that way. Hell, he even sounded fat. In a nice, plump voice, he said, "I see you've decided to try your luck with Haskell."

His smile was as nice and plump as a barracuda's.

Come to think of it, I didn't much like him either.

But Ginny just looked at him. "How do you figure that?" she asked calmly.

Smithsonian went on smiling. "You asked Haskell where he got your name. Even you wouldn't miss a simple thing like that. But you wouldn't bother to come here to try to get help unless you were working for him."

She studied him up and down. She was taller than he was, and he didn't care for that, but he was too good at what he did to back off. "You're smart, Lawrence," she said after a moment. "I've always said that. Haven't I, Brew?"

I gave Smithsonian a nod. "She always says that."

"But this time," she went on, "I think we can handle it by ourselves." I was glad to hear that, even though I knew she didn't mean it. "Thanks for offering. I was just curious. Why did you give Haskell my name?"

Smithsonian's grin got broader. He was looking positively voracious. "I didn't want the case myself. I thought it was something a female investigator with only one hand deserved."

I couldn't help myself—I've never been any good at holding back when anybody insults or hurts Ginny. In my case, it was a triumph of common sense that I didn't try to jump over the desk. Instead, I slapped my hand down hard in front of him. "Watch your mouth, sucker," I said. "You're going to look a hell of a lot uglier without any teeth."

Before Smithsonian could react, Ginny said, "Heel, Brew." She sounded amused.

I whirled on her. I had my hands locked into fists so I wouldn't hit her. But the way she looked stopped me. I knew that look. And it wasn't directed at me. It was aimed straight at Smithsonian.

"He has a point, Brew," she said almost casually. "But

I don't think that's the real reason he gave us a reference."

Well, it was worth a try. I had to admit he wasn't likely to tell us the truth if I rearranged his face for him. Making me look ridiculous might have better luck. It might be the sort of thing he just couldn't resist.

Because I didn't have anything better to do at the moment, I crossed my arms on my chest like I was sulking and hitched my butt onto the desk with my back to Smithsonian.

"I'd have him put to sleep if I were you," he said to Ginny. He didn't sound like he was smiling. "If he bites you, you'll get rabies."

All in all, I was having a wonderful time. But I went on sitting there and let her handle it.

Her mouth laughed, but her eyes didn't. Softly, she said, "Tell me the real reason, Lawrence."

At first, he didn't answer. But I guess the chance to be superior and make us both look stupid was too good to pass up. "You figure it out." His malice was so thick, you could've spread it around with a trowel. "If you were el Señor, and some minor punk welshed on you, would you call him up and warn him? Give him time to get out of town? Or hire protection?" He snorted his contempt. "I'm surprised you actually let him tell you a story like that. I know plastic flowers with more brains."

Ginny was concentrating hard—she let the insults pass. So did I. All of a sudden, my guts were twisted in fear. Slowly, she said, "So either el Señor doesn't have anything to do with this—"

She didn't need to finish. I knew the rest.

Or else it was some kind of ritual hit. El Señor had been betrayed—his honor had been stained—and he wanted his victim to know exactly what was coming.

And a ritual hit couldn't be stopped. Because el Señor wouldn't care how much it cost—in time, or money, or blood. He'd bury any number of people to avenge himself.

Abruptly, Smithsonian thudded me in the back. "Get off my desk. You're wasting my time."

I got off the desk and turned to face him. Maybe my stomach was knotted up, but I was still able to look fatass Smithsonian in the eye. "So you turned Haskell down," I said conversationally, "because you think somebody like his wife has it in for him and it's all too small and messy for you. Or because you think el Señor wants him dead and the bare idea of tangling with el Señor scares you shitless. And you gave him Ginny's name because you think whatever happens we're going to come up manure. You're a credit to your profession, Lawrence."

"You're wasting my time," he repeated. At least he wasn't smiling anymore. "Leave. Or I'll have you thrown out."

"Poor scared Lawrence Smithsonian," Ginny said. "Go back to sleep. We're leaving."

I went to the door and opened it for her. We left. I even closed it politely behind me.

In the hallway, I said, "Next time, I'm going to take his heart out through his ear."

She didn't apologize for the way she'd treated me. She just said, "Next time, I'm going to let you."

"Are we even now?" I asked.

She didn't hesitate. "Not by a long shot."

Oh, well. At least we were working together. That was an improvement, anyway.

The receptionist didn't give us a glance as we walked past. She might've forgotten all about us. Maybe she was verging on senility. Or maybe her job just wasn't enough to keep the mind alive.

Except for the left forearm jammed into her coat pocket, Ginny was carrying herself like the woman I used to know. But when we got out into the cold and the thin sunlight, she stopped. Even though she didn't look at me, but I could see the fight leaving her eyes. The way she felt about Smithsonian wasn't enough to sustain her.

"Brew," she said, "if he's right—if el Señor has some

reason to want Haskell dead—we've got to get out. While we still can. We can't deal with this."

Usually, things like ritual hits don't seem possible while the sun's shining. They need darkness to make them real. But not this time. This time, I didn't have any trouble hearing what she meant instead of what she said. She meant she only had one hand—and no self-confidence—and she was dependent on a man who might change back into a drunk any time she turned her head to the left.

I didn't try insulting her again. I tried being reasonable. "If all that's true," I said, "tell me why Haskell isn't scared. Even one of Smithsonian's plastic flowers would have the common sense to be scared, if el Señor wanted it dead."

"Maybe he's immune to fear."

"Then we'd better get him locked away before he hurts himself."

Finally, she looked at me. Her gray eyes made me want to fall all over myself. "So what's your theory?"

To keep my self-control, I took her arm and steered her toward the Olds. "Oddly enough, in this day and age," I said, "some people still get mad when the people they love screw around. I think somebody is just threatening the irresistible Reg Haskell to make him stop whatever he's doing. And I think he knows what's going on. That's why he isn't scared. He didn't tell us the truth because he was afraid we wouldn't take him on, but what he really wants us to do is find out who's behind it. He probably hopes it'll turn out to be his wife. That way he can get himself a nice injured-party divorce. He'll be free to chase all the women he wants."

Actually, I didn't think any of that. I didn't believe it—or not believe it either, for that matter. I didn't have a theory. I just had a gut hunch this case was important. I was talking to keep my panic under control—and to keep Ginny from backing out.

She knew what I was doing. After the amount of time

we'd spent together, I wasn't exactly a mystery to her. But she went along with it. "All right," she said. "We'll check out Reston Cole. Then we'll go see Mrs. Haskell."

That should've been fine with me, but it wasn't. I had other things on my mind. I looked at my watch. Almost noon. Trying not to sound like I expected her to yell at me, I said, "We don't have time."

She thought about that for a second. "Probably not," she agreed. "We'll go see Mrs. Haskell tomorrow."

I took a deep breath. Very carefully, I said, "What happens if he gets knocked off tonight, and she turns out to be responsible for it?"

She threw a glare at me. "You think we should split up?" She wasn't surprised—just furious. "What a peachy idea."

"Ginny." I was so careful, I was practically on tiptoe. "We're going to have to take shifts on this thing anyway. We can't both stay awake for the rest of the week. And while he's at work is our only chance to do any investigating. We might as well get started."

She was building up a head of steam that looked strong enough to blow me away. I kept talking, trying to fend her off.

"Let's go someplace where I can rent a car. Then you can go talk to Cole. You're the one with the license." Also the one who knew how to talk to executive banking types. "He won't throw you out on your ear like he would me. And you'll still have time to do some of the spadework we haven't done yet. Like talk to the cops. Find out if Haskell has any kind of background." Her license gave her a legal right to certain kinds of police access, and most of the cops in Puerta del Sol didn't like me. My dead brother'd been a cop.

"I'll go talk to Mrs. Haskell," I went on. "If she gives me anything we can use, I'll follow it up. Otherwise, I'll go back to the bank and see if I can spot anybody keeping a watch on Haskell."

She wanted to explode, but I was making it hard for

her. I was telling her exactly what she would've told me, back in the days before she got maimed. On the other hand, I would've preferred an explosion.

For a second, her eyes filled with tears. Then she blinked them back. "You know I can't drive."

"No," I said bluntly, "I don't know that." I had to be hard on her. It was either that or go step in front of a bus. "This is an automatic transmission." As if she didn't know. "You've been driving it with one hand for years."

Her mouth twisted like the beginning of a sob—or maybe the start of something obscene. Then she pulled it white and straight.

"Get out of the car."

I stared at her.

"I said, get out of the fucking car!"

So I'm not very smart. What do you expect from a temporarily sober alcoholic? I got out of the car.

When I closed the door, she slid over into the driver's seat and cranked down the window. Rattlesnake venom would've been friendlier than the way she looked at me.

"Don't be late. If you show up at the bank drunk, I will personally feed your liver to the coyotes."

She started the car, wrenched the shift into drive so hard I thought it was going to come off in her hand. The only thing I could think of to say was, "How am I supposed to find Mrs. Haskell?" Even her husband didn't know where she was.

"You're the one with all the ideas about how I should run my business," she snapped while she revved the engine. "You figure it out."

She took her foot off the brake, and the Olds squealed its tires as she headed it out of the parking lot.

If Smithsonian had been watching us, he would've laughed out loud. He never would've understood why I suddenly felt lightheaded and the pain in my stomach eased back a couple notches.

Ginny Fistoulari, I thought. By damn. I know that woman.

Chapter Five

Finally I kicked my head into gear and started to think about what I had to do.

For some reason, the hardest part was remembering where the nearest gas station was. But after a minute I seemed to recall seeing one a few blocks south. Hugging my coat against the cold, I began to walk.

Being abandoned by Ginny must've been good for my memory. The gas station was right where I remembered it. And my luck was good, too. The pay phone worked—and it had an intact phone book chained to the booth.

The book gave me the number of the Jiffy Cab Co., and also the location of a convenient rent-a-relic agency. I called for a cab. Then, while I was waiting, I dialed up Ginny's answering service.

One reason she uses that particular service is they keep good records. And she has my name current with them, so when I call they treat me almost like an actual person. After fumbling around for a few seconds, they gave me the number they'd given Ginny this morning for Mrs. Sara Haskell.

It was almost too easy. When I called that number, it turned out to be the Regency Hotel. Which was a little pricier than I'd been expecting. After all, Mrs. Haskell was the wife of a chief accountant, not a bank president.

But I didn't stop to be surprised. I was on a roll. I asked the switchboard to connect me to Mrs. Haskell's room.

She answered before the second ring—she must've been waiting by the phone, waiting for somebody to call, for somebody to tell her what was going on, something. There was a small tremble in her voice as she said, "Yes?"

"Mrs. Haskell?" I didn't like the sound of that voice. It worried me. "Mrs. Sara Haskell?"

"Yes?"

"My name is Axbrewder." Plunging right in. "I work for Fistoulari Investigations. You talked to Ginny Fistoulari earlier this morning."

She didn't say anything. She just waited.

"Ms. Fistoulari turned you down. But since then something's come up. I'd like to talk to you."

I could almost feel the clutch of panic at the other end of the line. Then she said, "Yes." At least this time it wasn't a question. "All right."

I asked for her room number. She gave it to me. I told her I'd be there in half an hour or forty-five minutes. We hung up.

Trusting soul, I thought. Then the cynical side of me answered, Well, of course. Haskell wouldn't've married her if she weren't.

That little tremble in her voice suddenly made the whole case seem more real. Maybe irresistible Reg wasn't taking things seriously, but his wife was. I was shivering in my clothes as I stood around waiting for the Jiffy Cab Co.

They weren't exactly quick about it, but eventually they showed up. The cab took me to the rent-a-relic agency, who allowed me to drive away in a lumbering old Buick with grease-stained seats and only two hubcaps. I was just ten minutes behind schedule as I started following deer tracks and blazed trees to find my way out of the North Valley and back to the beltway.

After that, I made better time. Trailing clouds of

smoke in protest, the Buick cranked itself up to fifty-five or thereabouts, and we went east up the long grade toward the edge of town, where the Regency Hotel lurked in ambush for unsuspecting motorists. It looks like every highway motel you've ever seen, and you don't realize until you're already caught that it gives you twice the luxury at four times the price. But in some ways it was a logical choice for Mrs. Haskell. It wasn't more than eight minutes by the mercy of the city planners from her husband's bank.

I wobbled the Buick into the parking lot around one o'clock. My stomach was starting to think about food—which meant the rest of me was starting to think about booze. Every drunk who's trying to stay sober knows the importance of food. For drunks, any kind of hunger almost magically changes itself into the hunger for booze. But I already knew I wasn't going to have time to eat. I scanned the room numbers nearby to orient myself, then headed around the swimming pool toward the "private" wing at the back of the hotel.

Mrs. Haskell's room was on the second floor, which was also the top floor. After the cold outside, the carpet in the halls felt as thick as quicksand and the air seemed warm enough to start growing a fungus in my underwear. A drink sounded like a better idea all the time.

But I usually felt that way when Ginny wasn't with me. The trick was to keep my priorities straight. The reason Ginny wasn't with me. Mrs. Haskell's voice over the phone. Get on with it, Axbrewder.

When I reached the right door, I raised my fist and knocked. I was sweating.

She answered the door the same way she'd answered the phone—right away.

She was a small, blond woman about my age—one of those attractive middle-aged women who can't seem to escape looking vaguely artificial. She had the kind of hair color that comes from beauty salons, and the kind of tan that comes from sunlamps, and the kind of trim figure that comes from Nautilus machines. The way she was dressed only made it worse. At one in the afternoon, she was still wearing a long chiffon nightgown with a pink satin robe over it. In one hand, she held a glass that smelled like heaven.

But the unsteadiness in her pale eyes wasn't caused by drink. "Mr. Axbrewder?" she said. "Has anything happened to my husband?"

For a few seconds, the smell of good scotch made my head swim. But I got it under control. I couldn't stand the way she was looking at me. Like she'd used up all her courage just asking that one question.

"He's fine," I said. "May I come in?"

A moment passed while she stared at the front of my coat and blinked her eyes. Then she said, "Excuse me. I can't see very well. I haven't got my contacts in." She stepped aside and held the door for me. "Would you like a drink?"

I started to shake my head before I realized she really couldn't see me that clearly. "No, thanks," I said as she closed the door. "Mrs. Haskell, I don't want to scare you"—not any worse than she was scared already—"but until we get this mess cleared up it'd be a good idea not to let anybody in here before you know who they are."

The drink in her hand wasn't the first one she'd had, and she wasn't dressed to face the day, and she hadn't even taken the trouble to put her contacts in—but she went right to the point. "Then he really is in danger?"

I couldn't tell which answer she wanted, yes or no. "He says he is. Until we learn anything different, we'll go on that assumption. Why would he lie?"

She sat down on the edge of the bed, still looking at me without seeing me. I took a chair from in front of the vanity. It was too small for me, but I made do with it. The room wasn't one of the Regency's more moderate accommodations. It had flowered wallpaper that matched the bedspread and brass fixtures that matched the bedstead. The bed itself looked big enough for a game of volleyball. And the liquor cabinet was so well stocked it made my back teeth hurt. Reg Haskell didn't pay for rooms like this on a chief accountant's salary.

His wife finished her drink, leaned one arm on the bedstead for support, and said, "To get me out of the house."

Sometimes it pays to be slow on the uptake. "Is that what he told you?" I asked obtusely.

"No," she said as if it hadn't been a stupid question. "He told me some men want to hurt him. He told me to leave so I wouldn't be in danger—so those men wouldn't try to get at him through me."

So far, so good. "Did he happen to say why anybody would want to hurt him?"

She nodded. "He said he beat those men to an investment they really wanted. They needed it to stay in business. It was too complicated to explain. But they're thugs, and until they calmed down or gave up they would want to hurt him."

Well, well, I thought. One story for the bodyguards, a different one for the wife. It might not mean anything—maybe Haskell was just ashamed to let his wife know how stupid he'd been—but it was sure as hell worth thinking about.

But not right then. I didn't want to lose the thread. As blandly as possible, so as not to sound threatening or judgmental, I asked, "You don't believe him?"

She rested her chin on the arm braced on the bedstead. "I don't know," she said. "I don't think I know anything about him anymore." She sighed. "He's been making these investments for four or five years. He's good at it." She didn't need to tell me that. All I had to do was look around. "But nobody's ever wanted to hurt him for it."

"Has he ever told you anything about these investments?" Carefully.

"No. I don't understand things like that." She gave me a lonely smile. "I don't even understand life insurance."

I smiled back at her. "Nobody understands life insurance."

But she couldn't see my smile. And she obviously didn't care whether God Himself understood life insurance. I went back to my questions.

"The fact he hasn't been threatened before—is that what makes you think he might not be telling the truth?"

"I don't know what I think." As she talked, I began to wonder just how much she'd had to drink. "I used to be sure. That was why I called you. Fistoulari Investigations. He's changed so much.

"Do you think I'm attractive, Mr. Axbrewder?" she asked without giving me any warning. But I didn't have to answer. She wasn't looking at me. "I ought to be," she went on. "I work at it. But he didn't change because of me. I started working at it because I saw him change and it scared me. I knew I was going to lose him.

"It had to be another woman. What else could make him so different?"

I did my level best to fade into the wallpaper. I wanted her to feel like she was just talking to herself. "How was he different?"

"He became charming," she said as if that explained everything. Luckily she didn't stop. "When we met—he was studying accounting, and I was one of the department secretaries—he was just an ordinary guy. Nice and conscientious and a little dull. I thought I was lucky to get him. Then he went to work for the bank, and he didn't exactly set the world on fire, but it was a good job, and he was moving up slowly. If he'd had more ambition, he would've moved faster. But I didn't care about that. I liked us the way we were. It didn't seem to bother him when I gained a little weight.

"But then he had to go away for a business trip one weekend, and when he came back he was excited. More excited than I'd ever seen. He said he'd gotten involved in some kind of investment and made a lot of money. I thought that was nice. I liked seeing him excited. It made him—I don't know how to describe it. It made him sparkle. It seemed to make him handsomer. And we'd never had a lot of money.

"So a few months later he took another trip and came back with even more money and he looked even more excited. He treated me like a queen, and we bought new clothes, and I could see the way other women started to look at him, and I was pleased and proud. But then he took another trip. And another one. And another one. And the way he glowed and laughed and teased got stronger and stronger. One day, I looked at the two of us in a mirror. He looked so good it almost broke my heart—and I looked like I already had too many grand-children."

Abruptly, she got off the bed, went to the liquor cabinet, and poured herself another glass of scotch. I watched her with my tongue hanging out, but I didn't say anything.

"We bought a new house." Back at the bed, she piled the pillows against the brass frame at the head and sat there, leaning back. She probably couldn't see me at all from that distance. "He started getting more promotions. He still treated me like a queen. I could buy anything I wanted. Do anything I wanted. He seemed to spend a lot of time courting me. But it wasn't any good anymore. The investments were just an excuse. Why did he have to go away to do them? Why couldn't he do them at home? But he was away practically every weekend. All I had to do was look in the mirror, and I knew he was involved with another woman. He was too excited and alive for anything else. How could any other woman resist him?

"So I started working at making myself more attractive. What else could I do? I wanted to win him back. That kept me going for a long time. But I guess I'm not very smart." Her bitterness was all for herself. None of it spilled over onto irresistible Reg. "I finally figured out that I wouldn't know the difference even if I did win him back. There was nothing wrong with the way he treated me. It couldn't get any better. Except for the trips—And I couldn't ask him to give them up. I couldn't ask him if he was having an affair. If I did, he might decide to divorce me. I couldn't stand that. Maybe I'd lost him, but at least he wasn't gone. Does that make any sense? He was still there. His eyes still sparkled when he looked at me. I didn't dare risk—

"But then he did something he'd never done before. He said some men wanted to hurt him, and he told me to get out of the house. What was I supposed to believe? I've never heard of people beating each other up over investments. I thought he wanted me out of the house so he could have that other woman visit him.

"That's why I called you. I couldn't stand it anymore. I wanted to find out the truth—without losing him. I didn't want to risk giving him a reason to divorce me.

"But Ms. Fistoulari said you don't do that kind of work. And then you called and said something had come up. Suddenly I thought something had happened to him, he was telling the truth and those men hurt him and I didn't even know where he was so I could go to him. I've been distrusting him all these years for nothing." Tears ran down her cheeks and made dark stains on the pink satin of her robe. "I deserve to lose him. I deserve it." Her mouth twisted, but she didn't sob. The tears just ran and ran down her cheeks.

Right there, I decided Reg Haskell was a shit.

Unfortunately, that didn't make my position any easier. I'd never taken the idea of Sara Haskell hiring goons to lean on her husband seriously. If that was what she had in mind, she never would've called Ginny in the first place. But I still had to do my job. And there was at least one too many coincidences running around in this case for my peace of mind.

Quietly, trying to sound natural and normal, I asked, "Mrs. Haskell, why did you call us? I mean, us personally. Why Fistoulari Investigations instead of some other agency?" I watched her closely. "Lawrence Smithsonian and Associates, for example?"

She didn't react to the name. With an aimless shrug, she said, "I don't know anything about detectives. I just looked in the yellow pages." Her head lolled on the pillows behind her, but we both knew she wasn't going to get any rest. "Did you know," she said, "that Ms. Fistoulari is the only woman in the yellow pages? The only woman detective. I wanted a woman. I thought she'd understand."

But now she didn't care—that was obvious. I got to my feet. She needed help, or at least some kind of comfort, but there were too many things I couldn't say to her. I couldn't tell her I thought her husband actually was screwing around. And I couldn't tell her I thought he was in real danger.

But she looked so lost, I didn't have the heart for the inane reassurance I'd given Eunice Wint. So I just said softly, "Thanks for your time. We'll let you know when we find out what's going on."

In response, she murmured, "Thank you," without seeing me and maybe without understanding what I'd said. She may not have noticed when I let myself out of the room.

She hadn't once asked me what I was doing there— what business I had asking her questions about her husband. She was that lonely.

Chapter Six

On my way back to the car, I wondered if maybe Haskell hired us just to make his wife believe he wasn't cheating on her. That sounded Byzantine enough for an accountant—somebody who lived by the tricks you can do with numbers. In that case, Ginny and I were completely wasting our time. But I couldn't think of any reason why Haskell needed his wife that badly. His position in the bank didn't depend on her. And she didn't have anything to do with his so-called investments.

It was too many for me. Ginny was better at sorting things like this out than I was. She was our expert on sifting the facts to get at the truth. I was the one who made intuitive leaps and landed in trouble. And my intuition wasn't saying much. It had probably gone south for the winter.

So I pushed the whole mess out of my mind and got busy with other things. After I persuaded the Buick to start, I hauled it up onto the beltway and then let it slide down the long slope toward the Flat River and the Valley.

I was going to talk to Pablo Santiago's parents.

Like any normal acquaintance of the family, I hoped they'd tell me he was home safe and sound and maybe

even a little bit reformed—chastened by experience, as
they say. But I didn't believe it. The disappearance of a
kid who ran numbers hardly a day before the numbers
boss turned up dead was more coincidence than I could
swallow.

The last time I'd seen Pablo, he'd been hard at work,
doing what numbers runners do—going from person to
person either collecting bets or paying out winnings, depending on the day of the week (Saturday night the win-
ners got paid). In my best Stern Uncle manner, I'd told
him, "A man does not run to do the bidding of those who
are themselves not men enough to do their own running." Which was probably pretty funny, coming from
me—even in Spanish. But you can't change the world by
giving it stern advice. Choosing between a quick buck
and the advice of an oversized drunk, even a saint
wouldn't hesitate. And so kids get caught up in it. After
a few quick bucks, they become loyal to el Señor and all
the opportunities he offers. In Pablo's case, I felt vaguely
responsible.

I took time I should've spent doing legwork for Ginny
to visit Rudolfo and Tatianna Santiago.

Their grocery store—the sign out front said "Grocery"
in chipped gray paint—was down in the old part of town,
at least half an hour and two entirely different worlds
away from the Regency Hotel. As distinct from what
Puerta del Sol calls Old Town (where most of the buildings aren't any older than I am, even if they are quaint as
all hell, and the tourists are thick as flies on manure—
except in this case it's the manure that eats the flies), the
old part of town is as close as you can get to a *barrio* built
out of three-hundred-year-old adobe.

A century or so ago, it was the actual center of the
city. But now it's just a warren of dirty bars and fleabag
rooming houses, abandoned buildings, businesses slowly
crumbling to ruin, defeated old chapels where women go
in the mornings to pray their men won't drink at night,
sweat-holes where you can get into any kind of trouble

your heart desires, and one cheap little park over on Tin
Street. That's just one more item in my long list of
grudges against the city fathers. Everywhere you go in
Puerta del Sol, the streets have names like Hidalgo and
Paseo Grande and Mesa Verde—except in some of the
newer developments, where the names are so cute they'll
give you diabetes. But in the old part of town, streets
with three hundred years of history are called Tin or Coal
or Seventh. And it's crowded to the teeth with Chicanos,
Mestizos, Indians, and bums of every description who
grub their lives away or sell their souls for sums of money
most Anglos think of as loose change.

Some days, it was the only part of town I understood.

It was where I did my drinking.

The Buick made good time getting there—it liked
going downhill. I didn't have to worry about where to
park it (your average Mercedes has a street-life of half an
hour in the old part of town, but the Buick looked like it
belonged), so I pulled it up in front of the Santiagos'
Grocery and left it there.

Sidewalks were few and far between here, but on this
block most of the buildings had low porches that served
the same function. A winter wind was blowing—not
hard, but full of implied bitterness—and dust and candy
wrappers and cigarette butts eddied halfheartedly past
my shoes. The sky wasn't clear anymore. It'd turned the
dead gray-white color of ashes. The temperature was
going to start dropping soon.

The Santiagos' store was one of those places that never
looks clean, even when it is. The stains were too deeply
ingrained in the plaster, and the adobes of the floor
didn't stand up well to hard use. The whole store was
only a little bigger than Ginny's office, and the shelves
were packed halfway to the ceiling. In spite of that, the
merchandise was hard to see. The Santiagos kept the
lights dim to save on electricity.

Both of them were there. The store needed them, and
they couldn't shut it down on a Monday. Their customers

would suffer. Today probably a couple of hundred black-shawled grandmothers would come in to buy all the nickel-and-dime staples they could carry home in their old arms, to make up for Sunday's cooking. If the grocery closed on Monday, those women'd have to try to carry twice as much on Tuesday.

Rudolfo and Tatianna were both short—at least compared to me. She was so plump the top of the apron tied around her waist disappeared into the folds of her body. She had a round face, and her coarse black hair with its white speckles was pulled into a bun at the back of her neck. But under her fat I knew she had the muscles of a stevedore. I'd seen the way she could throw cases of canned beans around the store. By contrast, her husband was thin. You could see the bones of his forearms shift under the leathered skin when he moved his hands. His eyes were always downcast with habitual politeness. But his moustache was assertive enough to tell anybody who looked at him that polite wasn't the same thing as meek. He'd used so much wax it was in danger of catching fire every time he lit a cigarette.

They both had the kind of faces Chicanos develop in an Anglo world—sad-eyed and weary, capable of almost any amount of sorrow. Under other circumstances, they might've been glad to see me. When faces like theirs smile, it's as good as a sunrise. This time they made the effort, but they couldn't pull it off.

"Señor Axbrewder," she said. "After so long a time. How good to see you."

"Señora Santiago." My Spanish was a little rusty, but I didn't have to sweat to bring it back. "Señor Santiago. The pleasure is mine. Are you well?"

"As well as God permits," she replied. "Life has many difficulties for everyone." Her unhappiness lay in her voice like a pile of rocks, but she was too polite—and reserved—to mention something that personal. "And the Señora Fistoulari? Is she well?"

I gave a shrug that wasn't anywhere near as eloquent

as it should've been. "Like yourself, as well as God permits. Her injury"—the grapevine being what it was, I was sure the Santiagos knew about Ginny's injury—"grieves her."

That was a bit more direct than they were used to. They stood there not looking me in the eye, politely sympathetic and just a little embarrassed. After all, I was an Anglo, even if I did have passable Spanish. They would've defended my merit with great loyalty—and high indignation if they were doubted. But everyone knows all Anglos are crazy.

To ease the situation, Santiago spoke for the first time. "Señor Axbrewder, what we have is yours. How may we serve you?"

A good question. Now that I was here, I wasn't so sure about what I was doing. On the other hand, my feeling of responsibility didn't go away. I should've spent ten minutes making polite conversation before I got to the point, but I didn't have either the time or the heart for it. Trying to strike the right balance between detachment and concern, I said, "I have read in the newspaper concerning the disappearance of young Pablo." I was asking them if he'd come home.

Their answer was as oblique as my question. They didn't say anything.

They didn't have to.

"Señor," I said. "Señora." Feeling my way. "I have done my work for you in the past, as you know. Now I wish to do such work again. If you will permit it, I wish to seek the whereabouts of young Pablo."

For an instant, Señora Santiago's gaze flicked up to my face. Then she looked at her husband. But he didn't look at either of us.

Neither of them spoke.

Their constraint didn't seem entirely natural. My offer didn't please them, even though they had every reason to be satisfied with the work Ginny and I'd done for them.

Either they knew something about Pablo's disappearance they didn't want to tell me, or they didn't trust me.

Or they couldn't afford to hire me?

"In this matter," I said with more bluntness than good manners, "I do not wish payment. I have conceived a fondness for Pablo. I wish to seek him out for the peace of my heart."

She turned away and started straightening the cans on a shelf beside her. But she couldn't keep it up. With both hands, she lifted her apron to cover her face.

I didn't know what to say, so I kept my mouth shut. The silence made my stomach hurt like a bad tooth, but I forced myself to keep quiet and wait.

Santiago stared at his wife's back for a long minute. Then some combination of decency and pain made him try to explain.

"Señor Axbrewder," he said softly, "among our people many tales are told. Some are true, some false. Some become false in the telling. But no harm is intended by them. With tales our people amuse themselves, to soften the difficulties of life."

He shifted uncomfortably. I had no idea what he was getting at.

Still watching his wife's back, he said, "One tale concerns a large *hombre* who labors among the sufferings of others and has become devoted to strong drink."

I almost gaped at him. So that was it. They weren't going to talk to me about Pablo because they didn't trust me. Suddenly, the store seemed to become too hot, and I was sweating again.

But Santiago wasn't finished. "I have heard another tale also." He sounded like he was actually trying to be kind to me. "I have heard that this same large *hombre* once sought speech with that unforgiven *pendejo*"—coming from him, the obscenity sounded extravagant and bitter—"whom the Anglos name el Señor. This the large *hombre* did in his need, because of a peril to his brother's daughter and other children. But el Señor forced drink upon him and caused him to be beaten and cast him out."

He shrugged delicately. "I know the truth of none of these things. But the *chota capitán* has spoken to us of our son. The police seek him as they are able. You need not trouble yourself, Señor Axbrewder."

It took me a minute to absorb what he meant. I was too mad to think straight. He was warning me. Trust didn't have anything to do with it. He was trying to tell me a drunk el Señor didn't like had better not go around asking questions about Pablo.

But why? What did Pablo's disappearance have to do with el Señor?

All at once, my intuition woke up and started jumping to conclusions in all directions. "Señor Santiago," I said, my voice as soft as his, "you have spoken with el Señor."

After a long moment, he nodded.

"What has he said to you?"

Abruptly, his wife whipped down her apron and swung toward me. Her eyes flared fury and grief. "He tells us that our son will be avenged. That Godless man speaks to us of vengeance, when the fault belongs to him and no other."

Avenged, I thought. Oh my God. But I didn't stop. "He is dead?" The way I said it made Santiago look at me. "You have knowledge of this?"

"Yes, Señor," he replied through his teeth. "I have knowledge."

The rational part of my mind plodded slowly along behind me, thinking, They don't know he's dead. They haven't found a body. If they found a body, the store'd be closed. They'd be in mourning. But the rest of me had already arrived somewhere else. They know Pablo's dead because el Señor told them. They went to el Señor because they knew Pablo was running numbers and they were afraid and didn't have anywhere else to turn, and he told them their son was dead.

Before Santiago could recover enough of his manners

and dignity to drop his eyes, I demanded, "Did you speak to the *chotas* of this?"

Señora Santiago snapped, "Is he a fool?" She made a gesture with her open hand that indicated her husband from head to foot. "Would he betray his son and his life to those who care nothing by naming el Señor to them? Then both the *chotas* and that evil man would fall upon us as vultures feast upon the lost."

I knew how she felt. Puerta del Sol's finest didn't exactly treat me with the milk of human kindness—and I wasn't even Chicano. But simple practicality, if not fairness, impelled me to say, "Some among them are worthy of trust."

Santiago nodded. Maybe he was just being polite to the crazy Anglo. But his wife was too angry and hurt to stop. "This one is not. He is vile among our people." She was raging so she wouldn't start to keen. "It would be an ill deed to tell such a one the name of his own father. That pig."

Well, I could think of maybe twenty detectives—and three times that many street cops—who fit the description. "Señora," I said, "who was that man who spoke to you of your son?"

She was mad enough to answer. But her people had been dealing with Anglos for better than two hundred years, and her instinct for caution ran deep. Clamping her mouth shut, she looked at her husband.

Slowly, he said, "Señor Axbrewder, our Pablo is dead. He set his feet to a bad way, but he was only a child. No good or evil will restore him. If you concern yourself in this sorrow, you also may die. What purpose will be served by a naming of names?"

I didn't know the answer to that, so I made one up. "I am Anglo. My voice is heard in places where yours is not." Which was half true, anyway. Ginny's been known to get the D.A.'s attention, when she wants it. "A name may do me no harm, and yet have great power in the ears of those who merit trust."

Santiago thought for a minute while his wife glared at the floor and knotted her hands in and out of her apron. Then his shoulders lifted in a shrug that might've been hope or despair.

"Cason," he said. "*Capitán* Cason."

Well, well. Captain Cason. Captain of Detectives Philip pig bastard Cason. That made sense. He was exactly the sort of man who'd be assigned to investigate Roscoe Chavez's murder. The sort of man you could trust not to learn more than you wanted him to find out. Not where people like el Señor were concerned, anyway. The bare idea made me sicker than I was already. I could imagine the way he'd behaved when he questioned the Santiagos.

"I know this *Capitán* Cason." To make myself feel better, I said obscenely, "He has the balls of a dog." Santiago acted like he hadn't heard me, but his wife let out one quick, flashing smile. "But better men stand over him," I went on. "If they are told what he does, they will not ignore it."

The whole thing made me livid. "My friends," I said, "I have had no drink for many months. I will do nothing that is foolish. But I swear to you that I will do all that I am able, so that those who cause the deaths of children will not continue."

He didn't respond. He was probably afraid he'd let me into more trouble than I could handle. But she wiped her eyes with the backs of her hands and said, "*Gracias*, Señor."

So I wouldn't start foaming at the mouth, I turned and walked out of the store.

I was thinking, el Señor knows Pablo is dead.

He knows Pablo was killed.

He knows why.

Chapter Seven

I didn't know why.

But I wasn't about to ask sweet old Captain Cason for an answer. I'd had a run-in with him once. Down in this neighborhood, I'd happened on a tourist dude from Cleveland or someplace while he was trying to rape a local woman. In an excess of zeal, as they say, I damn near put my whole foot through one of his kidneys. Cason didn't like that. In his mind, a ruptured kidney was too high a price to pay for trying to give some Mex chippy what she had coming. Since this particular Mex chippy happened to be a decent and hard-working woman, he hadn't had any trouble leaning on her until she dropped the charges. What I wanted to do with Captain Cason didn't involve asking questions.

For that matter, I wasn't going to talk to any of his superiors. Not yet—not when I didn't have anything solid to go on. And not when I couldn't imagine any kind of man or woman stupid or reckless or even just ignorant enough to hurt one of el Señor's numbers runners. That was like putting your entire hand in an active garbage disposal. Like most good criminal operations, a successful numbers racket runs on trust. In other words, if you do anything to mess it up, you can trust el Señor to cut your heart out and feed it to your loved ones with *salsa*. A kid like Pablo carrying bets or winnings is usually safer than a bank vault. Whatever happened to Pablo, whoever did it was so out of touch with reality it took my breath away.

No, I didn't want to talk to anybody in Captain Cason's chain of command. The man I wanted to talk to was Sergeant Raul Encino of Missing Persons. Not because the case was on his desk, but because he was a good cop and he might be able to tell me what was going on in the department. He didn't really owe me any favors, but he thought he did because he cared about his work and Ginny and I had helped him out once.

Unfortunately, he was on the night shift, so I wasn't going to be able to call him for a few hours yet.

That galled me. At the moment, I was a hell of a lot more interested in Pablo Santiago than in threats to Reg Haskell's legs—which I wasn't sure I believed in anyway. But I didn't have much choice. Trailing cigarette butts and dust, I went back to the Buick, fired it up, and began the long drive toward Haskell's branch of the First Puerta del Sol National Bank.

I made it with fifteen minutes to spare. At a quarter after four, I lumbered into the ice cream parlor parking lot and found a space near the one where Ginny sat glaring at me in the Olds. What with winter and the cloud cover, dusk was coming early, and the air had a gray, grainy quality, like amateur photography. The wind was getting sharper, and the temperature was starting to drop. The combination made my eyes water as I got out of the Buick and headed toward the Olds. By the time I got into the passenger seat beside Ginny where I belonged, I must've looked like I was crying.

Even that didn't work. The sight of a man six foot five and a quarter of a thousand pounds dripping like an orphaned four-year-old has been known to make her laugh out loud, but not this time. Her face was the same color as the air, and she didn't look at me. Her left forearm lay in her lap like a dead piece of meat, but her right kept squeezing the wheel as if she couldn't find a way to grip it hard enough.

In one of my pockets, I found a clean handkerchief. After I blew my nose, my eyes stopped watering. With as much gentleness as I could muster, I asked, "Been here long?"

She didn't answer that. In a tone she held deliberately flat, keeping herself under control, she said, "Brew, I don't like fighting with you."

I couldn't bear the way she looked. It took me through the middle like a drill bit. I folded my arms protectively over my stomach and tried not to sound too brittle as I commented, "That's never stopped you before."

She didn't turn her head. I had a perfect view of the way the muscles at the corner of her jaw bunched. But she didn't say anything until she was sure of her self-command. Then she sounded soft and hard, like being tapped lightly with a truncheon.

"You're living in a dream world, Axbrewder. Face facts. We aren't equipped to handle this. It scared Smithsonian off, and he has a hell of a lot more resources than we do. If it's for real, it's too dangerous. And if it isn't, we're wasting our time."

I absolutely couldn't bear it. "Don't tell me." Sonof-abitch Axbrewder in full cry. "Don't tell me Reston Cole refused to see you—and you let him get away with it."

Her control scared me. It was too tight. When she broke, the explosion was going to do something terrible.

Carefully, she unclosed her hand from the wheel and stared at the stress lines on her palm and fingers. "Reston Cole," she said, "is on vacation. He left two days ago. His secretary says he's gone white-water rafting in the Grand Canyon. Won't be back for two weeks. I found that out before anybody in the building knew who I was or why I wanted to see him, so his secretary didn't have any reason to lie to me. Anyway, she sounded too cheerful and helpful about it. And too many other people heard her."

Oh, well. Scratch one perfectly decent source of information. It all seemed a little too convenient for me, but there wasn't anything I could do about it.

"What about the cops?" I asked. "Have they got anything on irresistible Reg?"

"Not even a parking ticket." She snorted bitterly. "It's Monday. They didn't feel much like working. I had to sit around for an hour and a half. But they finally called back. He's cleaner than we are."

That wasn't saying much. Most of the population of the state pen is cleaner than I am. But I had to admit we weren't getting anywhere.

I didn't say anything. It was my turn to talk, but I didn't volunteer. I needed Ginny to ask. I needed her to do something that would indicate some kind of decision.

Nobody ever said she was stupid. After a minute, she finally looked at me. She didn't say, If you think I'm going to let you do this alone you're out of your mind. I couldn't read her face or her voice. But she gave me what I wanted.

"All right," she said. "I'll go along. At least for a while. What did you get from Mrs. Haskell?"

I let out a private sigh of relief. Then I told her all about my conversation with Sara Haskell.

I'm good at things like that. When I was done, Ginny had the whole thing almost word for word.

While I talked, she went back to staring out the windshield. Her eyes matched the dusk. Before I finished, she began tapping her fingers on the wheel. A light touch without any rhythm—just thinking. I was so relieved I almost kissed her.

To be honest, I was also relieved because she was thinking too hard to ask me how I'd spent the rest of the afternoon.

"I wonder what changed him," she murmured finally. The cold outside was leaking into the Olds, but she didn't seem to notice. "How does a boring accountant turn into a lady-killer?"

"Success?" I suggested. I knew her mind was somewhere else, but I didn't care. "This is America. Success is supposed to be magic."

She shook her head. "Risk." For a second, I thought she was answering me. Then she went on, "There's no way to make that kind of money that fast without a lot of risk."

"Not to mention breaking the law," I muttered. I've never understood how people make money legally.

"Brew," she said slowly, "can you think of any kind of investment in the whole world that makes you rich over the weekend?"

That little improbability had occurred to me, but the way she mentioned it made me realize it hadn't occurred to me hard enough. For something to say, I said, "I bet Smithsonian knows exactly what kind of investments those were."

"Fatass," she growled automatically. But she was thinking something else. "Or maybe," she said, "he's been lying to his wife all along."

Lying to her for five years now. "Makes you wonder, doesn't it," I drawled. "Makes you wonder what the truth is like, if it's enough for him to tell his own wife lies a brick wall'd have trouble believing."

She snorted again. "It makes me wonder about his opinion of her."

There was an obvious point to be made about all this. So maybe Reg Haskell had been lying to his wife. So maybe he thought she had all the brains of a well-preserved artichoke. And maybe he was even screwing around with every woman in San Reno County. So what? None of that proved he wasn't in real danger. And if he was in danger, then we had to protect him.

It was an obvious point, so I didn't make it. I didn't want Ginny to go back to thinking about el Señor and ritual hits—and about dropping the case. Instead, I pointed at the door of the ice cream parlor. "Let's ask him. Here he comes."

It was 4:30 on the dot, and Haskell came walking out of the bank like he didn't have an enemy or a worry within a hundred miles.

As we got out of the car, Ginny muttered, "You ask him. I'm already too mad to be civil about it."

Haskell waved and moved toward us, carrying his briefcase. He wore the sort of elegant camel's hair coat that makes you think the man inside it has all the money in the world—which reminded me for some reason that he hadn't sounded all that rich when Ginny told him about her fee. Cash poor? I had no way of knowing. But he sure as hell wasn't cold, not in that coat. He didn't have the night's chill starting to poke at him through his clothes the way I did.

Damned if he didn't look glad to see us. Not because we were protection. Because he liked us.

But he put on his sober face when he reached us. After a discreet look around to be sure none of the other people leaving the bank could hear him, he asked, "Was Reston able to tell you anything?" There was something in his voice that might've been eagerness or anxiety or even humor.

Brusquely, Ginny told him Reston Cole was on vacation.

Haskell managed to look crestfallen, but I felt sure we hadn't ruined his day. He glanced up at my face, then back to Ginny. "So what do we do now?"

"Get your car," she said. "We'll follow you home." She wasn't making any particular effort to sound congenial toward our client. "When we get there, stay in your car. One of us'll go in first—make sure it's safe. Your playmates have had all day to set up for you, if that's the way they work. Then we'll all go in and see what we can do about turning your house into a fort."

That didn't seem to be exactly what Haskell had in mind. Maybe it wasn't enough like playing cowboys-and-Indians. But Ginny was using her nobody-argues-with-me voice, and he didn't try. With a shrug, he turned away and started walking toward a Continental the size of a yacht at the other end of the lot.

He looked too exposed for his own good. Instinctively, Ginny and I both scanned the area, hoping we wouldn't see anybody who might be classed as suspicious.

We didn't. When Haskell reached his car, unlocked it, and climbed in, Ginny let her breath out through her teeth. "If we are honest to God going to work on this case," she said softly, "we'd better stop letting him walk around like that."

I nodded. My heart was beating a little funny. I was out of practice for this kind of job.

Ginny got into the Olds. I went back to the Buick. Haskell pulled his boat out of its parking space ahead of us and sailed away like the captain of his soul, leading us farther into the Heights toward the mountains.

All of a sudden, I wasn't so sure I wanted this case anymore. The afternoon was getting dark fast. And at night everything changed. For no good reason, I was starting to believe in the danger again.

In less than a mile, the Buick's heater had me sweating. I wanted to blare my horn at the other drivers, maybe try a little demolition derby, anything to clear the road so our private procession could get to Haskell's house before dark. I hate walking into unfamiliar houses in the dark when they might be full of goons. But thanks to the way Puerta del Sol's laid out, half the people in the Western Hemisphere live in the Heights, and they all want to get home between 4:30 and 5:30.

Fortunately, Haskell turned off the main roads after ten or twelve stoplights, and we started moving up into the kind of suburban development where Puerta del Sol's new money hangs out on its way to even better real estate. We didn't go all the way to the foothills, but by the time we reached Cactus Blossom Court, off Foothill Drive, we were close enough to see what we were missing. Cactus Blossom left Foothill on the spine of a ridge and dropped almost straight down back toward the city for a hundred yards before it became a cul-de-sac. From there, you could see the sunset turning the mountains pink above you and, in the other direction, the whole city changing into lights and jewels.

I didn't get a very good view of the neighborhood— just enough to see the houses were pretty tightly crammed together, no more than six feet from each other or fifteen from the sidewalk. In this part of town, you paid for view and size, not land. Haskell's house was on the south side of the cul-de-sac at the bottom of the hill. In fact, it was built back into a deep erosion gully called Arroyo Hombre, which used to overflow every spring, when the snow on the mountains melted, until the Corps of Engineers built a flood-control project that routed all the water somewhere else. As a result, Haskell's house had a dramatic—if not very convenient—place to sit.

He wheeled his Continental up into the driveway with considerable élan. But then he had enough sense to wait for us to catch up with him.

Ginny parked beside him. I snapped off my headlights and pulled in behind him. His lights and Ginny's shone on the doors of the double garage, but there was enough reflection to show a front yard landscaped with gravel and scrub piñon, low walls separating the properties on either side, and a recessed entryway bracketed by young cedars so well groomed they looked like artificial Christmas trees.

Ginny ditched her lights. Haskell did the same. She and I met at the driver's window of the Continental. After the heat and frustration of driving, I seemed to feel the cold slide into my clothes like a shiv.

"Stay here," Ginny said. Only somebody who knew her as well as I did could've heard the edge of fear in her voice. Dusk hid the details of her face, but her purse hung from her right shoulder, and her hand was in her purse, gripping her .357. Neither of us could see what Haskell looked like. "I'll be right back."

"Don't be silly," I replied with my usual tact. "You got to be the hero last time. It's my turn."

She didn't say anything. But she didn't try to stop me.

Well, nobody ever said I was smart. I took the key from Haskell. Trying not to shiver, I went to check out the house.

When I reached the cedars, I paused to loosen my .45 in its holster. But I didn't pull it out. I just instinctively trust size and muscle more than firepower. You'd be surprised how many people are afraid to shoot at something as big as I am.

I took one more look at the last pink light gleaming from the snow on the mountains. My heart seemed to be stumbling around in my chest like a drunk as I started for the door.

The door wasn't just recessed—it was downright bashful. It hid at the end of an aisle twenty feet long set into the house. Overhead was a trellis covered with something, probably wisteria, but without leaves it let in enough light to give me some vague idea of what I was doing. I felt like I was walking into a shooting gallery as I went to the door as quietly as I could.

At the door, I stopped. All right, Axbrewder. Just take it easy. This is why they pay you the big bucks.

I put the key in the lock and opened the door a few inches. Then I reached my arm in through the crack, feeling along the wall for the light switches.

Luckier than I deserved. I found a panel of three or four switches. So I wouldn't have time to panic, I flipped them all at once, pushed the door open, and started inside.

Lights came on behind me along the aisle and in the room I'd entered, a kind of off-center atrium with a big, dark hole in the floor (actually, it was a stairway to the lower level) and a railed walk around it giving access to other rooms on this floor. No thanks to my light-footedness, I wasn't making a sound. The carpet was so thick small children could've hidden in it. The decor was new—

money garish—rococo wrought iron for the railing, gilt on
the door frames, Spanish bordello light fixtures. But the
stairwell in front of me looked as ominous as a cave.

Nobody here but us chickens. So far.

As it turned out, there was nobody in the house at all.
But I was at least six years older before I was sure. The
whole place was a maze, and by the time I'd searched it
all I was expecting to find the skeletons of lost explorers.
One wall of the entryway aisle proved, obviously enough,
to be part of the garage. But the opposite wing was so
confused with closets and bathrooms and doors in odd
places that I almost didn't find the master bedroom. The
rest of the upper floor was easier. To the left of the
atrium, a living room with a spectacularly tasteless wetbar and several large windows staring out at the privacy
wall. Across the stairwell, a study and a solarium. Opposite the living room, a combination utility and laundry
room.

The lower floor, on the other hand, was heaven for
people who like to jump out at other people. There was
only one large room, a den with enormous, overstuffed
furniture and two picture windows, one for Arroyo
Hombre, the other for the lights of the city. Everything
else was built into, around, or behind itself. Even the
kitchen was hard to find without a compass. I kept turning left at the wrong bathroom and ending up in the
room with the pool table. And I needed three tries to
reach the dining room, even though it shared one wall
with the den.

When I was sure the place was empty, it wasn't because I'd searched every room. Maybe I had—or maybe
not. I just didn't believe anybody hiding in there could
stand to wait that long without shooting me in the back.

Fortunately, I didn't get lost on my way to the front
door.

Ginny and Haskell were waiting for me in the aisle. I
thought that was a pretty exposed place for just standing
around—until I saw all the light flooding the gravel yard

and realized I must've turned on the lights across the front of the house when I went in. Here Ginny could at least stand between Haskell and the street and keep her eyes open.

Something about the angle of her right arm gave me the impression she was gripping her .357 too hard. Anxiety made her skin look tight across the bones of her face.

For something to say, I muttered, "We don't get paid enough for this kind of work."

She took her hand out of her purse and hugged the front of her coat. "What took you so long?" she said unsteadily. "We're freezing out here."

Haskell wasn't cold. He looked like he was pleased about something. "It's a big house."

I wanted to say, Don't be too proud of it. You're going to have a lot of fun getting around here with two broken legs. But he was the client, so I kept my mouth shut.

A funny thing happened when he walked into the house. Somehow, he made the furnishings look less garish. They all belonged to him, and he was at home.

While I locked the door and Ginny glanced around the atrium, trying not to let what she was thinking show, Haskell hung up his coat in a closet I'd missed, then walked into the study to drop off his briefcase and came back rubbing his hands. "Your partner has the advantage of you, Ms. Fistoulari," he said with the smile of a happy man. "Why not let me show you around?"

"Fine," Ginny said. "I need to look at the locks. See how many different ways there are in here." But she didn't do any unbending for his benefit.

Like a professional tour guide, he started right in. "The garage is over here. Doesn't do us much good, I'm afraid." A smile full of wry charm and self-deprecation. It's hard, I thought, to dislike somebody who enjoys himself that much. "It's still full of our old furniture. We just haven't gotten around to getting rid of what we don't need."

I left him to it. Back down the stairs, I went hunting for the kitchen again to see what I could do about making some supper. I felt like I hadn't had anything to eat for days now.

At first, I couldn't find anything except liquor and wine—gallons of the stuff, backup supplies for the wet-bar in the living room and at least two cabinets, one in the den, one in the game room. That didn't seem fair to a man with my problems. Luckily, I opened what I remembered as a broom closet, and it turned out to be the refrigerator. It was big enough to be a morgue, even if it wasn't particularly well stocked. But I managed to locate a slab of ham and plenty of eggs and cheese. By the time Haskell had given Ginny the tour, I'd made enough omelets to feed six people.

We ate in the dining room like formal guests. Our host tried to get us to share a bottle of wine with him, but Ginny said she didn't drink while she was working, and I said I didn't drink. Then he entertained himself by telling us the exciting story of how he and Sara found and bought this house. We didn't listen. I didn't know about Ginny, but I was straining my ears to the noises of the house. I wanted to believe I was going to be able to tell the difference between the creak of contracting joists and the snap of a forced window latch.

I've said it before. At night I believe in cases like this.

Before we were done eating, Haskell ran out of one-sided conversation. Watching him obliquely, I saw the lines of his face start to sag into something that looked like creeping unhappiness. Contrast made the difference more obvious than it would've been otherwise. If he'd looked like this when I first met him, I would've assumed his expression was normal for a chief accountant. Dull and vaguely charmless, tired of numbers. Just like the man Sara Haskell thought she married.

Finally, he pushed his plate away, gulped the last of his wine, and asked, "So what do we do now?"

Ginny studied him for a while. Maybe she thought he

looked more like a man should when both his legs were in danger. She'd been as stiff as Sheetrock with him from the beginning, but now she eased back a bit. "This is the boring part," she said. "We sit here and wait for something to happen. We'll stay with you all night. The doors and locks look pretty sturdy. If you keep out of the den and the living room"—the only rooms in the house with ground-level windows—"they'll have to break in to get at you. When you go to bed, Brew and I'll take turns on guard duty. Probably in the atrium. That's the strategic center of the house. If nothing happens, we'll take you in to work tomorrow." She made an empty gesture with her hand. "It's really that simple. The complicated part is trying to track down the people who want to hurt you. We'll tackle that problem while you're at work."

Haskell began to look a little nauseated. Maybe he hadn't thought through what he was doing when he hired us. "You mean to tell me," he said slowly, "that I have to just sit here and do nothing all tonight, and all tomorrow night, and all the next night—until something happens?" His eyes were dark with unhappiness or anger. "I'll go out of my mind."

Even though he was my age, he looked for all the world like a rebellious four-year-old. But Ginny knew how to handle that. In her punishing-parent voice, she said, "It's up to you. All you have to do is fire us. Then we won't be in your way, and you can do anything you want."

When she said that, I went stiff in my chair. She still wanted to get out of this case. And at the moment he looked just childish or careless or convinced of his own immortality enough to take her up on it.

I should've known better. Sure, she wanted out of this case. But she was a responsible private investigator, and she took her work seriously. "But before you make up your mind," she said straight at Haskell, "let me tell you something. You say you got into this mess by welshing on a bet at El Machismo." She implied just enough disbelief to keep him on his toes. "As it happens, El Machismo belongs to a man who runs a whole series of illegal operations in Puerta del Sol. Some people call him el Señor. Ever heard of him?"

Haskell didn't react. He just stared at her, his eyes wide.

"For people like you," she went on like the edge of a knife, "people who get sucked into one of those operations, he's the power in this town. The cops can throw you in jail. El Señor can throw you in the river. And he gets that power by violence. People obey him because they know if they don't the consequences are going to be worse than they can stand.

"Violence, Mr. Haskell." Her own emotions made her fierce. "He depends on it. It holds his whole rotten empire together. So there's no chance of any kind in the world that he's going to let you off the hook—even if you are just one small sucker. At this point, he won't even let you pay him back. He can't afford to. You cheated him, and the price is blood. He's going to keep after you until he gets what he wants."

Haskell must've been crazy. While he listened to Ginny, I could see he was trying not to smile. A bit of his old gleam came back. Maybe he was going to get to play cowboys-and-Indians after all. Whenever anybody raised the ante, the game got better. When she was finished, he asked like a secret joke, "Where do you want to sleep? You can use the guest bedroom." It was hidden somewhere behind the game room. "Or I have a cot we can set up in the atrium."

Ginny sighed. "We'll think of something." She didn't know what to make of him any more than I did. And it was only 6:00. We had the whole night ahead of us yet.

"Fine." He got up, went to the nearest liquor cabinet, and poured himself a snifter of brandy. This time, he didn't offer us any. To my hungry nerves, it smelled like VSOP. Trying to keep the initiative, Ginny asked him for copies of all his house and car keys. He got a set for each of us. Then he led us into the game room and sat down on one of the sofas like he was suddenly content to spend the rest of the evening staring at the wall.

That lasted for nearly an hour. My mood was getting worse by the minute. Ginny was taking the only intelligent approach to this job—but I hated it. I hated the pale, tight, unreachable way she sat in her chair without so much as reading a magazine. Even though I knew exactly what she was doing. She was listening the same way I was listening. I wanted a drink just to prove I deserved it. Every ten minutes or so, I took a tour of the house, checked the locks on the doors and the latches on the windows, made sure the curtains were closed (the picture windows in the den didn't have any curtains). Every time I passed one of the liquor cabinets or the wetbar, I felt more like murder.

Haskell had good timing. He waited until my tension was almost boiling. Then he looked at Ginny and me and asked out of nowhere, "Do either of you play bridge?"

I nodded. Ginny shook her head. Surprise'll do that to you.

Before I could try to un-nod, he turned up the rheostat on his smile. "You do?"

"I did. Twenty years ago, for a couple of semesters in college." Talking to him like he was dangerously insane. "I wasn't very good."

"That doesn't matter. Believe me, your size alone will be good for at least one trick every board." He was on his feet. "Ms. Fistoulari," he said briskly, "I belong to Jousters. It's a private bridge club here in the Heights. They have a duplicate game at seven-thirty tonight. I'd like to go. Mr. Axbrewder can be my partner."

She practically gaped at him. After a second, she started to say, "Maybe you weren't listening—"

"I was listening." His confidence was so strong I could almost smell it. "I understand the situation. But there'll be a lot of people at the club tonight. Jousters has good security and plenty of light." He smiled. "It even has valet parking. I'll be perfectly safe.

"But that's not all," he went on, sounding like the sort of salesman who specializes in Eiffel Towers. "I'm not suggesting this simply because I can't bear to sit still. Isn't it better to be a moving target than a stationary one? A moving target attracts attention, but it's harder to hit."

"A moving target," Ginny cut in roughly, "is also harder to protect. In case you've lost count, there're only two of us on this job."

"I understand that." He was almost sparkling. "But if we do this your way—and you do it well enough—it could take weeks. I really can't afford that. I want to attract attention. I want to get this over with, so I can go back to leading a normal life. I don't mind taking a few chances."

He fascinated me. I'd never met anybody brave or lunatic enough to call exposing himself to el Señor's goons "taking a few chances." What did he call "leading a normal life"—standing in front of freight trains to see if they could stop in time?

But Ginny was less thrilled. I could see her getting ready to roast him in his socks. So I decided to share the fun. Cheerfully, I said, "That sounds like a terrible idea."

Like a piece of steel, she said, "It is a terrible idea."

"Let's do it."

She snapped her glare at me so hard I almost lost an appendage. But I wasn't just being perverse. Haskell didn't make sense to me. He was the wild card in the deck, and that made him dangerous. I wanted to find out what kind of game he was really playing.

And I was feeling too savage to just sit still for the rest of the night. If I did, I was going to start hurting things. Carefully, I said, "There's one other advantage. If Haskell and I go out, whoever's out there might go after us. Or they might try to get in here." I wanted to look at anything except the hot dismay in her eyes. But I forced myself. This case was too important. "If they try to get in, you'll be waiting for them. We'll double our chances to get what we want tonight."

She didn't look away. I thought she was going to take her stump out of her pocket and wave it around to show me what was wrong with my idea. But she didn't. Bitterly, she said, "You're really enjoying this, aren't you."

I was gripping the arm of the sofa hard. Any minute now, it was going to come off in my hands.

"Tell you what," Haskell said. "We'll flip for it." He fished a half-dollar out of his pocket. "Heads we all stay here. Tails Axbrewder and I go play bridge."

Ginny and I opened our mouths at him, like hooked fish. We couldn't help ourselves. He wasn't living in the real world.

He didn't wait for an answer. With a flick of his thumb, he made the coin dance and flash in the lights of the game room. It was just an ordinary coin toss, but the way he did it made it look like magic.

The half-dollar bounced on the carpet, rolled toward Ginny's feet—and came up tails.

She looked at the coin, at Haskell, at me. Softly, she said, "Oh, go to hell. Try to come back in one piece."

I had to admire the way he'd maneuvered us into giving him what he wanted.

Chapter Eight

I 'll get my coat." Haskell left the room before I could ask him if he had any idea—any idea at all—what he was doing. As he ran up them, I noticed unhappily that the stairs didn't make a sound.

I should've gone with him—even in his own house, I shouldn't have left him alone. But I couldn't stand to see Ginny looking like that. I said, "Is he out of his mind? Or is he just that eager to get out of the house?"

She didn't answer—or look at me, either. I got the distinct impression she was fighting back a desire to flay the skin off my bones.

I was too miserable and furious to think of anything better, so I said, "You've always used that .357 with one hand. You'll be all right."

She'd had all she could take. "If somebody gets hurt tonight," she said suddenly, aiming each word at me like a piece of broken glass, "make sure it's you."

Swearing at myself and her and everybody else I could think of, I turned my back and went after Haskell.

He was waiting in the atrium, all decked out in his camel's hair coat. He gave me a smile, but I didn't give it back. Roughly, I pushed past him, went to the switch panel, and flipped them all, turning off the entryway lights outside and inside.

"I'm going first," I muttered. "Stay close." Then I unlocked the front door and eased it open.

I was in no mood to be cautious, but I did it anyway. Fortunately, the aisle and the street lights on Cactus Blossom Court made it easy. All I really had to worry about was the walk from the cover of the cedars to the car.

I relocked the front door, then led Haskell to the end of the aisle. From there, I scanned the cul-de-sac. Several cars were parked around the curb, and the wind seemed to be getting stronger, but nothing set off any alarms in my head. I wrapped one fist around Haskell's upper arm and marched him between me and the wall of the house toward the driveway. After all, that was my job. But I didn't like it much. When we got into the Buick, I felt safer.

"Why not take my car?" he asked.

"This clunker'll be harder to follow. Less recognizable." The Buick must've liked cold and wind. It started as soon as I touched the ignition. "And we can always hope somebody'll see that showboat of yours and think you're still at home."

I backed out of the driveway and started up the steep hill toward Foothill Drive. I didn't turn on my headlights. And I didn't see any of the parked cars start moving behind me. But at the intersection I had to hit the lights so the oncoming traffic wouldn't plow into us. While my eyes adjusted, I couldn't see the road behind me. I didn't know what (if anything) was happening there as I pulled up onto Foothill and began following Haskell's directions toward his private club.

I could've stood the strain if he'd kept his mouth shut and let me concentrate on the road and my self-control. But he didn't have it in him. Halfway to the end of Foothill, he said conversationally, "One thing bothers me, Axbrewder." No Mr. now. We were becoming buddies. "Your partner doesn't want this job. I mean, she really doesn't want this job. I think she's afraid of it." I distinctly heard an implied contempt in his tone. "Why do you work for her?"

So much for self-control. I stomped down on the brake, wrenched the Buick onto the shoulder, slapped it into park. My arm swung toward him. With my index finger, I pointed out the spot in the center of his face where I wanted to hit him. My voice shook, but my arm and hand were steady. "If you have any complaints, you take them to her. She's the boss. I'm perfectly capable of breaking both your legs myself."

For a long minute, he measured me in the glow of the dashboard lights. His eyes didn't waver from my face. I don't think he even blinked. Then, quietly, he said, "Understood."

Damn right. Pulling the shift back into drive, I made the Buick spit dirt like a hotrod back onto the road. Damn fucking sonofabitch right. If anything happened to Ginny while I was away, I was going to have to do something really drastic to myself.

On the other hand, Haskell still didn't act like he was in any kind of danger. That was some consolation, anyway. I just hoped Ginny and I weren't going out on a limb to protect a man who'd already lost or thrown away all his marbles.

For a while, I watched a pair of headlights in the rearview mirror. But I couldn't tell if they were following us.

Jousters turned out to be on the far side of the Canyon del Oro golf course. Money being no object for the people who recreated in this part of the Heights, the course was actually lit all night—even in the dead of winter—and I saw several duffers beating iridescent orange balls up and down the fairways. The club was everything Haskell said it was. It looked like a colonial mansion (in Puerta del Sol, of all places—go figure that out), and it was lit like a national monument. Each blade of winter-brown grass in the lawns sweeping around it had been individually manicured. Its parking lot was opposite the building's colonnaded portico, on the other side of the road beyond the wide arc of the driveway. It looked as safe as a bank.

Approaching the driveway, the traffic nearly stopped, blocked by cars waiting their turn for valet parking. The car behind us came right up on our bumper. Instinctively, I loosened the .45 again—but nothing happened.

"By the way," Haskell said, "I should tell you. This is a private club. Sometimes quite a bit of money changes hands."

It took me a minute to absorb that. "Let me get this straight," I said. "You're planning to risk money on my bridge game?"

He smiled.

Terrific, I muttered. That's just peachy-keen. This is going to be such fun. "Are you out of your mind?" I asked him. "Or do you just like to throw money away?"

"Don't underestimate yourself." He chuckled. "I anticipate a profitable evening."

I didn't like the attitude of the car behind me. On impulse, I turned left into the parking lot instead of up the driveway. Maybe whoever it was would do something stupid. But the car just revved angrily and roared on past. All I got out of the deal was a chance to park the Buick myself, instead of having to bother with the convenience and luxury of the valets.

Haskell had the decency not to say anything, but he looked amused.

Walking briskly in the cold, we crossed the road and hiked up the arc to the club. On the marble steps under the high span of the portico, we were greeted by a man who dressed like a butler and looked like a bouncer. He knew Haskell by name. Haskell told him who I was, and he let us through the tall white doors into the club.

Inside, the place was all gilt and crystal and burgundy—and ceilings so far away you couldn't hit them with a slingshot. Another butler/bouncer type took our coats, and Haskell guided me up a long, curving stairway toward the second floor. As we climbed, I murmured,

"Tell me one more time about how you can't afford to pay us very long. Membership in this place must cost half the national debt."

He chuckled again. "That's true. But I didn't pay for it myself. I came here once as a guest. My partner thought I wasn't very good, so he told me not to worry about winning. I bet him we'd come in first. If we did, he'd have to buy me a membership."

I wanted to ask him how a man who did well risking money on bridge managed to lose his head and end up welshing at El Machismo, but I didn't get the chance. At the top of the stairs, we went through another set of high white doors and entered the playing area.

It was a huge, round room with the kind of decor you'd expect to see in a high-priced cathouse in San Francisco a hundred years ago. At least two dozen mahogany card tables were set in a wide circle around the director's table in the center, all of them square to the points of the compass. Most of them were already occupied. A large screen was set on one wall to display the scores.

Haskell got a table assignment from the director, and I found myself sitting South opposite his North. It was a duplicate game, which meant the same hands were played over and over again around the room. The cards were dealt into holders called boards, and for each round the boards moved counterclockwise while the East-West teams moved clockwise. The final scoring was comparative, North-South against North-South, East-West against East-West.

After twenty years, that was just about all I remembered about bridge. The only thing I had going for me was that I made the table and most of the players look small.

Our first opponents were a white-haired man with a Colonel Coot moustache and a woman dressed like a front for a diamond-smuggling operation. They both knew Haskell. "New partner?" the man asked him casually. "Any good?"

Haskell was in his element. I swear to God, he looked even handsomer than he did at the bank. Shuffling the first hand of the night, he winked at me and replied, "Let's find out."

"Stakes?"

Haskell smiled. "I feel lucky. How about a hundred dollars a point?"

The woman snatched up her cards like a swooping vulture. "Luck won't do you the least bit of good," she said severely.

For a minute, I couldn't look at my cards. I was fighting too hard to hold off a coughing fit.

By the time I had my hand sorted, the bidding was over—I just passed whenever it was my turn to say anything—and Colonel Coot on my right was playing a spade slam. I was so full of disaster I could hardly swallow. A hundred dollars a point! For one thing, I had to make the opening lead. For another, I only had twelve cards.

Somewhere in my hand, I located a singleton diamond and a lone king of spades, so I led the diamond. Colonel Coot won in dummy and led another diamond. I didn't know what else to do, so I ruffed with my king of spades. Then I led something else.

By the time Colonel Coot got around to drawing trump, I found my thirteenth card. It was hiding behind the clubs. The jack of spades. Having seen my king and drawn the obvious conclusion, Colonel Coot took a deep finesse against Haskell, and my jack won. The slam was down.

Colonel Coot muttered imprecations through his moustache. "If you'd ruffed with your jack, I could've dropped your king." The diamond smuggler glared at the ceiling. Haskell didn't say anything. He didn't even smile. He just glowed like an incandescent shark.

A few hands later, I trumped one of his aces and

ended up blocking the declarer away from four good tricks in dummy. And a few hands later, I pulled the wrong card from my hand and accidentally end-played the woman on my right. The rest of the time, I didn't have the faintest idea what was happening. My bidding didn't bear any resemblance to the cards in my hand, and I was playing off the wall. Under my jacket, my shirt was soaked with sweat. We were halfway through the game before I figured out what was going on.

Haskell was using my ignorance. He was counting on my mistakes. He played like he knew everything I was going to do wrong. And that gave him a tremendous advantage over every team we played. None of them knew what the hell I was doing. Three times during the game, he offered our opponents the same bet he had with Colonel Coot and the diamond smuggler. It would've been more honest if he'd brought in a professional and not told anybody. I didn't know whether to congratulate him or call the cops.

By eleven, the game was over. I felt like I'd spent the night in a gravel factory. When I stood up, my legs were cramped, and I almost lost my balance. If somebody offered me just one more hand of bridge, I was going to run screaming into the night. But Haskell won all his bets.

We didn't win the game. But we were second North-South—and second overall. Which meant we beat all the East-West teams.

I was dying to get out of there—get back to Ginny and hide my head under a pillow. But Haskell stood around the room for a while and graciously let people pay him his winnings. Colonel Coot was bitter about it. He gave me a glare and muttered, "Be watching for you next time," then marched away to vent his spleen on some hapless subaltern. I read the scores off the screen, did a little rough math in my head, and realized Haskell'd taken in over four thousand dollars.

He didn't smile the whole time. He didn't have to. His entire body did it for him.

On the way down the stairs, I made my brains stop rattling long enough to ask him, quietly, "How did you do that?"

Without me towering over him, he would've looked like a conquering hero. At my question, he cocked an eyebrow and thought for a few steps. Then he said, "It's difficult to explain. I don't really play cards. I play people. You gave me a lot to work with."

What a nice compliment, I growled to myself. I'm so proud I could just shit. But he was still the client, so I kept a civil tongue in my head.

Together, we collected our coats from the butler/bouncer and went out through the portico.

Outside, all the wind was gone. Behind the noises of the cars as valets brought them up the driveway and bridge players drove them away, the night was still. Poised and quiet, like your first kiss. On the other hand, it was cold as a meat-locker. I had to hug my coat to keep my bones from falling out on the ground. People stood in knots around the columns as if they were trying to share warmth. Over on the golf course, a few hardy souls were still playing. What few stars were able to show through the lights of the city looked like chips of ice.

I gave the Buick's keys to the next valet, a kid with hopeful eyes and an unsuccessful moustache, and told him what it looked like. He sprinted away toward the parking lot, working for a good tip.

"Don't take it personally," Haskell said. He'd already proved he was more observant than I gave him credit for. "I play that way because it works. It's the only way to win."

I didn't really listen. For some reason, I kept watching that kid. The way his coat flapped behind him as he ran made him look like a valiant child, too full of energy to be cold—and trying too hard to please. He reached the lot and began dodging between the cars toward the back row.

"Tell the truth, now," Haskell went on. Deep in his heart, he probably wanted me to admit how brilliant he was. "You enjoyed yourself. Didn't you."

"Give me a choice next time," I said absently. Still watching the kid. "I'd rather have my kneecaps dislocated."

The kid reached the Buick—I could see it between two other cars. He got the door open and jumped into the driver's seat. Before he closed the door, he reached for the ignition.

I wasn't ready for it. In all my grubby and sometimes violent life, I've never been ready for things like that. With a special crumpling noise you never forget once you've heard it, the rear of the Buick turned into a fireball.

I should've stayed with Haskell. That was my job. I was supposed to protect him. But I didn't. With every ounce of strength I had, I started for the parking lot.

Long legs help. And I'm fast for my size. In what felt like no more than half an hour, maximum, I reached the fire.

A couple of valets were there ahead of me. Yelling, they pointed me at their friend.

The whole Buick was burning now, but the blast'd blown him clear. He was lying beside the next car. All his clothes were on fire. He wasn't moving.

The heat was terrible, but I didn't think about it. He was only three steps away. Three steps with flame whipping in all directions. The important thing was not to breathe. I ripped off my coat and went to him. Used the coat to smother his clothes. Picked him up and carried him back out of the heat. Even though I knew it was too late.

His friends took him from me. Somebody said the manager was calling the fire department, the cops, everybody. With a piece of fire still burning inside me, I walked back to the club.

Haskell met me on the steps. "I called a cab," he said. "It should be here in a few minutes."

He couldn't help himself. He was grinning like a little boy after a successful raid on the cookie jar.

Chapter Nine

In an ideal world, I would've taken his head off for him, just on general principles. But he was still the client. And a second murder in less than three minutes was bound to attract a little attention, even though most of the people waiting in front of the club had gone to get a closer look at the fire and the few lazy, timid, or reasonable individuals who hadn't moved were staring in that direction. Somehow, I kept all that in mind. Instead of hitting him, I knotted my fists in his fine camel's hair coat and practically carried him around behind one of the columns. We weren't exactly invisible, but the pillar and the fire hid us pretty well.

Holding him up on the tips of his toes with his back against the column, I hissed down into his face, "You called a cab? That was quick thinking. We can just go home like none of this ever happened. What the hell are you trying to get away with?"

He wasn't smiling anymore. He may've even been a little afraid of me. But he didn't flinch or look away. He watched me like an expert, measuring me. Through the bunched collar of his coat, he breathed, "I don't want to talk to the police."

"What makes you think you can get out of it?" The Buick was starting to burn down, but I wasn't. "That car's rented in my name. I'm not exactly hard to recognize, and you're known here. As soon as the cops trace the car, they'll start asking questions around here. They'll be sitting in your office by noon tomorrow at the latest."

Haskell shrugged inside his coat. "Maybe—" The cold turned his breath to puffs of steam. "Maybe by then I can persuade you to cover for me."

"Cover for you?" I was so mad I lifted him all the way off the ground. "Cover for you?"

"You can tell them this el Señor has some grudge against you. We can make up a reason why we're together. Maybe I hired you to work on a security problem at the bank. Or maybe"—he flicked up a smile, dropped it again—"you just like to play bridge. Anything to keep them from investigating me."

"Fat chance," I snarled. "You're breaking the law. If I cover for you, I'll go to jail. Ginny'll be put out of business." I was too mad to think—but I didn't need brains to figure out some of what was going on. "I may have cement in my head, but I'm not deaf and blind. That car wasn't blown up by somebody who wants to break your legs. It was blown up by somebody who wants you dead. I'm not going to tell any lies for you. You've been lying to us from the beginning."

"Of course I've been lying to you," he wheezed. I think I was making it a little hard for him to breathe. "Don't you understand? I had to."

I glared at him for a minute. In the lights of the club, he was starting to look slightly purple. Slowly, I eased him down onto his feet. But I didn't stop leaning on him against the pillar. "All right, Mr. Haskell." Axbrewder dripping sarcasm. "Just for kicks, why don't you try explaining it to me."

He took a couple of deep breaths and straightened his coat. "Do you have any idea how many investigators I called before I called you?" He tried to sound indignant instead of defensive, but his eyes gave him away. They weren't either one. They were still measuring me. "I tried telling them the truth. They refused to help me. As soon as you and Ms. Fistoulari walked into my office, I knew you were going to walk right out again if I told you what was really going on. So I made something up."

"Damn right," I growled. "That whole phony story about El Machismo. Including Reston Cole." Ginny was going to be charmed.

He didn't say anything.

"Take your time," I went on. "Maybe you'd like to bet on whether your cab is going to get here before the cops. If the cops get here first, they'll talk to the valets. They'll find out about the big, crazy guy who pulled the kid out of the fire. May take them all of two minutes to come up here looking for us. I'm in no hurry."

I had to admire his nerves. I just couldn't seem to fluster him. "Axbrewder," he said evenly, "I told you I play people. It's the only way to win. And I'm good at it. I saw you and Ms. Fistoulari wouldn't touch the truth. So I had to bet you weren't quitters. I had to bet you don't drop things once you get involved in them. If I lied to you long enough to get you involved, you'd help me. Then I'd be able to tell you the truth."

I hated that. It was too much like the way he played bridge. But we could both hear sirens in the distance. And, because of the way I was holding him, I could see something he couldn't—a Jiffy Cab pulling up in front of the portico. I had him where I wanted him, and I wasn't about to let him go.

"You like to take chances," I commented sourly. "Don't stop now. Tell me the truth. See what happens."

For a few seconds longer, he studied me and didn't say anything. Then he sighed. "This is complicated. How much do you know about laundering money?"

Laundering money. By damn. I gave him a grin full of teeth and malice. "Not a thing."

I could tell he didn't believe me. But he bowed to the inevitable, as they say.

"Suppose you have ten thousand dollars," he began, "but it's in marked bills. Or it's counterfeit. Or it came from a source you have to keep secret—like a bribe. What do you do? You can't spend it. You can't simply deposit it in your account and write checks—you can't afford to admit you ever saw or touched that money. So you need to launder it. In essence, you need to exchange your money for other money that can't be traced.

"Most of the time, there are two steps. First, you need to get rid of the physical money. You need to deposit it somewhere, change it into numbers on a ledger or in a computer. That gets rid of the physical evidence. But it doesn't disguise your connection to that sum of money. So the second thing you have to do is confuse the numbers. Usually, you put the money into some kind of dummy account, and then you transfer the numbers back to yourself through as many different stages as you can think of—stock certificates, bearer bonds, selling your own products or belongings to yourself, whatever.

"There are a lot of different systems, none foolproof. Most of the time, the safest thing is to work through foreign banks. But even foreign banks keep records. And they occasionally let investigators look at their records. With enough luck, ingenuity, and sweat, any laundry can be traced."

I didn't want him to stop—he still hadn't gotten to the good part—but I was running out of time. An ambulance and two prowl cars were pulling into the Jousters parking lot. I could see a firetruck coming up the road. And the cab driver was getting restless. Any minute now, he was going to start calling for Haskell. Or else he'd get out of his cab and come up the steps to talk to one of the bouncers, and Haskell might see him. Soon I was going to have to do some gambling of my own.

But not yet. Haskell's explanation was still going on.

"What protects most money laundries most of the time is the sheer complexity of the records banks and credit unions and savings and loans and brokers keep. In retrospect—when you already know what a given laundry does—the trail sometimes looks pretty clear, even if it would be hard to prove in court. But when you don't know the answer, you could use a dozen accountants and spend thousands of hours of computer time and still not find it."

Past the edge of the column, I saw the cab driver get out of his hack. I was starting to feel the cold. Swearing to myself, I tightened my grip on Haskell. "That's marvelous," I growled. "I could listen to you sing and dance all night. Get to the point."

With perfect timing, the driver yelled, "Haskell? Mr. Haskell?"

Haskell jerked his head to the side, tried to respond. I kept him quiet by thumping him against the stone. "The cops'll be here in just about a minute," I whispered down at him. That was true—a couple of them were already walking across the parking lot in our direction. "Get to the point."

I would've given my back teeth to make him lose his self-possession. But it didn't happen. He sounded almost avuncular, like I was some kind of half-witted kid he couldn't help being fond of anyway, as he said, "I know how el Señor launders some of his money."

Well, I was expecting something like that. I may be a moth-eaten old drunk with no license and less good sense, but I can smell something rotten when you stuff my head in a sack of dead fish. Still, it rocked me back on my heels. Because now I had the whole picture—the whole grimy set-up that made Smithsonian give us a recommendation and then laugh about it. No wonder nobody in their right mind wanted this case. There was no way we were going to be able to protect Haskell. Not without going right to the source and putting el Señor himself out of business.

As Ginny kept telling me, she and I weren't equipped for the job.

And yet it only took me about two seconds to decide

which way I was going. I had an alternative. I could turn
Haskell over to the cops.

I shifted my grip from his coat to his arm. "Come on,"
I muttered. "We don't want to keep your cab waiting."

Haskell actually laughed. The excitement was back in
his eyes. But for a lunatic he was pretty smart. He didn't
say, I knew you wouldn't let me down. If he had, I probably would've broken his arm.

Two cops were walking up toward the club. They
weren't more than twenty yards away. By rights, they
should've stopped us. They don't like it when people
leave the scene of a crime. But they were human—and
back in the parking lot the firetruck was starting to hose
down what was left of the Buick. They turned to watch.

Haskell told the driver who he was, and we got into
the back of the cab. He mentioned an address I didn't
quite catch—I just heard it well enough to know it wasn't
Cactus Blossom Court. But I let that pass for the time
being. Instead of asking questions, I held my breath until
we were out of range if the cops yelled at us to stop.

After that, I went back to work. I wasn't getting no-
ticeably more patient with age. And every time I closed
my eyes, I saw the Buick go up in flames again. I saw
that poor kid lying beside the next car, his clothes on fire
and him not moving at all. The cab driver could probably
hear everything we said, but at the moment I didn't care.

"Dozens of accountants and thousands of hours of
computer time." Not making any effort to sound calm.
"And you just happen to know how el Señor launders his
money. What do you do in your spare time—walk on
water?"

Now that he thought we were safe from the cops,
Haskell seemed to twinkle like an elf. "It was an accident. Somebody told me about El Machismo. Actually, it
was Reston Cole. That's what made me think of him. He
didn't say he'd ever been there. We were just having a
drink, and he happened to mention that he'd heard there
was an illegal gambling club in town. A few days later, I

stumbled across the name again. El Machismo uses the Old Town branch of my bank."

He mused for a minute, then said slowly, "Axbrewder, being an accountant gets painfully boring. Every once in a while, I get so desperate for some excitement that I play little games with it, just so"—he paused briefly— "just so I won't go back to being as dead as I was a few years ago." The way he said it made it sound genuine. "When I saw El Machismo has an account with the bank I work for, I decided to play investigator. That's how I learned about laundering money." He grinned. "On-the-job training. It took me several months. But when I saw where the profits from that account were going, I knew I'd found something.

"As it turns out, El Machismo is a wholly owned sub-sidiary of a corporation that doesn't exist. The profits go into an investment portfolio managed by our trust de-partment. The returns are distributed to the four people who hold all the stock in that nonexistent corporation. They don't exist, either. Nevertheless, two of them invest heavily in a mortgage exchange. One uses a big bro-kerage firm here in town. One backs a small, private lending company. And all four feed back into another investment portfolio managed by our trust department."

He glanced at me. Then he said, "The owner of that account does exist. It's el Señor."

I couldn't see him very well in the back seat of the cab. But he looked almighty proud of himself.

The hack was wandering into a part of the Heights I wasn't familiar with. We definitely weren't going back to Haskell's house. The reasonable part of my mind won-dered what new game he was playing. But the reasonable part of my mind was pretty far away at the moment. The rest of me was seething. Old cauldron-of-emotions Ax-brewder. Being sober didn't make me calm, just bitter. I would've given a couple of fingers—and any number of toes—for the ability (and the access) to muster the kind of information Haskell was talking about. Even Ginny would've been willing to go out on a limb for it. For the chance to drive at least one nail into el Señor's coffin. But the one thing we would never have done—not in a million years—not as long as we had so much as half a wit between us—was tell him what we were doing.

"Clever you," I rasped at Haskell. "For a smart man, you've got more stupid in you than any other three people I know." The only reason I didn't yell at him was because of the cab driver. "What's the matter with you? You've got some kind of death wish?"

At least he had the decency to look insulted. "What are you talking about?"

"You found out how he launders his money. So what did you do? Did you go to the cops? The D.A.? The FBI? Not you—not Reg Haskell, boy investigator." I could see the whole thing. "What wildass logic made you think trying to blackmail el Señor was a good idea?"

I was so sure I was right, I would've been surprised if he'd tried to deny it. He didn't. He was frowning, but that was just because he didn't like my attitude.

"Two reasons." There was a hint of iron in his voice, something he usually kept hidden. "First, I can't prove any of it. I can't prove there's anything illegal about El Machismo's money. And I certainly can't prove that those four people really don't exist.

"Second—" He shrugged. In the faint glow of the dash lights, his face looked hard and maybe even a little bit fanatical. "I needed the money."

"He needed the money," I explained to the window beside me. "I love it." We were riding into an area of apartment complexes and condos. The Heights has dozens of them. And some are actually inexpensive. Not everybody needs money badly enough to be as well off as Haskell. "It's going to look great on my tombstone."

Abruptly, Haskell told the driver to stop. We pulled over to the curb in front of a place called Territorial Apartments. Haskell got out and nearly slammed the door on me. I told the driver to wait and went after my client.

The cold seemed to soak into my clothes like water. Without a coat, my jacket wasn't much protection. "So what're we doing here?"

He stood in the outside lights of the building—it was an ersatz chalet-style structure, probably affordable—and glared up at me. If nothing else, he was letting me see the side of him his wife was afraid of. "What do you care?" he snapped. "A friend of mine lives here. I'll be safe for the night."

"Listen to me, Haskell." I made a real effort to keep myself from boiling over. "It's just luck you and I aren't dead instead of that poor kid. El Señor isn't going to let any of us get away with this. He can't afford to. And he can send an army after you if he wants to. He may blow up your whole house. Your only chance is to go to the police." They wouldn't exactly be amused when they heard his story. But they'd want his information. "They might be able to protect you."

He didn't flinch or hesitate. He didn't even blink. "It's my life," he said. "I'll take my chances. Just tell me whether you're in or out. Fish or cut bait, Axbrewder."

I stared at him. For a minute there, I almost told him to blow the whole thing out his ass. Would've given me no end of satisfaction. But the plain fact was, as opportunities went he was too good to miss. Ginny was going to hate me for it, but I did it anyway.

"Since you ask so nicely," I said, "I'll fish. Ginny and I don't drop clients when things get tough." Then I stepped closer to him and pointed a finger at the front of his coat, just to remind him I could throw him across the street if I wanted to. "But we don't like being lied to. You'd better be telling the truth this time. If you aren't, I'm going to take you apart piece by piece until I find it."

"Fine." Unflappable as all hell. You'd think he ate being threatened with bodily harm for breakfast. "I have to be at work by eight-thirty. Pick me up here at eight-fifteen."

Just like that, he turned and walked away. The Territorial Apartments didn't have a security gate. He strode through the entryway out of sight like he'd been here a lot and knew exactly what he was doing.

For a while, I stood where I was, puffing vapor in the cold and thinking, He needed the money. The same man who just made four thousand dollars playing bridge.

Chapter Ten

Maybe I was losing my mind. Maybe the car that got blown up wasn't really my rented Buick. The night was too cold to hold all that fire. Maybe Haskell actually did know what he was doing. Maybe I hadn't just agreed to go on trying to protect a man who seemed determined to get himself killed.

And maybe Ginny was going to have a fit when she heard about it.

But I couldn't just stand there and let my blood freeze. And anyway, you still have to function. You still have to do what you can. Feeling dissociated and crazy, I went back to the cab, got in, and told the driver to find a phone booth.

"There's one back the way we came," he said. "About half a mile."

I said, "Fine." But I couldn't put the same decision and certainty in it that Haskell did.

At the phone booth, I left the hack again, fumbled out some coins, and called Sergeant Raul Encino of Missing Persons.

Crazy people do things like that.

And God watches over crazy people. After only three or four rings, I got an answer.

"Missing Persons. Sergeant Encino."

He sounded bored—and nobody sounds as bored or indifferent or just plain world-weary as a Chicano duty officer in the middle of the night. But he perked up when I identified myself. Deep in his heart, he was an old-world Spanish gentleman. He even looked like it, despite his uniform—every hair and shirttail was so well behaved it looked like he held it at gunpoint. That meant he was just a little bit arrogant, with exaggerated ideas of honor and dignity. That was why he thought he owed me a favor.

"Señor Axbrewder," he said. "How good of you to call." I couldn't miss his sarcasm—he was speaking Spanish for my benefit. And possibly because there were people listening around him. "I am at your service. How many lost children do you wish to discover tonight?"

I winced at that. Last time, it was seven—nine, if you count the two who survived. "Nice try," I replied. In English, for his benefit. "But this time you can't cheer me up by being charming. I'm in over my head, and I need somebody to tell me a few straight facts."

"*Bueno*," he said without hesitation. "Speak."

There was some static on the line. It sounded like fire. That poor kid hadn't even had a chance to scream. But I tried to push burning Buicks out of my mind. He couldn't've been more than a year or two older than Pablo.

"In the paper this morning," I plunged in, "I read about a missing kid. Pablo Santiago. I know his family—Ginny and I did some work for them a couple of years ago. So I went to see them today." Well, yesterday, actually, according to my watch. "They don't think he's missing. They think he's dead." I took a deep breath. Encino was going to love this. "They think he's been killed."

There was a long silence at the other end of the line. Then he said softly, "What do you desire to know?"

From a technical point of view, he had no business knowing the answers I wanted. Hell, he wasn't even supposed to be talking to me. I didn't have a license. But I was counting on the department grapevine. "I want to know if he's been found. I want to know if he's still alive." My grip on myself was slipping. I fought my voice back under control again. "If he's dead, I want to know how he died."

Encino thought about that for a minute. Then he said, "Señor, I must put you on hold."

I heard the click as he disengaged the receiver. The fire on the line got a lot louder.

What fun, I muttered to myself. Joy and party hats. Back in the cab, the driver kept warm by running the engine. He looked like he was taking a nap. The skin of my face felt as stiff as sandpaper, and all my joints ached. I needed to beat somebody up, just to keep my blood moving. But you can never find muggers or rapists when you need them. I tried to imagine what Encino was doing, but all I got was phone static like roasting children.

He was gone for a long time. But I went on waiting, and eventually he came back on the line. "Axbrewder?" he said. "This is a different phone." In English. "I can talk here."

"And not a minute too soon." To explain the shiver in my voice, I said, "I'm freezing to death." Then I asked, "What've you got?"

The background crackle made him sound distant and unconcerned. "For an Anglo, you are not a bad man. Are you certain you want to involve yourself in this?"

"Ask me that some other time." I didn't want to come unglued right there in the phone booth. "I'm never sure. What've you got?"

"All right." He really did think he owed me something. "A boy tentatively identified as Pablo Santiago was found early Sunday morning, just a few hours after his family reported him missing."

I couldn't help myself. I cut in, "What do you mean, 'tentatively'? Didn't you call in the family?"

He didn't answer that. "He was found down in the

South Valley, on Trujillo, lying in the road. The preliminary report says, 'Death consistent with fall from moving vehicle.' A broken neck. The whole body bruised and scraped. The medical examiner considers it an accident. The boy is presumed to have been joyriding with some buddies. Doped or drunk. I'll be unable to look at the autopsy report until I go off duty."

Through my teeth, I said, "So it was an accident. So why didn't you call in the family?" In the name of simple decency, for God's sake.

Encino chewed his end of the line for a while. I heard him tapping his fingers on the receiver. Then he said carefully, "The detective in charge of the case is Captain Cason."

I already knew that. It explained everything—and nothing. Holding onto myself as hard as I could, I said, "I know Cason. You know I know Cason. He's crazy. Also a bad cop. What's he got to do with Pablo Santiago?"

His shrug was almost audible. "The preliminary report is clear. The M.E. considers this an accident. But Cason is working on the death of Roscoe Chavez. He learned that Pablo ran numbers for Chavez, so he believes the two are connected. He told the newspapers Pablo was still missing. And he refuses to call in the family. He wishes to conceal his knowledge. He believes this secret will assist his investigation."

That bastard. I wanted to yell—but Encino didn't deserve to be yelled at. None of this was his business. Softly, I said, "I can identify Pablo for you."

He laughed—a short, humorless bark. "Imagine Captain Cason's delight. He will ask how you heard that Pablo had been found. You will reply that I informed you. I will be suspended. I am Chicano." And very conscious of prejudice in the department. "Perhaps I will lose my job altogether."

"All right," I said. "It was a bad idea. When can you tell me what's in the autopsy report?"

A sigh. "I will try to steal a look when I go off duty. Call me at home during the day." Sounding especially world-weary, he gave me his home phone number.

"Thanks," I said. Inadequate gratitude. "Remind me I owe you five or six favors for this."

He didn't have to say I'd be doing him a favor by causing trouble for Cason. I already knew that, too. He just hung up.

I did the same and walked like an old man back to the warmth of the cab.

The driver asked me where I wanted to go. I almost told him to take me to the Santiagos' home in the old part of town. Fortunately, I got my common sense back in time. Instead of doing anything rash, I gave him Haskell's address.

The ride was bearable. The heat in the cab helped my mind go blank—which was a big improvement. But when we turned down into the cul-de-sac of Cactus Blossom and I saw Haskell's house, my stomach started hurting again. Ginny'd been there alone for better than five hours now. I didn't expect she'd had any trouble. Most people don't try to kill you a second time until after they find out they didn't succeed the first time. But I was afraid she might've talked herself into a really poisonous frame of mind. And there was no way around the stuff I was going to have to tell her.

I didn't try to buy the cab driver off so he wouldn't tell the cops where he took me. I knew better. They weren't going to have any trouble tracking either me or Haskell down. Anyway, there're only so many things you can worry about at any one time. I just gave him what I owed him, got out of the hack, and walked between the cedars into the black aisle toward the house.

Not knowing how else to get in without scaring Ginny and maybe getting shot, I knocked on the front door and rang the doorbell.

She took a long time answering. Long enough for me to think maybe she was trying to tell me something. Then I heard her faintly around the edges of the frame.

"Who is it?"

The muffling made her sound faraway and frightened.

I tried to pitch my voice to reach her without disturbing the neighbors. "It's Brew. I'm alone."

I felt the door shift slightly, like she was leaning on it. Then the locks clicked, and the door swung into the darkness of the house.

I closed it behind me, relocked it.

When I snapped on the atrium lights, I found her standing near the switch panel, her back against the wall. Her right hand was aimed in the direction of my belly.

But she wasn't holding her .357. She was holding a glass. The stuff in the glass looked amber and beautiful. It smelled like fine Irish whiskey.

Waiting for me all evening alone in Haskell's house had done something to her.

Her clothes were a little rumpled. Her gray eyes looked vaguely out of focus. For some reason, the lines of her face seemed slightly smeared, like a photograph with a thumbprint on the negative.

"Where is he?"

"Ginny"—my wit never fails me—"you're drunk."

She tried to glare at me, but couldn't quite pull it off. "So what? Where is he?"

"What's the matter with you?" My stomach hurt so bad I could hardly stand up straight. "You trying to get yourself killed? What would you've done if they tried to break in here?"

She actually giggled. "Offered them a drink." I hated her giggle. "They don't know we're working for him yet. Why would they kill me?" But her amusement didn't last. Like she didn't realize she was repeating herself, she asked, "Where is he?"

For a second, I almost started to argue. Then I thought better of it. Taking hold of her arm, I said, "I think you need to lie down."

That took a little while to reach her through the fog. Then she wrenched her arm out of my hand. I wasn't holding her hard, but the effort nearly made her lose her balance. "God damn you entirely to hell, Mick Ax-brewder," she said, articulating each word as precisely as a piece of glass. "I asked you a question."

When I didn't answer, she looked for something even angrier to say. But nothing particularly scathing occurred to her. After a minute, her whole body seemed to sag.

"I'm not in good shape, Brew," she said dully. "I wasn't in good shape before tonight, and I won't be in good shape tomorrow. I can't seem to think straight. Nothing makes sense anymore. Please don't try to mother me."

It was enough to make a grown man weep. The problem was, I was so used to depending on her to carry me over the rough spots. And the smell of whiskey burned in all my nerves. For a while there, I didn't think I could stand it. But people sometimes do remarkable things because they have to. Softly, I said, "He's staying with a friend. He thinks he'll be safe there." Then, because she obviously needed more than that from me, I added, "Why don't we go to the den? You can at least sit down. I'll tell you all about it."

She didn't move. The blur in her eyes made me think she hadn't heard me.

"Ginny, this whole mess is a lot worse than he told us."

At that, she nodded. Carrying herself as carefully as her glass, she turned and started down the stairs toward the den.

I wanted to catch up with her, hold her to keep her from falling. But I made myself stay a couple of steps back.

In the den, she sat on one end of the long, overstuffed couch facing the picture window and the arroyo. She leaned herself against the arm of the couch for support. So we wouldn't be too exposed, I didn't turn on any lights. From the other end of the couch, I couldn't see anything more than her silhouette in the faint glow from the atrium.

"So," she said, a million miles away, "how was the bridge game?"

"I had a wonderful time." I had too much to tell her—and no idea where to start. "He says he doesn't play games. He plays people. And he's good at it. He used me to sucker the opposition into bad bets. When it was over, he was four thousand dollars richer."

After that, the fire came back—I could see the Buick burning in the arroyo like an auto-da-fé—and the rest of it was easy to tell. I just babbled until it all came out. (All except Pablo and the Santiagos and Encino. That was mine. And I didn't need Ginny to tell me we couldn't work on two cases at once.) I didn't forget anything—I have a good memory for details that scare me. The only part I left out was the part where I promised Haskell we wouldn't drop him. I wanted to find out what she was thinking first.

But when I was done I couldn't tell whether she'd heard a word. She sat against the arm of the couch without moving—without even drinking—and didn't say anything the whole time. I might've been talking to myself, like a kid at a campfire telling ghost stories to explain the dark.

Finally, I asked quietly, "Ginny, are you asleep?"

She turned her head slightly toward me. In a lifeless voice, she said, "I searched the house while you were gone. I didn't find anything. He doesn't even keep personal financial records around here. If his wife wants to know anything, she has to take his word for it."

I sat with my arms wrapped over my stomach and waited for her to go on.

"I even checked his briefcase. But it was empty. He carries a briefcase without a single scrap of paper in it."

That surprised me, more because she seemed to think it was important than because it meant anything. "Maybe he carries it just for show."

"Sure," she said without inflection. "And maybe it was full when he took it in to work this morning."

I didn't understand. "So what?"

Abruptly, she lifted her glass and drank the rest of the whiskey. Then she dropped the glass on the carpet. "Brew"—there was a dying breeze in her voice— "somebody wants him dead. More people are going to get hurt. What're we going to do?"

I wanted to ask, You mean, somebody besides el Señor? Do you still think Haskell's lying? But I didn't have the heart for it. Softly, I asked, "What do you want to do?"

"This is your case," she said. "I'm just along for the ride." She didn't move, but she was going away. Leaving me alone. "We've traded places. I used to be the one who went out and did things. Now I'm the one who sits around and drinks." Slowly, she pulled her legs up onto the cushions and curled herself against the arm of the couch. "We'll do whatever you decide. I'm going to sleep now."

I waited until I was sure she was asleep. Then I picked her up and carried her back upstairs to the master bedroom. Her face was wet with tears, and she went on crying while I undressed her and eased her under the sheets. But she didn't make a sound.

After that, I spent what felt like the hardest night of my life. Staying awake to keep her safe, in case Haskell's enemies came to cause trouble. And not drinking.

By the time dawn finally crept into the Heights, I wasn't in a very good mood. I felt old and burned out, and I'd occupied the whole night thinking about things that scared me. Just along for the ride, huh? I was too bitter to be civil about it, so I put one foot on the bed and bounced her up and down. "Get up," I muttered. "The ride's about to start."

She came awake slowly, her face puffy with sleep and too much booze. Raising her head, she looked at me. Registered the fact she was naked under the covers in Haskell's bed while I stood in front of her with all my clothes on. "What time is it?" Even her voice sounded blurred.

"Around seven."

First thing in the morning, with that broken nose, and not enough rest, and too much to drink the night before, maybe she wasn't the best-looking woman in the world. But she still made my back teeth hurt.

Peering at me, she asked, "You haven't had any sleep yet?"

I turned my back on her, started out of the bedroom. "Get up. We've got work to do." I was an especially nice guy this morning, but there didn't seem to be anything I could do about it. Trying to calm down, I went to make some breakfast.

Showered and dressed, she joined me in the kitchen sooner than I expected. She had the decency not to want any breakfast, but she swallowed about a quart of orange juice, ate a handful of vitamins, then started on the coffee. For a while, she watched me eat. Then she said, "Sorry about last night. I thought I told you not to mother me."

In the privacy of my head, I replied, I'm not your mother. At the rate I'm going, I'm not even your lover. What the hell do you think you're doing to yourself? But I really didn't want to have that conversation with her. Not the way I was feeling. So I said, "I'm surprised you remember even that much about last night." Charming as always.

She shot a glare at me. But instead of snapping she said quietly, "I remember. Try me."

I didn't feel much like eating anyway—I had a belly full of sand and too many things stuck in my throat. I picked up the dishes and put them in the sink. For once, I left them for somebody else. "What's so important about his briefcase?"

She sighed. "I don't know. Probably nothing. It just seems strange that the chief accountant of a bank carries a briefcase with nothing in it."

I didn't look at her. "What did we decide about this case?"

"We didn't decide anything." She was getting some of

her acid back. "I said it was up to you. You gave the distinct impression we're still working for him. Or why did we spend the night here?" I could feel her watching me. "Brew, what's the matter?"

I couldn't answer that. But I did the next best thing. "When the Buick blew up." Trying not to let my voice quiver. "I've seen something like that before. It was a gas fire."

"Meaning what?"

"Meaning it doesn't take explosives, or detonators, or anything fancy. All you need is enough wire and maybe a metal punch. A half-wit can do it. And it's almost impossible to prove because the wire usually gets burned or melted too badly."

She was still a step behind me, so she didn't say anything. I didn't like the way her silence felt.

"Whoever followed us to that bridge club saw we weren't using Haskell's car. It probably only took them a couple of hours after the Buick went up to find out he wasn't in it." After stewing for most of the night, I still came to the same conclusion. "They don't know he isn't here. They've had plenty of time to try again."

She tried for some of that famous Fistoulari self-control. But this morning it didn't sound right. "So what's the problem? You know what to look for. Why don't you check the cars?"

That made me turn around. "The problem," I hissed so I wouldn't shout at her, "is this time they might try something fancier. They know we've been warned. To sucker us, they might try to booby-trap it. All they have to do is hot-wire the cars and make a contact at the hood latch. Or set up any kind of trembler switch." I didn't really know that much about bombs. Just enough to be scared spitless. "I can't just lift the hood. And I'm too big to fit under cars. Using a jack might be as bad as trying the hood. I'll kill myself before I even find out I'm in trouble."

For a minute, her eyes drifted out of focus. Automatically—she probably wasn't aware she was doing it—she hugged her left stump protectively under her right arm. How do we get out of this one? Let me count the ways. Call the cops? That'd be as good as turning Haskell in—something we'd apparently agreed we wouldn't do, at least for the time being. And from the point of view of professional ethics, we had to tell him what we were going to do first. Not to mention quitting working for him if he ordered us not to tell the cops. Use cabs? That'd leave trails anybody with the right kind of clout could follow. Rent more cars? Ginny's insurance company was going to be mad enough about the Buick (the kind of insurance you buy when you rent a car doesn't cover things like having the car blown up by somebody who wants to kill you). Any more property damage, and her policy might be cancelled. The rates would sure as hell go through the roof.

I watched her think it through. The look in her eyes slowly got sharper and sharper, and the end of her nose went white with anger. But she came to the same conclusion I did.

"You want me to crawl under those cars. I'm the one who already knows what it's like to get blown apart. By now I ought to be used to it."

Yessir. I had every reason to be in a good mood this morning. "If you've got any better ideas," I said, trying to keep my own anger down, "spit them out. I don't like this much myself."

She gave me a murderous glare. "The hell you don't." Fiercely, she snatched up her purse. "Come on. Let's get it over with."

Private investigators sometimes do stupid things because they don't have any choice.

She retrieved her coat, put it on. I didn't have anything except a jacket over my stale shirt and the dead weight of the .45. Following her up the stairs, I was so light-headed with fear and lack of sleep I had the sound of fire in my ears. But now it was the Olds burning, and Ginny was stuck under it.

At the top of the stairs, I stopped to sweat for a minute. "Sometime today," I murmured wanly, "one of us has got to go back to the apartment for some clean clothes. I'm starting to stink."

She didn't look at me. Her attention was aimed out toward the cars.

We made sure we had all the keys we needed. We weren't particularly cautious about the way we left the house, but that didn't bother me. At the moment, we weren't in any danger of being shot.

Outside, the weather felt like snow. The cold wasn't quite as sharp, and the air had a wet smell that's rare in Puerta del Sol. Clouds the color of lead piled over the mountains, making the morning look dull and hopeless. The perfect day for a firebomb. Dust and paper scraps blew like they were falling down Cactus Blossom into the cul-de-sac.

Ginny handed me her purse. Bleak as the weather, she asked, "What do I do?"

"All right." With my free hand, I gripped my jacket closed over my chest. "What you're looking for is a pair of wires." All of a sudden, I wasn't sure anymore I knew how the Buick was blown. "They run from the starter—or the distributor—or even the spark plugs—back to the gas tank. They go into the tank right at the top, through either the breather vent or a new hole. They'll be taped close together, so any juice from the engine'll make a spark in the tank. The safest thing to do is pull the wires out of the tank."

She didn't move. With her head, she indicated the Olds. "There's a flashlight in the glove compartment."

Oh, terrific, I thought. What if the doors've been wired? But that was one too many things to worry about. Grimly, I went to the passenger side of the Olds and unlocked it. Holding my breath, I opened the door.

Nothing happened. I got the flashlight and gave it to Ginny. The sweat felt like ice under my arms.

"Maybe you ought to stand back." Her face was tight and pale. She hefted the flashlight as if she wanted a weapon. Then she went to the rear of the Olds and got down on her back on the cement. Using her arms for leverage, she wedged herself under the car.

I couldn't watch. Lifting my face to the mountains, I stared into the wind until my eyes ran. She muttered curses while she searched. With any luck at all, I wouldn't feel the blast when it hit me.

Maybe if I died I'd get to go to heaven. That'd be nice. In heaven, they drink good scotch. Right then, I could've used a little scotch.

Then I heard the scuffling sound as Ginny pried herself out from under the Olds. I turned around quickly and squatted to look.

She'd left a pair of wires lying on the cement behind her. They had bared ends, and they were taped close together, and they ran up toward the engine.

She was breathing hard as she got to her feet. For a minute, she leaned against me while I put my arms around her.

I wanted to stand there and hold her for a long time. But she pulled away—too angry to stand still. Panting fury, she knelt beside the car, reached under it, and swung the wires out where we could see them. Then I went to the hood and unlatched it.

We both heard the starter grind. The ignition had been jumped. A spark snapped at the ends of the wires.

To be honest, I could've used a lot of scotch.

I couldn't stand still either. Trembling quietly to myself, I disconnected all the extra wires under the hood of the Olds while she got down on her back again and squirmed under the gas tank of Haskell's Continental.

This time, she knew what she was looking for and found it quicker. Another set of wires feeding into the gas tank. Another jumped ignition, another contact at the hood latch. Maybe it was the cold. I couldn't say anything because I thought my teeth were going to chatter.

She rested her weight against the car, her expression

half rage, half nausea. She looked tight and flushed, like a woman with a high fever. She was holding her left forearm clamped under her right elbow like it was hurting her.

Trying to recover a little calm, I asked, "Are you sure you wouldn't like some breakfast now?"

Abruptly, she pushed herself straight and looked at me. Her voice shook. "I don't believe el Señor has anything to do with this. Do you hear me, Axbrewder? I don't care what Haskell says. I don't care what evidence you think you've come up with. You can play this case any way you want, and I'll go along. But I don't *believe it*!" Her shout was so sudden it practically rocked me back on my heels. She was right on the edge. "It's too messy and *stupid*! It doesn't make any sense."

"Ginny——" I didn't have anything to say. I just wanted to reach out to her somehow.

"Don't talk to me," she snapped. "I don't care how big you are. Next time it's *your* turn to get under the damn car."

For a second, she raised her hand to her face while her expression knotted. Then she forced herself to let out a long, slow breath. When she dropped her hand, she didn't look at me.

"Let's go get Haskell," she muttered softly. "I want to ask him some questions."

It's just reaction, I said to myself. That's all. She'll be fine in a few minutes. But I didn't believe that.

I believed she was losing it—whatever it was that used to make her tough, clearheaded, capable. She couldn't bear the idea of el Señor. Fear and her stump were eroding the conviction or self-esteem or something that held her together. Right in front of me, she was coming apart at the seams.

Under the circumstances, I was in no mood to go get Haskell. I had my own kind of reaction to deal with. But she was right. Even I could think of a few questions to ask him. So I made an effort to pull myself together. We took the Continental—let his insurance company worry about it if anything happened. I drove—at least it's usually called driving. In spite of the crushed velour seats and the leather dashboard, the climate control and the digital clock, I felt more like I was holding a rudder while several hundred galley slaves rowed for their lives—at least it's usually called driving. In spite. Up Cactus Blossom to Foothill, south to the nearest useful cross street, then west toward the neighborhood of the Territorial Apartments.

We weren't more than three minutes early when I pulled up in front of the fake chalet building and parked. Ginny got out, opened the rear door, and climbed into the back seat. That's where the textbook says one of you is supposed to sit when you're doing a bodyguard job. I slumped behind the wheel, feeling like a sack of dirty laundry. Since I didn't have anything bright or cheerful to say, I didn't say it.

Right on cue, Haskell came out of the Apartments. He looked scrubbed and fresh and ready to take on the world. Even though there wasn't any sunlight, and the clouds piling overhead were about as friendly as steel wool, his camel's hair coat seemed to glow like it was brand new. He could've been a headline in the morning paper:

**Bank Executive Conquers City
Virgins Sacrificed In Honor**

Before he reached the car, Ginny leaned forward abruptly and said, "He's wearing a clean suit."

Just for a second, I wondered how she knew that. Then I noticed his dark brown pants. The suit he'd been wearing when I left him here was light blue.

He came to my side of the car. When I rolled down the window, he said, "As long as you're using my car, I'll drive."

My smile felt about as charming as I did. "As long as

you're paying us to protect you," I said, "I'll drive." I pointed at the passenger seat. "Sit over there."

I thought he was going to argue, but he didn't. With a shrug, he ambled around the Continental and let himself in. After he closed the door, he turned to look at Ginny, then glanced toward me. The gleam in his eyes reminded me I hadn't shaved. "You two are in a good mood this morning," he commented. "What's the matter? Has anything happened?"

I started the engine. "Whoever blew up the Buick"—pulled away from the curb—"tried the same thing with this car." Heading the wrong way to get to the bank. "That always cheers us up."

He watched me for a minute. Then he said, "The bank's back that way."

"Well, hush my mouth," I said. "So it is."

After five blocks, I made a U-turn in an intersection and went back toward the Territorial Apartments. A block before we got there, I pulled to the curb again and parked. I could almost feel him trying to figure out what was going on.

Finally, he said, "All right, I give up. What are you doing?"

"Waiting," Ginny replied. "We'd like to see who else comes out of that apartment building."

Haskell's tan turned darker. "Don't," he snapped. "This is none of your business. I'm not paying you to pry into my private life."

"That's funny," she murmured in a distant voice, not really paying attention to him. "I thought it was your private life that got you into this mess."

He gave her a look that would've split a pine board. "You're wrong. Don't do this." I still couldn't claim we had him flustered, but this was as close as we'd come so far. "Take me to work. I'll fire you."

I smiled again. I was getting good at it. "Fire away."

I didn't want him to call my bluff. Playing people was his game, not mine—he could probably get around me.

But he made the mistake of looking at Ginny again. Her eyes were hard and gray as lead shot.

He didn't fire us. We went on waiting.

It didn't take long. After a few more minutes, a woman came out of the Apartments and hurried toward her car. In spite of the weather, she was dressed like a daisy. The glow of having Reg Haskell to herself all night left her too happy for dull colors.

Eunice Wint.

Chapter Eleven

More for Haskell's benefit than anything else, I said to Ginny, "I told you so."

"I believed you." Already, her mind was somewhere else—probably trying to figure out how this case didn't have anything to do with el Señor. "I always believe you when you tell me things like that."

Haskell stopped acting angry. His skin was still flushed under his tan, but his manner changed. "Was that Eunice? I didn't know she lives here."

"Nice try," I muttered as I put the Continental in drive. Smoothly, the galley slaves rowed us away from the curb. We headed in the direction of the bank.

Ginny went on thinking for a minute. Then she said, "Mr. Haskell, Brew told me what happened last night. It was a gas fire. Somebody hot-wired the ignition to make a spark in the gas tank. Now, to be honest, that doesn't sound like el Señor's style." She wasn't being honest at all. El Señor hired all kinds of muscle, all with different styles. But she was fishing for something. "It was something anybody could've done. Anybody who was angry or desperate enough to sneak into the parking lot with some wire and maybe a metal punch.

"That's why we're prying into your private life." She was making a calculated effort to soothe and unsettle him at the same time. I hoped he didn't realize it. "We have to consider the possibility that this case doesn't have anything to do with el Señor—that you have a personal enemy who wants to kill you."

He turned in the seat and hooked an arm over the back so he could look at both of us more easily. He was taking us seriously again. Or acting like it, anyway. "Why would anybody I know want to kill me?"

"We don't know that. But look at it from our point of view. Last night, you told Brew that you've been trying to blackmail el Señor. He'd certainly want to kill you for that. But how does he know it's you?

"I'm sure you've done some stupid things in your life." A touch of acid under the sweet reason. "But I can't believe you're stupid enough to attempt this kind of scam without taking precautions. You certainly didn't walk into El Machismo and announce that you wanted to blackmail the boss. And I assume you didn't tell him your name and address when you contacted him.

"Maybe," she said, "you'd better tell us what you did do."

I approved. Maybe she was ragged and fretting, trying to deny what was going on, but she was playing his own game for him pretty well. Now he was going to have to give us some straight answers. Unless he wanted us to go on prying into his private life.

His eyes shifted back and forth between us. His expression was faintly speculative—measuring us again. For some reason, I remembered the way he sabotaged our opponents in that bridge game.

After a minute, he let out a short laugh. "Well, I thought I took precautions. By the time I finished tracing his laundry, I knew he wasn't kidding around. A man who goes that far to protect his income is probably willing to go further. So I got his address out of the file on his account and wrote him a letter.

"But first I went to the downtown post office and rented a box under an assumed name. I used that for a return address. Then I told the post office I was going to be out of town for a while. I filled out one of those cards, asking them to forward my mail to my brother-in-law." His own cleverness tickled him no end. "As it happens, my brother-in-law's name was Reg Haskell. He had a box at the Heights branch post office.

"When I wrote to el Señor, I used bank stationery—to show him my credentials—but I told him to reply to the downtown box. I thought he might be able to find some way to have that box watched, but since the mail would be forwarded to the Heights, I'd be safe." Then he frowned. Or at least the lower half of his face frowned. I wasn't sure about his eyes. "Apparently, I underestimated him."

Well, I suppose if I'd been that clever I would've been tickled, too. It could've worked. In fact, it should've worked. Believe it or not, it's not that easy to suborn the post office.

But Ginny didn't waste her time on questions like that. And she didn't say anything nice about Haskell's cleverness, either. For a minute or two, she scowled out the window. Then she looked him in the face again.

"How long ago was this?"

He turned on a wry smile. "Actually, I just started. I mailed him my first letter last Wednesday. I was going to give him a week, then follow up with a few photocopies to show him I knew what I was talking about. I never expected him to track me down. I certainly never expected him to do it that quickly."

Last Wednesday? I thought. That wasn't quick, that was almost instantaneous. In Puerta del Sol, a letter mailed on Wednesday never arrives before Friday. And Saturday none of the post offices have counter service— just delivery. And yet by Sunday night Haskell was getting phone threats. If el Señor had his very own postal inspector, he still might not've been able to trace Haskell's mail that fast.

But Ginny was thinking something else. "Mr.

Haskell," she said slowly, looking right at him, "how much did you want him to pay you to keep your mouth shut?"

At that, he laughed out loud. Couldn't seem to help himself. "I knew how much El Machismo was taking in a week. I thought he could spare ten percent of that. Ten thousand dollars—give or take for seasonal variations."

Well, no wonder my stomach hurt. "Haskell"—for a minute there, I had trouble making the Continental behave normally in traffic—"how in hell can you possibly need that much money?"

Now at least I knew how to make him stop laughing. The humor disappeared from his face like I'd wiped it away with a sponge. The muscles at the corners of his eyes knotted hard. In a tone like an iron bar, he said, "You know I can't afford that house and this car on what I earn as an accountant. I've been lucky with some investments. But recently I took some risks that turned sour on me. I've got a lot to lose. Including my job. The bank doesn't smile on accountants who get in trouble with their investments. Why shouldn't I try to solve my problems by getting money where I can?"

I'd hit a nerve. I wanted to hit it again by asking him about those investments. But the Continental was swimming into the parking lot of the ice cream parlor, and Ginny had something to say to him. I eased the car into a landing slip. Then I sat and kept my eyes on the people arriving for work while she talked.

"Mr. Haskell," she said in a detached voice, sounding slightly bored, "it's not my job to tell you just how stupid you've been. Anybody in el Señor's position would try to have you killed. And he doesn't fail. That's how he gets away with it. It's self-perpetuating. In essence, he got his power by killing people. And his power makes it possible for him to go on killing people. Keeping you alive is going to be about as easy as changing the laws of nature.

"We need a lever. We can't match his muscle and resources. You don't want us to go to the police. We need

some threat that's strong enough to make him back off."
Her detachment didn't make her especially persuasive.
Maybe she really didn't believe what she was saying. "We
need that laundry.

"I want all the documentation you can get your hands
on. Copies, addresses, account numbers—whatever. I
want it today. First we'll make him believe we have the
same information you do. Then we'll convince him we've
got it protected, so that the cops and everybody else will
get it if anything happens to any of us. And then"—her
tone was still distant, but her gray eyes nailed Haskell—
"we'll find out just how dependent on violence he is."

He didn't look happy. When she was done, he shook
his head. "That won't work. I told Axbrewder last night
that I can't prove what I've found. It's too inferential. It
wouldn't stand up in court."

"That doesn't matter," she replied. "What matters is
what we can make him believe. As long as he thinks we
can prove it, he'll have to pay attention."

If I were Haskell, I would've been cheered right up by
the way her mind worked. But he didn't seem to get any
pleasure out of it. Maybe it wasn't enough like cowboys-
and-Indians. He stared out at the bank for a long minute.
Then he said, "I'll try." Gleaming, irresistible Reg actually sounded morose. "I might not be able to do it today.
I don't have regular access to all those files and records."

Ginny let the acid back into her voice. "Give it your
best shot. You're a walking dead man until we get some
kind of lever."

"All right." He didn't like being talked to like that.
"Pick me up at four-thirty." Swinging the door open, he
got out and slammed it behind him. As he walked toward
the bank, he looked like he could feel the sky leaning
down on him.

I turned around, got both arms over the back of the
seat. Knotting my fists in Ginny's coat, I pulled her to me
and kissed her.

She didn't know whether to kiss me back or get mad.

There was too much going on. When I let her go, she leaned back against the upholstery. Her face looked like the skin was stretched too tight over the bones of her skull. "Someday," she muttered, "you're going to meet a woman who isn't scared blind by your sheer size, and she's going to break her hand trying to slap your face."

I almost laughed. But I was distracted by a car pulling into the space beside the Continental. I'd seen that car before. It was driven by a woman dressed like a daisy.

"With your permission," I said to Ginny. Mock deference. Every once in a while, I'm faster than she is. A second after Eunice Wint closed the door of her car, I got out of the Continental.

She was in a hurry—late to work—but my sudden appearance stopped her. She gave me a quick smile. "Mr. Axbrewder." She still had the radiant look of a puppy in love. I would've felt sorry for her if I'd had the time. "You're early. We don't open until nine."

I met her smile with my harmless-galoot grin. "No problem. Just one question. Mr. Haskell forgot his briefcase. Left it at home. Do you think we should go get it for him?"

Poor Eunice. She never had a chance. She was too happy and young, and maybe just a little slow. Haskell seemed to like women who didn't exhibit what you might call penetrating intellect. "Oh, no," she said promptly. "Don't worry about it. He doesn't need it."

Then she realized what she was doing.

The way her skin burned was painful to watch. Even the sides of her neck blushed. Without meaning to, she told me more than I thought she knew. She made a lame effort to cover herself by saying, "He only takes work home over the weekends." But it was too late for that.

Still, I did what I could to help her out. "He's a lucky man," I said. Trying to make my grin suggest more than one kind of envy. "That saves us a trip. Thanks." Then— to let her off the hook—I climbed back into the Continental.

"Someday," I growled to Ginny, "one of us has simply got to poke him in the eye with a sharp stick. She knows exactly why he carries an empty briefcase."

Softly, she asked, "Do you think she'll tell us?"

"You ask her. I'm sick of picking on children."

Ginny didn't react to that. Instead, she pointed across the street at a restaurant called Granny Good's Family Food. "Let's go get a cup of coffee."

Snarling inane obscenities to myself, I started up the car and drove over to the restaurant. That way, Haskell might think we were going to leave him alone.

Inside, the restaurant was identical to every other so-called "family-style" joint in the city, with bright, vinyl-covered benches, a menu offering twenty different kinds of pancakes, hamburgers, and leather steaks, and waitresses so young they can hardly spell their own names. I took a booth while Ginny went to use the phone. When she came back, she seemed more brittle than ever. Her nose was too pale, and her cheeks were too red, and the muscles around her eyes were tight with strain. She was working on this case because I wanted her to, but she wasn't getting any less scared.

With her left forearm stuffed protectively into the pocket of her coat, she sat down opposite me. We ordered a pot of coffee. She swallowed a few more vitamins. I stared out through the window at the bank, watching the weather congeal. The heavy clouds and the threat of snow made the ice cream parlor look like a loony bin—the kind of place where ax murderers and Presidential assassins are locked up for their own good. It was probably the most successful bank branch in the whole city.

We didn't have to wait long. Ginny still knew how to get results over the phone. No more than five minutes after our coffee arrived, a tall, thin man wearing an immaculate old-school banker's pinstripe came out of the ice cream parlor. She'd gotten his attention, all right—he wasn't even wearing a coat. Hunching his shoulders against the cold, he crossed the street in our direction.

I waved at him through the window. He came into Granny Good's and found his way to our booth.

Jordan Canthorpe, Eunice Wint's fiancé.

Up close, the prim way he carried his hands seemed about right, but his face looked too young for the suit. His hair was so blond and fine it was almost invisible, and his moustache was self-effacing to the point of nonexistence. Even though he was thin, he had the kind of smooth, soft skin that was going to make people think he was his wife's son in about ten years—if he ever succeeded at getting married. Still, he was doing his best to age himself with worry, and it showed. His pale eyes had a harried cast.

In spite of that, he was feeling too much internal pressure to be easily handled. "Ms. Fistoulari?" he asked in a high voice, as tight as a wire. "I don't like phone calls like that. I have work to do. The bank opens in eighteen minutes. Why can't you come talk to me normally in my office?"

Neither of us got up. Ginny gave him her woman-of-steel look. "Because if we did that, Reg Haskell would see us talking to you."

I smiled and offered him a seat beside me. "Want some coffee?"

Automatically, he said, "No, thank you." For a minute, his gaze shifted back and forth between me and Ginny. Then, abruptly, he folded himself into the booth. "Reg Haskell is our chief accountant," he said unsteadily. "He does excellent work and has for years. We're fortunate to have him. You have no business asking me questions about him. I shouldn't be talking to you at all."

It was Ginny's turn to smile. She did it, but it didn't soften her eyes at all. "Mr. Canthorpe, Reg Haskell is in danger. He hired us to protect him. Somebody wants to kill him."

Canthorpe stared at her. If he could've seen himself, he would've cringed at the way his mouth hung open. His voice almost cracked when he said, "I don't believe it."

Conversationally—and still smiling—I said, "Last

night, they blew up my car. They tried the same thing with his this morning. I don't think they're going to keep missing much longer."

He looked at me, gulped a little air, turned a face full of distress back toward Ginny. "I don't believe it," he repeated. But he believed it, all right. He'd probably given more than a little thought to killing Haskell himself.

We just watched him and waited while he thought himself into a sweat. He wasn't a stupid man by any stretch, but he wasn't used to what he was faced with. A few seconds passed before he started to look horrified. Then he said, "I don't know anything about it. Why would I know anything about it?" His long, clean hands hugged each other on the tabletop. "Why do you think I know anything about it?"

Left to myself, I would've said, He's screwing your fiancée. That girl's never going to marry you now—not after she's had a taste of irresistible Reg. Why wouldn't you know anything about it? But Ginny was smoother.

"This is a complicated case, Mr. Canthorpe. Mr. Haskell is in serious danger, but we don't know from whom. That makes our job difficult." Old master-of-understatement Fistoulari. "We have to investigate every lead we can find." As she talked, she began to let herself sound less formal. "If we can, we want to get at his enemies before they get at him.

"What we need from you is information. There are two crucial points we have to track down. You can help us with both of them."

Canthorpe squinted at her. He didn't seem especially aware she hadn't answered his question, but he was getting his dismay under control anyway. Very carefully, he said, "Ms. Fistoulari, you surely realize that the private lives of our people are just that—private. They deserve confidentiality. And I certainly can't discuss the bank's business with you."

She didn't so much as blink. "Before you decide that, don't you think you should hear what we have to say?"

Now he remembered she hadn't answered his question. He took a tighter grip on himself and nodded slowly.

I leaned into the corner of the booth to watch and wait. I think the seats in restaurants like that are deliberately designed to be uncomfortable so people'll eat fast and get out, make room for somebody else. But I kept my kindly-uncle smile glued on my face and tried to be stoical. I was watching Canthorpe. That's part of my job—help make people nervous while Ginny talks to them. It's surprising how nervous people can get when a man my size just sits there and smiles at them. And I was waiting to hear what story she was going to tell him. She certainly couldn't tell him the truth. Even private investigators have ethics of one kind or another.

She has more scruples than most people in the business, but she wasn't wearing them where Canthorpe could see them. "As I say, Mr. Haskell has hired us to protect him. We're licensed by the state for this kind of work. Naturally, one of the most important questions we have to answer is, why would anybody want to kill him?

"He tells us he only knows of one reason. Apparently, during the past few months he's stumbled onto what he calls a money laundry—a way of concealing sources of illegal income. He believes one of the leading criminal figures in the city is using your bank to process his profits from gambling, prostitution, and drugs." She was laying it on pretty thick. "Through a series of dummy accounts and companies, he makes his income hard to trace, disguising his involvement in criminal activities."

She hadn't reached the point yet, but Canthorpe couldn't resist a banker's question. "How is it done?"

She told him what Haskell'd told me.

"That's quite possible." He was nodding to himself, thinking furiously. When he didn't watch what they were doing, his hands made little stroking gestures along his moustache. "But it's highly unlikely that such a laundry would be discovered by accident." He wasn't used to this kind of reasoning. It took him a moment to catch up. "Hasn't Haskell gone to the police?"

Ginny shook her head. "He says he doesn't have enough proof yet."

"But if he lacks sufficient proof, and he hasn't made his findings public in any way"—he was getting confused—"then this criminal can't know about them. Why would he try to kill him for knowing something he doesn't know he knows?"

She didn't waver. Making it up out of whole cloth, she said, "Mr. Haskell thinks somebody at the bank found out what he was doing and stooled on him."

I went on smiling. In the privacy of my head, I gave her a round of applause.

Canthorpe gaped at her. "That's preposterous!"

She put a little more bite in her voice. "Mr. Canthorpe, do you mean to tell me that if Mr. Haskell stumbled on a money laundry and began to trace it, nobody else would be able to do the same to him? That it would be impossible to discover what he was doing?"

"Well, no." Her tone made him retreat a step. "I don't mean that precisely. Logs are kept. Access to files is limited or supervised. He would have to go rather far afield from his normal duties in order to trace such a laundry. An observer might become suspicious—especially if the observer had prior knowledge of the laundry's existence." I was right—Canthorpe wasn't stupid. For a second there, I wondered if Ginny was going to be able to get around him. He was recovering his indignation. "But that in itself is preposterous. No one who works for the First Puerta del Sol National Bank would ever—"

"Oh, spare me," Ginny cut in. "I'm sure everybody who has ever worked for any bank anywhere is pure as the driven snow. But there's only one way to be sure, isn't there?"

"To be sure?"

"Trace the laundry yourself. Check back on what Mr. Haskell's been doing. Find out who might've been in a position to realize what he was up to."

If I'd said that, it would've sounded like I was reading

it off a cereal box. But from her it made a queer kind of sense. For him, I mean. For me, there was nothing queer about it. She was just trying to verify Haskell's story. And to set Canthorpe up for what she really wanted. But from a banker's point of view, what she was suggesting held together only by force of personality.

"That might be possible," he said slowly. He didn't have any idea what he was getting into. On the other hand, I suspected Haskell was a subject he wouldn't be able to leave alone. "It would be easier for me," he went on, "if you could give me a name."

Ginny nodded fractionally and glanced at me.

Softly, so I wouldn't sound too much like I was swearing, I said, "Hector Jesus Fria de la Sancha." El Señor.

Fumbling, Canthorpe pulled a notepad and a silver pen out of his breast pocket and wrote the name down.

She didn't need me to tell her he was ready. When he finished writing, she said, "I told you there're two crucial points you can help us with. The money laundry is one. The other's much easier."

He looked at her like he was going to be sick. This was all too much for him—which was exactly what she wanted. He couldn't've walked out on us then to save his soul.

"We have to investigate every possibility," she said. "It's Mr. Haskell's idea that somebody found out he was tracing Señor Fria's money. Personally, I consider that farfetched." She could afford to admit it now. Just made her sound more plausible. Now he'd probably never figure out he'd been lied to. "It's more likely, I think"—her eyes were hard, but she didn't give him any warning—"that somebody he knows—somebody he works with—wants him dead for personal reasons."

Canthorpe's whole body went rigid. We were back to the subject that got his attention in the first place. Holding on to the edge of the table with both hands, he said, "What personal reasons?"

It was my turn. I didn't have any trouble making my

smile look sad. "We're just trying to do our job. You know what personal reasons as well as we do. We saw Haskell come out of your fiancée's apartment this morning."

He had the opposite problem Eunice Wint did. When something hit him that hard, all the blood rushed out of him. He turned so pale he looked like he might evaporate. For a minute, he shoved the heels of his hands into his eyes. It wouldn't've surprised me if he'd started to cry.

But then he dropped his hands back to the table. They left red marks under his eyes like scars on his white skin. His voice shook, but it wasn't because he was in danger of crying.

"I'm a conservative man," he said. "Banking is a conservative profession. I earn a good income. I value traditional things—honesty, family, security, fidelity. Kindness. Reg Haskell has no moral sense at all.

"He considers himself some kind of sexual buccaneer. For two or three years now, he's been cutting a swath through our staff of tellers and receptionists. He has them standing in line. No amount of promiscuity satisfies him, and he makes the women around him promiscuous simply by smiling at them.

"I thought Eunice would be different. She seemed too pure for him." Even though his voice was shaking, he said that with dignity. "I had no wish to fall in love with one of his discards. A man like that has no business working in a bank."

"A man like that," Ginny said quietly, "must've hurt a lot of people. Were any of them hurt badly enough to want to kill him?" *Any of them besides yourself, Mr. Canthorpe?*

The clarity of his anger was fading. "That's the terrible part," he said with more self-pity. "His women don't act as if they're hurt. They're grateful." Then a spasm of memory twisted his face for a second. "Most of them."

"Most of them?" Ginny asked.

"There was one who wasn't." The quiver in his voice began to sound like disgust. "About six months ago. She took it to heart—the way Eunice does. But I'm afraid she wasn't very stable. We had to let her go. We try not to impose our standards on the private lives of our employees, but the way she dithered around after him affected her work. One day, she made a scene in the lobby." His face twitched again. "We had no choice."

"What was her name?"

"Gail Harmon." Remembering her made him distant. He didn't seem to realize what he was implying about her. "The other tellers called her Frail Gail. She was beautiful in such a fragile way."

"Do you know where we can find her?"

Without thinking about it, he gave us the address—a house number down on Bosque in the South Valley. Right in the middle of Puerta del Sol's *barrio*. He said it like he'd been meditating on it for hours, using it for some kind of mantra.

That surprised me. The branch manager of a major bank has better things to do with his time than sit around memorizing the addresses of people who don't work for him anymore. But I thought I understood it. Almost casually, I asked, "Were you engaged to her, too?"

That brought him back. He sat up straighter. He didn't seem to have any blood in his whole body, but something about his eyes suddenly made him look capable of spilling some. "I saw what Haskell did to her," he whispered fiercely, "and I felt sorry for her. I thought I might help her find another job, so I called the address she used when she worked for us. That was her parents' home. They told me how to locate her. I think they were sick of worrying about her."

But he couldn't keep it going. He was in too deep. After a minute, he sagged, and the truth came out.

"She took him so much to heart. I thought she might be able to explain Eunice to me. She might help me understand. But I haven't called her, haven't gone to see her. Every day, I promise myself that today I'll do it. Every day, I believe that I can't bear any more. But I lack the nerve." Then, as if it were irrelevant, he said, "Her parents told me she's living with somebody."

I didn't know what else to do, so I put my hand on his shoulder. "Maybe she'll wake up," I said. "It's been known to happen." Axbrewder on the verge of getting maudlin. "Maybe she'll realize what she's doing and come back to you."

I thought he was going to say, I wouldn't have her. But he just sighed. "That would be nice."

With her hand, Ginny pinched the bridge of her broken nose, trying to keep her priorities straight. "Mr. Canthorpe," she said, sounding tired and a little beaten, "Reg Haskell may not be a nice man, but murder is murder. He has a right to hire protection. We do this kind of work because we want to keep the number of people who get hurt to a minimum."

I hoped he wasn't going to try for some kind of sarcastic comeback, but he just asked, "Is that all?"

She nodded.

He said, "Call me around four." Then he got up and walked away. Through the window, I watched him return to the bank. He didn't look back.

After a while, I said, "Is Haskell really all that irresistible?"

"No." She was bitter and brittle—and angrier than she knew what to do with. "Canthorpe's just one of the victims. It makes him exaggerate."

Outside, the clouds looked too heavy to carry their own weight. The air was dead gray. Nothing had any color. Mostly to myself, I said, "Some days I love this job so much I could puke."

Chapter Twelve

That was the wrong thing to say. She was in no mood for it. She put her one hand flat on the tabletop, her palm against the Formica. "All this," she said, pushing down so hard her fingers splayed, "was your idea, remember? You wanted this case. Don't tell me you're sick of it. I don't give a shit."

Well, she had a point. The whole thing *was* my idea. But I hadn't exactly been enjoying it so far. "Yes, sir, Ms. Fistoulari, sir," I muttered sourly. "I disembowel myself in shame. Do forgive me."

"All right." Her voice was as white as the skin of her nose. "All right. Go over there"—she nodded at the bank—"and tell Haskell we quit. Then I'll drop you off at the nearest bar."

I stared at her. Maybe she was bluffing. But I couldn't think of any way to call her on it. I couldn't risk flushing everything down the toilet like that. I just stared at her and held my breath and didn't make any effort to hide the hurt in my eyes.

After a minute, she sighed and looked away. "Either that," she said, "or go back to the apartment and get some rest. You don't look like you can hold your head up much longer."

Slowly, I scrubbed my hands over my face to pull what

was left of my brains back together. I hadn't shaved, and my whiskers felt like sandpaper against my palms. But that helped. When I'd rubbed some of the anguish out of the muscles of my cheeks, I dropped my hands back onto the table.

"I can't," I said. "The cops aren't going to just sit on their butts while people go around blowing up rented cars in parking lots and killing innocent kids." That was too much to expect, even from Puerta del Sol's finest. "They're going to get our address off the rental contract. And they'll get Haskell's address by asking people at his club what I was doing there. If they get mad enough about the fact I haven't gone in to talk to them, they might stake out both places." Eventually, we were going to have to tell the cops what we were doing. There was no way around it. But I wanted to put it off as long as possible. "If they catch me, they might hold me as a material witness."

I didn't point out the obvious. If the cops held me, Ginny would have to cope with this case all by herself.

"Besides," I added, "I want to go see Gail Harmon."

Something about the way that came out told her more than I actually said. "What do you mean, *you* want to go see Gail Harmon? What about me? What do you expect me to do?" She looked like she wanted to take the skin off my bones. "Spend the day the way I spent last night—sitting around waiting for you to come back beat up, stupid, or drunk?"

"No." I was too tired, and she was hitting too hard. I kept myself from yelling at her, but I couldn't keep my anger down. Sounding about as savage as I felt, I said, "I expect you to find proof el Señor doesn't have anything to do with this. You believe it, you prove it. Stop whining about it and *do* something."

Then I wanted to turn around and do the same thing to myself because there was nothing she could do to conceal the way she flinched. Her mouth twisted like she was going to spit at me—but her voice wasn't even sarcastic. "I suppose that's fair." Just dead flat. "I'll try to disprove your theory while you tear holes in mine. What a great idea. When we took this case, I didn't know you were going to use it to get away from me so much. I didn't realize I was going to get to do so much alone."

A sharp intake of breath pulled her lips back from her teeth. She knotted her fist. "It's so much fun working for you. This time I don't even have a car."

For a second there, I felt about as rotten as I deserved. Then I dug down into a pocket and tossed the keys to the Continental onto the table. "I'll take a cab back to Haskell's house and use the Olds."

She didn't look at me. Her face was pale, and the expression in her eyes was faraway, harried, and miserable. For a moment, she pressed the knuckles of her fist against her forehead. "Brew," she said in a tight voice, "when was the last time we actually told each other the truth?"

I hadn't told her any direct lies—and precious few indirect ones. But suddenly all the things I hadn't told her made my pulse throb in my throat. Through my teeth, I gritted, "I am not going out to get drunk. You know me better than that."

"No," she muttered. "Not anymore. I don't know you at all anymore. I don't know what's going on with you. You pressured me into taking this case. You won't let me get out of it. But the only thing *you* do is figure out excuses to go off on your own. You want me in this case, but you don't want me with you. What kind of sense do you expect me to make of that?" Frustration and pain turned her voice as harsh as the cut of a crosscut saw. "So far, I haven't seen any sign that you're drinking. That's true. So what? *You* give me another explanation."

She sounded so fierce I started to stare at her, dumbfounded, and almost didn't answer. "What do you mean, 'another explanation'? I already gave you one. Weren't you listening?"

"Oh, I was listening," she snarled back. "I've been listening all along. You talk about the case. You insult and manipulate me. But you don't *say* anything. Well, give it a try. Give me one reason why I shouldn't believe you and Haskell are doing this together."

Then I did stare at her. My mouth actually hung open. *You and Haskell*. I wanted to say, Stop it. Stop this. But I couldn't.

She didn't stop. "Or maybe," she said, "this is all just some clever way to get rid of me. You've got some girl on the side, and you're tired of taking care of the angry old cripple, so you want to use this case to solve the problem. Maybe get me shot by el Señor's goons. I had my hand blown off for your niece, but that isn't enough for you. You're leaving me alone so I'll be a better target."

It was too much. The more I gaped at her, trying not to believe what I was hearing, the more she seemed to be going out of her head right in front of me. She looked so hurt, so abandoned, that I wanted to break my fists on the table just so she wouldn't be alone. I'd done this to her. And I was doing it deliberately. It was too much by a long shot.

I heaved myself out of the booth. I couldn't stand to sit there with her anymore and admit her abuse was justified, even if it was completely wrong. "By my count," I said, "we're just about even right now." Then I stomped away toward the phone.

By the time I got to it, I was mad enough to rip it out of the wall.

Lucky for me I was housebroken at a young age. Instead of demolishing the phone, I used it to call a cab. Then I went out into the cold to wait.

Lucky again—Jiffy had a cab free in the neighborhood. I only had to wait a few minutes. But that was long enough. The wind wasn't hard, but it was coming down off the mountains like the edge of a knife. The clouds were heavy as lead, overdue for snow. With-out a coat, I didn't have anything except my tired metab-olism to hold out the cold. During those few minutes, I realized I didn't have any idea what Ginny was going to do.

There was no need for me to tell myself she didn't mean it. That was the point. I didn't think she knew what she meant.

Whatever she did might be as crazy as what she said.

When the cab arrived, I pulled myself into the blast of its heater and tried to absorb as much warmth as possible while the driver took me over to Foothill in the direction of Haskell's house.

I wanted to stay in the cab forever. Just sprawl out on the back seat and sleep in the warmth and the lulling sound of tires on concrete until all my problems went away. But if I did that I was going to get a terrible crick in my neck. And anyway, I had my job to do. That's why they give us private investigators all that money and glory—because we're tough as nails, true as steel, and about as intelligent as overcooked turnips. I told the driver to stop at the corner of Foothill and Cactus Blos-som—above the cul-de-sac, where I had a good view of the house. Before I paid him, I made sure there weren't any suspicious-looking vehicles parked nearby. Then I sent him on his way and walked down the hill toward the Olds in Haskell's driveway.

Maybe I was getting sloppy in my old age. Maybe fa-tigue was turning what few brains I had left to sawdust. Or maybe I was just thinking too hard about not getting caught by the cops. I got into the Olds, put my key in the ignition, and turned it before I remembered anything about spark wires and gas tanks.

Nothing happened. The people who'd wired the car during the night hadn't come back. I tried not to tremble or throw up while I cranked the engine. Then, devoutly careful, I backed out of the driveway and drove up out of Cactus Blossom Court.

So far, so good. I was awake, anyway, my heart stewing in useless adrenaline. And the cops hadn't caught me yet. It occurred to me I was starting to go a little crazy around the edges, but there didn't seem to be anything I could do about it. What I really wanted to do was go back to Granny Good's and throw myself on Ginny's mercy. But I didn't think the waitresses were old enough to stand the sight of a man as big as me acting like that. No doubt about it, I was losing my mind. Dependency cut both ways. I was fundamentally lost without her.

But I hung onto the wheel with a kind of religious fervor and kept the Olds on the road while I worked down through the Heights. When I reached the beltway, I had the wind behind me. My pulse slowed down a bit, and I began to feel better. About as stable as a bottle of gin, maybe, but less like I was close to falling off the fence.

A few flakes of snow paced me along the highway. But most of them stayed up in the clouds, considering the possibilities. A cop passed me without slowing down.

I was headed for the South Valley. Which is where the people the tourists aren't supposed to see live.

Funny how these things happen—the kind of funny that makes you feel there isn't much hope for human civilization after all. In all the history of Puerta del Sol, there was probably never a time when anybody sat down and actually decided, We're going to put all the really poor people *here*, all the dirt farmers who've lost their land, all the wetbacks who never found work, all the hippies who gooned out on drugs in the '60s and never recovered, all the Indians who left their reservations and then started drinking too much, every ruined, degraded or helpless sod in the city *here*, and then we'll build the rest of the city so nobody ever has to go where these people live. But that's the way it turned out. Pure social instinct put Puerta del Sol's *barrio* in the South Valley and then encysted it, closed it off from everywhere else. If you live in the South Valley, the only way you can even hope to find work is if you have a car—and money for gas. And if you have a car—and money for gas—you probably live somewhere else.

At least they don't have organized crime in the South Valley. They don't have enough money to make it worth el Señor's while.

From the beltway, I found Trujillo and headed south. It was a long drive. I went through a transitional region where every trucking company in the state had some kind of warehouse, then through an area where all the warehouses were abandoned and I'd almost gotten myself killed once when Ginny was in the hospital after losing her hand. Then I angled onto Bosque closer to the river and began peeling away layers of destitution toward the hard core of the *barrio*.

There used to be a lot of cottonwood, juniper, and russian olive that close to the river, before the trees got cut down for firewood by people who couldn't pay their gas bills. The stumps still stood there, giving the city an excuse not to invest in sidewalks. The houses were built of either mud bricks—in which case, only the exterior plaster kept them from washing away when it rained—or cinder blocks. At any other time of year, the bare dirt around them would've sprouted with despondent little crops of tumbleweed, chamisa, and goathead. But winter and wind made the ground look like it'd been scoured down to hard clay.

When I found the number Canthorpe'd given me, I saw it must've been more prosperous once, maybe fifty years ago. The house had at least three or four rooms, judging by its size. It had a pitched roof covered with actual tin instead of tarpaper shingles. It even had what was left of a screened front porch. But that degree of gentility hadn't meant anything for decades. The wood of

the porch frame was so far gone only its own rot and
termites held it together. The door hung abjectly from its
one remaining hinge, and the screening looked like it'd
been used for target practice by half the shotguns in
Puerta del Sol.

Gail Harmon had come a long way down.

I parked the Olds in the dirt beside the road. Got out.
Made sure all the doors were locked. The cold cut into
me again, but this time it made me feel a bit more
awake. Surreptitiously—in case I was being watched—I
slid my hand under my jacket and checked the .45. (It
was a pretty good bet I was being watched by somebody.
People who survive in *barrios* are good at looking out for
trouble.) Then I went up to the house.

The boards of the steps and porch held my weight
more out of habit than conviction. I shifted the hanging
screen door out of my way and crossed to the inner door,
making the whole front of the house shiver. It was
as good as a burglar alarm. Before I had a chance to
knock on the cracked panels of the door, a man's voice
from inside barked, "Go away, *cojones*. I gave at the
office."

I could tell by the way he said it he wasn't Mexican or
Chicano.

Well, Canthorpe had warned me, even if he hadn't
known what he was warning me about. Since I was being
given the tough-guy approach, I took the same line myself. "Good for you," I said. "Too bad that's not why I'm
here. I want to see Gail Harmon."

A rustling noise from the other side of the door. People changing positions. "Go away," the voice repeated.
Tough—and getting angry. "I don't know no Gail Harmon."

Maybe he didn't. But two could play that game.
"Neither do I. What difference does it make? I want to
talk to her."

"You don't hear so good, *cojones*. I said, Go away. I
won't warn you again."

"Oh, come off it." Ignoring the way the wood sagged, I leaned my shoulder on the frame of the door. "If I go away, you'll never find out what I want to talk to her about."

Another rustle. I figured there were at least two people on the other side of the door. The man thought about it for a minute. Then he said, "Tell me from there." His voice was raw with the kind of stress you sometimes hear from burnt-out cops.

I decided to chance it. Nobody ever accused me of having too much sense for my own good. A bit more softly, I replied, "Reg Haskell."

That got a reaction. A woman's voice started to say something. Then a pair of heavy boots thudded down on the floor-boards, and the woman yelped. I heard a particular clicking sound.

"Open it slow," the man said, "or I'll blow you in half." For some reason, he sounded happy.

Blow me in half, I thought. Oh, good. What fun. I'd heard that clicking sound before. In spite of the cold, my palms were sweating.

I didn't pull out the .45. But I didn't hesitate, either. I didn't like the idea of what was happening to the woman in there. The knob rattled loosely in my hand as I unlatched the door and eased it open.

It let me into a living room about the size of your average jail cell. Tattered curtains stiff with grime covered the windows. The gas heater was working too hard, and the whole place stank like a witch doctor's brew—cigarettes and dope, generations of spilled beer, sweat, urine, and despair. There was only one chair. The rest of the furniture consisted of pillows on the floor. Between the pillows, the boards were littered with cigarette butts, beer cans, and magazines—*Guns & Ammo, Argosy, Soldier of Fortune*.

A man sat in the chair facing me and the door. He was as thin as a bayonet and looked about as tall as I am. He wore combat boots, jeans, and a black T-shirt. One

sleeve of the shirt was rolled up to hold a pack of cigarettes. He had a cigarette hanging from his thin mouth,
the smoke curling into his eyes. His skin was like stained
parchment, and both his arms were blue with tattoos—a
naked woman on one bicep, a dragon curving down his
left forearm, a rifle lovingly etched on his right. His face
looked flat and heartless and a little crazy.

With his right hand, he held an M-16 pointed at my
belly, its bolt cocked and ready.

His left was clenched in the hair of a young woman,
gripping her so she whimpered on her knees beside him.

"Haskell?" he said. "Haskell? I knew Reg. I never
knew Haskell. This I'm gonna love."

The muzzle of the M-16 left my stomach in knots. But
I didn't like the way he was treating the woman. Carefully, I closed the door to keep the heat in and the neighbors out. Then I faced the woman. "Ms. Harmon? My
name is Axbrewder. I'd like to talk to you about Reg
Haskell."

She couldn't react. "*Cojones*!" the man spat—still
happy, but more than a little disappointed. "You're not
Haskell? Fuck it."

"If you want," I said to her quietly, "I'll make him let
go of you."

"Please, Mase," she whimpered. "Please."

His eyes narrowed as he raised the rifle and pointed it
at my head. He looked like a snake.

I didn't make any threatening moves. "That dragon," I
said, nodding toward his left forearm. "Cambodia, right?
Special Forces." My brother was in the Army in south-
east Asia for a while. He used to talk about things like
that. "You must've earned it the hard way."

He was at least as dangerous as a stirred-up rattler, but
he wasn't any smarter than I was. Surprised by my recog-
nition, he loosened his grip on the rifle just a little. "You
know about that?"

"Sure."

I was still nodding when I kicked the rifle out of his

hands. Instinctively, trying to defend himself, he let the woman go. Then I heaved him out of the chair by the front of his shirt, jerked him into the air, and slammed him to the floor with a jolt that rattled his bones. Clamping my left foot on the back of his neck, I pushed his face against the floorboards. For a second, he struggled. Then he stopped—he could feel how easy it'd be for me to break his neck. He started frothing obscenities, but I put more weight on him until he stopped that, too.

While I was still bending over him, I took a quick glance at the subscription labels on the magazines. They were all addressed to Mase Novick.

If I was right about him, he was a mercenary, or had been recently. He didn't live here because he was poor. He lived here because he was professionally paranoid. He felt safer in the *barrio*, where people like cops, customs agents, and the FBI weren't likely to come looking for him. Not to mention agents of foreign governments. And if he happened to shoot one of his neighbors by accident, nobody'd know the difference.

He was exactly the kind of man you'd hire to kill somebody if you didn't have el Señor's resources.

With Mase Novick pinned to the floor, I got my first good look at Gail Harmon. At the bank, they'd called her Frail Gail, and she looked more than ever like that now. She was wearing a ragged old flannel shirt that only had one button left to keep it closed over her breasts, jeans that probably fit her right before she lost too much weight, no shoes. If she'd washed her hair anytime in the past month, it didn't show. Her face was covered with freckles that would've appeared perky and fresh if she'd had any kind of health at all to back them up. But behind them, her skin was the color of stale dough, and her eyes looked like they were in the process of being erased from her head by dope, beer, and exhaustion.

She didn't seem particularly aware of what I was doing to her boyfriend. Still on her knees, she gave me a white stare and asked in a voice like a little girl's, "Do you know Reg? Have you seen him? Does he want me back?"

She made my insides hurt worse than the M-16. I didn't need a doctor to come along and tell me I was out of my depth. I knew that as soon as I got a good look at her eyes and heard her voice. Inside her skull, she was already a wasteland—and the rest of her was going that way fast.

All of a sudden, I wanted Ginny, wanted her so badly it closed my throat and I couldn't say anything.

When I didn't answer, Gail got to her feet. "You said you wanted to talk about Reg. I heard you." She was starting to sound wild. "You said his name."

Out of my depth—and close to drowning. Her desire to hear me say something about Haskell made her breathe harder and harder. Her eyes didn't seem to have any focus at all. I thought she was going to try to hit me. To keep her back, I pulled out the .45. Then I took my foot off Novick's neck.

He rolled into fighting position fast. But I had him covered. Directing him with the barrel of the .45, I moved him to his chair and made him sit down. After that, I picked up the M-16, cleared it, and leaned it against the wall in the corner. He watched every move, his eyes blank with hate, but he didn't try to jump me.

Finally, I forced the muscles of my throat to unclamp. "Novick," I said, and didn't care how my voice shook, "what the hell's going on here?"

He didn't say anything. He didn't move. He just fixed his hate on me and waited.

I had a hard time keeping myself from shouting. "Whatever it is, she doesn't know anything about it. She probably doesn't know her own name half the time anymore. You're the one who knows. You may be so strung out with drugs and paranoia you can't think, but you haven't lost your mind yet." For a second, I almost lost control. "What the fucking hell is going on?"

A bit of a smile touched his thin lips. He liked seeing me upset. But he didn't answer.

Gail went to him, stood beside him, put her hands on his shoulders. "Mase," she whispered softly, pleading with him, "he said he wanted to talk to me about Reg. I heard him." Her fingers stroked the side of his neck, the back of his head. "Make him talk to me about Reg."

Because I didn't have any better ideas, I said the simplest and most direct thing I could think of. "Novick, she needs help. She needs help bad."

At that, something I wasn't expecting came into his face. Something like a snarl of rage—or a cry of grief. "You think I don't know that, *cojones*? You think I look at her and don't know that?"

"Then do something about it, for God's sake! Take her back to her parents. Take her to a doctor. Something. She isn't going to last much longer."

"Do something." He laughed softly, like a splash of acid. "You big fucker. You think you understand. You understand nothing. That Reg bastard fucker kicks her out. I take her in. I take care of her. Whatever I got, we share. What do I get? She lets me do what I want." Abruptly, he reached into her shirt, squeezed one of her breasts. Then he knotted his hand in her hair again and pulled her down to her knees beside him. He had a virtuoso range of endearments—but she didn't react to either of them. She just kept watching me, waiting for me to say what she wanted to hear. "But she don't want me. She wants Reg. She thinks Reg—sleeps Reg—smokes Reg. You think I like that?"

Without warning, he pushed her away so hard she sprawled into the magazines and pillows. "Do something. *Cojones*, I'll do something. She don't need no parents— and no doctor, either. I'll give her what she needs. I'll give her Reg Haskell's balls on a stick."

On some important level, Gail wasn't aware of what he said, or even of what he did. She climbed out of the pillows and got to her feet, hardly strong enough to keep her balance. Her face was pale and venomous. "You said you wanted to talk to me about Reg." In her frail way, she hated me worse than Mase Novick did. "You lied.

You don't know him at all. If you knew him, you would've told me he wants me back." Then she turned toward Novick. "Make him go away, Mase. I don't like him."

He grinned at me. He didn't have all his teeth.

By then, a mongoloid idiot could've told you I'd botched the whole thing. I'd come all this way, and all I'd learned was Gail Harmon didn't have any of her oars in the water and Novick liked his work. If I didn't start doing better soon, I was going to end up laughing myself out of Puerta del Sol. So I did something a little crazy. I said, "Gail, somebody's trying to kill Reg. I came here to find out who it is."

At least I was in good company. She didn't have any expression on her face as she bent down and picked up one of the pillows. She wasn't looking at me, wasn't seeing me. I didn't have any warning when she flung the pillow at my head with all her little strength.

Faster than I thought she could move, she snatched up a beer can and threw it. Another pillow. A magazine.

While I was fending that stuff away from my face, Novick came out of his chair at me like the slam of a piston.

I was back on my heels, couldn't pull all my muscle together. But I managed to get my arm around in time. Swinging hard, I clubbed him across the shoulder and deflected him past me on one side.

Toward the corner where his M-16 was.

As he grabbed his rifle, I pivoted after him and raised the .45 so it would be the first thing he saw when he turned.

And Gail jumped onto my back. Reaching for my head, she clawed her fingernails at my eyes.

For a temporarily sober drunk, my reflexes were still pretty good. And they were a whole lot better when I didn't have a chance to think about what I was doing. Just in time, I got my eyes squeezed shut.

Her nails raked my eyebrows and cheeks. Novick

brought the rifle into line on my chest and grabbed for the bolt. I opened my eyes again.

Somehow, my right hand went on pointing the .45 into Novick's face. With my left, I caught Gail's wrist and swung her around me, pitching her against him and the rifle.

That saved me. Before he had a chance to recover, I thumbed back the hammer of the .45 and shouted, "Don't even think it!"

He froze. Force of habit, probably—good mercenaries have to know when to take orders.

I could already feel blood on my face, but I ignored it. "You're both insane," I panted, out of breath more from fear than exertion. "You're too sick to live. You should be put out of your misery."

Saying that made me feel better. But it didn't get me out of there in one piece. They were both watching me like cornered rats, waiting for their chance.

I had two choices. Drag them out of the house with me so I could keep them covered while I got to the Olds. Or gamble. Choosing self-respect over caution, I decided to gamble.

"Well, today you're lucky." A drop of blood ran into my left eye, smeared my vision. I blinked it away. "I'm not going to shoot you." Lowering the .45, I uncocked it and put it back in its holster. "If you stop and think about it, you don't have any reason to shoot me, either."

Which probably wasn't true—but I trusted it anyway. I gave Novick one last chance. "Get her some help." Then I pulled the door open and let myself out onto the porch, out of the overcooked heat into the cold.

The blood felt like sweat on my face. Closing the door behind me, I crossed the splintered porch to the bare dirt of the front yard and strode toward the Olds without looking back. I was moving briskly, but I didn't run.

That wasn't as stupid as it sounds. I knew I was going to be able to hear the door if they opened it.

They didn't. I reached the Olds, got in. For once, the

engine started as soon as I touched the key. I drove a few blocks farther down Bosque before I stopped to see what I could do about the state of my face.

The rearview mirror didn't raise my opinion of myself much. Seven or eight bright weals oozing blood started in the middle of my forehead and ran down across my eyes into my cheeks. They were beginning to feel like fire. And they made my face look ghoulish, like some kind of death mask. Like I was staring wildly out at the world through streaks of pain. I dabbed up most of the blood with a handkerchief, but I couldn't wash the welts until I got to some place with soap and water. And washing them wasn't going to improve my appearance any.

Reaction was setting in. I felt nauseous with disgust. My hands shook, and my clothes were starting to smell like a sweat locker. If there was any way to have screwed up my encounter with Gail Harmon and Mase Novick worse than I did, I couldn't think of it.

On the other hand—looking on the bright side—I wasn't sleepy anymore.

Since I didn't have any better ideas, I decided to risk going back to Ginny's apartment. If the cops were there, I was out of luck. But if they weren't, I could get a shower, shave, put on some clean clothes. Pack the suit-case Ginny wanted. Take care of my face. The other things I had to do could wait that long.

It was a nice plan, but I was interrupted. Before I put the Olds in gear, I readjusted the rearview mirror—and saw a tan-and-white, a Puerta del Sol Department of Po-lice prowl car, cruising down Bosque toward me.

After what I'd just been through, I wasn't particularly thrilled. You don't see cops very often in the South Val-ley. Keeping my fingers crossed, I sat where I was and waited for the prowl car to drive on past.

Instead of driving on past, it pulled to a stop in front of me, blocking the Olds. Then another car, a baby blue Dodge with a powerful exhaust and anonymous city plates, came up and parked on my rear.

Cops are like that. Now I wasn't going anywhere without permission.

Two street cops got out of the tan-and-white. They had their riot sticks out and ready. They came around to my door and planted themselves there, standing well back so I couldn't surprise them. I thought I recognized one of them, but I wasn't sure—I might've known him back in the days when my brother was a cop. There was something familiar and not very kindly about the way he said, "Get out of the car, Axbrewder."

They'd been looking for me, all right. At the moment, I didn't have any idea how they'd found me.

I wanted to know. That was normal, I suppose. When trouble falls on you out of the sky, you naturally want to know how it found you. But there was something else I wanted to know a hell of a lot more.

"What's wrong, officer?" I asked, doing my best to pretend I wasn't scratched up like a punk rocker.

Good as twins, both cops tapped their palms with their sticks. "I said," the familiar one repeated, "get out of the car."

I couldn't help it—I just had to get cute with them. "As long as we're here," I said, "do you mind if I get out of the car? I don't want to scare you. I just want to stretch my legs."

They swore at me with varying degrees of subtlety while I opened the door of the Olds.

Right away, they let me know they weren't here to arrest me. That decision probably hadn't been made yet. One of them jabbed me with his stick before I had both legs under me, hit me hard enough to rock me back against the side of the car. But they didn't read me my rights. They didn't make me assume the position. And they didn't take the .45 away. They were just making sure they had me under control.

I gave them a smile that would've curdled milk, but they ignored it.

Once I was safely pinned to the side of the Olds, two

more of Puerta del Sol's finest got out of the Dodge. Plainclothes detectives. One of them was a small individual with the secret, harried look of a man whose wife doesn't like his line of work. The other was Captain Philip Cason.

Which told me right away what I wanted to know. It told me the story I had planned—the one Haskell suggested to me—wasn't going to wash.

I didn't have to reason it out by the numbers. Cason was investigating the death of Roscoe Chavez, and he had an interest in Pablo's disappearance. So why would he care who blew up a car I rented? Only one reason. The cops checking that explosion must've found Haskell's cab. And the driver must've told them what Haskell and I were talking about. When el Señor's name came up, those detectives just naturally passed the investigation over to Cason.

None of which explained why the cops hadn't decided to arrest me. But it was a start. At least I had that much to go on when I began lying.

As he sauntered toward me, Cason was grinning like the blade of a can opener. He was a short, fleshy man who didn't mind carrying a little fat because he already knew how much muscle he had. He had hands like shovels, burying hands, and eyes the color of blindness. A dapper hat perched on the back of his head, and his suit and coat looked so expensive you couldn't wrinkle them with a steamroller.

Like the street cops, he kept a safe distance. Still grinning, he scanned the damage on my face. Then he said, "Well, well." His voice had a hoarse rasp that came from too much interrogation. "Fistoulari do that to you? She must be one hot screw."

"Captain of Detectives Philip Cason," I replied conversationally. To restrain myself, I folded my arms over my chest. "I see you're just as charming as ever. If you weren't carrying a badge, I'd take your face off."

He must've wanted something from me. Instead of

coming down hard, he concentrated on his homicidal smile.

"I'm curious," he remarked. "What brings you way down here? You were always a bum, but this is low even for you. This isn't where you usually drink."

Not to be outdone, I replied, "I'm curious, too. How did you find me way down here? I thought cops were scared of this part of the city." I hoped the cold made me look like I was hugging myself to keep warm, instead of to prevent myself from doing something stupid.

He didn't like my attitude. His grin was fading. To compensate, he made his voice tougher. "You figure it out, smartass."

"All right." Under the circumstances, an educated guess wasn't hard. "You had an unmarked car watching the entrance to Cactus Blossom from Foothill. When I drove out, I was followed. Nothing obvious." In the Police Academy, they call it a *sector tail*. "All you wanted was my general direction. You just had your people report where I was headed and then leave me alone." Even in my condition, I would've noticed anything closer. "You didn't care exactly where I was going. You just wanted to be able to close in when you were ready.

"What I don't know is why you're wasting all this time and manpower on a two-bit case like me."

The look of blindness in his eyes made Cason hard to read in some ways. But I was reasonably sure he hadn't found me because he already had Gail Harmon and Mase Novick staked out. Novick was the sort of man who'd notice being staked out—even if he wasn't. So Cason wasn't that far ahead of me. The way he dismissed my explanation was downright reassuring.

"One thing at a time," he growled. "You haven't told me what you're doing here."

I was tempted to retort, You figure it out. But that might make him too mad to let me go. Instead, I tried to see how many lies he was going to swallow.

Mumbling and looking embarrassed, I said, "Ginny

and I haven't been getting along. I came down here to see a former girlfriend." I made a brusque gesture toward my face. "She wasn't amused to see me."

One of the street cops gave a short laugh like a pistol shot. Cason's partner studied the scuffed tops of his shoes. But I didn't care what they thought. I was waiting for Cason's reaction.

The idea that I came to the South Valley looking for love gave him his smile back. "You always did like Mex chippies," he rasped happily.

He was such a nice man. But I knotted the muscles of my arms and didn't take him up on it. "Cason," I said, "I don't have a coat, and I'm freezing." Injured-pride Axbrewder. "How much longer do you want me to stand here?"

He raised one fist, glanced with approval at the scars on his knuckles. "Long enough for you to tell me why you've been on the run ever since that Buick you rented got blown up in the Jousters parking lot last night."

If I'd had time to stop and think, I wouldn't've known what to say. Was he trying to get me to admit knowing too much about things I wasn't supposed to? Or was he just blindly giving me a chance to find out how much he knew himself? But I was already in a counterpunching mood, so I just kept going.

"What do you care? Did some hot-wired stoolie tell you I've got something to do with whoever wasted Roscoe Chavez, or are you just getting paranoid in your old age?"

His grin disappeared again. Easy come, easy go. In some states, the glare he gave me would've been classified as police brutality. "You're cute, Axbrewder," he chewed out. "I didn't know what to do about you. I thought I ought to give you the benefit of the doubt. But to hell with that. I'm going to take you in for concealing information of a crime."

Any con'll tell you a good lie is its own reward. I snorted a laugh. "Too bad it won't stick. I haven't concealed any information. I've already made a statement."

His whole body seemed to swell up inside his clothes. He looked like he'd invented apoplexy all by himself. "The hell you have, you sonofabitch. I didn't hear anything about it."

"Why, Captain," I said maliciously, "didn't you get a copy of the report? I guess I'm not the only one in Puerta del Sol who doesn't trust you."

For just a second, he started toward me. His fists looked hard enough to powder bricks. Then the implications of what I was saying got through to him. Good lies are like that. He froze. His expression became as flat as his eyes. "That's bullshit. Who took the report?"

I didn't even blink. "Detective-Lieutenant Acton." Acton didn't like me much. But—unlike Sergeant Encino—he really did owe me a favor. "I talked to him because he's an honest cop." With a smile of my own, I added, "Why do you suppose he didn't pass it on to you?" Then, just to keep the pressure on, I finished softly, "Talk to him, Cason. Check it out." With any luck at all, he wouldn't believe the truth when he heard it. "You'll be surprised by what's going on behind your back."

To be perfectly honest, I didn't know why he swallowed that one. I didn't know why it struck such a spark when I tossed out Chavez's name. I was just glad it worked. "Axbrewder," he snarled, jabbing a heavy forefinger in the direction of my face, "you're on a tightrope this time. Any minute now, you're going to lose your balance. When you do, I'm going to make damn sure there's no net under you."

Abruptly, he turned and stomped back to the Dodge. After a moment, the small detective with the scuffed shoes followed him glumly.

When they were both in the car, the small man said something. Cason started yelling, but I couldn't make out the words.

I felt like I was turning blue in the cold, so I didn't stand on ceremony. I climbed back into the Olds and fired up the engine to get the heater working.

The Dodge pulled out, spewing dust along the wind.

Trying not to look too mystified, the street cops sauntered back to their tan-and-white. They took their time,
but after a couple of minutes, they drove off, leaving me
to do whatever I wanted.

At first, I didn't do anything. I sat and shivered while
the car tried to warm up. Cason hadn't told me why he
was interested in me. I thought I knew the answer to
that.

But I still didn't have any idea why I hadn't been arrested.

Chapter Thirteen

For that matter, I didn't have any idea why Haskell hadn't been arrested. The same things that had Cason chasing around after me would go double for Reg Haskell.

The combination of Novick and Harmon and Cason and no sleep had me more strung out than I realized. A few minutes passed, and I was driving back the other way on Bosque, heading out of the South Valley, and the heater was finally starting to do me some good, when I finally realized I didn't know whether Haskell'd been arrested or not.

If Cason went to all that trouble to find out what I was doing, he must've already had men working on Haskell, one way or another.

For a while, I was so astonished by my own stupidity I didn't even swear about it. Then I leaned down on the gas and made the Olds rattle for acceleration as if there was something to be gained by setting some kind of record on my way back to the bank. As if I could do anybody any good when I got there.

Fortunately, that didn't last long. By the time I got off Bosque back onto Trujillo, I was thinking a little better. With an effort of will, I made the car and my heart slow down. Respecting the legal speed limits—and the haphazard way people drive in the South Valley—I headed up Trujillo and started hunting for a phone booth.

At first, I couldn't find one. What with vandalism and other forms of human frustration, the phone company doesn't find the South Valley a very cost-effective place to leave its equipment. But after I'd gone a mile or two past the abandoned warehouses, I spotted what I needed—a seedy-looking Muchoburger joint with a pay phone.

I parked the Olds, went inside, and changed a dollar bill to get some coins. Then I looked up the number for the First Puerta del Sol National ice cream parlor and dialed it. When the bank came on the line, I recognized Eunice Wint, so I pitched my voice up a couple notches and asked her in Spanish if I could speak to Señor Haskell.

She didn't speak Spanish, but she caught the name. "Mr. Haskell? Do you wish to speak to Mr. Haskell?"

"*Sí*, Señorita."

"Just a moment, please."

I heard the clicking while she connected me. Then Haskell's phone rang.

He picked it up right away. I listened to him ask if he could help me, who I was, what the hell was going on, until I was dead sure it was him. Then I hung up.

So he hadn't been arrested either. Not yet, anyway. Probably for the same reason I was still running around loose—whatever that was.

Relief made me feel exhausted all of a sudden. And the smell of greasy hamburgers made me look at my watch. It was already a little after noon. You could lose your whole life just driving in and out of the South Valley. I still had things to do, but I decided in my condition food was probably the better part of valor. I bought a couple of hamburgers and about a quart of strong coffee. Then I sat down and tried to pull myself together while I ate.

Why in the name of all the hamburgers in the world

that ever tasted like lard held together by sawdust hadn't Cason hauled Haskell if not me in to find out what the hell we thought we were doing? All that coffee and any amount of heartburn later, I still didn't have any idea. Since I wasn't making any progress, I gave up on it. I didn't have to pick our client up until 4:30—which meant I had four entire hours (minus driving time) free to get some sleep. Or to work on what'd happened to Pablo Santiago.

After stuffing my trash in a can that hadn't been emptied for a while, I went back to the phone.

For a second, my brain refused to cooperate. Then I kicked it, and it coughed up Sergeant Raul Encino's home phone number.

When I dialed it, it rang a dozen times or so with no answer. That didn't cheer me up, but I hung on. After all, what do night-shift cops do during the day? They sleep, that's what they do. And maybe his family—if he had a family—was out. In school, grocery shopping, something. I let the phone ring.

Finally, the line opened. A fatigue-numb voice said, "Encino."

"Axbrewder." For some reason, I wasn't relieved. I was scared. Those hamburgers felt like buckshot in my stomach. "Sorry about this. Tell me what was in Pablo Santiago's autopsy report, and I'll get out of your life."

"Axbrewder." I heard the distinct thunk of the receiver being put down on a hard surface. He went away. The phone didn't pick up any breathing, or even any movement. When he came back, he didn't sound asleep anymore. He sounded like he had a gun in one hand and a riot stick in the other. "Axbrewder?"

"I'm still here." It wasn't witty, but it was the best I could do on short notice.

"Are you sure you wish to stick your nose in this?" The stiffness in his English contrasted ominously with his fluid Spanish. "For an Anglo, you have some decency. Consider what will happen if you hinder Captain Cason's investigation. Anything you do will make enemies. To find the killer of a man like Roscoe Chavez—even a bad cop will jump for the chance. Consider what will happen if they find I leaked this autopsy to you."

I understood him, and it made tiredness swim around in my head. Oh damn it all to fucking hell. His poor parents. They could probably stand it if he was just dead. "In other words," I said from some distance away, "he was killed. It wasn't an accident. He was killed, and it has something to do with running numbers."

"Listen to me," Encino said sharply. "Even such a man as Cason will jump for the chance to pin a crime on el Señor. Leave it for him."

"No, you listen," I retorted. Somehow, I made myself sound like my mind wasn't out there flapping in the wind. "I know Pablo's parents. They have a stake in this, and I seem to be the only one who's paying any attention to that. I'm just a crazy Anglo—what harm can I do? If I screw up, you can at least be sure I'll never tell where I got my information. And if I haven't got enough sense to cover my own ass, that's not your fault. What does the autopsy say?"

There was a long silence. Then Encino sighed. "Pablo Santiago died of a broken neck."

I waited. When he didn't go on, I said, "I already knew that. You told me."

"I told you," he replied with old-world asperity, "he died of a broken neck, bruises, and injuries consistent with an accidental fall from a moving vehicle. That remains true. However, the M.E. is now sure the neck was broken before the fall. Partially crushed windpipe and other internal damage to the throat indicate strangulation."

Now it was my turn not to say anything. Encino spelled it out for me. "Someone killed the boy"—as if I needed it spelled out—"and then dumped him from a car to make it appear accidental."

"Shit," I muttered profoundly. "Shit on everything."

I could almost hear him shrug over the phone. "You asked. I told you."

"I know." My head was going in eight directions at once. "Has anybody told the family yet?"

"Would I be informed?" In his own way, he was about as pleased as I was. "This case is not mine."

"All right," I said. "All right." I needed to get off the phone. "Thanks. I owe you. Remember that."

"Go away," he replied. "I call it even."

I didn't thank him again. I just hung up.

My reaction probably would've been pretty entertaining to watch. There was this huge clown with raked eyes in a Muchoburger joint, of all places. First he put the receiver back in its cradle like it was a snake that just bit him. Then he went outside, flapping his arms wildly at the doors and the cold. He kicked one of the tires of his car as hard as he could, and he was so big the tire should've at least ruptured and with any justice at all the whole car would've flipped over, but all that happened was he damn near broke a bone in his foot and almost fell down. Finally he fumbled the door open and stumbled into the seat and spent a little while with his eyes fierce and his teeth gleaming and his hands trying to pull the steering wheel to pieces. What fun. I couldn't've been happier if I'd fallen into a cement mixer.

So naturally what I wanted was a drink. To be precise, what I wanted was Ever-Clear. The closest thing I could get to intravenous alcohol. Axbrewder, I said, get a hold on yourself. You're not doing anybody any good. But talk was no substitute for being drunk.

What'd happened to Pablo made me sick enough. But what really made me rage was, the cops'd found his body more than two days ago now and they still hadn't bothered to tell the family.

As soon as I had myself steady enough to put the key in the ignition, I started the Olds in the direction of the old part of town.

There was still a lot of lunchtime traffic—and no good

roads between me and where I was going. But after I did a few stupid things and nearly got hit once, the frustration restored some of my grasp on reality. I managed to become a little less manic. After all, I was in over my head—and I was used to taking orders—and I didn't have Ginny with me. On top of which, I was slaphappy from lack of sleep. Being reminded of all that helped me realize I had to start being more careful. By the time I reached the narrow streets of the old part of town, I was at least a loose approximation of a responsible citizen.

When I pulled the Olds to a stop in front of the Santiagos' grocery, I saw right away the store was closed.

Closed. On Tuesday. At 1:20 in the afternoon. While I stared at the door, an old woman with a basket on one arm rattled the knob as if she couldn't believe the evidence of her senses, as they say, then wandered away muttering toothlessly to herself.

By then, I'd been feeling sick so long it was becoming metaphysical. Trying not to hunch over, I got out of the Olds and walked into the alley that led to the back of the building.

A small flurry went past me, but the clouds were still holding on to most of the snow. The wind felt like it left my clothes in ribbons. Fortunately, I didn't have far to go. Behind the store, beside the small delivery dock, there was a weathered old stair leading up to the apartment where the Santiagos lived. It didn't look like it could carry my weight, but I trusted it anyway. I thumped my way up the treads and knocked on the door as soon as I reached the landing.

For a while, there was no answer. Then Rudolfo Santiago unlocked the door, opened it a crack, and peered out at me. When he saw who I was, he closed the door again.

Faintly through the wood, I heard him call to his wife, "Sēnor Axbrewder comes to speak to us concerning our Pablo."

At once, he pulled the door open all the way. "Sēnor

Axbrewder." His sad eyes flicked to my face, then settled on the middle of my chest, too polite to stare at or react to the way my mug had been redecorated. "Enter. Enter."

"*Gracias*." As I went in, I added in Spanish, "Such cold chills my heart."

Sēnora Santiago was there to greet me. While her husband closed the door, she gave me a frank, anxious scrutiny before she remembered her manners and lowered her gaze. "Sēnor Axbrewder," she said, "be welcome. Come to the fire. Will you drink coffee with us?"

Even in her home, she wore an apron knotted around her waist. But that fit—she was a woman who worked. The small living room showed the effects of attention and love instead of money. It was spotlessly clean, even the vigas holding up the latia-and-plaster ceiling. There were no rugs on the floor, but the boards had been cleaned and waxed so often they'd acquired an antique glow. A massive frame couch and a similar chair piled with old pillows instead of upholstery filled the space in front of the beehive fireplace in the corner. I could smell piñon from the fire. A few *santos* presided over the room from niches cut into the adobe walls. The ceiling was uncomfortably low for me—but still the whole place tugged at my heart. It felt like a home.

As cold as I was, I couldn't resist moving toward the fire. But I couldn't accept more hospitality than that. "My thanks, Señora," I said. I didn't like the way my voice sounded in that room. "Please pardon my rudeness. I have not come for courtesy."

The weight of what they wanted to know oppressed the air. But they were too polite—and too reserved—to say it out loud. Instead, Santiago seconded his wife. "A little coffee, surely? To ease the cold?" At the same time, with a gesture that betrayed his tension, he offered me a cigarette.

I shook my head. "Again my thanks. I have no claim upon your kindness."

Señora Santiago knew what to say to that. "A man who has served us so well in the past, and who now wishes to aid us in our sorrow, he has no claim? What we have is yours. Some coffee at least you must have." She started out of the room, bustling in a way that suggested she'd already cooked six meals and cleaned the apartment twice today—holding back the grief by keeping herself busy.

Her husband stopped her. "My wife, Señor Axbrewder has another matter in his heart. He wishes only to speak of that."

Ignoring the slight tremor in his hands, he inserted a cigarette under his moustache and struck a match. Then he moved closer to the fireplace so he could flick his ash into the hearth.

"Señor Axbrewder," he said quietly, "say what brings you to us."

For a second there, in the warmth of the fire and the hominess of the room, I almost lost the handle. I wanted to say, I found someone who saw Pablo. Two days ago. Alive. On a bus. Heading south. For Mexico. He'll be all right. I should never have come here—I didn't have the right. But that wasn't one of my choices. There was some reason why the store was closed. Pablo's parents weren't going to believe any phony consolations.

"Señor—Señora—why do you not work in your store today?"

At that, her face twisted. Abruptly, he threw his cigarette into the fire. At first, I thought they weren't going to answer me. Then I saw he was waiting until he was sure he had himself under control.

In a voice as flat as a board, he said, "That one who is named el Señor considers it unseemly that we labor in our store when our son has died. Has he not spoken to us of Pablo's death? At his word, we must grieve. Tomorrow a funeral will be held, though we know nothing of our son's end. For this"—traces of bitterness spilled past his restraint—"el Señor pays from his own pocket."

Well, I suppose I should've expected that. I already knew el Señor knew why Pablo was killed. And el Señor ruled the old part of town like some kind of private fiefdom. When he told his people their sons were dead, he expected them to by God grieve. He could even afford to be magnanimous about it. After all, he wouldn't notice the cost of the vigil and the prayers, the funeral and the candles. I could've probably afforded them myself on what Ginny pays me.

But it still hurt. The arrogance of that bastard made me want to go back to kicking tires. I couldn't hold down my bitterness anywhere near as well as Santiago did.

"In this," I said, hating myself and everything I had to say, with el Señor and Pablo's killer at the top of the list, "he speaks truth. Pardon me that I must bring such news to you. I have learned that the *chotas* have found the body of Pablo. A broken neck caused his death. They seek the one who did this evil, but they do not find him."

Me they believed. I had that one advantage over el Señor. Until I spoke, some kind of hope had kept from going. I took it away. For a moment, her eyes went wide as if she was having a stroke. Then she cried out sharply, "Ayyy!" and snatched up her apron to cover her face. Her whole body clenched, and she didn't seem to be breathing anymore.

Her husband closed his eyes. Slowly, he sank down to sit on the hearth. Neither of them moved.

It felt like my doing. But I wasn't done. There was something else I had to say.

"Your pardon." How could I stop apologizing to them? She was rigid with the effort not to let out what she was feeling. He couldn't seem to bear to open his eyes on the world. "I must speak of this. I beg of you that you do not go to the *chotas* and ask the return of your son's body."

At that, she whipped down her apron. Her face was livid—it seemed to hold about three hundred years of outrage. "Not? You say that we must not? He is my son. My son! His neck has been broken, and the *chotas* hold him from us, and they say nothing to us, having no decency and no heart and no honor, and you say that we must not ask his return? Have you become such as they are? Have you resumed drinking?"

"My wife," her husband said softly. "My wife."

But she couldn't stop. "It is my right! To hold the son of my body in my arms and to mourn him as he should be mourned, it is my right! Of what use is his death, if he is not mourned?"

"Señora, hear me." It hurt to have to defend what the cops were doing, but I owed it to Encino. And to the Santiagos. They could get themselves into terrible trouble now, if they did anything rash. "For what they do, the *chotas* have reason. They wish to conceal from Pablo's killer that his crime is known. Considering himself safe, he will be careless—and more easily snared. This they believe. You must permit them to work as they will. For that they have withheld your son from you."

I didn't say the rest. I didn't tell her there might be a reason why el Señor insisted on a funeral for Pablo. He might be making a deliberate effort to sabotage the cops. To clear the field for himself. All I wanted was to persuade the Santiagos to be passive, so they wouldn't stick their heads on the block by defying either el Señor or Cason.

But Señora Santiago wasn't interested. "A great and worthy reason," she shot back. The force of her outrage made me feel crude and ugly. "For this a mother and father are denied their grief? For a secret which is known even to you?"

"Señora." In simple self-defense, I put some bite into my voice. "He who revealed this secret to me will suffer greatly if what he has done becomes known to *Capitán* Cason."

She stopped. She didn't acknowledge my point or make any promises, but she didn't aim any more of her pain at me. For a minute, I was afraid her face was going to fall apart. But she held it together in front of me.

After all, I was little better than a stranger. Dignity counts for something. She turned to her husband. In a thin, strained voice, she asked him to invite me to Pablo's vigil. Then, slowly, as if she knew how fragile she was now, she left the room.

He didn't respond. His eyes were squeezed tight, but the rest of his body was slack and useless. Moving like they had minds of their own, his hands took out his cigarettes, stuck one between his lips. He didn't light it.

I wanted to apologize again, but there wasn't much point. I gave him a moment to say anything he might want me to hear. Then, so he could let go in peace if that was what he needed, I crossed the room toward the door.

"Señor Axbrewder." His voice sounded like dust settling.

I paused at the door and waited for him to go on.

"When you discover the killer of my son," he said after a while, "I wish to assist you."

I thought he might have something foolish in mind, so I said, as gently as I could, "Leave the *chotas* to their work, Señor Santiago."

"I spit on the *chotas*," he replied without any inflection—or even any energy. "When you discover the killer of my son, I wish to assist you."

I couldn't promise that, so I opened the door and let myself back out into Puerta del Sol's leaden and threatening winter.

Chapter Fourteen

From the old part of town, I went back to Ginny's apartment. Funny how I still thought of it as her apartment, even though I'd been living there for six months—and even though I was the one who took care of it. Since I didn't find any cops staking out the place, I let myself in like normal—as if anything about my whole life was normal. The impersonal tidiness felt safe to me, made me want to go to bed and not wake up again for about six weeks. But I fought that off. Instead, I took a shower. Ran water as hot as I could stand onto my face until the marks of Gail Harmon's nails burned like stigmata and the bones of my skull felt like cracked glass. Then, trying for a little self-respect, I shaved and put on clean clothes.

After that, I packed a suitcase for Ginny and me. Since I wasn't thinking very clearly, I had to go through it several times like a catechism before I could believe I had everything we were likely to need for a couple of days. I left her prosthetic hand where it was. At the time, it didn't seem like my responsibility. By a little after three, I was ready to leave. I couldn't come up with anything useful to get done in the time I had left before I was due at Haskell's bank, so I decided to go and wait for him.

Left entirely to myself, my personal way to solve this

case would've been to give up trying to solve it and instead just go ask somebody for the answer. Somewhere in Puerta del Sol—if you knew where to look for them, and how to talk to them—there was some old Mestizo or Chicano drunk with a grizzled face, cirrhosis of the liver, and no experience at all with personal hygiene, who knew exactly why Pablo was killed, or what Roscoe Chavez did to get himself thrown in the river, or maybe even who wanted Reg Haskell dead. And they might sell that information—if they were offered the right price. And if they trusted the one who did the offering. Well, I knew how to find men like that. And I'd spent enough time lying in my own puke with them to be trusted. But they only came out at night, and so far I hadn't had a chance to go talk to them.

So instead of reasoning or even intuiting my way to brilliant answers for all the questions I had in front of me, I spent the drive wondering why it wasn't really snowing yet when the weather looked as angry as a high sea and the wind coming down off the mountains made the Olds rock like a rowboat. That helped keep me awake until I got up into the Heights and reached the ice cream parlor.

The Continental wasn't there—which didn't exactly surprise my socks off. The fact that I had no idea in the world what Ginny was doing made a small worm of fear crawl across my stomach, but that was all right. A little fear was the price I had to pay.

Unfortunately, when I pulled the Olds into a parking space where I could watch the front of the bank, I still had almost an hour to kill. Saying to myself I was going to sit there and wait for Haskell was easy. Doing it was harder. Without quite meaning to, I slumped farther and farther down in the seat. Before long, I was asleep.

Which was a mistake. I knew it was a mistake as soon as it happened, because I was standing alone in the bank parking lot and all the cars were gone—except for my rented Buick, which was down at the far end—and I heard an explosion. When it hit, the car filled up with fire. I could see the kid inside, clawing at the door, trying to scream.

At the same time, all the concrete of the lot powdered and turned into snowflakes. Snow blew into my face from all sides. I could hardly see the Buick. When I headed toward it, somebody started shooting.

I turned. I could see muzzle flashes and a dark shape behind them—the snow hid who it was. But whoever it was wasn't shooting at me. The shots were aimed at the Buick.

Suddenly I understood—Ginny was pinned down behind the Buick. She was being shot at to hold her there until the car exploded. I couldn't figure out why she wasn't shooting back. I ran to help her. Now the bullets came after me, tugging through my clothes like snow. But I didn't feel them. After I ran for a while, I reached the Buick and dodged around behind it.

Ginny was there. On her knees near the car. She had her .357 out, but it was lying on the ground in front of her.

"Pick it up!" I shouted. "Shoot back!"

She gave me a look like a lash of hate and shoved her arms in my direction. Both arms.

Both her hands were gone. Both of them. The stumps were still bleeding.

"This is your fault," she said like the snow in the air and the fire in the car. "You did this to me."

Then something grabbed me by the shoulder, and I think I yelled.

When I got my eyes open, the snow was gone. I was sprawled down in the seat of the Olds, one hip wedged under the wheel. The door was open, letting cold blow into my bones.

Haskell stood there in his rich man's coat, one hand on the door, the other just leaving my shoulder. Past him, I could see people from the bank on the way to their cars. They were hurrying, hunched into their coats and scarves against the weather.

Haskell looked angry enough to start shooting himself. Oh, good, I thought. Just what I need.

"What happened to you?" he demanded. "Is that how you do your job? You go around brawling?"

It took me a few seconds to realize he was talking about the marks on my face.

I couldn't resist. "Actually," I rasped, pulling myself up in the seat, "it was a former girlfriend of yours. Remember Gail Harmon?"

"Damn it!" he snapped back, "I didn't hire you to dig up my life." I knew the signs—I could tell he wasn't afraid of me. "First you browbeat Eunice. Then you drag Gail into this, God only knows why. I've had enough. You're fired. Hear me? You and Fistoulari aren't working for me anymore." That was the trouble with him—he didn't seem to be afraid of anybody.

I didn't care. I'd had all I could stand. "Do tell," I growled. "What do you suppose your wife's going to say when we tell her you fired us because we found out about your girlfriends?"

Inside his coat, he became as still as a poised snake. "Don't tell me," he said like the edge of a straight razor, "you've been talking to my wife."

Maybe he was as good as he said at playing people. His tone made me ashamed of myself. "What're you afraid of?" I retorted angrily. "The woodpile's full of people who want you dead. She's bound to find out about them sooner or later. What difference does it make if we get to them first? We're still trying to save your life."

"No, you're not." He was so good at outraged innocence you'd think he practiced in front of a mirror. "You've been fired. Leave my wife out of this."

The cold made the raw skin around my eyes hurt worse. Parts of my brain were still muzzy with sleep and nightmares. I didn't know how to argue with him. And I knew it wasn't going to do any good if I just grabbed him and threw him into the car. "Oh, come off it," I said intelligently. "You can't fire me."

"It's already done."

"You can't," I repeated. For some reason, I didn't shout at him. "I'm just the hired help. You can't fire me. You can only fire Ginny." A snarl came out of him, but I cut through it. "Until she tells me she's been fired, you're not going to be able to get rid of me."

The wind ruffled his hair, giving him a look of wildness he didn't usually have. "Stuff it," he said. As obscenities go, it made me want to laugh. "I don't need you."

"Of course you don't." Suddenly, I wasn't angry at him anymore. Anybody who could make a statement like *I don't need you* and believe it needed all the help he could get. "But in the meantime, how're you going to get home? Ginny has your car. As long as you're stuck with me anyway, you might as well let me give you a ride."

He chewed on that for a minute. His face was red with cold and tight with anger, but something about the way he stared at me reminded me of playing bridge. Abruptly, he nodded. "All right. I'll take it up with Fistoulari." He walked around the hood, pulled open the passenger door, and got in. Preserving his air of righteous indignation, he didn't look at me. "Let's go."

With a mental snarl, I closed my door and started the engine. The Olds coughed a few times—sympathy pains for the way I felt. Haskell sneered at the dashboard, which didn't make me or the car any more cheerful. I made a special effort to be on my good behavior while I drove him home.

But on the way, I couldn't stand the silence. That nightmare kept playing across the back of my mind, and I needed distraction. So after a few blocks I said as conversationally as I could, "Explain something. I've met your wife. I don't think I told her anything you wouldn't want her to hear. But I talked to her long enough to find out how she feels about you. I don't understand why you want to involve yourself with all these other women."

He cocked an eyebrow. He looked like he was amused by my naïveté. "Wouldn't you sleep with every woman you could get your hands on?"

Driving carefully, I said, "I'm not that predatory."

He snorted. "You mean you're afraid of the consequences." His tone suggested disdain for consequences of all kinds. "Let me tell you something, Axbrewder. I love my wife. I know how loyal and trusting she is. She gives me exactly what I want in a wife. But that isn't all I want. I want everything." The way he said it made it sound special rather than unreasonable, like the size of what he wanted was a virtue—part of what made him attractive. "All of life. I want to make love to every woman. I want to have the best of everything. I want to stretch myself right to the limit and prove I can do anything." I could feel him watching me sidelong to see how I took it. "Accounting doesn't provide many opportunities for that."

"So you play bridge."

I wasn't exactly raising his opinion of me. "I told you. I don't play games. I play people."

Trying to get even, I asked, "What does that have to do with those investments you've been having trouble with?"

"Forget it," he retorted. "You're going to be off this case as soon as I talk to Fistoulari. Stop trying to pry into my life."

Well, at least he still had that raw nerve. Maliciously, I said, "I'll tell you what I really don't understand. You talk a good game, but any moron can see you wouldn't want to fire Ginny and me unless you're afraid of what we might find out. You'd rather take the chance of being killed. I don't understand how what you've got hidden can be worse than being killed."

In reaction, he swung toward me on the seat. "Listen, Axbrewder," he said like the wind thumping against the side of the Olds. "Pay attention. I'm going to say this so that even you can follow it. I'm not afraid of you. I don't have anything hidden. I just don't like what you're doing. You're meddling with my privacy. I'm living the life I want, and I'm not going to permit two airhead detectives to mess it up. If you were actually trying to protect me, that would be fine. But you're investigating this case as if I'm the enemy. I can't think of one good reason why I should put up with that. The only thing el Señor can do to me is kill me. At the rate you're going, you're going to wreck my life. Any moron can see that I'm better off without you."

Coming from him, that was quite a speech. I didn't care whether he meant it or not. "Too bad," I replied acidly. "You know, you're really not as smart as you think. Instead of sitting there feeling threatened, you should be asking what Ginny and I've found out." I wanted to make him ask. But I was afraid he wouldn't, so I spelled it out. "Maybe el Señor wants you dead, and maybe he doesn't. But Gail Harmon has a boyfriend who wants to kill you so bad it keeps him awake at night. And he's a Special Forces vet. He's perfectly capable of doing it."

Haskell didn't respond. Abruptly, he straightened himself in his seat and stopped looking at me, his face expressionless. But that was all I needed. While he stared out through the windshield, I could hardly keep myself from smiling.

By then, we were on Foothill, getting close to the turn down into Cactus Blossom Court. I can't say I was paying the best attention in the world, but instinctively I slowed down. Just for the exercise, I drove past Cactus Blossom to see if there were any parked cars with people in them on Foothill nearby—any sign of a stake-out. But there weren't. Cason'd apparently given up being interested in either of us. So I turned around in a driveway, went back to Cactus Blossom, and nosed the Olds over the hill.

As soon as we started down the slope, I saw the Continental parked in Haskell's driveway.

There were other cars in other driveways around the Court. And one black Cadillac the size of a hearse parked on the street—above Haskell's house and across the road.

In the cold, I could see exhaust wisping away from the Caddy's tailpipe. There was somebody in that car.

All of a sudden, my hands were sweating on the wheel. As we coasted slowly down the hill, I muttered to Haskell, "Don't get out. If anything happens, duck down under the dash."

He snapped a look at me. "Why?"

Maybe I was scaring myself for nothing. Maybe the Cadillac was just waiting for somebody to come out of the house it was parked in front of.

I couldn't afford the chance.

I pulled in behind the car and stopped. Didn't turn off the engine. The man in the driver's seat looked short and squat through his rear window, and he wasn't wearing a hat, but I couldn't tell anything else about him. He may've been watching me in one of his mirrors—I couldn't tell that, either.

I checked the .45, just to reassure myself. Then I opened my door. I was going to go like a good neighbor and ask the man in the hearse if I could help him. At least see who he was.

As soon as I stuck my head and shoulders out of the Olds, the Caddy started to roar. Tires screaming, it burst away from the curb and went accelerating wildly down into the cul-de-sac.

Just for a second, I watched him go—not so much surprised as simply wondering whether he was going to plow between a couple of houses and end up in somebody's back yard or maybe the arroyo. Then I saw him begin to turn, and I realized what was happening.

He made the kind of squealing, fishtailing turn you see in the movies, tires tearing their hearts out on the pavement, and came clawing back up the hill at us.

I could already see what looked like the barrel of a shotgun sticking out through the driver's open window.

Fortunately, I wasn't all the way out of the Olds. With my right hand still on the wheel, I wrenched myself back into my seat.

The Caddy was closing fast. He was going to pass right by me and fire at point-blank range, blow me halfway to next Saturday. I didn't even have time to close the door.

I didn't try. Jamming the gearshift into drive, I stomped all my strength down on the gas pedal.

My heart beat once while I sat there thinking the Olds was going to stall. I couldn't see the man's face, but I could sure as hell see the shotgun.

Then the Olds moved. It sounded asthmatic and miserable, but it did its best to match the Caddy's haul-ass start down into the cul-de-sac. Momentum slammed my door for me.

By guess or by God, my timing was perfect. The shotgun seemed to go off right in my ear—but all that happened was, some shot licked the trunk of the Olds. Most of the blast tore a huge clump of dry pampas grass in the nearest yard to shreds.

Haskell clung to his door and the edge of his seat. I couldn't tell whether he was scared or excited.

Careening down the hill, I snatched a look in the mirror and saw the Caddy smoke into reverse. The driver was backing up after us.

I stood on the brakes. While the Olds tried to stop, screeching like tortured steel, I twitched the wheel to the right. Damn near flipped us, but I got what I wanted. I made us look like we were trying to turn in that direction. The way we hit the curb helped—almost hard enough to burst a tire.

The Caddy angled over to that side to cut us off.

This time, I got the timing right all by myself. With the Caddy hammering down toward us, I fisted the Olds into reverse and floored the accelerator again.

Before we went twenty feet, I stopped. Now I was ready. Out of the way of the Caddy. And in position to ram it if it didn't crush its wheels when it slammed the curb.

It had good brakes. It came down the hill like a cart of bricks, but somehow it slowed enough so hitting the curb just made it bounce a little.

For a few seconds, we stayed where we were and looked at each other. The goon in the Caddy had his shotgun up in front of his face, aiming at us. But he was on the wrong side now. His passenger window was closed. And he couldn't help seeing what I was about to do to him. He made up his mind almost immediately. Gunning his engine for all it was worth, he did his best to get back up the hill before I could run into him.

I let him go. The Olds was never going to catch him, anyway. And I didn't particularly want to shoot it out with him right there in the street. I was peripherally aware of all the people coming out of their houses to see what the commotion was about.

So instead of trying to be a hero, I got the Olds moving again and rolled it into Haskell's driveway. Then I stopped. "Come on," I said to Haskell. My voice sounded too tight and breakable, but I couldn't help it. "Let's get inside before somebody decides to come over and ask us what the hell we're doing."

He didn't look anywhere near as sick as I felt. His eyes shone with some kind of tension I couldn't read—it could've been adrenaline or stroke. Without a word, he got out of the car and started toward the house.

I followed him, feeling stiff and cramped and cursing myself because I hadn't managed to see the face of the goon in the Caddy.

Haskell was passing the cedars into the aisle toward the front door ahead of me before it occurred to me to wonder why Ginny hadn't come to investigate who was doing what to whom outside the house.

All that caterwauling of tires wasn't the sort of thing she usually ignored.

Faster than I could think it through, I jumped after Haskell, caught him by the arm. Maybe it'd all been too quick, she hadn't had time to get out here before it was over. But surely by now—

"What is it?" Haskell demanded. "What's the matter?" I couldn't see his face clearly in the relative dusk of the aisle, but he sounded like a man with a fever.

I ignored him. Blocking him against the wall to keep him out of my way, I pulled out the .45.

What I was thinking didn't make any sense. Why set a trap for Haskell outside the house if the inside was already set up? Maybe two bad days and no sleep were making me paranoid. But if she was all right, why wasn't she out here by now? I could've used her a couple minutes ago.

"Axbrewder—"

"Don't ask," I hissed. "Shut up. Stay here."

As quietly as I could with my muscles stiff and my kneecaps quivering, I moved toward the door.

When I touched the knob, a voice from inside snapped, "If you try to come in here, I'll blow you in half."

She sounded too demented to be the woman I knew.

"Ginny." Her voice twisted a knife under my ribcage. What was happening to her? "It's Brew. I've got Haskell with me. We're all right."

She didn't answer. I said, "Ginny, we're coming in." In spite of the way my hands shook, I holstered the .45, got out the keys, and unlocked the door.

When I opened it, I saw her leaning half-slumped against the wall near the light switches. None of the lights were on—I couldn't make out her face. But I couldn't miss the .357 hanging like a dead weight from the end of her right arm. She could hardly keep her grip on it.

She had the stump of her left forearm clamped over her heart.

My throat was full of acid, and I couldn't swallow it. She hadn't come outside to see what was going on, see if we needed help, because she'd been too scared. She looked like she'd gone over the edge. Like fear and incapacity had finally pushed her farther than she could go.

Like she'd learned something that made this case worse than anything she could possibly stand.

I would've gone to her—I wanted to put my arms around her, hold her as hard as I could, just so my bones would stop shaking. But Haskell shoved his way into the house between us.

I closed the door behind him, relocked it. He reached past her to snap on the lights. The sudden glare made her battered expression and her tight face go through me like a cry.

Haskell faced her, his back to me. The way he studied her reminded me he'd never seen her stump before—she'd always had her left forearm hidden in a pocket. I bunched my fists. If he said anything I didn't like, I was going to deck him. At the moment, I didn't care whether he survived the experience or not.

But he didn't say anything about how she looked. He didn't say anything about her hand. He didn't even say anything about firing us. Softly, kindly, like he was actually a friend of hers, he said, "I need a drink. You want one?"

She couldn't meet his eyes. Dumbly, she shook her head.

He shrugged. Still with a spring in his steps, he turned and went down the stairs, leaving us alone.

"Ginny." I didn't know how to say it. I needed you out there. How did it get this bad? "What happened?"

"I heard the cars," she said dully. "I'm getting to be like you. Intuitive. Somehow—without any reason for it—I knew you were in trouble. I grabbed my gun and ran up the stairs." She was too ashamed to look at me. "But when I got up here, I couldn't—I just couldn't—"

Abruptly, she threw her .357 at the floor. It bounced once, but the carpet absorbed the impact. Tears spilled from her eyes as she looked at her empty hand and her stump. "You know, it's funny," she said past the knot in her throat. "I didn't want this case from the beginning. But up until today I never really believed el Señor had anything to do with it. It didn't make sense to me. For God's sake, Haskell's just an accountant who works in a bank that looks like an ice cream parlor. How could he possibly be involved with a hood like el Señor?"

Almost holding my breath, I asked, "What changed your mind?"

She looked at me then. With all her fear and pain and disgust, her eyes still had room for a flash of wild anger.

"Haskell's been lying to us all along. I think I know why el Señor wants him dead."

Chapter Fifteen

A minute later, she said, "Brew, what happened to your face?"

I dismissed that. "I'll tell you about it later." But then I didn't say anything. I stood there like a dummy and stared at her.

I was confused. Not by her announcement—I can understand plain English, if you enunciate clearly and don't use big words. No, I was confused by the way I felt about it. Any other time, I would've been at least relieved. She thought she knew the answer. And she was usually right. It didn't matter how bad the answer was. Just having something solid to work with helped.

But I didn't feel relieved. The way she looked left my insides in a knot.

She was studying me for some kind of reaction, practically hanging onto me with her eyes. She was counting on me for something. She probably thought she was counting on me to hold her in one piece. I couldn't afford to let her down.

So I went to the head of the stairs and checked for some indication of what Haskell was doing. I thought I heard a clink of glass—he was fixing himself a drink. With any luck, he might stay down there for a few minutes before he started to wonder what we were doing.

Turning back to Ginny, I said quietly, "Don't let him hear you. When I picked him up, he said he was going to fire us. He doesn't like us prying into his personal life."

She was still leaning against the wall as if she couldn't hold up her own weight. But her brain kept functioning, and she was making an effort to cope. "Has he changed his mind?"

"I don't know." I moved back across the atrium to stand in front of her. To be perfectly honest, I wanted to be close enough to put my arms around her if I got the chance. But I knew that wasn't what she needed—even if she thought it was. She needed to find her way back to the woman she used to be. Take-no-prisoners Fistoulari. "Maybe that little demolition derby out there made him reconsider. But we might be better off if he doesn't know how much we know."

She nodded. What she was thinking brought the misery back into her eyes, but she forced herself to say it. "Did you see who it was—out there?" She indicated the street with a jerk of her head. She hadn't had a shower for two days, and her hair looked stringy and un-loved.

The phone rang. I waited until Haskell picked up an extension downstairs. His voice came vaguely up from below. He sounded like he was telling a neighbor that car chases and shooting on Cactus Blossom Court were nothing to worry about.

"No." I wasn't exactly feeling gentle, and it showed. "Every time I looked at him, he had a shotgun pointed at me." But I had to admit the man in the Cadillac hadn't looked much like Mase Novick. I didn't worry about where Novick could've gotten a Caddy. He wouldn't think twice about stealing one.

But Ginny was in no shape to consider I might be disgusted at myself. She took my tone as a comment on her failure to come to my rescue. "Brew," she said softly, "please don't." Her face was pale with anger and anguish. "I've already got more than I can stand."

I understood. Folding my arms over my chest to keep them out of the way, I murmured, "Don't worry about it. If you count the three or four thousand times I've let you down, I don't really have much to complain about."

She took a deep breath, held it. Running her fingers through her hair, she straightened it a bit. Slowly, she got herself under control. Her broken nose, and the slight flaring of wildness in her eyes, kept her from looking calm. But she did everything she could to turn off her desperation.

"So tell me," she said, trying to sound normal. "How was your day?"

I shook my head. If we didn't find our way through this mess soon, watching her struggle with herself was going to be the death of me. "You first. I want to hear about it before Haskell gets curious."

She made an effort to produce a sour smile. Apparently, her day hadn't turned bad right away. "I'm not like you," she said almost steadily. "I don't like to wait for God or intuition to tell me what's going on. I'd rather do some old-fashioned investigating.

"Sara Haskell said her husband made his money with investments during business trips. Weekend business trips. I had a hunch I knew what that meant—I mean, try to think of some kind of investment where you can buy in, make money, and cash out again over the weekend— but I didn't need hunches. I came back here, picked up a few family pictures of our client"—she was recovering herself enough to drip sarcasm on Reg Haskell—"and drove out to the airport."

I asked, "Why?"

"A lot of people fly into and out of Puerta del Sol. There're seven airlines, not counting the commuters, and who knows how many counter personnel. But I thought that if a man made a lot of trips, and always went to the same place, and always used the same airline, he might get himself remembered. Especially if he tried to make every female employee he met go weak at the knees."

I knew from the way she was telling it she'd found what she was looking for. I made an effort to listen for Haskell without missing what she was saying.

"Brew," she said, her voice so soft she was almost whispering, "where do you suppose he goes to invest his money over the weekend?"

I was feeling stupid, partly because she thought the answer was so obvious. I didn't say anything.

"He goes," she said, "to Las Vegas."

That surprised me in several different ways at once. But the first thing out of my mouth was, "And he wins?"

"Not necessarily. But I think he did at first. I think that's how he got into this. Anyway, I can prove he's been to Vegas at least thirty times in the past few years. One of the ticket clerks for Southair recognized his picture. And I'm sure at least two other women there know him, even if they didn't want to admit it. So I leaned on the station manager a bit, and he finally let me pull passenger manifests out of their computer. Southair has more direct flights from here to Las Vegas than anybody else, and his name turned up on a lot of them. Out on Friday evening, home on Sunday."

"He didn't bother to use a different name?"

"Why should he? It's not exactly illegal to go to Vegas over the weekend."

I digested that for a moment—and kicked myself for not thinking of it. It wasn't quite what you'd expect from the chief accountant of a bank, but other than that, it fit. It explained where he got his money, explained his "investments." And poker was probably his game, because it was even better than bridge for a man who liked to play people, especially if he could get into a private game where he didn't have to face the house odds. Come to think of it, Vegas was the perfect place for the man who wanted to have everything—and wanted to get it with as much excitement as possible.

And Haskell admitted some of his "investments" had gone bad recently. If he'd gotten himself into a game with some pros, they might've given him quite a bit of line before reeling him in. But they were reeling him in now. For a second, I had a flash of where the implications were going. A few years ago, a friend, an acquaintance, or maybe just a brochure in full color persuaded him to break out of the boredom of being an accountant, go to Vegas for some thrills. And while he was there, he did well because he didn't make the mistake of playing the cards—he played the people. He had power. He had control. He was alive. It was like magic. So he went back. Again. And again. And started getting used to it. He began counting on winning. He began spending more and more money at home. He began feeling like he could do anything—which made him look like he could do anything—which helped him succeed whenever he tried. And then, ever so slowly, the pros started to pull the rug out from under him. All that power, control, magic—slipping away. Of course, he didn't believe it. He was Reg Haskell. Nobody outplays Reg Haskell. So he turned to other kinds of games to get the money he wasn't winning in Vegas anymore. And that led—

But I was getting ahead of myself. With an effort, I pulled back. Ginny still had things to tell me. "All right," I murmured. "So he went to Vegas a lot. That doesn't prove he's been lying about el Señor."

"No," she said, "it doesn't."

"In fact, it fits. After he began to think he could outplay the big boys—and maybe he even got addicted to it—he started to lose. So when he stumbled on that money laundry, he decided to try el Señor himself. That way, he gets the money he needs, and he proves he can do anything."

"Slow down," she said impatiently. "It sounds good, but it doesn't hold up. I'm not done."

Fine. I was just saying the same thing myself. Tightening my grip on myself, I waited for her to go on.

"When I was done at the airport," she explained, "I finally got around to calling the answering service. They said Canthorpe had been trying to get in touch with me all morning. So I called him.

"He was in a lather. I guess he wasn't having the kind of day he was used to. He said the cops had paid him a visit. In fact, it was your old friend Captain Cason. He asked Canthorpe the same questions we did about that money laundry."

"They tracked down the cab driver," I put in.

She nodded. "I figured that. Anyway, Canthorpe says he gave Cason the same answer he was going to give me. There is no money laundry. Haskell made the whole thing up."

"He did what?" No doubt about it, I was bright today. Even though she'd warned me. And I really should've been expecting something of the sort. "How did Canthorpe find that out so fast?"

She was looking at me hard. "It was easy. Nobody in his right mind banks under a name like el Señor. And Hector Jesus Fria de la Sancha doesn't have an account anywhere with the First Puerta del Sol National Bank."

It was that simple. Haskell's story couldn't be true.

When I thought back, I could see Ginny and I didn't have any reason to believe Haskell even knew el Señor's real name.

The sheer audacity of his latest lie was dazzling. No wonder he didn't want us to pry anymore.

At least now I knew why Cason hadn't arrested either me or Haskell. In effect, Canthorpe told him this case didn't have anything to do with the one he was working on. Cason probably rousted me just to double-check—or maybe to warn me out of his way.

If Haskell wasn't curious yet about what we were doing, there was something the matter with him. But as long as he left us alone, I was going to keep talking about him. It was easier to start with minor points. "Did Cason talk to Haskell?"

She shrugged. "I asked Canthorpe that." She was waiting for me to get to the important stuff. "He said no."

"Did Canthorpe happen to mention to Cason we'd been asking him the same questions?"

"I asked that too. Same answer."

"No?" I didn't know what it meant. Canthorpe might have any one of several different reasons for giving the cops as little information as possible—and some of them I didn't like much. But I let it go for the time being and did my best to face the issues Ginny had in mind. "Well, at least now we know why Haskell wanted to fire us. He must've seen Cason go in to talk to Canthorpe, so he jumped to the obvious conclusion we were siccing the cops on him. But he can't admit that's the real reason he wants to fire us without also admitting he's done something the cops'd be interested in." I was spinning more inferences than I could keep track of all at once. I had one other idea I wanted to pursue, but it could wait. "What's he trying to hide with all these lies?"

"His ego," she snapped. "He wants us to think he's a big deal, and he isn't. He's just a petty philanderer who's gotten in over his head and can't give up his delusions of grandeur."

Well, maybe. I didn't know what she was getting at. "You said you've finally started to believe el Señor wants Haskell dead. But if the money laundry story's a fake, then Haskell's no threat to him. Why try to kill somebody who doesn't have anything to do with you?"

"I know," she sighed. "It doesn't sound like it makes sense. But that's the way it hit me." For some reason, she stopped watching my face. When she dropped her eyes, she saw her .357 lying on the carpet. Grimacing to herself, she bent down and picked it up. Then she didn't know what to do with it, so she let it dangle loosely from her hand.

"Haskell goes to Las Vegas," she said. "For a while, he wins. Long enough to get hooked. Then he starts to lose. He's a small fish with sharks on his tail, and all the nice life he's bought for himself is going to get taken away from him. What does he do for money?

"Brew." Slowly, her eyes came back up to mine. "I don't know whether it's true. But it's the kind of story I can understand." Her gaze was full of pain and fear. A little thing like that—a story she could understand—took the heart out of her. It made her afraid because it made what she was up against seem real. "Where can he get that kind of money? Loan sharks, that's where. From el Señor."

"And since he keeps losing," I finished for her, "he doesn't pay the money back. El Señor's finally gotten tired of it, and he wants his pound of flesh."

She nodded. "And Haskell doesn't tell the truth because he doesn't want to admit he's gotten himself into something that grubby and useless. He's got some kind of glamorous image of himself—a pirate or something—and he likes to live dangerously."

It seemed to fit. I had to give her that. And it got rid of a lot of nagging questions—like how el Señor could've possibly tracked Haskell down so fast. I just couldn't shake the feeling there was something wrong with it. A sore place in my gut kept telling me over and over again we were underestimating somebody. Who, I didn't know—just somebody.

My personal candidate was Jordan Canthorpe, but I didn't get a chance to say so. While I was opening my mouth to tell Ginny not to jump to any conclusions until she heard about my day, feet-on-carpet sounds from the stairs stopped me. We shut up and watched as Haskell's head showed past the rim. He paused there for a second, then came the rest of the way toward us.

"Am I interrupting something?" His eyes were sharp and wary, and his manner was careful. Somehow, he consistently managed to give the impression he was taller than he was. He was wearing a casual khaki suit I hadn't seen before, and his hair was damp—he'd been in the shower—which explained why he'd left us alone so long. "It's my life you two insist on investigating. And I heard one of you mention danger. I think I have a right to know what's going on."

His audacity was wonderful. As they say, he had brass balls. Apparently he hadn't told us one true thing except his name in two days, and here he was acting like we were in the process of abusing his trust.

But Ginny didn't bother to admire the show. For no particular reason, she tightened her grip on the .357. Facing him, she said in a voice like a scalpel, "Brew tells me you want to fire us, Mr. Haskell."

She made the statement into an attack, but he met it without any trouble. In fact, he looked like he might be sneering quietly to himself. "I've changed my mind."

"Why is that?"

Almost smiling, he said, "I was wrong to question the way you're handling this case. I think I'm a pretty good judge of people. I can see now that I don't need to worry about what you're doing."

There was more than one way to take that, and I thought I knew which way he meant it. I was just getting ready to yell at him when Ginny stopped me.

"In that case"—her tone might've made Genghis Khan sit up and take notice—"maybe you'll leave us alone to finish our conversation. We'll let you know when we've decided what we're going to do."

He carried it off better than I would've. He didn't try to argue, protest, or fight back. He didn't say anything else about his rights. He didn't even ask what kind of decision it was we had to make. On the other hand, he didn't look the least bit ruffled or unhappy, either. "I'll be in the den," he said with just a touch of what you might call hauteur. Then he turned on his heel and went back down the stairs.

When I figured he was out of earshot, I murmured, "I wonder how long it's been since that man told anybody the truth about anything."

"I'm not sure," Ginny said distantly. "I think he just told me the truth about myself."

I looked at her. Suddenly, I was mad at her, too. "The hell he did."

I would've gone on. But she made a gesture that cut me off. "We really can't spend the rest of the night standing here." Back to being reasonable. "We've got to get to work. Maybe you'd better tell me how you got your face scratched up like that."

Good point. That was exactly what I wanted to do. The only thing we knew for sure here was, Haskell was lying. Other than that, Ginny's theory fit well enough, but it didn't seem particularly inevitable. We didn't have anything as handy as evidence to go on, so we couldn't afford to rule out other possibilities. Like one or two of the inferences I'd been in the middle of a few minutes earlier.

But when I started talking, the way I felt—angry and tired and reeling—mixed me up. What I really wanted to do was tell her about Pablo and the Santiagos, not Gail Harmon and Mase Novick. On top of that, she had no business looking so damn breakable. By the time I'd said two sentences, I was talking such gibberish I had to go back and start over.

Squeezing down hard on my brain to make it behave, I told her about my run-in with Frail Gail and her head-hunter boyfriend. Then I described my little chat with Captain of Detectives Philip Cason. To make sense out of it for her, I had to give her some news she'd missed— the news about how Bambino Chavez got killed and Cason was in charge of the investigation. But when I was done, she let that side of the question go. It became irrelevant when we knew Haskell was lying about that money laundry. Instead, she concentrated on the obvious implications of what I was saying and made every effort she could not to feel relieved.

I was giving her exactly what she wanted most. "That's quite a coincidence," she commented. A reason not to believe we were trying to stand in the way of a ritual hit. "There's a man in Puerta del Sol who'd like nothing better than a chance to waste our client—and Jordan Canthorpe just happens to have his address memorized." But she didn't say it. She didn't want to hope that hard. "What's your theory?"

I shrugged. "Simple, as far as Canthorpe's concerned. Haskell's been screwing around with his fiancée. Looking for a little consolation, Canthorpe goes to a former girlfriend, Gail Harmon, and meets Novick. Next thing you know, he's pointing Novick like a loaded gun at Haskell's head. Too good an opportunity to pass up.

"On Haskell's side, it's more complicated. When you stop and think about it, having el Señor after you isn't something you can be wrong about. You either have or you haven't—and if you have, there're lots of intermediate steps. You know what you've done, the loan shark gets mad, you get threats, harassment, nasty phone calls. When the goons come after you, you know about it. No matter what he tells us, Haskell would know if el Señor was after him.

"So if Canthorpe is, then el Señor isn't. If I had to guess, I'd say Haskell's trying to use us to solve two different problems at once. He wants us to protect him from Novick. At the same time, he is in trouble with el Señor—he's into the sharks for more than he can cover, and they're starting to get mean. By lying to us, making us concentrate on el Señor, he's gambling we'll be able to do something violent, stupid, or maybe even brilliant enough to get the sharks off his tail without actually letting Novick kill him."

Then I stopped. After I said all that, I didn't believe it anymore. No particular reason—I just didn't like the way

Ginny couldn't keep the relief and eagerness out of her face. Somehow, we'd traded places. Now I wanted to believe the explanation that scared her so bad she couldn't force herself out of the house. She pounced on the one I was ready to give up.

Again, I didn't tell her the driver of that Cadillac hadn't looked much like Mase Novick.

But at least she was still playing fair. It cost her an effort, but after a minute she said, "Haskell's probably capable of anything. But why would Canthorpe tell the cops Haskell was lying about the money laundry? It was a perfect chance to cause trouble for Haskell, get him tied up with the cops, and misdirect everybody, make us focus on el Señor. Instead, he let Haskell off the hook."

Since she was playing fair, I had to do the same. "That one's simple. Haskell's story was too easy to check. As soon as the cops brought in their own accountant, they'd find out the truth. Which might make trouble for Canthorpe. Anyway, he didn't want Haskell taken into protective custody where Novick couldn't get at him."

"All right," she said. Her forehead knotted while she concentrated on not jumping to conclusions. "That's fine so far. But if Canthorpe's really that smart, why did he give us Novick's address in the first place? Why try to get Haskell killed and then tell us what we need to know to protect him?"

I spread my hands. It was just a theory. "Maybe he panicked. You sure as hell took him by surprise this morning." She shook her head. I tried to do better. "Or maybe he's even smarter than that. Maybe he's smart enough to know Novick's an unguided missile. He might do anything, go off anywhere. When you launch something like that, the best thing to do next is dig yourself a hole, climb in, and pull the hole in after you. Maybe that's what Canthorpe's doing. Making himself look as innocent as possible."

That was what she wanted to hear. It gave me a quicksand feeling in my stomach to see how much she needed to believe what I was saying. From the look of things, I was doing her a favor. I was making what we were up against small enough for her to handle. But I knew better. The woman I loved was getting farther and farther away, and I didn't know what to do about it.

So I didn't respond when she straightened her back, shook the slack out of her muscles, made an attempt to smile at me. I didn't respond when she stepped closer to me and looked at my scratches again. "After we nail Novick," she said softly, "I think I'll go find Frail Gail Harmon and break her fingers." I wanted to kiss her, but I didn't.

As well as I could, I said, "That'll be fine. What're we going to do in the meantime?"

My lack of response hurt her. Frowning, she peered into my face. Then she drew back. Whatever she saw in my eyes made her stop looking at me. She waggled her .357 aimlessly in front of her. "First, I'm going to go get my purse. Put this thing away. After that—" I could almost see the way she struggled inside to pull herself together, be as strong as she remembered being. "I'll go have a talk with Sara Haskell. Before it gets dark and late enough for Novick to try again. I want to see if I can get her permission to look at lover-boy's bank accounts and financial records. They might tell us a lot—if we hired somebody to interpret them for us. I know she's probably too loyal to do it, but it's worth a try.

"What about you?"

By the time she asked me that, the misery was back in her face. And it was my doing—which naturally made me as proud as horseshit. What would it've cost me to comfort her a little, even if I hardly knew who she was anymore? But I was still mad inside, fuming mad and barely able to keep a lid on it. I'd gotten us into this case to try to recover the Ginny Fistoulari I used to know, and it wasn't working.

Until she asked, I hadn't thought about what I was going to do. But right away several ideas occurred to me.

They must've been percolating in the back of my head, waiting for me to feel as savage as they did. I picked the one she wasn't likely to argue with and said, "I think I'll take Haskell to visit Eunice Wint." Ms. Wint didn't deserve that, but I was too mad to worry about her. "She might be able to tell us something useful about her fiancé."

Ginny nodded. She still couldn't look at me. "Good luck."

All alone, she went downstairs to get her purse and her coat.

Chapter Sixteen

But I didn't go see Eunice Wint. Not right away. I waited until Ginny left the house. Then I went downstairs myself.

Haskell was in the den on the couch, turning a drink around and around between his palms. For some reason, he was able to look more relaxed when he was moving than he could when he was sitting still. His tension showed in the way he turned his head as I walked into the room.

"That took long enough," he commented. "I thought I'd have to sit here while you two negotiated world peace." Then he noticed my expression. Adjusting his tone, he said, "Fistoulari didn't tell me anything. What've you decided?"

"Come on," I said. The pain of my scratches seemed to come and go. At the moment, they felt like I'd been raked by a tiger. "Let's take a ride."

He didn't get up. "I've got a better idea. It's been a long day. You look like you could use some rest. Why don't we stay home and unwind for a while? Have a drink." He waved his glass. "Put your feet up. Do you play poker? We could try a few hands. It'll make you feel better. Take your mind off your troubles. Loser pays for dinner."

"You're going to pay for it anyway." Even at my best, I'm not exactly a scintillating conversationalist. "It's a business expense—part of the bill. Come on."

"What's the hurry?" Apparently, he didn't want to move. "It's only"—he glanced at his watch—"five-thirty. The trouble with you is that you never give yourself a break. We're safe here. What can happen? The door's locked, isn't it?" He nodded toward the picture window. "Nobody's going to shoot at us from the arroyo." That was true—for a while. The light was still in our favor. But it wouldn't last. Dusk was coming on fast, and the weather looked like maybe it'd finally made up its mind to start snowing. "So relax. Have a drink. I'm serious.

"I'll tell you what. If you'll unbend enough to join me, I'll entertain you for a few minutes. I'll bet you"—he dug into his pocket, pulled out his half-dollar—"you can't flip a coin ten times and have it come up heads more than three or less than seven times. What would you say the odds are?"

Haskell was doing a little research, trying to find out where he stood. But I didn't care. "The odds are," I said, "if you don't come with me, I'm going to drag you."

He stared into his glass and swirled the amber from side to side. "You still haven't told me what you've decided."

"That's true." I didn't really want to muscle him, but I was ready to do it if I had to. "You still haven't told us what happened to the records on that money laundry. You were supposed to get us copies, documentation, so we'd have something to fight with. Where are they?"

He looked at me—a long, hard look as steady as a steel probe. Then he said, "I left them at the bank. Where they'll be safe. If I brought them here, anything could happen to them while you and Fistoulari were out prying into my private life."

He was good. I had to admit it. I almost believed him, even though I knew he was bluffing. If he looked at me like that and told me my mother was a cocker spaniel, I'd be tempted to believe him.

So I had to tell him something. But I couldn't tell him what I had in mind. He'd never go along with it. Holding his gaze, I said, "We don't like to leave things in the middle. You've decided not to fire us—we've decided not to quit. We're going to keep working until we find out what's going on here." Just trying to keep him nervous. "Until we take care of whoever's after you.

"In the meantime, I've got errands to run. I can't leave you alone, so you're going to come with me. If you don't like the way I pry into your life, this is your chance for a little damage control."

I wasn't as good as he was. But I was sincere, at any rate. He kept me waiting while he finished his drink. Then he got to his feet and gave me a smile that made my scalp itch. "You're in luck," he said brightly. "I didn't have any other plans for this evening."

I resisted the temptation to poke him in the stomach once, just to remind him of his mortality. Instead, I told him to get his coat.

When we left the house—carefully leaving the lights on and locking the door—we found Ginny'd taken the Olds. We had to make do with Haskell's showboat Continental. Considering where we were going, that didn't cheer me up. But it was still better than walking. Haskell wanted to drive, as usual, but I wasn't that dumb. Once I'd talked him into the passenger seat, I fired up the Continental—which was like turning on your own private hydroelectric power station—and drove out of Cactus Blossom Court in the direction of the beltway.

Even that car's luxurious suspension felt the wind. On the exposed surface of the beltway, heading west, the car made small lurching movements in the gusts. I had the unsteady feeling we were about to spin out of control. Outside the range of the headlights, all we could see was the thickening dusk, as if the wind was slowly turning black.

Haskell rode in silence for a while, watching the day go out. But he wasn't any good at sitting still. He had his half-dollar in his hands, turning it back and forth between his fingers. Every now and then, he flipped it gently. Then, abruptly, he stuffed the coin back into his pocket.

"You're an unusual man, Axbrewder." He made it sound like he was just continuing an earlier conversation. "I don't always know what to expect from you. You're in what seems to be a relatively grubby job, but you act like you've never forgiven yourself for not being a saint. You're big and tough, you carry a gun, you throw your weight around, and yet you're as touchy as a cat. Tell me something. Why don't you drink?"

That was why he was good at playing people. His accuracy was frightening. I think he did it with radar. I wanted to spit something nasty at him, but I stopped myself in time. As what you might call an act of self-mortification, I told him the truth. "I'm an alcoholic."

"Ah," he breathed. For a second there, I could've tricked myself into thinking he sympathized. But then he laughed. "That's perfect. Somebody is trying to kill me, and who do I get for protection? A drunk and a cripple. If I were counting on luck to keep me alive, I'd be as good as dead."

I almost ran off the road. "Ginny isn't a cripple. She's just lost her left hand."

"I'm not talking about her hand," he retorted. "She's going to pieces in front of you. If you can't see that, you're in worse trouble than I thought."

I measured the distance between us, wondering if I could hit him hard enough to do some damage without losing control of the car. Then I had a better idea. I let out a loony sound that was supposed to be a laugh. "Oh, come off it, Haskell. You're just upset because she doesn't find you irresistible. Every now and then, people make the mistake of underestimating her. Some of them are dead."

"Is that a fact?" His tone made his opinion clear. But he didn't say anything else for a while.

Rush-hour traffic was starting to thin out as I turned

off the beltway and pointed the Continental south on Trujillo. The headlights didn't show much of the way the city was changing around us, but I could feel the difference. Down in the South Valley, people were starting to huddle together to keep themselves from freezing to death.

Eventually, Haskell asked me where we were going. I told him to wait and see. After that, he forced himself to keep his mouth shut.

I found Bosque easily enough, but in the dark I almost missed Gail Harmon's house. I spotted it as I was going past. Lights showed at the windows.

Feeling as savage as I did, I intended to stir up quite a bit of trouble. But I didn't want to be stupid about it, so I drove by without stopping. After a bit of groping on the unfamiliar streets, I managed to work my way around and back in the other direction until I hit Bosque again. Then I turned off all my lights, eased the Continental down the road, and parked in front of the house beside the one I wanted.

"Are you sure you know what you're doing?" Haskell asked. "If you want to pry into my life, you've come to the wrong place. I've never been down here. I don't think I know anybody who's ever been in this part of town."

You'd be surprised. It's amazing what pain and loss do to people. But I didn't try to answer him. At the moment, I had better things to do.

I took out the .45, checked the cylinder just to be on the safe side. Then I looked at Haskell. "Stay quiet. Don't get out of the car. I'll be back in a few minutes. If anything happens, try not to be seen."

He started to say something, then stopped. He must've noticed I was already ignoring him.

I found the switch for the courtesy lights and turned them off. Easing the door open, I got out. I left the door partway open so I could get back in quickly. The cold went through my clothes like I was standing there naked.

My fist clamping the butt of the .45, I moved carefully toward the side of the house to look in one of the windows.

If I was as smart as I needed to be—or maybe if I was just a bit saner—I would've been there looking for Novick. My timing was good. This was the time of night when a man who planned to go out and kill somebody might be at home getting ready. So after locating him I would've staked out his house until he left. Then I would've followed him to find out what he was going to do. If he went to Haskell's house, I would've been in position to nail him.

But that wasn't why I was there. I wasn't that smart—or that sane. In fact, when I looked in the window, I was praying I wouldn't see him.

I didn't. The window showed me a bedroom lit by a dim red bulb hanging from the ceiling and decorated in beer cans and gun magazines. Nobody was in the room. But a shadow moving past the doorway told me the house wasn't empty.

Not wanting to put my weight on that front porch if I didn't have to, I moved around to the back of the house.

Back there, Novick and Harmon had collected enough garbage to start their own landfill. I needed both hands for caution and balance, so I put the .45 away. I was doing pretty damn good to navigate the piles of cans and stacks of broken furniture and pools of slop without crashing into anything or breaking a leg. Still, I was never going to get my Boy Scout skulking badge. By the time I reached the back door, I heard Gail's voice.

"Is that you, Mase?"

She sounded small and vulnerable, but not particularly afraid.

Before I could react, she opened the door and looked out at me.

The steps up to the door put her slightly above me. There was enough light in the kitchen behind her so she could see me a lot better than I could see her. But that was all right—as long as Novick wasn't in the house.

She'd taken me by surprise, but I didn't let that slow me down. "Hi," I said like I did this kind of thing every day. "Remember me? I'm the man who wanted to talk to you about Reg Haskell."

She didn't say anything. Her silhouette didn't move. But at least she didn't close the door.

"I couldn't talk this morning," I said, "not with Mase here. I couldn't let him hear me. He wants to kill Reg."

"So do I," she said. She sounded far away, made tiny by distance. "I love him."

I resisted an urge to ask her which one. Neither of them was what I would've called a logical candidate.

"You said you wanted to talk to me about Reg"—a note of bitterness came into her voice—"but you didn't. You just wanted to hurt Mase."

"No," I countered. "I work for Reg. I don't want Mase to hurt him. So I couldn't talk to you while Mase was there." Since she didn't seem likely to panic at the moment, I decided to take a chance. "Where is Mase?"

Slowly, she turned to look behind her. Then she peered out at me again. Everything she did was slow. "He went out," she said. "I thought he came back, but it was you."

I could hear the ruin of her life in the way she spoke. That and the cold made it hard for me to keep sounding calm. "Gail, let me tell you why Reg sent me."

She considered that. She was in a different mind than she'd been this morning. "If you do," she said finally, "Mase'll kill you, too."

You mean, I thought, me in addition to Haskell? Or me in addition to you? But I couldn't sort it out. "No, he won't," I said. "I want you to come with me. That's why I'm here. I want to take you to Reg."

Her outline stiffened against the light. "To Reg?"

"He's waiting for you. We want to take you someplace where you'll be safe." Not to mention poking a stick into the hornet's nest of Novick's mind. Stirring up trouble, as they say. The quick way to find out who your enemies are. Ugly, brutal—and quick. "Will you come with me?"

"To Reg?" she repeated. She seemed to be breathing hard. "You'll take me to Reg?"

I nodded. "Yes."

"Just a minute." Moving like a figure in a dream, she shut the door on me.

While I stood there hesitating, I heard what sounded like a drawer opening, closing. Then, before I had a chance to make the wrong decision, she swung the door the other way and came down the steps to me. "I'm ready."

Now that she wasn't between me and the light, I saw she was wearing the same clothes I'd seen her in earlier—a ratty flannel shirt with only one button, jeans that made her look anorexic, no shoes. If I'd had any confidence at all in what I was doing, I would've taken her back in the house to get a coat. As it was, I wrapped one hand around her thin arm so she wouldn't get away and used the light to help me navigate through the trash, heading for the warmth of the car.

Some of the stuff she stepped on must've hurt her feet, but she didn't seem to feel it.

I felt it for her. I felt the cold for her, too. But mostly I made her hurry because I was afraid if Haskell saw us coming and had time to react, he'd drive away. A lot of what I was doing was aimed at him.

But the dark shielded us enough. We reached the Continental. I jerked open the rear door, steered Gail into the back seat, then strode around to the door I'd left open.

By the time I got in and pulled the door closed, Gail had her arms around Haskell's neck over the back of the seat. She made muffled noises, crying into his ear.

Without light, I couldn't see Haskell's face. But he had his hands on Gail's arms like he was wrestling to keep her from strangling him. "Axbrewder, you bastard," he gasped at me, "you bastard."

Grinning maliciously, I snapped on the dashboard lights.

Her crying changed into words. "Oh, Reg, I love you, I love you, Reg, I love you." The grip of her arms was frantic.

Haskell looked like he was about to do something violent to make her let go.

"Listen to me, Haskell," I said, putting all the conviction I could muster into my voice. "You helped create this mess, and you're going to help clean it up. She's killing herself with malnutrition, booze, and dope, and she hasn't got enough mental balance left to know it. The clown she lives with is wild enough to put us all in the morgue just for kicks, and she doesn't seem to understand that, either. Your name is the only thing I can say to her she'll pay attention to."

Haskell managed to loosen Gail's grip enough so he could breathe and turn his head. "You bastard," he repeated softly, "I didn't cause this. I'm not responsible for her."

I ignored that. "She needs all kinds of professional help. I want to take her to a hospital. But there's nothing I can say to persuade her to go with me. And nobody can force her to sign herself in for treatment. She has to do that herself." I faced him like a set of brass knuckles. "You're going to talk her into it."

In the faint glow of the lights, he looked dark and menacing, his face covered with shadows. "How?"

"I don't care," I said. "Tell her you love her. Tell her she's going to save your life. Tell her any damn lie you want. Just talk her into it."

She murmured his name over and over again, desperately pleading for some response. Quietly, he said, "I can't. I got tired of her months ago."

"Fake it!" I snapped. "You're the one who's so good at playing people. Play her."

For a minute longer, he went on staring at me with pieces of murder hidden in the shadows on his face. Then he turned around, reached his arms toward Gail. One hand stroked her hair, the other hugged her shoulder, while he met her feverish kissing. "Gail," he breathed to her, "I'm sorry. I was wrong. I'm sorry."

She replied by clinging to him for her life.

I started the Continental, hit the lights, pulled the automatic transmission into drive, and headed back up Bosque toward Trujillo. In the direction of San Reno County Public Hospital.

While I drove, I concentrated on not hearing the way Haskell and Gail mooned at each other. She was out of her mind, and he was too good at it. He made me want to gag with revulsion—except for the simple fact I'd forced him into this. There weren't too many rational ways to justify what I was doing. On the other hand, I've never been especially rational. After a while, Haskell's endearments began to fray around the edges. He was showing the strain. I gritted my teeth and kept going.

Fortunately, San Reno County Public Hospital (affectionately known as *SaRCoPH*—short for sarcophagus) is in the South Valley, in the marginal area where the respectable part of Puerta del Sol begins to dwindle toward the *barrio*. The drive seemed to take a week or ten days, but we actually arrived around seven. SaRCoPH isn't the best hospital in the city, but it isn't the worst, either, even though it looks like a cross between a steel foundry and a vivisectionist's lab. And it's the only one where they don't look at you crosseyed if you've got no visible means of support. But once we got there, the tricky part started.

I didn't have too much trouble with the starched personage on the other side of the emergency admitting desk. Her eyes were good enough to see Gail needed help, so she listened to the part where I explained Gail Harmon was spacey with dope and neglect and had to have treatment for malnutrition as well as psychiatric evaluation, and she ignored the part where I explained Haskell and I were friends of Gail's who found her half-comatose in her apartment. The nurse probably thought we were a couple of good-time bozos who'd picked up a susceptible-looking woman, realized she was in worse shape than we thought, and now wanted to get out with as little involvement as possible. Instead of bothering to make me feel like a bad liar, she simply filled out the required forms and passed them over for Gail's signature.

That was the problem. Gail didn't seem to have the first idea where she was or why, but somewhere in some dim corner of her mind she'd figured out we were going to leave her. She had one arm curled like a C-clamp around Haskell's right arm. With the other, she pulled at his neck, trying to bring his head down where she could reach it for more kisses. "No, don't leave me here, don't, please, take me with you, Reg," she begged softly, "don't leave me again." But her eyes somehow failed to focus on his face, giving her a vacant look. The tone of her voice already sounded lost.

Haskell was near the end of his rope—which may have been how she knew she didn't like what we were planning. He didn't look at her. He was facing me, and there was a gleam of desperate fury in his eyes.

I cocked my fists on my hips and glared back. The woman in the starched uniform rustled her papers. "We need your signature on these forms, Miss Harmon," she said. "We can't help you without your permission."

"Sign them, Gail," Haskell said. Maybe it was having the nurse for an audience, or maybe he'd had about all he could take. The gentleness, the fake affection was gone. He still didn't look at her. "I want you to sign those forms."

"No," she pleaded. "You're going to leave me again. Why are you going to leave me? What've I done? I don't understand. Please tell me what I've done. I won't do it again, I promise, I swear. Please don't leave me again."

I couldn't stand to watch. I was already hours past the end of my own rope and into the kind of grim, helpless rage that keeps some people swimming long after they should've drowned. So I rasped at him, "Get on with it.

We haven't got all night." At that, his face seemed to go blank. But I didn't stop. "You're the expert on getting women to do what you want. You're the one who wants to prove he can do anything. Get on with it."

With no expression at all, he glanced down into Gail's urgent face. Nothing about him gave me any warning.

Suddenly, he swung the arm she was hanging on, wrenched it away from her so hard she almost fell. "Stop clinging!" he shouted like the door of a furnace opening. "All you ever do is cling! You suck all the life out of me. You beg and wheedle and whine! You demand everything! You're going to cling me to death!" As full of righteousness and fire as the Wrath of God, he roared, "Sign those papers!"

Her whole body seemed to cry out to him in chagrin, remorse, contrition. But her face didn't. It was empty, deserted. Her eyes didn't focus on anything.

"Yes, Reg," she said. "Of course."

She went to the desk. The nurse handed her a pen. She signed her name somewhere on the nearest piece of paper.

Haskell turned his back on her. "You lousy bastard," he hissed at me. "You're going to pay for this."

For maybe the first time since I'd met him, I felt like I was seeing the real Reg Haskell instead of one of his lies or bluffs or manipulations.

But I didn't pay any attention to him. Gail left the desk, moving toward him—ignoring the starched woman who tried to call her in the other direction—and something started to hum in the back of my mind like a wire in a high wind. At the back door of her house—

I couldn't talk this morning, I said, *not with Mase here. He wants to kill Reg.*

So do I, she said.

—I'd heard a drawer in the kitchen opening and closing.

She didn't hurry, but she was so close to him I was almost too late. Somehow, I shouldered him aside and caught her wrist as she drove the paring knife toward the small of his back.

As soon as I stopped her, she went wild. Screaming like a demented cat, she tried to repeat what she'd already done to my face. I was strong enough to hold her, but she seemed to have more arms and legs than I could keep track of. Fortunately, the nurse had enough presence of mind to call for help fast, and pretty soon a couple of orderlies came running. They got Gail off me with my clothes and most of my skin still intact.

Haskell didn't say anything. I didn't say anything. I wanted to hit him so bad my arms felt like they were going to fall off. And I couldn't bear to look at Gail Harmon's betrayed face as the orderlies wrestled her away. The woman in the starched uniform was the only person nearby I could stand to deal with, so I talked to her.

"I know none of this makes sense." I gave her one of Ginny's business cards. "Call us in the morning. We'll tell you everything we can. By then, we should be able to put you in touch with her parents."

She just nodded. She'd probably seen crazier people than me in her time. She dismissed me by going back to her paperwork. I turned away.

One hornet's nest stirred up. One more to go—a subtler one. I closed a fist around Haskell's arm so I wouldn't take a swing at him and steered him back out into the cold toward the car.

I felt him watching me sidelong while we walked, gauging me. After a minute, he said, "Say something, Axbrewder. I did what you told me. I got her to sign." Maybe he was actually proud of himself. For some reason, I didn't think so. I thought he was trying to cover up the fact for a moment there he'd lost control.

When I didn't respond, he started to get mean. "I hope you like the results. I imagine this is how you compensate for being in such a grubby line of work. You put on your Good Samaritan suit and go around helping people who are too far gone to stop you. Well, congratulations. I think you've just cost her what was left of her sanity."

Without quite meaning to, I ground my fingers into his arm until he gasped. "Just remember this, Haskell. You're the one she tried to kill. At this point, your life's nothing but a list of people who want you dead."

He didn't answer. Maybe he didn't have an answer. Or maybe his arm was about to snap. Gritting my teeth to take up the slack, I forced myself to unsqueeze my fingers.

When I let him go, a thin sigh leaked up out of his chest. Other than that, he kept his composure.

We got back into the Continental. It started so easily I didn't trust it. That instant ignition made me think of sparks and gas tanks. Haskell was right—I hadn't done Gail Harmon any favors. Fortunately, he'd exhausted his capacity for social conversation. He sat, slumped a bit more than usual, and tried to rub his arm without letting me see him do it while I drove us onto the beltway again and up into the Heights toward the Territorial Apartments.

He didn't question where we were going. For most of the drive, we might've been on our way back to his house. Gusts of wind hit us head-on as we climbed the long grade, making the car shudder slightly like it was too well bred to work this hard. Bits of snow came like crazy down the tunnel of the headlights. Cars going the other way lit the almost horizontal slash of the flakes. Still, the snowfall looked thicker than it was. I had trouble seeing through the reflection, but I didn't need to turn on the wipers.

Off the beltway, the visibility was better. Buildings broke up the straight blast of the wind a bit. And there wasn't much traffic. The sane, normal, daytime population of the Heights had apparently decided this was a good night to stay home. I found the way to Eunice Wint's apartment easily enough.

Before we got there, Haskell saw where we were

headed. He straightened up in his seat. The faint light of the dash made his face look stiff as a mask.

When I parked in front of the Territorial Apartments, he turned to look at me. Like his face, his voice didn't have any expression I could read. "Your last stop was such a roaring success," he said. "What do you have in mind this time? Do you think it's possible Eunice is working with el Señor? If you loan me a gun, we could go in shooting. We might catch them red-handed."

I bit back an impulse to ask him what el Señor's name was. Ginny and I weren't ready to spring what we knew on him yet. Shrugging his sarcasm aside, I gave him as much of an answer as I was willing to part with.

"I want to ask her a few questions about Jordan Canthorpe. You may or may not be any good at keeping your infidelities secret, but she's lousy at it. Half the people you work with know exactly what's going on. And jealous fiancés have been known to carry things to extremes.

"Ginny and I've already established he had motive, opportunity, and means. What we don't know is whether he's the kind of man who'd go that far."

What I said didn't ruffle him. But at least it made him stop throwing acid at me. In a steady tone, he asked, "So why bother Eunice? She's not much more than a kid. Ask me. I can probably tell you more about Jordan Canthorpe's character than he knows himself."

"Because you might be wrong. It's been known to happen."

Buttoning my jacket across my chest to create at least the illusion I was dressed for the weather, I climbed out of the Continental.

I didn't try to stop him from joining me. I had a strong sense he might drive off and leave me if I pushed him too far. And I didn't have any idea which one of the Territorial Apartments Eunice Wint lived in. So I let him go with me. In fact, I let him lead the way.

The building was a standard apartment complex, square cinder-block construction behind the ersatz chalet

style. The entryway led to a central courtyard which held
an untended swimming pool, its scum freezing in the
cold. The apartments were ranked around the pool in
two layers, like a cross between Alcatraz and *Better
Homes and Gardens*. The management had spent enough
on lights to keep strangers from falling into the pool, but
not enough to make the place look habitable.

Haskell took me up some chipped cement stairs to a
door on the upper level. The light made the door look
badly faded and unloved. It rattled on its hinges when
Haskell knocked.

Trusting and innocent as usual, Eunice didn't ask who
was there before she opened up. She just undid the lock
and swung the door out of our way. When she saw
Haskell, her face lit up like a touch of sunlight. Then she
noticed me, and her pleasure turned to embarrassment.

"May we come in, Eunice?" he asked gently, as if he
really cared about her. "Mr. Axbrewder wants to ask you
a few questions."

Just like that, as smooth as oil, he took control of the
situation, left me gaping in the doorway with the impression he and Eunice were going to humor me because it
was Be Kind to Dumb Animals Week. Just by being
there, he seemed to take possession of the room. The
way he slipped his arm around her and kissed her was
proprietary and protective. I closed the door behind us—
I think I could've knocked it out of its frame with one
hand—and wondered what she knew about him that he
wanted to hide.

She was wearing a worn terrycloth bathrobe. It was as
threadbare as the carpet and looked like it'd attended too
many high-school slumber parties. An elastic band held
her hair back from her face. A manicure set on an end
table beside the dispirited couch suggested we'd interrupted her in the process of beautifying herself for the
night. Which in turn made me think she'd been hoping
for a visit from Haskell later on.

She was making an obvious effort to rise to the occasion, but her surprise and uncertainty were too much for her. Intending something polite and appropriate, she opened her mouth and asked, "Mr. Axbrewder, what happened to your face?"

Haskell laughed contentment and malice. "Axbrewder has a part-time job. He puts on makeup at night and goes around scaring children into obeying their parents. A professional boogeyman. Or semi-professional, anyway. But tonight he forgot his makeup."

Eunice tittered nervously. She didn't know what else to do.

Neither did I. In less than a minute, Haskell'd made my questions impossible. With that introduction, they were going to sound like ravings. I felt like an idiot—I never should've let him into the apartment ahead of me. But it wasn't any good to just stand there until smoke started coming out my ears. I had to do something. That's the first rule. Do something. It's better to walk into the front of a train than get run over standing still.

So I put on my avuncular expression to hide what was inside and said, "Mr. Haskell likes to kid around, Ms. Wint. Unfortunately, my business is a little more serious than that. Do you know Gail Harmon?"

Haskell's relaxed posture and superior smile didn't change. But I saw the small muscles around his eyes go tight.

Eunice considered the name for a moment. Then she shook her head. I believed her. If she'd tried to lie to me, she would've blushed for three days.

"She used to have a job at the bank where you work," I explained. "I wanted to ask her the same questions I'd like to ask you. She's the one who scratched my face."

That confused her. She didn't know which end to tackle first. "Why did she—? What questions—?"

"She used to know Mr. Haskell fairly well," I told her. I was pretty close to the edge of professional ethics—the part where it says you keep your client's dirt to yourself—but I didn't much care at the moment. Still, I made an effort to watch my step. "I'm talking to all kinds of people about him. Perhaps he hasn't told you what I'm doing here." She shook her head again. He hadn't explained anything about me. "I work for him, Ms. Wint. I'm essentially a bodyguard. I'm trying to protect him. I asked Gail Harmon if she knew anyone who might want him killed."

"Killed?" Her hands fluttered to her face in alarm. "Reg?" The look she cast at him was horrified to the bone. "You didn't tell me—" Back to me. "Is somebody trying to kill him?"

"I'm afraid so."

"Oh my God." Instead of going her usual red, she turned pale—for a second, I thought she was going to faint. But she lowered herself to the couch and stayed there, her eyes staring wide at something I couldn't see. Maybe it was the face of someone who wanted Haskell dead. Or maybe she was just confronting the idea her lover might die. "Oh my God."

"Nice going, Axbrewder," Haskell rasped. I couldn't tell whether he was angry or amused. "You've got all the finesse of a bulldozer, do you know that? What good do you think you're doing?"

I gave him a glare that would've chipped paint, but I didn't let him deflect me. "Ms. Wint," I said—gambling a little, but what the hell—"forgive me if I seem callous. I'm just trying to do my job. For some reason, women who know Reg Haskell don't react normally when I tell them he's in danger. Gail Harmon tried to tear my face off. And you—"

"You believed me right away, didn't you, Ms. Wint. As soon as I said it, you knew it was true. And you haven't asked me why." Haskell tried to interrupt, but I stopped him by grabbing hold of his bruised arm and digging in a bit. "You know what I think? I think as soon as I said somebody wants him dead a name leaped into your mind. An answer. You know somebody who'd like to see him killed, and you know why.

"Who're you thinking of, Ms. Wint? Who is it?"

She didn't look up. She wasn't avoiding me—it just didn't occur to her to look at me. She was transfixed by whatever images were unreeling in her head.

"Ms. Wint." Quietly, but with an edge in my voice. "I need the help. I'm trying to protect him."

Her lips moved. Her eyes shifted to my face and away again. She seemed to be trying to pull her thoughts together from a dozen different directions at once.

"Is it Jordan Canthorpe? Your fiancé?"

Without knowing how, I'd touched something deep in her—some loyalty to her own choices and mistakes, some kind of dignity. A bit of her color came back, and she looked at me straight.

"Mr. Axbrewder, I think every other man in the world must want Reg dead. He's the only one who's really alive. The rest of you are just going through the motions."

That was it. I couldn't ask her any more questions. If anybody else—even Sara Haskell—offered me that load of horseshit, I would've laughed at it. But from Eunice Wint I accepted it. She was nothing more than an innocent bystander, after all. She had the right. And I'd pushed my own meanness as far as I could stand it. Jumping up and down on a girl who'd fallen in love with somebody who wasn't her fiancé was more than I could stomach.

And maybe she was right. I sure as hell didn't have anything in me to match the gleam of Haskell's grin.

So I let go of his arm. I said, "Thank you, Ms. Wint." I gestured for him to follow me, and I let myself out of the apartment, making a special effort not to pull the door off its hinges.

He caught up with me at the bottom of the stairs. He looked ready for anything in his nice, warm coat. From where I stood, it felt like the temperature had actually gone up a couple of degrees. Poised for some serious snow. He didn't make the mistake of smiling at me, but he couldn't keep the bounce out of his stride, couldn't hide his eagerness. Somebody was trying to kill him. It was even more fun than bridge.

As we walked out to the car, he said, "So tell me, Axbrewder. When have I ever been wrong?"

Reg Haskell, old buddy, old pal. You were wrong when you hired Ginny and me.

Chapter Seventeen

Nosing the Continental off Foothill over the crest into Cactus Blossom Court, I saw Ginny's Olds parked in Haskell's driveway. All the exterior lights of the house were on. And there was a car I didn't recognize beside the Olds.

I didn't like the look of that. A little abruptly, I pulled over to the curb. The car was a late-model beige Mercury sedan, and I had the feeling maybe I'd seen it somewhere before. That was a big help—there probably weren't more than five hundred cars just like it in Puerta del Sol.

Of course, I had to consider the possibility it belonged to Sara Haskell. That was a dizzying prospect, as they say. I turned to Haskell. "You recognize that car?"

He shrugged. "It looks like Jordan Canthorpe's."

Muttering curses to myself, I jerked the Continental into reverse, backed into the nearest driveway across the street, and headed back up toward Foothill.

Haskell was watching me like I was an amusing and slightly dangerous lunatic. "Don't tell me," he said, "let me guess. You think it's a trap. You think the branch manager of the First Puerta del Sol National Bank is holding your partner in my house, waiting there with a gun to shoot me when we walk in. You're getting paranoid, Axbrewder. You should've asked me whether Jordan's capable of that."

I didn't answer. I was thinking, Canthorpe. Or Canthorpe and Novick. Or Novick alone. All of the above. I
couldn't afford to take the chance. So I did one of the
few smart things I'd done all day. I drove a mile back
down Foothill to a gas station and used the pay phone to
call Haskell's house.

Ginny answered after the fourth ring. "Hello?" The
way her voice twitched on the word scared me. Suddenly
all the things I was afraid of didn't seem paranoid at all.

I braced myself inside the phone booth, clamped the
receiver to the side of my head. "Ginny. You all right?"

"Brew." Relief and exasperation—and a small,
stretched tremor like a hint of hysteria. "Where are
you?"

"Are you all right?" Please, Ginny, tell me you're not
in trouble and make me believe it.

"Of course I'm all right. Or I was until I had to spend
an hour sitting here waiting for you. What're you doing?
Where the hell are you?"

She didn't sound all right. She sounded ragged and
overwrought, close to craziness with too much strain and
fear. But she wouldn't've talked that way if she'd been in
any danger. I let a sigh slip through my teeth. "There's a
car parked next to yours. I don't know whose it is, so I
thought I'd better check before I went barging into the
house."

"That's Canthorpe." She didn't seem particularly interested in how smart and cautious I was. "Get over here.
You're going to love this."

I said, "Five minutes," but she didn't hear me. She'd
already hung up.

I'm fine, I thought. Thanks for asking. Actually, my
evening's been pretty entertaining. I'll be glad to tell you
about it. Since you're so interested.

I put the receiver back in its cradle—gently, Axbrewder, gently—and went back to the car, trying to believe what I was feeling didn't matter.

As I got into the Continental, Haskell gave me a

quizzical look. His air of sardonic superiority wasn't what I needed at the moment. When I didn't say anything, he murmured, "Don't keep me in suspense. What's going on? Is Fistoulari being held hostage? Are we going to storm the house?"

Damn him, anyway. "Better than that," I muttered as I wrenched the car away from the gas station and aimed it back up Foothill. Snowflakes did crazy little dances in the headlights as we rushed through them. "You're a bridge player. We're going to do what's called tabling the dummy. We're going to put your cards down where everybody can look at them."

He replied with a moment of frozen silence. Then, slowly, he shook his head. "It's amazing," he mused. "I don't know how you stay in business. Do you always treat your clients like this?"

No. Just the ones who lie to us a lot.

Gritting my teeth, I wheeled the Continental down into Cactus Blossom.

There weren't any cars besides Ginny's and Canthorpe's outside. The rest of the neighborhood either wasn't at home or had already put its cars away. So I wasn't particularly cautious. I parked the Continental and got out. Together, we walked into the aisle leading to the front door. I used my key to let us in.

When I got the door open, I heard Ginny call from downstairs, "Is that you, Brew?" She sounded the way a knife starts to look after you've used its edge to turn screws for a while. "We're in the den."

I answered to reassure her. Smiling slightly, Haskell took off his coat, hung it up in the closet. Behind the smile, he was wearing his sober, serious face. But the shine in his eyes just made him look like a kid playing some keen game he thought he was going to win. After I relocked the door, I gestured him ahead of me, and we went down the stairs.

When we reached the den, with its picture window

blind against the darkness of the arroyo, we found Ginny and Canthorpe on their feet waiting for us.

Canthorpe's pinstripe didn't look quite so immaculate anymore. It was slightly rumpled, like he'd been wrestling in it. And his self-effacing moustache seemed even thinner than before. His pale eyes showed strain and anger.

In contrast, Ginny's eyes looked sunken and hollow. The skin of her broken nose was white against the high, hot patch of color on each cheek. She wasn't making any effort to conceal her stump.

"Jordan," Haskell said amiably, "what brings you here?"

Canthorpe didn't respond. His fingers twitched at his sides.

"Would you like a drink?" Haskell went on. Polite and amused, on top of his game. "I need one. Ms. Fistoulari? Axbrewder, you deserve a drink by now."

"Mr. Haskell," Ginny said carefully, "this isn't a social occasion."

"I know that." Not ruffled at all. "Somebody is trying to kill me, and all you've done since I hired you to protect me is dig into my life and attack me with what you find. This will be more of the same. But we can still be courteous about it."

He repeated his offer of drinks. None of us accepted. He shrugged to say it was our loss, not his, and left the room. When he came back a minute later, he had a tall glass full of liquor and ice cubes in one hand. For an irrational moment, I hated him because I needed that drink more than he did and I couldn't have it.

"Now," he said, glancing around casually at us, "what is it this time?"

I think he was having fun.

But Ginny'd had all of him she could stand. The same pressure that pushed her so far she didn't even care what I'd done with my evening also put a lash like a lick of venom in her voice. "Mr. Haskell"—soft and poisonous—"before you go off the deep end and start accusing us of unprofessional conduct, I want to say just once that we did not tell Mr. Canthorpe the half-assed story you told us about el Señor's money laundry. We talked to him because we thought he could help us locate the leak—el Señor's source of information that helped him find you so fast." And because he still has reason to want you dead, Reg Haskell, even though you aren't worried about that at all. "We did not bring him into this in order to attack you."

Haskell couldn't argue. He couldn't claim the question of how he'd been found wasn't crucial. So he didn't try. He sat down on the couch facing the window, made himself comfortable, sipped his drink, and waited for her to go on.

"When I called him this afternoon to see if he'd made any progress," she said, "he informed me that your entire story was a lie. There is no money laundry. You've been stringing us along from the beginning."

Haskell widened his eyes. He lowered his glass to his knee. He looked at Canthorpe. "That's cheap, Jordan," he said softly. Then he looked at Ginny. "I told you from the start that I couldn't prove anything. That doesn't mean I'm lying. It just means the connections are tenuous. And there's no way that he could have checked my research in just one morning—not without asking me for details to put him on the right track." It was a good performance. He did righteousness well. "Before you take his word over mine, you ought to consider his reasons for wanting to hurt me."

"Damn you, Haskell," Canthorpe snapped tightly. "Not everybody in the world is as unscrupulous as you are. I wouldn't stoop to lies because of you. And let me tell you something. I know—"

Ginny cut him off. "As it happens," she said sharply, "I don't need to take anybody's word for anything. We've been talking about el Señor all day"—she was aimed straight at Haskell—"but we've never mentioned his name. Obviously, he does his banking under his own name. If he didn't, you wouldn't know it was him.

"Mr. Haskell, why don't you tell us el Señor's real name? Just to prove you know what it is."

He met her glare without blinking. As a precaution, I shifted positions slowly, moving around behind the couch so I could grab at him if he tried anything stupid. For a long minute, he didn't say anything. The fact he'd been caught lying again was apparently a matter of intellectual rather than personal interest. When he spoke, he didn't sound worried, just curious and thoughtful. "That's clever. You told Jordan the name, and he checked the account computer. He found out that nobody by that name banks with us."

"That's right," she said. "But that's not all."

He raised an eyebrow. "Really? I would've thought you had enough by now to keep you entertained."

In response, she raised her left forearm like she'd forgotten it didn't have a fist anymore. Maybe she didn't realize what she was doing. She was too tense, too close to the edge. "This isn't entertainment," she gritted. "It's my job. I believe in doing it right.

"But for that I need the truth. All you've given us is lies. Not because you have any reason to lie. You don't tell lies because you need to. If you did—if we were dangerous to you—you wouldn't have hired us in the first place. No, you tell lies because you think it's fun. Part of the game. You get your jollies by manipulating people, jerking them around. You've been playing with us ever since yesterday morning.

"Well, grow up, Reg." She turned his name into a snarl. "The game's over. When I got back this evening, Mr. Canthorpe was here waiting for me. Your lies about a money laundry made him suspicious, so he did some checking of his own. We know where you've been getting your money, Reg."

"My money?" he asked innocently. "You mean my investments?" But he didn't look particularly innocent—or guilty either, for that matter. Just interested. Curious about what was coming next.

"Investments, shit," Canthorpe put in. From him, the obscenity sounded quaint. But his face was pale with vehemence, and his hands clenched at his sides. "You've been using the bank's money to finance your gambling habit."

"Now, wait a minute," Haskell retorted. "Hold it right there." Oddly enough, his protest sounded more genuine this time. "I do not have a gambling habit."

If he thought he could stop Canthorpe that way, he'd misjudged his boss. "I don't care what you call it," Canthorpe snapped. Anger quavered in his boyish voice. "You've been risking the bank's money for personal gain. I've seen the records.

"This Friday, when the books were closed at three-thirty, you had exactly $112.82 in your account. But you have overdraft protection for your account on your bank credit card. You stayed a little late, and you persuaded Eunice"—he stumbled over the name—"Eunice Wint to cash a check for you. For five thousand dollars.

"You knew, of course, that your withdrawal wouldn't go onto the books until Monday morning. And when it did, it would show up as exceeding the limit on your card instead of as passing a bad check. So you'd have a few days' grace to pay it back.

"But this time you didn't need grace—not the way you have sometimes in the past. This time you came in early Monday morning with twenty thousand dollars in cash and put it in your account to cover your check.

"You haven't always been that lucky. I haven't had time to check the whole history of your account, but I've been over the records for the past six months. You've pulled this stunt fifteen times—nearly two weekends out of three. The average balance in your account has gone from something over ten-thousand to just $112.82, and last month your credit card carried you for three weeks before you got the money back.

"You've been pouring your own money down the drain. And you've been risking the bank's money along with it. On top of that"—he looked like his collar was choking him—"you've implicated my fiancée in some kind of gambling scam.

"What's the matter with you, Haskell?" he demanded with more force than I thought he had in him. "How sick are you?"

Well, I had to admit that came as a jolt. No wonder Ginny looked like she'd gone too far out on the wire and was losing her balance. Canthorpe's information punctured a lot of theories. For instance, it left us with absolutely no reason to believe Haskell'd ever had anything to do with el Señor—not even indirectly, through loan sharks. On the other hand, it didn't make Canthorpe look like he had anything to do with whoever was trying to plant Haskell. If Canthorpe had already put Novick onto Haskell, why bother coming here tonight and acting righteous over a few thousand dollars of bank money? It didn't make sense. I suppose it was possible Canthorpe was doing this precisely to make himself look innocent. But that was a little too ornate for me. It didn't fit the way I felt.

However I looked at it, it still left us with no explanation for what we were up against. We only had two hard facts to go on. Haskell was lying. And somebody was trying to kill him. Well, three facts, maybe—if you count the way Smithsonian sneered at us when we took this case. What fun. I was having a great time.

At least now we knew why Haskell carried an empty briefcase home from work on Monday. Friday morning he took an empty briefcase in to work. Friday evening he came home with a briefcase full of money. Reverse it on Monday. I suppose I should've been grateful for small favors.

But Haskell didn't swallow Canthorpe's accusation. Looking bright-eyed and bushy-tailed, he watched Canthorpe until the branch manager stopped. Then he shrugged and took a pull at his drink. His insouciance was perfect. "Jordan," he said almost kindly when he lowered his glass, "you're just upset. None of that proves I've been gambling."

I think I looked as blank and amazed as Canthorpe did. Haskell's reply was like defending yourself against a murder rap by claiming you hadn't had anything to drink. To the bank, it didn't matter what he'd done with the money. He was still in trouble. Either he was starting to lose what was left of his grasp on reality—or there was a whole new side to this case we didn't know about yet.

But Ginny didn't seem surprised or baffled by Haskell's attitude. One way or another, it apparently made sense to her. "That's true," she said harshly. "None of that proves you've been gambling. But Mr. Canthorpe isn't the only one who's been doing some checking."

Slowly, he turned his head to look at her like he wasn't sure she was worth his attention.

"I spent this morning out at the airport," she said. "And this evening I had a talk with your wife."

He stiffened just enough to make a difference. "You know"—his voice was soft and dangerous—"I could have sworn I told you to leave her out of this."

"Just for the record," I murmured, "no, you didn't." But nobody took any notice of me.

Ginny smiled like the edge of a hacksaw. "Just doing my job." Before he could interrupt, she went on, "At first, I thought she wasn't going to be able to tell me anything. She's going quietly crazy all by herself in that hotel, alone hour after hour with no idea what in hell's going on. You've kept so much secret from her—and she wants to trust you so badly—she's practically blind and paralyzed. All she can do is talk to total strangers about you, asking them for reassurance because she thinks you're getting ready to dump her. She really doesn't know anything at all about what you do with your time when you're not with her.

"But finally I asked the right question. A simple, practical question." She watched Haskell sharply. Canthorpe had moved back a few steps to lean against the wall beside the window, studying his fiancée's lover—but mostly waiting for his chance to talk again. "She told me who your travel agent is.

"After that, it was easy. I went to your travel agent. I flashed my license around, offered to get a few subpoenas, and they let me look at their records. I know which flights you took to Las Vegas on which weekends for the past year. I know the hotel you stayed in. If you push me that far, I can go there, show people your picture, and find out exactly what you did—what game you played in, how much money you lost, the whole thing.

"I'm going to do that, Haskell." She chewed the words at him. "I'm going to find out so much about you you'll never get a job again with any bank or accounting firm in the state. Unless you start telling us the truth."

I couldn't see his face anymore—I'd moved myself right behind him—but he didn't seem particularly upset. His hand was steady as he raised his glass and finished his drink. After a minute, he said evenly, "It looks like I underestimated you a bit." He wasn't exactly filled with chagrin by the idea. "I didn't think you'd get so wrapped up in investigating me instead of the people who're trying to kill me. I thought I could get you to protect me without having to tell you how much trouble I'm really in. I didn't want to take that chance. I've never dealt with private investigators before. I didn't know how much you'd tell, or who you'd tell it to. And I knew I'd lose my job if anybody at the bank found out what I'd been doing." He shrugged. "Now I'm going to lose it anyway. You've cost me that. If you don't do your job and start protecting me, you're going to cost me my life. So I'll tell you the truth." He put rat poison in his voice. "That way, you won't have any more excuses."

But he didn't start right away. He stared out at the cold black night and thought until Ginny said in exasperation, "Get on with it, Haskell. I've had all I can stand." Then he pulled himself together to tell his story.

"Do you people read the paper?" he asked with obvious sarcasm. "Do you know who Roscoe Chavez is?"

That went through me like the stroke of a knife. "Front page news yesterday," I said for no reason except to help myself handle the shock. "Bambino Chavez was one of el Señor's main lieutenants. He turned up dead on Sunday." I had to stop. If I went on babbling, I was going to say something about Pablo.

"That's right," Haskell commented drily. "If you check back far enough and hard enough, you'll learn that Roscoe Chavez and I went to high school together." He snorted a laugh. "You'd never know it to look at them, but even hoods go to high school when they're kids. Roscoe and I were on the soccer team together. In fact, I gave him the assist that let him score the winning goal in the conference championship. It would've surprised me if he ever forgot who I was.

"Anyway, I started going to Vegas a while back. I was looking for some relief. Being an accountant was going to bore me into an early grave, and I knew I had to spice it up somehow. Vegas gave me a chance to feel alive for the first time in years. It practically resurrected me. And I made a lot of money.

"About a year ago, I ran into Roscoe in Vegas. He was staying at the same hotel. We had an old soccer team reunion, commemorating his moment of glory—took in a show, played some poker, had a lot to drink. It was fun. I hadn't expected to enjoy it that much, but Roscoe knew how to have a good time.

"If you still think I'm lying"—poison again—"go and check. You'll find it's easy to learn who I spent my time with. It was always the same. First Roscoe and I got together whenever we were there. Then we started planning our trips together. He had an interesting life, and he liked to talk about it—especially to his old soccer buddy.

He wasn't the brightest man I ever met, but he was exciting company.

"Then, about six months ago, we both hit a streak of bad luck. We were playing poker with a group of regulars at the hotel, and we'd been taking them to the cleaners for months. But when our luck shifted we started to lose a bit. I mean I lost a bit. Roscoe lost a lot. He was shoveling money out of his pockets with both hands. In fact"—there was a smile in his tone—"what winnings I got came from him.

"After a few months, he began to get desperate. He told me he'd used up all his reserves. He needed a stake so he could win his money back. Since I'd been losing right along with him, I didn't have anything to spare. I couldn't help him. We spent a while commiserating, and then he suggested that maybe I could help him after all. He knew how he could get his hands on some money by ripping off his boss. El Señor."

Oh God. I had to brace my hands on the back of the couch to keep myself on my feet. "And you bought it?" Ginny snapped. "He offered you a scam to rip off el Señor, and you bought it? What do you use for brains? Oatmeal?"

"I couldn't see anything wrong with it," Haskell shot back at her. "I needed money myself, you know. What better place to get it? Besides, his scheme looked good. He ran el Señor's numbers racket. He knew the whole operation inside out. All he needed was a secret partner, somebody that nobody in Puerta del Sol could connect to him. Then it was simple. He'd give his partner the winning number a few days in advance. His partner would bet that number and collect the winnings. They could split the take later. What could go wrong?"

As he talked, he recovered his composure. Maybe it was the sound of his own voice that steadied him. "I assume you noticed I didn't go to Vegas last weekend." Ginny nodded stiffly. Canthorpe was watching Haskell with a kind of fascinated nausea. "Friday evening I used my bank card to borrow five thousand dollars, and I placed the bet. We knew we had to be cautious because I wasn't one of their regulars, so we didn't try to get greedy. I didn't put all the money down on the right number. I spread it around.

"I don't know if you know how the numbers work. You have a choice. You can buy a straight number for a dollar and have a chance to win the pool for the week. Or you can stack your bets with however much money you want to risk, and they pay odds instead of the pool. The hundred bucks I put on the right number got forty-to-one."

He spread his hands. "I picked up my winnings Saturday night. Sunday I gave Roscoe his half. I thought we were all set." The memory seemed to sadden him. "Sunday night I got the phone call I told you about. Monday morning I read in the paper that Roscoe was dead.

"I guess his boss must've found out what he was doing."

Must've found out. I guess so. Jesus Christ. For once, we had a story that seemed to cover everything. It was a terrible story. I couldn't keep my kneecaps from trembling.

"Who did you place your bets with?" I was trying to sound nonchalant, but I didn't come close.

"Huh?" Haskell craned his neck to look up at me behind him. "What do you mean?"

Ginny went on staring at him. Something in her eyes looked vague and lost. Her worst fears were landing like vultures on her shoulders.

"I'm talking English, aren't I?" I returned. "It's a simple question." I may very well have been losing my mind, but I couldn't stop. "Who did you place your bets with?"

"I told you—I spread my money around." He didn't like peering up at me, so he looked away. "I went everywhere Roscoe told me to go. I must've seen ten different runners."

"Haskell." I was having a little trouble breathing. Lack of sleep and too much panic do funny things to you. "I know how the numbers work in this city." Don't try lying to me. "I know some of the runners. Where did you go?"

He may've been cocky, but he wasn't stupid. He didn't miss my point. "The old part of town," he said warily. "Phone booths. Bars. Alleys. I can't tell you addresses or names. But if you go with me, I can take you every place I went."

"The runners," I said. "Describe some of them."

"Come off it, Axbrewder." Heavy disdain. "I was down there at night. They're all Chicano kids. They all look alike to me. There wasn't one of them I could swear to if I saw him again."

Damn him. Damn everything. I wanted to take him by the throat and shake him until he learned a few decent lessons about fear. It was just possible he was responsible for Pablo's death. If Pablo figured out or stumbled onto what the Bambino and Haskell were up to, Chavez was perfectly capable of breaking his neck and dumping him out of a fast car in self-defense. And if el Señor found out about it, that would explain his attitude toward the Santiagos—his insistence on an honorable funeral, his promise he would avenge Pablo's killing.

It was all pure speculation, nothing but moonshine. But it fit. It fit so good it hurt.

I wanted to ask Ginny what she was thinking. Then I wanted to kick myself in the head because I hadn't told her anything at all about Pablo. Whatever she was thinking, she was in a completely different world than I was.

Whatever it was, she didn't know how to deal with it. Her face was pale, and her eyes didn't seem to be in focus. She was probably considering the obvious implications of what we'd heard—the implications I was ignoring. El Señor wanted Haskell dead for the same reasons Roscoe Chavez had been killed. A ritual hit. And we were supposed to protect him.

Abruptly, she said, "I need a drink after all." She

didn't look at me or anybody else as she left the den like she was fleeing inside and barely able to keep it from showing.

I almost went after her. I'd never seen her like this before, and it appalled me.

But before I could turn away, Haskell said to Canthorpe, "I hope you're satisfied." His tone held me. It was too quiet. I could hear venom. "You'll be able to fire me now. You've endangered my marriage. Sara isn't going to know what to think about all this. And you may even get me killed. If Fistoulari and Axbrewder don't trust me, they aren't going to be very effective at keeping me alive. You must have waited a long time for a chance to do something like this to me. I wonder"—he looked casually at his hands, his fingernails—"what I'm going to do to get even."

Canthorpe came off the wall like he'd been hit with a cattle prod. But a couple of steps later he snatched himself under control again. The blackness of the window framed him. His pale, boyish face looked as fierce as it could—which wasn't very fierce. But his eyes weren't stupid, or weak either, and the bone behind his expression was hard. He was a better enemy than he probably realized. Maybe he was better than I'd given him credit for.

Deliberately, he straightened his jacket and his tie. In a cold voice, he said, "You simply don't understand, do you, Haskell? You're in every conceivable kind of trouble, and all you can think of to do about it is threaten me. Well, your threats aren't frightening, Haskell. They're asinine. For all your charm and talent and philandering, you're an empty hull instead of a man. It shouldn't surprise me that you don't understand. Your conception of love is no better than a goat's."

Haskell started to laugh. "Ah, the injured pride of the impotent man. You shouldn't let yourself be vindictive, Jordan. It makes you ridiculous."

"*Listen* for a minute," Canthorpe snapped back at him. "I'll add it up for you."

Ginny'd come back into the den. She stood beside me, a glass of straight scotch—I knew it by smell—in her hand. Her grip was white, like a mute call for help.

"You can't threaten me," Canthorpe went on, "because you've already cost me what I care about most. There's no significant harm left for you to do me. The best you can hope for is to minimize your own losses.

"Keeping you alive is none of my business. I couldn't help you with that if I wanted to. But the bank is my business. You've made dishonest use of the bank's money, and you deserve to lose your job.

"However"—some of his vehemence faded—"the bank hasn't lost any money that I can see." His gaze was nailed to Haskell's face. "I'd be willing to let it pass. I'll keep what you've been doing to myself. On one condition." Unexpected color came into his cheeks. He sounded like his heart was trip-hammering. "Leave Eunice alone. Stop seeing her. Tell her it's finished, you don't love her, you don't want her anymore." What he was saying made his mouth quiver. "Give me a chance to win her back."

At that, Haskell began laughing. "A chance?" He could hardly get the words out. "To win her back?" He was laughing so hard I thought he was going to pop something. Or I was going to pop it for him. "You're dreaming." Slowly, he wrestled himself under control. "Some people are content to eat cardboard all their lives. But not after they've tasted steak. You can't go back. Nobody can go back."

"You bastard," Canthorpe panted. "You bastard." Suddenly, his face was covered with tears. "I hope they cut your heart out." Jerking himself away, he walked unsteadily toward the end of the room.

Moving so he wasn't between Haskell and the picture window anymore.

That was all the warning we had. It wasn't much.

As soon as Canthorpe was out of the way, a brick came in through the window. It seemed to appear out of nowhere against the glass, a piece of night that suddenly turned hard and heavy enough to shatter panes. The window burst into splinters, and a spray of glass followed the brick.

Straight for where Haskell was sitting.

The window was double-glazed for insulation. Those two heavy layers of glass took most of the steam off the brick. It thudded to the carpet a good ten feet from Haskell's shoes. Chips and splinters carried farther, but they didn't reach him either. Bits of snow swirled in out of the darkness.

That was the whole point, of course. You couldn't tell how thick the window was unless you looked at it close in good light. Some of the energy-conscious homes in Puerta del Sol have triple- and even quadruple-glazed windows. That much glass can deflect even a high-powered rifle bullet—and you'd only get one shot because it'd make the entire window crazy with cracks. Since there were four of us in the room, you probably wouldn't want to use a rifle at all. You'd want some way to take us all out at once. And that'd make it even more important to get the glass out of the way first.

While we stared like paralytics at the brick, and shards of cold made moaning noises past the ragged edges of the window, a hand grenade took a casual flip through the opening, hit the carpet, and rolled to a stop in front of Haskell.

The pin and the handle were gone. We could all see that as plain as the glass glittering in the nap of the carpet.

It was an old army surplus grenade, the kind you can order by sending in coupons from *Soldier of Fortune*. It probably wasn't powerful enough to gut the room, but that many screaming steel fragments were going to do a nice job on the four of us.

Ginny barked, "Move!" in a voice that went through all my muscles like a jolt of electricity.

Like we'd been practicing it together for months, she bent down to get her hands under the edge of the couch while I reached for Haskell.

My part was easy. Under the circumstances, he didn't feel particularly heavy. I latched onto his shoulders and heaved him over the back of the couch. He hit the wall pretty hard, but I didn't waste time worrying about that.

For Ginny, it was tougher. Apparently, she forgot she only had one hand. She didn't brace herself right for the leverage she needed. Both wrists under the edge of the couch, she jerked upward—and her hand failed. She lost her balance. As she stumbled backward, she hit the wall about the same time Haskell did—and almost as hard.

Those old grenades give you seven seconds before they tear you to pieces. I didn't know how much time was gone, and anyway I wasn't counting. Why bother? There wasn't anything I could do except try to beat the detonation.

I jammed my hands under the couch and pitched it forward, shoving it upside down on top of the grenade.

That was when the grenade went off.

It made a muffled crumpling noise like popping a paper bag underwater. The couch burst stuffing at the ceiling. I felt the shock of the explosion and did my best to fall backward, away from it. Wood and cloth went to shreds. Metal springs twanged louder than the grenade. The walls spit chips in a few places. But the couch absorbed enough of the blast.

As I landed on the floor, silence clapped back through the room. The innards of the couch seemed to geyser everywhere, obscuring the hole in the window so I couldn't see out—and whoever was out there couldn't see in. Haskell lay against the wall, his eyes wide. Across the room, Canthorpe gaped at the couch like he was going to throw up just as soon as he figured out what'd happened. He was the only one of us on his feet. Ginny knelt near me, bracing herself with her good arm. She didn't seem aware of anything around her. She was hitting her stump on the wall as hard as she could. "Damn this thing," she panted. "Damn it. Damn it."

First things first. I was so calm I felt like a lunatic. "Canthorpe," I said. My voice was quiet and conversational, crazy in the aftermath of the grenade. "Get the lights." But something in my tone made him move toward the switches. His direct path to them kept him out of the line of sight of the broken window.

I turned to Ginny. "Stop it. This is no time for hysteria. Get your gun."

The stuffing settled like snow in the center of the room. When Canthorpe reached the switches, the lights went out.

Ginny stopped.

"Don't move," I breathed to Haskell and Canthorpe. "Don't say anything. He knows this is a trap." Ditching the lights was a gamble. It warned whoever was out there. But it was the only way to even the odds. I got up on my hands and knees, reached under my jacket and pulled out the .45. "I think he's going to come in after us anyway."

Ginny crawled past me in the dark. When she stopped moving, I thought I heard somebody start up the hill in the narrow lane between the privacy wall and the side of the house.

That made sense. Circle around and try to take us from behind. I headed for the stairs, hoping to cut him off.

Behind me, Ginny whispered hoarsely, "Brew! Wait for me." She got to the stairs a few steps after I did.

The atrium and entryway lights were still on. I didn't even think about trying to get them off. I didn't want the man outside to know where we were. Near the top of the stairs, I tightened my grip on the .45 and paused. If I were him, I'd try to break in through the living room window. It was on ground level before the hill sloped down toward the arroyo. It wasn't exposed to the outside lights of the house and the street. And the atrium lit the doorway to the living room but left the window dark. He could watch for us—and we'd have a hard time surprising him.

Keeping out of the line of the light, so my shadow didn't touch the doorway into the living room, I left the stairway and moved to stand beside the frame.

Ginny followed me. Her face was as pale as bone. A smear of blood oozed from the abrasions on her stump. Behind her clenched teeth, she looked like she was hyperventilating.

I waited for the sound of breaking glass. We'd left all the windows locked. The goon'd knock in one pane to reach the latch. Or he'd just charge the window and crash through it.

He didn't. I didn't hear anything. Nothing at all. Not even a car out in the street.

I was wrong. He wasn't coming in this way. Then where? Where were the other windows on this level?

"Shit," I sighed to Ginny through my teeth. "The bedroom."

Just to be on the safe side, I jumped in front of the doorway to the living room, leading with the .45—just to reassure myself the window there was closed and intact.

It wasn't. Nothing was broken. But it was wide open.

Before I could react, the goon came out at me. With all his weight and strength behind the blow, he hammered me in the chest with the butt of his rifle. I went down like I'd been kicked by a horse.

No way to defend myself. My lungs felt like they'd been nailed to the floor. Somewhere on the other side of a wall of pain, my arm struggled to do something with the .45. But my muscles might as well've been cut—I couldn't even raise my hand. All I could do was watch him raise the M-16 to swing it again. This time it was going to crush my skull.

"Don't do it!" Ginny shouted. She sounded wild—so

wild Novick froze in mid-swing. Her .357 was aimed right into his face. From that range, the muzzle must've looked like the snout of a howitzer.

Somewhere under the dope or fever in his eyes, his instinct for survival still functioned. When she kicked the rifle away, his hands made twitching movements toward his belt. Maybe he wanted the knife sheathed on his left hip—maybe one of the grenades clipped on the other side. But she rasped, "I mean it. I've killed people this way before."

Slowly, he pulled his hands back until his weapons were out of reach.

Somehow, I took a breath. After a minute or so, I figured out how to move again.

Chapter Eighteen

By the time I got to my feet, I was starting to think maybe Novick had cracked a couple of ribs, and Haskell and Canthorpe were standing up near the head of the stairs, staring. For different reasons, they both looked like kids—Canthorpe because he had that kind of face, Haskell because this was probably as close as he'd ever been to a real live game of cops-and-robbers. Just judging by appearances, neither of them could've possibly had anything to do with Mase Novick, with his tattoos and his murderous cornered-animal expression—or with Ginny either, for that matter, who looked like a whisky bottle with the bottom broken out of it and the jagged glass ready to slash in any direction.

"Who is he?" Canthorpe asked softly.

"Cover him," she panted at me. She was breathing hard—too hard. Her aim at Novick was starting to wobble.

I pulled up the .45. The stress hurt my chest, but I didn't let that bother me. Lining up the barrel on Novick's guts, I said tightly, "I hope you try something." My voice sounded like it had to squeeze its way through a pile of rocks. "I'd love to get even."

Ginny sagged a bit. But she didn't lower her gun. "Haskell," she said like she was fighting suffocation, "get some rope."

He nodded. He was glad to participate.

As soon as Haskell crossed the atrium and went into the garage, she swung her .357 on Jordan Canthorpe.

"Don't move." She was practically gasping. "Don't talk. Don't think. You've already had your chance."

His face went wide. His mouth gaped open. All the color ran out of his skin. If he wasn't innocent, he was sure as hell surprised to get caught.

Two things went through my head like ricochets. Either she was wrong. Or Haskell had lied to us again. Wait a minute, I wanted to say. Let's think this through. But Ginny wasn't in any shape to hear me. She had her teeth locked on the air like that was all that kept her from passing out, and the lines of her face looked too sharp. I forced myself to concentrate on Novick.

Feeling a kind of polite, demented detachment, I advised him to lie down with his nose in the carpet. Canthorpe tried to find his voice to make some protest, but Ginny's white grip on the .357 stopped him. By the time I had Novick stretched out the way I wanted him, Haskell came back with a coil of clothesline.

When he saw what was going on, he stopped. "Jordan?" He'd probably done any number of stupid things recently, but that didn't make him a stupid man. He seemed to catch up with the implications almost immediately. "Fistoulari, what the hell are you doing?"

Circling so I could keep the .45 aimed at Novick's spine, I went over to Haskell and took the rope. "If I were you, Mr. Haskell"—a bit of friendly advice—"I'd keep my mouth shut for a while. There's nobody here who gives a flying fuck at the moon for your opinion." Then I went back to Novick.

Keeping him pinned with one knee, I lashed his wrists together behind him. "*Cojones*," he rasped at me. "Motherfucker." With the .45, I gave him a lick on the side of the head that shut him up. Just to be on the safe side, I tied his wrists to his ankles, bowing his back until his shoulders looked like they were going to pop.

"Now him," Ginny panted. The barrel of the .357 indicated Canthorpe.

Oh, good. If you have to go off the deep end, you might as well go all the way.

"Ms. Fistoulari, I don't know what you think I've done"—Canthorpe sounded steadier than I was expecting—"but you're wrong. I don't even know who this man is."

"Now him," she repeated through her teeth. "Come on, Brew."

I didn't argue. I wasn't ready. My chest hurt, and cold air from the broken window downstairs only made it worse. I was still trying to figure out how much I was responsible for what'd happened. I was the one who'd stirred up that beehive Novick used for a brain. So I did what she told me. Canthorpe gave me a glare of outrage and appeal, but he didn't try to resist. In a few minutes, I had him trussed up too—like Novick, but not as hard.

That gave her at least a bit of what she needed. She lowered her gun. Taking a deep breath, she held it and stopped breathing so hard. With her sore stump, she wiped her face. Sweat made the hair on either side of her face stringy. Her eyes were out of focus—relieved and lost.

I knew what was coming—and didn't know how to deal with it. Trying to postpone it, I went into the living room and snapped on the lights to see how Novick had gotten in.

The window was open all the way. The damage around the latch made it look like the window'd been forced with the blade of a knife. A heavy-duty knife, like the one Novick was carrying. But that still would've made enough noise to tell me what was going on. He must've gotten to the house before Ginny and Canthorpe, and started to break in when they arrived. But they'd gone down to the den, so he must've followed to keep an eye on them, leaving the window open in case he needed it. And Ginny'd been so close to the edge—not to mention so interested in what Canthorpe was saying—she'd never thought to check the house.

When I went back to the atrium, she was sitting on the floor, her gun in front of her. Haskell was watching her like he wouldn't've been surprised if she'd started to sing Christmas carols. Canthorpe was saying over and over again softly, "You are out of your mind, Ms. Fistoulari. You are out of your mind." She didn't look at either of them. As soon as I left the living room, she said, "Call the police, Brew."

She didn't look at me, either.

"Ginny." There was no good way to say it. "Maybe we ought to go over this once or twice. I'm not sure we've got it right."

"I said, call the police." Her voice was acid. "This bastard almost broke you in half. He threw a hand grenade at us. How innocent do you think he's likely to be?"

I shrugged. "More than you do, anyway." I wasn't primarily interested in Novick. But the whole situation hinged on him.

"I don't care." Her hand curled into a fist. "I'm not going to tell you again. Call the police."

Well, that wasn't a bad idea as far as it went. And it still might leave me time to talk her out of giving Canthorpe grounds to sue us. I said, "You're the boss," and went back into the living room to use the phone.

I called Detective-Lieutenant Acton. I was stretching the favor he owed us pretty thin by now, but I counted on him to at least listen to what we had to say before he jumped to any conclusions. Maybe he'd even forgive me for getting him in trouble with Cason.

He had a voice like the exhaust of a Mack truck, and when he got on the line he tried to tear my ear off with it. I let the first couple of blasts go by, then told him enough about what was going on to get his attention. Finally, he snarled, "All right, all right. I'm on my way. Give me half an hour. But when I get there, you better be ready to tell me the whole story. You hear me, Axbrewder? I want the whole story."

I said, "Sure," and hung up.

While I was on the phone, I heard voices from the atrium—sounded like Canthorpe and Haskell—but when I went back to Ginny they stopped. Haskell had moved closer to her. The excitement was gone from his face—he looked almost unnaturally serious. And Canthorpe had squirmed around into a position where he could watch her. Novick lay where he was, muttering to himself. Ginny was still on the floor, sitting with her back against the wall beside the doorway to the living room. She kept running her fingers through her hair, trying to pull it back from her face.

Softly, I said, "Acton's on the way."

"Want to hear something crazy, Brew?" I wasn't sure she'd absorbed what I said. "Our client here wants us to believe Canthorpe's innocent. Novick just tried to kill him, and Canthorpe knew about Novick and Harmon, and he's got the only proven motive in this whole mess, and our client still wants us to believe his boss didn't sic Novick on him."

"It's true," Canthorpe protested. "I swear it." Her attitude scared him worse than being tied up.

But she dismissed him with a humorless snort. "Our client," she went on, "just can't bear it that we've caught him lying again. All that bullshit about being involved with Roscoe Chavez. He's just been trying to make himself feel important. As if anybody besides a jilted fiancé would even consider him worth threatening. I've been thinking back on it. As I remember, our client didn't so much as know the name el Señor until he heard it from us. He probably got Roscoe Chavez out of the newspaper."

"Damn it, Fistoulari." Haskell was angry now—or faking it well. "I'm not that stupid. Nobody's dumb enough to invent trouble like this. I'm good at games, but that's all they are, games. I wouldn't lie about something this serious. It's too unpredictable, too dangerous. I've been trying to manipulate you before tonight. I admit it. But I didn't know how much I could trust you. I didn't want to have to tell you what I'd done. I was afraid you might turn me in.

"But now I've told you the truth. You're looking in the wrong direction. El Señor is trying to kill me. Because Roscoe and I ripped him off. I don't care about motive. Jordan is not the kind of man who would try to have anybody killed, for any reason."

She ignored him. "I'll tell you something, Brew." She sounded like she wanted to laugh and couldn't pull it off. "I've had enough. I'm getting out of this business. As soon as the cops get here, this case is closed. I'm going to quit. Find myself some other line of work." Maybe instead of laughing what she wanted to do was cry. "I can't take any more of this shit."

"Ginny." I had to stop her somehow. She was going to break my heart. "We've got to think this through again. Before Acton gets here. It isn't as simple as it looks."

She didn't even glance up at me. For a long minute, she didn't say anything. Then her voice came past the edge of her hair like a flick of hate. "Mick Axbrewder, what in hell are you talking about?"

Sweet Christ on a stick. This was going to be fun.

As steadily as I could, I said, "I haven't had a chance to tell you about my evening yet."

"What's to tell?" She really didn't want to hear it. "You went to talk to Eunice Wint. You took your precious good time—but it didn't get you anywhere. You blew it somehow. If you'd gone at it right, she would've told you enough to prove Canthorpe's guilty. But she's pretty and stupid, so you felt sorry for her and your head turned to mush. You don't need to tell me about it. I'm not interested."

"I can see that," I snarled. My unbalanced calm was gone. Now I was just unbalanced. "But you ought to be. You ought to know by now it doesn't take all evening for a pretty and stupid girl to turn my head to mush. What do you suppose I did with the rest of the time?"

Bitterly, she said, "I'm afraid to ask."

I bent over Novick and turned him so I could see his face. I was rougher than I meant to be—when I was done, there was sweat on his face and a white glare of pain in his eyes. "*Pendejo*," he hissed at me. "You're tearing my arms out." But I didn't pay any attention to that. I just wanted to be able to watch his expression.

"Before Haskell and I talked to Eunice," I said to Ginny, "we went to Novick's house. The house he shares with Gail Harmon. We took her and checked her into a hospital."

That didn't hit him for a second or two. Pain and craziness made him slow. Then a spasm of fury convulsed his face. "Bastard!" he coughed. "Fucker!" All his muscles corded, trying to break the clothesline. "Cocksucker! You took my woman? My woman? I'll kill you. I swear I'll kill you." I thought he was going to froth at the mouth.

Which answered one question. He wasn't here because of what I'd done. He must've already been on his way when Haskell and I went to his house. That gave me a queer, useless sense of relief.

On the other hand, the implications made what I was trying to say look a lot weaker. And Ginny didn't miss them. "Don't tell me," she said fiercely. "Let me guess. You were going to say the only reason he came here tonight and tried to kill us all was because you snatched his girlfriend. He was just an innocent bystander until you made him mad. By the way, that was brilliant, Axbrewder. Real genius. Sawdust is smarter than that. But never mind. It isn't true. He didn't know you took his girlfriend until you told him."

Now it was my turn not to look at her. I couldn't stand it. Instead, I concentrated on Novick. Both Canthorpe and Haskell were watching me with various degrees of alarm and hope, but I ignored them.

"Novick," I said through his cursing, "listen for a minute. Bite your tongue and listen. This is your life we're talking about. How many years of hard time you're going to do for attempted murder. Listen."

"Go fuck yourself, *pendejo*," he responded. "I'm so scared I shit my pants."

"I know. You're as tough as a whole regiment. Listen anyway. Somebody's been trying to kill Reg Haskell for two days now. There've been three tries so far. We're not going to have any trouble proving it was you the third time. But what about the other two? Can you think of any reason why we shouldn't pin those on you, too?"

From my point of view, that was the crucial question. I thought I knew the answer. But I couldn't risk putting words in his mouth. And if he refused to say it—if he decided to play belligerent all the way to the state pen—then I was stuck.

But apparently there's nothing killers like less than being blamed for things they didn't do. "Yeah, *cojones*," he spat. "I can think of a reason. I didn't know his fucking name before you told me. Gail called him Reg. She never told me who he was. She didn't want him killed. You told me Haskell. I looked him up in the phone book." There was a glitter of triumph in his eyes.

But Ginny wasn't having any. "That's a crock. He's lying. Why not? What's he got to lose?"

Somehow, I forced myself to turn around and look at the fever in her face. "It's true," I said. She looked like she was being eaten alive from the inside. "I told him the name. I didn't have any way of knowing it was a mistake. But as soon as I said it, I could see I'd done something wrong. He couldn't've boobytrapped the Buick last night. And he wasn't—"

She cut me off. "I'm not going to argue with you. You're out of your head. You need professional help. Novick tried to kill us, and we caught him. With a little research, the cops are going to be able to prove Canthorpe hired him to kill Haskell. We've done our job. It's over. I don't care how many dumb mistakes you've made, or how responsible you feel. It's over. As soon as the cops get here—"

"Ginny—"

"—this case is closed."

I opened my mouth. She almost jabbed me in the face with her index finger. "Shut it. You've said enough. I don't want to hear any more. You had better sense when you were a drunk." Abruptly, she wrenched herself to her feet, scooping her .357 off the carpet as she stood up. Maybe without realizing it, she pointed the gun in the direction of my stomach. To Haskell, she said, "You'll get my bill in the morning."

He threw up his hands in exasperation. "I should've fired you this afternoon while I was thinking about it," he muttered angrily. "I changed my mind because I thought I was safe. I thought you were too stupid or out of control to stumble onto the truth. And I thought you were brave or honest enough to stick with me. I was wrong both times."

"Ginny." I had to lock both fists to keep myself from howling. "God damn it, it wasn't Novick in the car that tried to nail us this afternoon."

She actually tightened her grip on the .357. "You bastard." Her voice shook. "What makes you so sure?"

"I was there, remember?" I couldn't help it—I was shouting at her. "He's too tall! And too thin! And he's in love with his M-16. The goon in the car had a shotgun."

"He probably has a shotgun," she fired back. "He probably has one of every gun known to man. And he was in a car. He was aiming a shotgun at you. You were trying to drive. You couldn't tell how tall or thin he was."

I wanted to hit myself in the head, just to make her stop. "I saw him. It wasn't Novick."

"What kind of car does Novick drive?" Haskell asked. "Maybe it wasn't the same car."

Ginny ignored him. "You saw him," she said like she was threatening me. "Sure you saw him. I bet you couldn't even tell whether it was a man or a woman."

I just stared at her for a second. Then I said, "Ginny, you know better than that."

"I do?" Something inside her seemed to snap—and all at once she sounded almost cheerful. Completely out of her skull. "Let's go outside." She waggled her gun at my stomach. "I'll prove it to you." A wild smile lit her face. "I'll prove you couldn't tell whether it was a man or a woman from even ten feet away."

Suddenly, my throat was too dry to talk, and my heart was knocking against my rib cage. Ginny, I thought. Oh my God.

Her cheerfulness only lasted a few seconds. When I didn't say anything, her expression turned savage. Before I could defend myself, she stepped forward and poked me with the muzzle of her gun. "I said, let's go outside."

The way I saw it, I only had two choices. I could take the .357 away and hit her a few times until she got her sanity back or passed out. Or I could do what she told me.

I did what she told me. With a shrug, I walked across the atrium to the front door. Unlocked it. Opened it.

All the outside lights were on. I could see everything. Reacting to the noise of the door, the sound of my shoes on the cement walk, a man came out of the snow around one of the cedars into the other end of the aisle. I recognized him right away.

He wasn't tall, but he was put together like a tank. Muscle bulged on him everywhere—he looked like he'd been packed into his coat at a sausage plant. A hairline moustache under his nose tried to make his face human, but the way his eyes protruded insisted he was really a reptile. I'd had a run-in with him once. It still gave me nightmares.

El Señor's bodyguard. Muy Estobal.

I wasn't what he was expecting. But he was ready. His hand was already in the pocket of his coat. He brought it out holding a snub-nosed Smith & Wesson .38. The lights lit the snow behind him so he stood against a background of swirling white bits that looked like the world was going to pieces.

I was still trying to claw the .45 out of its holster when he started shooting.

Something that felt like a cannonball took hold of my belly and slammed me off my feet. The jolt when I hit seemed to turn every bone in my body to powder.

I heard Ginny yell behind me. Then she began to lay down fire in the aisle as if she'd lost her mind.

Chapter Nineteen

For what seemed like a long time (but it could've been anything, long or short—I was in no condition to keep an eye on my watch), I thought I was conscious when I really wasn't. I must've been unconscious because I missed all the transitions. When I landed on the cement of the walkway, it turned out to be a hospital gurney going somewhere in a hurry, and Ginny and Muy Estobal had somehow changed themselves into people wearing green robes and caps. Later, the gurney was transformed into a big bed with high railings all around it, and the white corridor walls were curtains hanging from runners in the ceiling to surround the bed. The people in green were holding me down by both arms—only now they looked suspiciously like IV stands with tubes that disappeared into layers of tape around my forearms.

But it didn't feel like being unconscious. It felt like walking wide-awake and terrified onto the business end of a harpoon—and then standing there helpless while somebody even bigger than me stirred the blade like a ladle until my guts became soup.

At first, there was nothing to it except red-gray pain wrapped around my mind and one long scream driven like a spike through the center of the world. The only problem with that was you need your stomach muscles to scream and I didn't seem to have any to speak of. But eventually I became more lucid. I began counting all the nerve cells that'd been torn apart by Estobal's bullet.

At least it felt like that. The way I hurt was impossibly precise. But I lost track after a while. By degrees, I came to understand I hadn't been shot at all. Oh, no—nothing that tidy and manageable. I'd been blown up. Like that rented Buick. With that poor innocent kid inside. It was always the innocent who got roasted. And it was always people like me who saw what was happening too late and failed to save them.

No question about it. I was having all kinds of fun.

But what I was conscious of most of all—with the complete certainty and conviction that only comes to you when you're drunk or crazy, all the way off your rocker with booze or grief—was that I didn't have time for this.

There were only so many hours in the night, and they were getting away from me. There were people I needed to talk to—two old men, probably together, drinking and dealing in an odd and half-unreconciled partnership because they were too old and too tired to try to compete with each other. Until the dives in the old part of town where grizzled *muchachos* like themselves were still welcome and even honored closed—2:00 A.M. in Puerta del Sol—they'd be following their exact and unpredictable circuit from place to place, receiving and dispensing wares in their relatively humble area of expertise, earning themselves bottles of indifferent mescal with what they knew or could deduce. After that, for maybe an hour or two—no, not that long, not tonight, it was snowing, remember?—one of the less useful parts of my mind insisted on remembering snow—so maybe for an hour, maybe less, maybe not at all, they'd go to that cheap little park down on Tin Street, the same place where I used to go spend the nights and wait for Ginny, and finish their last bottle together. And then they'd be gone. They'd evaporate into the dwindling night, and with every cop in the city on your side you'd never be able to prove they even existed.

I needed to talk to them. I needed to get from wherever I was down to the old part of town and find them and talk to them before time ran out. I couldn't afford to lie around like a side of beef in an abattoir and let the night get away from me.

So I almost started babbling when I finally got my eyes open and saw Ginny standing over me, near the head of the bed. What saved me was my mouth and throat were so dry I couldn't dredge up anything more than a croak. That held me back long enough to realize I couldn't say anything to her. If I did, she wouldn't help me. Just because I happened to be in pain, she'd stop me. In my condition, I didn't have the strength to tell her why she was wrong.

When she heard the faint strangling noises I made instead of conversation, she leaned over the bed. Her fingers stroked my face, running gently around the marks Gail Harmon made on my cheeks. "Mick Axbrewder," she said, even though nobody calls me Mick, not even her, "you look awful." I couldn't actually get my eyes into focus on her face—but her voice had a damp, blurred sound, like tears. "I did this to you."

That didn't compute, as they say. But I was in no shape to argue with her. With an effort, I managed to make my croaking sound a bit more like words.

"Where am I?"

"Don't worry about it." She was trying to be comforting. Maybe she was even trying to smile. "You've done enough for one night. Everything's taken care of. Just relax and get some rest."

I persisted. Stubborn old Axbrewder. "What time is it?"

"Late," she said. "You got out of surgery about half an hour ago. You were lucky again. Half the rest of the people in the world would be dead by now. The other half would have some kind of serious damage to their internal

organs. Not you. That slug just tore up your guts a bit."
She sounded brittle and lonely, like a woman standing on
the edge of a wasteland. But she was fighting to put a
good face on it. "The doctor told me more than I wanted
to hear about it. You got hit just low enough to miss your
ribs and lungs, just high enough not to take out a kidney,
just far enough to the side not to damage your liver.
Since it didn't hit bone, the slug didn't mushroom. And
the surgery went well. You're in surprisingly good shape.
You're going to hurt like hell for a while. Then you're
going to be all right."

Damn woman. She couldn't possibly know what I was
thinking about, but she still wouldn't give me a straight
answer. For a minute there, frustration and pain made
me so mad I had actual tears in my eyes. She leaned on
her arms on the rail of the bed. With her hand, she took
hold of one of my forearms. "Brew," she said softly, "I'm
so sorry. This is my fault. I was so bloody determined to
prove you were wrong about the driver of that Cadillac. I
wanted to prove Haskell was still lying. I couldn't think
about anything else. So I set you up to get shot at point-
blank range." Her voice bit in like the edge of a saw,
ripping across the grain of her self-respect. It was lucky
for me I still couldn't get her face all the way in focus.
God knows how bad she looked. "When I saw Estobal
there and he started shooting at you before you could do
anything—when you went down and I knew you were
hit—

"We should never have taken this case."

Well, maybe. She was probably right. But that didn't
matter. I was running out of time. If it wasn't already too
late. I didn't know how to get through to her. And one of
those IVs was feeding stuff into my veins that made me
want to go to sleep for three or four weeks. So far, the
only thing keeping me awake was the pain—and that was
starting to fade. I tried again. "Where am I?"

She didn't seem to hear me. "I used to think I was
tough," she said, far away with hurt. "Not physically.

Mentally. I used to think my mind was sharp and hard enough for anything. I never knew I was so dependent on my hands. When I really understood that I was never going to get my hand back—that the best I was going to be able to do was a clumsy, ugly, almost useless *prosthetic device* that made me look like I was only half human, not a person at all, never mind how I looked as a woman—" She caught herself, the words like barbs in her throat. "Something went out of me. Whatever it was that used to hold me together. And then I found out I wasn't tough at all. I've been using you to carry me ever since." Softly, she swore at herself—vicious, down-to-the-marrow curses, swearing to hold back the grief. "We never should've taken this case."

I wanted to scream at her. Silly of me—I didn't have the stomach for it. The whole situation was getting away from me. Hell, even consciousness was getting away from me. I could hardly remember what I had in mind that was so important.

As clearly as I could, I said, "I don't care about that. What time is it?"

Her reaction sent a quiver through the bed. Pieces of something wet landed on my face and trickled down my cheeks. "Fuck you, Axbrewder," she said stiffly. But then she softened. She stroked my face again, spreading the wet around. "Ah, hell. They've got you so doped up, you probably don't have any idea what I'm saying. We'll talk about it later." That was a lie, and I knew it. The loss in her voice was too obvious. She was never going to talk about this again. "In the meantime, you're not going anywhere." Now she was trying to be kind. "This one over here"—she pointed at the IV on my left, a large plastic packet full of red stuff—"is going to replace the blood you lost and give you something to live on. That one"—the other IV—"is your medication—antibiotics to keep you from developing peritonitis, dope for the pain, sedatives. You're going to spend a lot of time asleep."

I was going to scream. I swear to God, pain or no pain. But finally she took pity on me.

"However," she sighed, "if it'll help you rest—you're in Intensive Care at University Hospital. It's a little after ten-thirty. The nurses are going to check on you in a couple of hours. If you're still stable, they'll transfer you to your room. I've arranged a private room for you. All that hospitalization I've been paying premiums on for years has got to be good for something."

Involuntarily, I groaned. University Hospital! It was too far from where I needed to go. I was in no condition to walk that many miles.

"I'm sorry, Brew," she said contritely. "The doctor warned me not to keep you awake. I'll leave now. If you need me, I'll be in the waiting room. I'll see you again after they transfer you to your room."

She seemed to be receding. Or maybe it was me. Wandering away from consciousness like I was trying to find my own pain. The bed had a distinct tendency to float. But I couldn't just let go. That'd be too easy. The road to hell—as they say—is easier than anything.

"Ginny," I croaked like I was dying. "Wait."

She didn't exactly come back into range, but at least she stopped receding.

"What did you do with Haskell?"

Her mommie probably taught her she ought to be nice to sick people. But Reg Haskell wasn't a subject that brought out her nice side. "He got lucky," she rasped. "If you hadn't been lying there bleeding like a geyser, I would've had time to redesign his vital organs before the cops arrived. If he'd told us the truth from the beginning—" She stopped herself. "As it was, I was too busy. And Acton got there before the ambulance did. So I turned the whole mess over to him—Haskell, Canthorpe, Novick, everything. We're out of it. You don't have to worry about any of that anymore."

Now, wait a minute, I wanted to say. It isn't that simple. Haskell's story about Chavez changes everything. As soon as that story gets around, Haskell's case is going to be turned over to Captain Cason. That'll be like flushing the whole thing down the toilet. You've never flushed a case down the toilet in your life.

It was amazing how lucid I felt, when you consider Ginny'd disappeared and I couldn't see anything anymore because my eyes were closed. I must've been three-quarters unconscious while I watched ideas and possibilities walk back and forth in front of me, as clear and primed for violence as muggers or rapists in a line-up. But somehow I forced my eyes open again. Somehow I got my left arm across my chest and used those thick, fumbling fingers to pull the IV needle out of my right forearm.

What came next was the detail I couldn't afford to screw up. It took an enormous effort of concentration to slip the needle back under the bandages so it looked like it was still plugged into my veins. If a nurse glanced at those bandages and saw what I'd done—

The exertion took everything I had left. When I was done, I could've sworn the bed tipped over and pitched me out into the black middle of the night.

But it worked. Sweet Christ my stomach oh the pain it worked. I wasn't getting any more painkillers or seda-tives, and the unintentional jostling when the nurses and aides eased me out of the ICU bed onto a gurney woke me up in a sweat of agony. This definitely wasn't sane. But after the first groan got past my teeth, I managed to keep myself quiet and limp. My guts felt like they were hanging out in shreds, but I had to fake being relaxed and practically asleep so the nurses wouldn't wonder why I was in so much pain and check the IV. If they checked the IV, they'd find what I'd done and they'd fix it—and I was never going to have the courage to pull that same stupid stunt twice in one night.

Fortunately—or unfortunately, depending on your point of view—nurses and aides are human, too, and they've been known to get tired and maybe even a little careless in the middle of the night. None of them noticed my IV was oozing into my bandages instead of dripping into my veins. They gave me an elevator ride that seemed to go on for three or four hundred floors, wheeled me along a few miles of corridor, and finally shunted me into a room. Lifting me by the sheet under me, they heaved me off the gurney into bed while I did my best to pretend I wasn't squeezing hot sweat out of every pore in my whole body.

I was afraid of passing out again, but this time I didn't. Instead, I heard a young woman whisper in surprise, "Did you see this?" Opening my eyes a slit, I saw an aide showing my .45 to the nurses. "Is he a cop?"

"I don't know," one of them replied. "But he has a license for it in his wallet. Put it back."

With a shrug, the aide dropped the .45 into a large grocery sack that sat on top of the bureau one of the amenities of a private room. Apparently, my clothes were in that sack. Soaked with blood. By now, the blood would be dry—crusted and harsh. The clean, tidy part of me wanted to throw up. The rest of me vetoed the idea. I should be glad I had any clothes at all. Now all I needed—

But I couldn't think of what I needed. It was amazing how keen and cunning having a four-hundred-pound gorilla in spiked shoes dancing on my gut made me feel. Pain does wonderful things for the intellect. It teaches concentration. I tried again. Now all I needed—

Was some way to get from wherever I was (oh, that's right—University Hospital) to the old part of town.

Bravo. Good for me.

Well, lessee. Put your mind to it, Axbrewder. Some way to get from here to there.

I couldn't walk. So I'd have to drive. (Good again. Doing fine. Keep it up.)

I couldn't drive. So I'd have to get a ride. (That's right. Go on.)

I couldn't call a taxi. No cab driver in his right mind

was going to drive a gut-shot man *away* from a hospital. (See? You're doing better than you thought. You even noticed there's a phone in the room. I'm proud of you.)

Who could I call who'd be willing to drive me all over town while I bled to death? Who did I know who might conceivably be that desperate?

I waited until the nurses and aides were gone, and the door was closed, and the only light in the room came faintly through the window from the city. Then I pulled the IV away from my right arm. Slowly, carefully—hurting like Satan and all his demons—I rolled out of bed to the left and got my feet to the floor, then rested there trying not to breathe because breathing tore like a heavy-duty sailfish lure at my guts. Braced myself. Stood up.

See? That wasn't so bad. (The hell it wasn't! Dear God, this'll kill me.) You can do it. Just use the pain. Make it help you.

For a while, the room swirled like a sink draining all the life out of me. But the pain was at the center of everything, and it didn't let me go. I got my hands on the side table at the head of the bed, held on there until the walls slowed down. Then I fumbled for the reading lamp.

When I snapped it on, the light hurt my eyes. But once the pain shifted from my eyeballs back into my skull, I was able to see. The phone was on the table right in front of me.

Good. Fine. Keep it up. One thing at a time.

I still had the other IV in my left arm. But that was OK—I couldn't dial with that hand anyway. So I used it to lift the receiver. Almost randomly, I stabbed fingers at the buttons until I finally got through to Information.

Information listed six Rudolfo Santiagos.

Six! I couldn't just stand there and call them all. However, the exasperation in the operator's voice brought me back. (Damn him, anyway. Didn't he know I'd been shot in the gut and couldn't think clearly?) Grimly, I made him read me the addresses until he hit one I recognized.

Then—God alone knows how—I managed to remember the number long enough to dial it for myself.

The phone rang forever. Three or four times at least. Then a man's voice answered in Spanish. My mouth and throat felt like I'd been living on a diet of nothing but wool socks. In fact (why hadn't I realized this earlier?), my whole body was stretched and urgent with thirst. My IV was practically empty. How much blood had I lost? The voice on the other end of the line demanded an answer three times before I figured out I had to say something.

"Señor Santiago?" I croaked.

"*Sí*?" A question—suspicious and bitter.

One thing at a time. Swallow. Clear your throat. Come on, Axbrewder.

"I must speak with Señor Santiago."

That's better.

"Ah, Señor Axbrewder." Thank God he recognized me. "What transpires? You do not come to the vigil of our son? A curse upon all telephones. Your voice does not sound well. Have you been harmed?"

He paused, giving me a chance to respond. But I couldn't pull myself together. In a whisper, he asked, "Have you discovered the killer of my son?"

Ah, God. Everything hurt, and I didn't know what to do about it. Had I discovered the killer of his son? Of course not. I couldn't bear it.

But there had to be some reason why I was standing there holding onto the phone when I should've been horizontal and unconscious, pumped to the gills with medication. Eventually I remembered what it was.

"Señor Santiago," I said, "I am injured. I must have someone to drive for me. Will you come?"

"I?" He tried not to show it, but he was shocked. "You desire that I should drive for you? My son has been slain, and even now we hold vigil for him"—shock turning quickly to outrage—"although his body is denied to us and all we are given for our grief is an empty coffin and fifty dollars of candles. Also the time is beyond one in the morning. I do not—"

"Rudolfo," I heard in the background, his wife's voice, "do not shout. It is unseemly. Some respect we must have, for those who watch with us at least."

Intensely, he whispered at me across the dark city, "Have you discovered the killer of my son?"

With elaborate care, as if I was responding directly to his anger and sorrow and incomprehension, I said in English, "I'm in University Hospital. Meet me outside Emergency. As soon as you can. Bring me an overcoat." Then I remembered something else. "And a pint of mescal."

For a minute, he didn't say anything. When he spoke, his voice shook with the effort he made to keep it quiet.

"Señor Axbrewder"—he sneered the words—"I will not leave the vigil of my son so that I may play the errand boy and chauffeur for a gringo whose heart is set on drink. Doubtless you are 'injured' by the excess of your drinking. For such as you I feel no pity."

Through the line, I could feel the force of his yearning to slam down the receiver, the pressure of his desire to shout, You promised to find the killer of my son!

The thought that he was about to hang up sent a sting of panic through me. I fought the pain out of the way. "I don't know who killed your son." I stayed with English because I didn't have the strength for Spanish. "But I know how to find out. There are two men who might know the answer. If I can get to them tonight." The silence at the other end of the line changed. Trying not to sound like a wild man, I kept going. "They won't talk to the cops. They wouldn't even talk to you. But they might talk to me." If I got to them before they disappeared for the night. And if I looked and talked and smelled like the Mick Axbrewder they remembered, Axbrewder the drunk, tanked to the scalp with mescal and tired self-contempt. "I can't get to them if you don't give me a ride."

He didn't answer right away. I could hear him breath-

ing, thinking. Fighting his way through his tangled emotions. I was an Anglo and a drunk. And I wasn't just
asking him to trust me. I was asking for his faith.

Abruptly, he said, "I will come." Then he hung up.

For some reason, I didn't put the phone down. "Don't
forget the mescal," I said. I could get by without the
overcoat. I wasn't particularly worried about freezing to
death. But I had to have that bottle of mescal.

After a while, however, I noticed I had a dial tone
clamped to the side of my head. Moving my arm with a
jerk, I clattered the receiver back into its cradle.

Now all I had to do was get myself dressed and sneak
out of the hospital before the nurses told Ginny my room
number and she came to check on me (they certainly
weren't going to be able to make her wait for regular
visiting hours). That was all. A mere bag of towels, as
some clown I once knew used to say. Child's play.

Well, so was the Spanish Inquisition, if you just
thought about it from the right point of view. After all,
what was the worst that could happen? I could bleed to
death before I got anything done. But I'd heard that
bleeding to death was a rather peaceful way to die.

Unfortunately, I wasn't that easily reassured. I wasn't
especially concerned about dying. What I was really
afraid of was being caught and stopped.

So I leaned myself against the bed while I untaped the
other IV and pulled it out of my arm. Then I eased my
weight back onto my feet and began to inch my way
across the room toward the bureau.

Actually, sneaking out of the hospital wasn't going to
be that hard. I already knew how to do it. I'd sneaked in
once to see Ginny the night after her hand was blown off.
All I needed was a little luck.

On the other hand, getting myself dressed promised to
be a pure gold immaculate and absolute sonofabitch.

Concentrate on something else. A few weeks after I
left the bed, I arrived at the bureau. All my clothes and
possessions were in the paper sack. It should've been

easy to think about how thirsty I was. My mouth and throat felt like I'd eaten a pound of alum. My hospital pajamas shrugged to the floor without too much difficulty, and I got my first look at the bandages on my stomach. They had small red stains in them. I was so fascinated—in a horrible sort of way—I wanted to stand there and stare at them.

But Ginny might show up any minute. By twisting my shoulders into positions that gave me cramps, I managed to get my shirt on. The fabric was stiff with dried blood, and it had nice, neat holes in it over the bandages, front and back. I buttoned it approximately and tackled my pants.

Putting my pants on was hell. Double-dipped fire-and-brimstone with chocolate sauce and peanuts. The only thing that kept me going was the pain made me mad—too angry to give up. Then, instead of passing out, I pushed my feet into my shoes and slipped my jacket up my arms to my shoulders. The holster for the .45 I left behind. I didn't have the heart for it. With the dead weight of the gun in my jacket pocket, I fixed my attention on the door of the room and started toward it.

With my luck, I thought, Ginny'd arrive right then. Sure. But she didn't. I got to the door, and nobody was there. I couldn't hear anything except the way I whimpered when I breathed. When I mustered my courage—not to mention what you might laughingly call my strength—I opened the door a few inches and scanned the corridor. Nobody there at all.

Halfway down the hall from me, I saw the red-lit "Exit" sign and the door labeled "Emergency Exit Only." I didn't hesitate. Couldn't afford to. Leaving the room, I limped toward the exit as if I knew what I was doing.

Amazing. The secret to overcoming your fear of pain is just to be more afraid of everything else.

Unfortunately, after each ordeal there was another one ahead, and it looked worse than what I'd already been through. For instance, stairs. Lots of them. At least three or four flights. That sort of thing could be the life of the party. Hey, gang, I've got an idea! Let's all shoot ourselves in the belly and walk down stairs! Even hanging onto the rail with both hands, I felt the jolt of every step like my guts were being punted out of the stadium. It would've been a whole lot easier to just fall and roll to the bottom. Only the simple logic of the situation kept me going. I'm doing it, aren't I? If I'm doing it, then it must be possible. In fact, if I can do it in this condition, it must not be very hard at all.

The last flight, I lured myself with promises of water. When you get to the bottom, Axbrewder, you can go find a drinking fountain and have all you want. But I didn't keep that promise any better than all the rest I'd made. Instead, I went into one of those curious lapses of awareness where your body keeps on moving but you can't remember anything about it afterward. Since I was presumably in the surgical wing of University Hospital, I must've come out of the stairwell opposite the Emergency waiting room. I must've gone straight out through Emergency to the parking lot. And there must've been enough other people there to keep me from being noticed by the nurses and security guards. As far as I could remember, I lost track of things somewhere in the stairwell and came back to myself in the snow outside. The night and the clouds were closed down hard over the city, making everything black and thick and beyond redemption. But the Emergency and parking lot lights reflected off the snow, creating quaint pockets of visibility in the darkness. The snow was falling almost straight down, gently, without any wind behind it. For some reason, it didn't seem cold.

Cocooned in pain, my shoelaces untied and no socks on, I shuffled through the accumulating slush and tried to look conspicuous so Rudolfo Santiago could find me. I hoped I wasn't going to have to wait very long.

The headlights that slapped at me through the snowfall

almost knocked me down. They came forward slowly. They were aimed right at me—I must've been standing like a derelict in the middle of the right-of-way. Knives of light cut through my eyes and did things to the inside of my head. Then they stopped moving. A car door opened.

"Señor Axbrewder," he said. "I am come."

I didn't have the strength to move. Now that he was here, I had trouble remembering what I was supposed to do about it. But he had a front-row view of the leftover bloodstains on my jacket and shirt. After a minute, I heard him cursing.

He got out and came over to me. In the headlights, he looked like somebody'd poured acid into the wrinkles of his face, making them deep and dark. "Ay, Señor Axbrewder," he murmured, squinting concern up at me, "this is madness. You are indeed sorely injured. You must return to the hospital for your life."

A vagrant eddy of wind swirled snow across my face, and I almost fell. I shut my eyes, put one hand on his shoulder for support. "It's not as bad as it looks," I said thinly. I owed him Spanish, but I didn't have it in me. "I'm just a little weak. This'll only take a couple of hours. Then you can bring me back."

He wasn't particularly persuaded. "Haste will not restore Pablo to life. I desire that the *pendejo* killer of my son be repaid for his evil. Yes, assuredly. But one day or two or a week will change nothing. Is it necessary that you suffer?"

If I'd had any muscles left intact in my belly, I might've laughed. Sure. Why not? Suffering maybe doesn't make people any better than they used to be, but it's sure as hell educational. Anyway, sometimes it's the only thing you can do to pay your debts. But this was no time to stand around discussing religion. On top of that, I was failing fast. "I don't call it suffering," I said. "I call it doing my job."

He hesitated a minute longer. Then I felt him shrug. "As you wish. I will assist you."

He let me lean more of my weight on his shoulders and slowly guided me around to the passenger side of his car. It was so old it didn't seem to have any specific make or model anymore—it was just a generic clunker. But the engine still ran. The doors still opened. One of the windshield wipers worked. Doing the best I could to keep the stress off my torso, I eased my bulk into the car. But there was no way to sit that didn't put pressure on my guts.

Santiago closed my door, walked around to his side of the car, and got in. "Now, Señor Axbrewder," he said. "Where does one go to speak with these two men who may have knowledge of my son's killer?"

"The old part of town." I was definitely on my way out. "The little park on Tin Street." There didn't seem to be any way I could hold myself together. "Get as close as you can." It was going to be downright humiliating if I started to cry in front of him. "But stop before you can see the park." On the other hand, if I passed out, I might not regain consciousness for weeks. "Don't let them see you bring me."

His silence didn't sound like he'd understood a word. But he put the car in gear anyway. All Anglos are crazy. With exaggerated care because he wasn't used to snow, he began to creep out of the parking lot.

As it happened, I didn't start crying. And I didn't go the way of the goony bird. Pain has more imagination than you might expect from a mere sensation. Or maybe it's the way the brain reacts to pain. In any case, I hadn't exhausted the possibilities—not by a long shot. This time, the way I hurt was like the snow. Blown against the windshield and set dancing by the movement of the car. As blind as a wall because of the reflected light. Delicate and impenetrable. Hypnotic. I stared into the snowfall until it seemed the whole world was composed of nothing but misery.

And eventually it came to an end, the way everything does which is probably the nicest thing God has ever

done for us. Santiago nosed his car to the curb just
around the corner from the Tin Street park. When we
weren't moving, the snow swirled less and I was able to
see better. I recognized the place with an ache of famil-
iarity. I'd spent a lot of my life there, drunk out of my
mind. But not just drunk. Desperate, too. That park was
where I used to go when my self-revulsion finally got too
strong to be ignored—where I used to go and wait like I
was praying for Ginny to come along and rescue me, call
me back to work. When the bars closed, I went to the
park with drunks and bums like myself, whoever happened to be in the neighborhood that night, and we
shared whatever was left of whatever booze we'd managed to procure for ourselves against the long, lonely
dark, and then the others wandered off to their private
hovels, *barrios*, or beds, but I stayed where I was, sleeping curled up on a bench with my arms and knees hugged
over my stomach and waiting in the passive hope of the
damned for Ginny to come. The sight of the old place
sent a lick of panic along my nerves, and my head cleared
a bit.

We were blocked from view of the park by the blunt
edge of an adobe building. Santiago ditched his headlights, killed the engine. Abruptly, our enclosed little
world turned quiet. When my ears adjusted, I could hear
the faint, wet sound of snow on the hood and roof.

Santiago struck a match to light a cigarette, and the
yellow flare showed his face for a second. He looked old
and tired. But his eyes caught the light like bits of glass.

Sucking on the coal of his cigarette, he reached into
one of his pockets and brought out a flat pint bottle.

My hands shook when I took it. He watched me hard
while I pushed the pain out of my way and forced my
fingers to screw off the bottlecap. Right away, I smelled
mescal. It was strong as a shout. Thirst clenched my
throat. It was just possible if I took a good, long drink I
wouldn't hurt anymore.

Covering most of the mouth of the bottle with my

thumb, I splashed mescal onto my clothes. Quite a bit of it. I wanted to hide the stink of blood. Gritting my teeth, I unlatched the door and opened it a few inches so I could pour about a quarter of the bottle onto the street. Then I put the cap back on and dropped the bottle into my other jacket pocket, opposite the .45.

Santiago still didn't say anything. He reached into the back seat and produced an overcoat. The old cloth was greasy and smelled like mildew.

I had to get going. No time like the present. Apprehension and the scent of mescal made me urgent. I nodded toward the park. "You can wait in the car. Or watch from the corner. Just don't be seen. I'll try to get them to talk to me."

Pain burning in every muscle, I levered myself out of the car and stood up. I couldn't seem to get my arms into the sleeves of the overcoat—and anyway, it was pretty small for me—so I just pulled it onto my shoulders and let it hang. I could feel the cold now—the overcoat didn't make any difference. But at least I could hold it closed so the bloodstains wouldn't show.

Softly, Santiago murmured, "*Vaya con Dios.*"

Stiff-legged, slow, and awkward, I started forward to try my luck.

The snow was falling without interference now, soft and silent, covering everything. We weren't more than five blocks from where the Santiagos had their store. But in the old part of town the night belonged to Puerta del Sol's other population, its midnight denizens. In winter, the park was nothing more than three scruffy aspens and a few loose-jointed benches marking out patches of bare dirt in the dry, brown, untended grass. But the snow gave the place a blanket of beauty and innocence. I could see that because there was some light from the few streetlamps erratically installed and randomly vandalized around the area.

As I got closer, I could also see two hunched figures sitting together on a bench in the middle of the park.

I didn't have to pretend I was under the influence. The way my gut hurt was enough. I lumbered ahead slowly, my shoes full of snow. When I reached the edge of the park, I stopped, pulled out my bottle, took off the cap, corked the mouth with my thumb, and went through the motions of drinking. Then I put the bottle away and moved closer to the two men on the bench.

I didn't deserve to be so lucky. Oh, I'd earned some of it. I had a right to know their habits—I'd paid for that knowledge. But it was months and months old, a long time in the life of a drunk. Anything could've changed. I didn't deserve to find them there, right where I'd left them.

But there they were, not quite looking at me the same way I wasn't quite looking at them—Luis and Jaime. They'd spent so long soaking themselves in alcohol that the rest of their names, along with most of their past, had dissolved out of them. Twenty years ago, they were both powers in Puerta del Sol, purveyors of fine secrets and competitors for the leverage secrets could buy. But the world got away from them. The population boom in the city produced a geometric increase in the number, complexity, and value of whispers. Younger men, more cunning men, specialists came along, reducing Jaime and Luis to the status of amateurs. To survive, they began specializing themselves. But the heart had gone out of them, so naturally they gravitated to the subject with the least competition because it was the least interesting and violent—numbers gambling. With what they knew, their ability to advise and forewarn, to sift rumors or start them, they kept themselves in tortillas and mescal. And after enough mescal the past was mostly forgotten.

Jaime claimed—for no obvious reason—he was a good decade older than Luis. He looked like a shrunken version of me, his clothes stained in front and rotting under his arms, his cheeks grizzled, most of his teeth gone. He had a constant, openmouthed smile that made him look like an idiot. In contrast, Luis would've appeared almost dapper if all his clothes hadn't been at least fifteen years old. Somehow, he contrived to keep clean-shaven, barbered, even manicured. He had the face of a grandee, and he frowned at the world with disapproval and dignity.

But behind the differences they were closer to each other than brothers. No kinship of blood could compete with the mescal they'd shared.

They greeted me by lowering their eyes and not saying anything. I used to be a true companion—the amount I drank with them made up for the fact I was Anglo, and on the one hand I was too big for decency, but on the other my Spanish was good and honorable. But I'd been away, and maybe they'd heard the story I was sober. Nothing'd forfeit their toleration, never mind their trust, like being sober.

And if they didn't trust me, I was lost. They wouldn't answer my questions. But they'd sure as hell let el Señor know I was asking those questions. And el Señor wasn't likely to be forgiving, not after I'd already offended him once. What I was doing was probably more dangerous than going to talk to him in person.

Jaime and Luis waited, courteous and noncommittal, for me to do something.

I didn't look at them directly, either. I was too far gone to have much grasp on the danger. But I needed answers. After a minute of mutual politeness, I took out my bottle again and offered it to them.

Jaime grinned into the snow. Luis gave me a nod like a bow, accepted the bottle gravely, and sampled it. Then he passed it to Jaime. Like his companion, Jaime drank precisely the right amount for good manners—enough to compliment the mescal, not enough to seriously lower the level in the bottle. Still grinning, he handed it back to me.

I screwed the cap onto the bottle. But I didn't put it away.

Their eyes on the mescal, Jaime and Luis shifted over, making room for me on the bench.

"*Gracias*." The screaming chainsaw in my stomach made the word come out blurred and thick. Carefully, I eased myself to the bench and tried to make my involuntary whimpering sound like a sigh. I felt like I was going to faint. "Are you well?"

"Very well," Luis replied. He had a bottle of his own propped between his thighs. That was why he and Jaime were here—their bottle wasn't finished. But it was nearly empty. I'd caught them just in time.

"Luis is heartless," Jaime put in at once. "Very well, he says. He is very well. Assuredly so. He does not suffer as I do. He has no piles to make his life a torment." His tone was as amiable as his smile. He'd been complaining for so many years it'd become a gesture of friendship. "He has been spared the canker which eats in the gums, causing the teeth to fall out. Unkindly, he says that he is well while my pain grows extreme."

That was a hint. "I, too, suffer," I said. "Providentially, there is solace." I uncapped my bottle and handed it to Luis.

He took a swig and gave the bottle to Jaime. While Jaime drank, Luis said to me, "This one lacks all fortitude. Others feel pain also, but they do not speak of it constantly."

"Truly." I needed a way to make the conversation do what I wanted. But my feet were freezing, and thirst and pain muddled my mind. "However, fortitude and honor are alike. Not all possess them equally." While part of my brain tried to concentrate, the rest kept yearning for drink. "As one man varies from another, so one people varies from another."

Jaime nodded, passing the bottle back to Luis. "It is so. Lacking my pain, you do not understand my fortitude."

Luis looked at him. "Without question it is true that your fortitude is either greater or less than any other. But that is as Señor Axbrewder has said. Not all possess fortitude and honor equally."

That was a step in the right direction. Luis used my

name, admitted he knew me. And while Luis drank from
my bottle, Jaime aimed what was left of his teeth at me
companionably. "And also one people varies from another," he agreed. "I have heard it said that the Anglos
know as little of courage and dignity as of good manners." He seemed to be insulting me. But there was no
insult in his tone. And he went on quickly, "But behold
Señor Axbrewder. He admits that he suffers. Yet he does
not speak of it. And his politeness is well known." In
demonstration, he took my bottle from Luis. "It becomes
necessary to think better of Anglos."

He was asking me obliquely to account for myself.

I didn't exactly feel equal to the occasion, as they say.
In front of me, the world seemed to be bleeding away at
the edges. Everything was muzzy with snow. But I'd already come this far. It was silly not to say something.

"Ah, it is nothing. I suffer loneliness only. It shames
one to speak of it."

Luis cocked an aristocratic eyebrow. "The woman," he
asked delicately, "the private *chota* who gave you em-
ployment—? A man must have a woman. Does she not
ease your loneliness?"

"That one," I murmured, hoping my pain sounded like
disgust and sorrow. "At one time, I took great gladness
in her. But since the loss of her hand"—it was a safe bet
Luis and Jaime knew the story of that bomb and Ginny's
injury—"she has become shrewish. She permits me no
rest. She demands my service in every way. It is not
enough that I must do her work. I must drive her car. I
must clean. I must cook. I am a servant to her." If I'd
told that story to anybody else, I'd've been met with embarrassment and male shame, men wondering how I
could let myself be humiliated like that. But Jaime and
Luis were drunks. Like me. They were intimately familiar with humiliation. As it was, I wasn't doing Ginny's
reputation any good—but that didn't matter at the moment. What mattered was to provide a reason why I'd
gone away—and why I was back. "*Compadres*, it is un-

believable. She requires me to kneel before her to place her shoes upon her feet.

"Also," I said, "she denies me a man's right of strong drink."

Luis understood implicitly. He handed me my bottle. And while I cradled it in my hands and wondered how to get rid of it, Jaime took the bait I was dangling in front of him.

"Plainly," he said, "she is a woman of no fortitude."

And Luis said, "All women are harridans. But the saints know that no woman of our people would behave thus to a man. To require that he kneel before her!"

"Your pardon. It is not my place to complain." Deferentially, I passed the bottle back. "But it becomes a man to be philosophical. I wish to understand the differences of our women. To me, it appears that all Anglo women are as mine, lacking fortitude and courage, and holding a great contempt for their men. Yet the women of your people are such as Señora Santiago, bearing herself with dignity and reserve even when her son is slain."

I was starting to rush. I stopped and held my breath while my heart thudded.

Luis took a long drink and gave the bottle to Jaime. I couldn't see any change in Jaime. But Luis's face seemed sharper, harder. The snow muffled everything around us. The only sounds we heard were our own voices and breathing. I could feel blood seeping from my bandages down into my pants.

Luis asked evenly, "Are you acquainted with Señora Santiago?"

"*Sí*, surely." I couldn't make myself sound casual, so I didn't try. "Señor and Señora Santiago hired service from me some years ago. In return, they honored me with their respect. I grieve for Pablo with them." Then I couldn't stop. I was out of my depth—and out of strength. Harshly, I demanded rhetorically, "What manner of man kills the son of such parents as Señor and Señora Santiago?"

Luis was still watching me like he'd caught a whiff of something he didn't like. But Jaime lowered the bottle—empty now—and grinned like a banshee.

"A gringo."

I wanted to pass out. A gringo? Not Chavez? *Not* Chavez? I gave an involuntary twitch of surprise, and the pain almost tore a yell past my teeth. "Ah, then it is simple," I said, trying to defuse my improper intensity. "Pablo was slain by a gringo. Therefore the matter is one of money."

"Assuredly." Jaime sounded almost happy. "The night was Saturday. Pablo bore with him the winnings for his numbers." In an almost simpleminded way, he seemed proud of his knowledge for its own sake. "Twenty thousands of dollars."

That was it. The whole thing. Just, *A gringo*. And, *Twenty thousands of dollars*. It proved exactly nothing. Nothing of any kind. And yet it gave me almost the entire story.

Almost. Never mind the fact I didn't think I was going to be able to walk as far as Santiago's car. There was one detail I might be wrong about. One bit of information that might change everything.

But I wasn't going to get to ask. Luis's eyes had gone hard. Whatever it was he didn't like had become clear to him. Even though he and Jaime were drunk, I was no match for either of them. And if they thought I was manipulating them, using them for some Anglo reason, they'd need no more than ten minutes, tops, to contact el Señor.

"Señor Axbrewder," Luis said softly, "you do not drink with us." He reached for the bottle Jaime held. But it was empty. He tossed it away into the snow and lifted his own. It still held an inch of mescal. "You have shared generously with us. Permit me to share with you."

He extended the bottle toward me.

Just like that, I was trapped. I hadn't thought this mess through before I got into it. With the radar of the drunk, he'd realized there was something wrong with me. This was the test. If I drank—and if I was careful—I was all right. If I refused, I might find myself installed in a storm drain before morning.

I wanted to drink. I was dying of thirst anyway. And I was the one who'd gotten us into trouble. I hadn't told Ginny about Pablo. I wanted to drink myself out of my skull—and to hell with it.

But there was something else I wanted worse. I wanted to get even with that bastard. I wanted to nail him to the wall for what he'd done. If I was right about him.

I reached for the bottle.

And fumbled it.

A quick lurch to try to catch it pulled a cry out of my chest, and I fell off the bench, face down into the snow.

On top of the bottle.

For a minute, the agony held me there. Then Luis and Jaime lifted me by my arms. At first, they weren't gentle. But then they saw the bloodstains on my shirt. Surprise changed everything for them, too. "Mother of God," Jaime breathed. "Shot. This is madness, Señor Axbrewder. Whose bullet have you caught?"

Panting hard and shallow, I fought for balance, strength, anything to keep me going. "Muy Estobal."

"*Pendejo!*" Jaime dropped my arm roughly. "You are truly mad. Do you believe I also wish to be shot?" Turning and cursing, he hurried away into the snowfall. I lost sight of him almost at once.

I should've fallen. But Luis didn't let me. When I swung my head around to look at him, he seemed to be smiling.

"You have fortitude, Señor Axbrewder," he said. "Also *cojones*. I honor that."

"Please." My Spanish was gone. I was almost gone. I felt like that fall did something terrible to me. "Tell me why Chavez was killed."

Luis gave a snort that might've been laughter. "El Señor came upon the Bambino making the beast of two backs with his daughter."

That fit. It all fit. I was going to go down. But Luis held me up until Santiago came out of the snow to take me away.

Chapter Twenty

For a while, snow seemed to be all there was. It fell everywhere in silence, the way dead men grieve. But then I felt something warmer against the welts around my eyes. The posture I was in put pressure on my guts, sharpening the hurt. I was sitting down. Apparently, I was in the passenger seat of Santiago's car. The heater blew at me, melting the snow in my hair, warming it away from my face. I'd lost my overcoat in the park.

"Now hear me, Señor Axbrewder." Santiago's voice was congested with emotion and uncertainty. "You are seriously unwell. If you do not speak to me, I must return you to the hospital."

Well, that made sense. After all, he had to take my word for the condition I was in. If I couldn't talk, he had every reason to assume the worst.

But I didn't want to go to the hospital. I didn't have any evidence. If I went back to the hospital, I could lie there and tell people what I thought to my heart's content, but nobody was going to do anything about it. Not as long as I couldn't produce one measly scrap of sane or at least concrete evidence to back me up.

And there was something else. Something itching at the back of my brain. Only I couldn't remember what it was. I was fine as long as I let the pain do my thinking for me. But when I tried to impose what I wanted on the process—

Not Luis. But Jaime. Jaime for sure. He was going to pass word to el Señor I was walking around the Tin Street park with a bullet hole in my belly, asking questions about Pablo.

That wasn't it. But it was important enough to get my attention. With an effort that made me want to puke, I lifted my head from the back of the seat. "I hear you," I breathed thinly. "I'll be all right. Just need a little rest. Don't take me back. Not yet."

He studied me closely. I couldn't look like I was really all right, so I tried to look like it didn't matter. After a minute, he demanded softly, "Have you learned who killed my son?"

"*Sí.*" I answered in Spanish to make him believe me. "I know him."

For an instant, his eyes widened. Then his face closed. All the pity that made him take care of me was gone. "Let us go. He must be made to pay for what he has done."

I agreed. It sounded simple enough, when you put it that way. Leaning my head on the seatback again like I couldn't carry the weight of what I was thinking, I gave him Reg Haskell's address and told him how to get there.

In response, he jerked his old clunker into gear and started so hard we went out of control around the corner and almost broke an axle on the opposite curb. That reminded him he didn't know how to drive on snow. He got a better grip on himself and tried again, slowly this time. We eased out onto the road and began to work northeast through the old part of town, heading for the Heights.

Of course, Haskell wasn't going to be there. I mused on that instead of watching where we were going. Ginny'd turned him over to the cops. To Acton, who was at least honest. But that was just as well. I was in no

condition to deal with Haskell. All I wanted was to tear
his house apart until I found something, anything, that
might pass for evidence. So he wouldn't have a chance to
lie his way out of trouble again.

But that connected to what I was trying to remember.
Ginny'd turned Haskell over to Acton. But she was
bound to mention Muy Estobal. And that implied el
Señor. And—now it was coming back to me—as soon as
el Señor's name came up, the case'd go over to Cason.

Bingo. Captain Cason. He rousted me for concealing
evidence of a crime—and then didn't bother to do anything about it. Because the real reason he was after me
was that the cab driver overheard Haskell and me talking
about el Señor. But when Canthorpe demonstrated that
Haskell was lying, Cason lost interest in both of us.

For the first time in what seemed like forever, I found
myself wondering whether that made any sense. Cason
was responsible for investigating the long-overdue demise
of Roscoe Chavez. So a rented car got blown up, and
neither the renter nor his passenger waited around to be
questioned, and the cab driver who took them home reported they spent the drive talking about an el Señor
money laundry. So the matter was passed to Cason because it might connect with his investigation. So he identified Axbrewder and Haskell and went to all the trouble
to tail and roust Axbrewder. And then he learned
Haskell's story was a fake. So he forgot the whole thing.

Oh, really?

Think about that for a minute, Axbrewder, old
buddy—I mean, since you don't have anything better to
do, and loss of blood is making you feel light-headed
anyway. Ask yourself what kind of man tries to give himself an alibi by inventing lies about el Señor. And ask
yourself how many Anglos in Puerta del Sol, *especially*
bank accountants, even know el Señor exists? If you
were Cason—who hates your guts, pardon the expression—wouldn't you be just the teeniest bit curious about
what the hell was going on?

Sure you would.

Either Cason wasn't. Or he had some other reason for letting us go.

I didn't like the sound of that much.

From time to time, I noticed where we were, but I didn't have the strength to concentrate on it. There probably wasn't much leftover painkiller in my system. And there was a damp sensation under my shirt that was probably blood. The only advantage was my head really did seem to be getting clearer. In other words, I was beginning to understand just how lunatic what I was trying to do was.

Also I was beginning to wonder how Ginny'd react when she went to my room and saw I was gone. Whatever she did, it wasn't likely to be gentle. For either of us.

I'd almost talked myself into doing something reasonable for a change, like stopping at a phone booth to call the hospital, talk to Ginny or leave a message, when Santiago's relic brought us up Foothill to the top of Cactus Blossom Court.

The snow was still falling. It was at least a couple of inches thick on the road. Santiago approached the slope carefully so he wouldn't start into a skid. I had plenty of time to see Ginny'd left all of Haskell's lights on.

His Continental was parked in the driveway.

That didn't mean anything. After hearing Ginny's story, Acton wasn't likely to let Haskell drive himself downtown. But seeing his car there reminded me of all the times I'd been wrong—and how easy it was to get into trouble just by walking into Haskell's house. With an effort, I pulled myself together and told Santiago to stop.

Still near the top of the hill, he slid the car to a halt against the curb. Some instinct prompted him to turn off the headlights and cut the engine. Darkness seemed to swallow us while my eyes adjusted, but soon I could see Haskell's house clearly through the snow.

Santiago eyed the house, then looked back at me. Automatically, he stuck a cigarette in his mouth. But he didn't light it. "This Anglo who killed my son—this 'Reg Haskell'—he lives there?"

I nodded.

He turned toward the house again. Roughly, he asked, "What is your intent?"

I had to come up with the right answer to keep him out of trouble, so he wouldn't end up paying for any of my mistakes. "I'm going down there." I tried to sound like I knew what I was doing, but the pain made me too harsh. "You're going to wait here."

The way he stared at me told me I had to do better than that. I tried again.

"He isn't home right now. The *chotas* have him. But they don't know he killed Pablo. They might keep him in protective custody for a while. Or they might let him go.

"I want to search his house. For evidence. I want to prove what he did. But if the *chotas* let him go and he comes back—or if they come to search his house themselves—or if Muy Estobal shows up again—and they catch me in there, I'm finished. If I don't end up dead, I'll be back in the hospital—or jail—and nobody'll believe you when you say he killed your son. You won't have any proof.

"Unless you stay here and watch. So you can warn me if anybody comes. If you see anybody walk up to the house, honk your horn. Twice, short and quick. But don't honk until you're sure of what they're doing. And make sure they don't see you. If they don't see you, they might not guess where the sound came from." And you won't be in as much danger.

Santiago didn't like that. But all this was new to him, and he didn't know how to argue with me. "You are certain this killer is not in his house?"

"No," I said in Spanish. "But I believe it. Yet because of the hazard I cannot go to search for evidence unless you consent to keep watch for me."

The end of his cigarette bobbed up and down as his jaw muscles knotted. This wasn't exactly his idea of revenge. "Señor Santiago," I said softly, "Pablo was your son. But we have no evidence. Without evidence it is possible to be mistaken. Any man may accuse another, out of malice or error. For that reason there is law. If you wish to commit murder yourself, return me to the hospital and go your own way."

He was a good man—angry as hell, hurt, bitter, and hungry for violence or relief, but a good man. After a long minute, he sighed and let his weight sag into the seat. "I will keep watch. Did not I myself attempt to teach my son the importance of law? Him I failed. I will not fail you."

I wanted to thank him, but I didn't know how. So I wouldn't change my mind or lose my nerve, I creaked open the door, put my feet into the snow, and lifted my torn guts out of the car.

The light from the streetlamps was full of snow. Flakes drifted heavily into my face. I closed the door with my hip and leaned against it, trying to call up reserves of strength or at least stubbornness that'd probably been exhausted two days ago. Then I hunched over the pain, folded my arms protectively across my stomach, and started down toward the house.

I had to move slowly, carefully—the footing was bad, and if I slipped the fall would rip what was left of my insides apart. But I made it. The snow covered my footsteps. I didn't make a sound as I crossed the gravel. Here the light was bright through the snowfall. There was no point in pretending to be stealthy—and I was in no shape for it anyway. Fumbling in my pockets for the keys, I passed the cedars and went straight down the aisle to the door.

It was a good thing the snow kept me so quiet. If he'd heard me coming, God knows what he would've done. But as it was, he only had a few seconds' warning while my key twisted the lock. Then I got the door open and found myself standing right in front of him.

Our client, Reg Haskell.

For a minute, we stared at each other. His eyes seemed to go blank at first. But then they got brighter and sharper, as if somewhere in the back of his head he was turning up a rheostat of adrenaline or excitement. "By God, Axbrewder," he said, "if you weren't right here I would've sworn nobody could walk around with a bullet in his stomach. You're astonishing. How do you do it?"

He was standing at the top of the stairs. He hadn't changed his clothes since the last time I saw him—but there was a suitcase on the floor on either side of him.

I closed the door (I couldn't see any point in relocking it, so I didn't bother) and took a few steps toward him, carrying the pain as well as I could. My right hand slipped into the pocket of my jacket and wrapped around the butt of the .45. A detached part of my mind wondered how far he was going. Did he mean to skip town completely, leave the state and maybe even the country? And if so, was he going to take his wife? Or did he just want to hide from el Señor for a while? But I didn't ask those questions out loud. I was still too surprised.

I stopped a few feet away from him, and he looked at me more closely. Concern that might conceivably have been genuine crossed his face. "Axbrewder, you look terrible. What are you doing to yourself? You're a wreck."

Panic and thirst closed my throat. I was in no condition to deal with him, no condition at all. When I got my voice working, it seemed to come through miles of cotton.

"Cason let you go."

He ignored me. "Can I get you something? I mean it. You look terrible. You ought to lie down. How about a glass of water?"

A glass of water would've been heaven. I had to glare at him until my skull throbbed in order to concentrate. "Why did Cason let you go?"

Haskell shrugged. "I told him the truth. He didn't have any reason to hold me."

"What was the truth? I've never heard it from you. I've never heard anything except lies." I wanted to cut into him somehow, lay him bare. But I didn't have the strength. I sounded like I'd swallowed a bucket of sand. "Lies are part of the game. That's how you play people. You don't really care about cards or dice or coins. The kind of gambling you're addicted to is manipulating people."

Then I stopped. I wasn't getting anywhere. He just stood there and looked at me like I'd gone out of my mind. I changed directions. "Never mind. I already know what you probably told him." Actually, I had no idea—but that didn't matter at the moment. "Tell me something else. Why did you hire Ginny and me in the first place? You must've known you were taking a risk. You talked to Smithsonian about us. He's slimy and unscrupulous, but he's not stupid. Why buy that kind of trouble for yourself?"

"Come on, Axbrewder." Haskell didn't show a flicker of uncertainty or fear. "You know the answer to that. I needed protection. So I needed somebody honest and tough enough to face el Señor, and I could see Smithsonian didn't fit that description. At the same time, I wanted somebody who didn't have the resources, either of money or personnel or intelligence"—he didn't mind calling a spade a spade—"to mess with things I wanted left alone. You and Fistoulari looked like exactly what I had in mind.

"You scared me for a while. I thought I'd made a mistake—and I don't make very many. You kept prying into my life instead of trying to nail the people who want me dead. I said I was going to fire you, and I meant it. But then I saw that Fistoulari was coming unglued." His contempt was plain in his voice. "She was panicked just thinking about el Señor. After that, I knew I didn't have to worry about her. And you were still too stubborn to give up trying to protect me."

Abruptly, he shrugged. "Now I don't need you anymore. Captain Cason's going to take care of el Señor for me. Your job's finished." Then his concern came back. "Why not let me call an ambulance? You ought to get back to the hospital."

He made me so mad I wanted to pull out the .45 and start shooting. But I didn't. Instead, I nodded at his suitcases. "Cason's going to take care of el Señor for you. Is that why you're on the run? Where do you think you can hide so el Señor can't find you?"

At first, he affected surprise. "On the run?" Then he gave me one of his laughs. I hated his laughs. "You have brain fever, Axbrewder. I'm not running anywhere. I'm going to join Sara. I'm going to check into her hotel, and we'll have a kind of mini-honeymoon. Celebrate the end of my problems. Captain Cason already has the room number, in case he needs us for anything."

He said it so well I almost wanted to believe him. There must've been a logical flaw in his lies. Or some way to trick him. But I didn't have the time or the stamina for either logic or cunning. I just had to trust my intuitions and do what came naturally.

"If Cason let you go," I said, "you must not've told him the whole truth. You must not've told him you killed Pablo Santiago."

At least I got his attention. His eyes went wide and his mouth opened. "Who?"

Then for the first time it occurred to me he might not know Pablo's name.

"Pablo Santiago." The last of my endurance was oozing out of me, and I didn't have anything that so much as resembled evidence. "That kid you killed. The numbers runner.

"All that crap about Roscoe Chavez. You got his name out of the newspaper. You never had anything to do with him. You just used him to give us a reason why el Señor's after you. Just like that crock about the money laundry. Or the one about welshing on a bet. The truth is, he

wants you dead because you murdered one of his runners."

Haskell looked shaken. Maybe he really was shaken.
"Axbrewder," he muttered. "What in hell—? You must
be out of your mind. Where did you *get* an idea like
that?"

"From you." Small dark spots were starting to swim
across my vision. My throat was raw for something to
drink. "Your priorities are so screwed up. You hire two
professionals to protect you, and then you handcuff them
with lies to keep them from doing their job. People who
don't have something serious to hide don't act like that.

"So you've been having trouble with your investments.
Gambling's like that. You got hooked on the excitement—and the fancy living—so you just kept digging
yourself in deeper. Like any other kind of addict." I
knew all about it. "And when things got bad enough, you
decided to try to clean up playing the numbers. So Friday
night you goosed your bank out of five thousand dollars
and went down to the old part of town for some more
investing.

"But Saturday night when you went to pick up your
winnings the very first runner you met told you there
weren't going to be any winnings. Imagine that. He had
packets of money stuffed all over his body, twenty thousand dollars—but none of it was for you. Only he didn't
realize you're such a hotshot nobody can beat you and
you're willing to take on any kind of odds just to prove
how virile and fucking *alive* you are." Between anger and
pain, I was close to passing out. "So he probably didn't
even try to resist when you took hold of him and broke
his neck and piled him into your car—or piled him into
your car and then broke his neck—and drove away.
Then, when you had all the money, you pitched him out
on Trujillo so the cops'd think he was killed by the fall
while maybe he and his buddies were out joyriding. It
was all so easy. Probably made you feel like a real man.
You only made about half a dozen mistakes."

"Mistakes?" He looked like he'd never heard the word before.

"You didn't stop to think runners are bound to have some kind of supervision. And whoever does the supervising has the job of knowing all the bettors—so if the runner quits, or gets fired or promoted, or dies, the supervisor can bring in a new kid without having to start from scratch. Also he sets up the runner's schedule. You had to use some kind of identifying word or name to place your bets. He got all that, along with your description. Only you were so clever, you went to a bunch of runners and placed a whole series of bets. And when the supervisor heard about one man placing all those different bets, he got suspicious. So he probably had Pablo tailed. There was probably an eyewitness when you killed him. That was how you were found so fast—the witness followed you home.

"On top of that, you went and put in your bank account Monday morning exactly the same amount of money el Señor lost when Pablo was killed. Also"—I was about at the end—"you made the mistake of killing a kid I knew and liked. His parents deserved a whole lot better than what you did to them."

For a minute, Haskell just stood there and stared at me. Then he chuckled softly. I didn't have any idea what was going on inside him. "You know," he said, "you have a hell of an imagination, Axbrewder. If Roscoe were alive, he'd laugh himself silly. He and I were willing to try a scam. But not murder!"

"No," I said. "That one isn't going to work, either. Chavez was killed because he got caught sleeping with el Señor's daughter. It didn't have anything to do with business."

"Really?" The thought fascinated him. "Then maybe we could've gotten away with it after all. Maybe I could've—" But abruptly he shook his head, made a dismissive gesture. "I don't care about that right now. You have to have some help. I can't just let you die in front of me like this. First I'm going to get you some water. Then I'm going to call an ambulance." He showed no hesitation as he started for the living room. "Come on. In here you can at least sit down." Decisively, he walked into the room and headed toward the wetbar.

I tightened my grip on the .45 and went after him. What else could I do? He was right—I needed a drink of water and an ambulance, in that order. Almost immediately. I was so thirsty, my whole head felt like it was on fire, and the dampness under the waist of my pants was getting worse.

Vaguely, I noticed it was cold in the living room. For a second there, I couldn't figure out why. Then I realized the window was still open. He hadn't bothered to close it. Snow was collecting on the sill and the carpet. Which meant—

Come on, Axbrewder. What does it mean?

It means he's in a hurry. That's it. He's in such a hurry to get out, he didn't even bother to close the window.

The analytical mind at work. A veritable steel trap.

He'd gone behind the wetbar. Stupid of me to let him do that. Now I couldn't see his hands. I tried to squeeze the .45 even harder, but my arm seemed to be losing sensation—all the blood was draining out of it. Fortunately, I could hear liquid, pouring sounds. Then he came out from behind the bar, carrying a full highball glass.

He pushed the glass in my direction. "Here. Drink this. I don't care if you think you're God Himself. You can't last much longer."

How did he know I was so thirsty?

My vision was going gray at the edges. All my senses contracted around the glass in his hand, focusing on it, shutting out everything else. After all, I'd lost a lot of blood. I needed fluids.

Still hanging onto the .45 with my right hand, I took the glass in my left. Haskell smiled like a cherub while I pulled the glass up to my face and drank.

But that wasn't water in the glass. It was vodka.

My reflexes were too slow to stop the first couple swallows. Then I started to gag and sputter, tearing up my stomach. The glass fell somewhere—vodka sprayed at Haskell. He ducked, backed away. I tugged the .45 out of my pocket—

—and alcohol bit into my guts like the business edge of a bandsaw.

I didn't scream. Not me. It was the whole room that screamed. The floor shrieked under my feet and the walls howled agony at each other and the dark, wooden bellow of the wetbar hit me like a club. The lights exploded in my head, bits of glass and anguish squalling back and forth until my brain was ripped to tatters. Some goon with a crane and a meathook caught me by the belly and yanked me off my feet, but I never saw him.

I couldn't see anything at all, except Haskell. He was the world—what was left of it, anyway—and he straddled me like a conquering hero. He had the .45 in both hands. It was pointed into my face.

"Actually"—he sounded like he was screaming too, but that couldn't be right, he must've been gloating—"it does make me feel *fucking* alive. You're tough, but you've never been a match for me. Didn't anybody ever tell you you can't drink anything when you have a hole in your stomach?"

No. Nobody ever told me.

Maybe I was finally out of my head. Behind the way the room seemed to yowl and screech, I could've sworn I heard a car horn. Two quick cries in the distance, like a wail with its throat cut.

Apparently, I was wrong. Haskell didn't react. He was aimed at me.

"But you're worth your pay," he smirked, "I'll give you that. You've finally saved me. Now I don't have to run. All I have to do is wait here until el Señor sends somebody after me again. I'll shoot him with your gun.

Just to be safe, I'll shoot you with his gun. That'll buy me enough time to figure out what I want to do next."

No, I wasn't out of my head. I should've been, but I wasn't. He heard the same thing I did.

A key in the lock of the front door.

It's always the trivial details that kill you. If Ginny had known I left the door unlocked, she could've walked right in and nailed Haskell. Or if I'd locked the door behind me, one turn of the key would've unlocked it and she still might've been quick enough to catch him. But her first twist locked the door. Then she spent a couple seconds rattling the knob before she tried turning the key the other way.

Haskell had enough time to catfoot into the atrium.

All he wanted was to shoot one of el Señor's men. But he knew none of them had a key to his front door. And he couldn't risk killing somebody else with my gun.

Her key still in her hand, Ginny got the door open. She was in a hurry—too much of a hurry to be careful. Her eyes scanned the atrium. Then she saw me through the doorway. Simple horror seemed to make my vision as clear as sunlight.

She was wearing her claw. Its stainless steel hooks caught the light and leered like a grin in double vision.

I tried to shout a warning. I tried with all my heart. But I couldn't control my diaphragm—or any of the other muscles in my chest, for that matter. Maybe I wasn't breathing at all. I really didn't know. I gaped in her direction like a stranded fish, but nothing came out of my mouth.

Then it was too late. Haskell hit her on the back of the neck with the butt of the .45, and she dove face first into the carpet.

When he saw she wasn't moving, he smiled as if he could hardly keep his laughter to himself. With the side of his foot, he pushed the door shut, but he didn't take his eyes off Ginny and me. "Better and better," he chortled softly. "I told you I don't need luck. Skill makes its own luck." He was having the time of his life.

But he didn't forget to be cautious. He kept Ginny covered while he went to her purse and helped himself to her .357. Then he disappeared into the bedroom while I gagged and retched up blood and tried to move and couldn't. When he returned, he had a thick roll of white bandage tape in one hand.

Deftly, like he'd been practicing for years, he taped Ginny's wrists together behind her. Still grinning, he dragged her by the shoulders of her coat into the living room and dropped her beside me. I was so paralyzed with pain I couldn't even twitch when he pushed me onto my front, tugged my arms behind me, and strapped my wrists with tape, too. Then—just to keep me from getting bored—he hooked a shoe under my rib cage and levered me onto my side.

(Did I scream that time? Not old man-of-steel Axbrewder. My mind went blank with complete, perfect, transcendental agony, and I just lay there and tried to be dead.)

"This is going to be quite a shootout," he said. He had a gun in each hand, for all the world like a kid playing the best game of cowboys-and-Indians. But he looked like he knew what the guns were for. "I should be able to take care of all my enemies at once. One of you is going to shoot whoever el Señor sends after me. Not her." Enjoying his own contempt, he kicked Ginny's artificial hand. "She doesn't deserve it. I'll give you that honor. It'll do wonders for your reputation. Unfortunately, you won't survive to take the credit. And el Señor won't be able to tackle me again for a while. He'll be too busy defending himself against a double murder charge. Even if the cops can't prove anything on him, I'll still be innocent. I'll be able to walk away with twenty thousand dollars and a fresh start.

"All I have to do is set it up and wait." Abruptly, he seemed to remember he still had things to do. He put the guns in his pockets, moved to the wall switch, and snapped off the living room lights. "Don't worry," he said back to me. "You probably won't have to stay in the dark very long. Just long enough for el Señor's hood to walk into the trap. With the lights off, they'll think I'm going to bed. They'll come after me soon." Then he left the room. In the atrium, he hit the switches for all the entryway and exterior lights.

A glow from the lower level of the house lit his way down the stairs. After that, I couldn't see him anymore. When he reached the bottom, he flipped more switches, and the last glow vanished. Night seemed to come rushing into the room through the open window—darkness as cold as the snow.

In the dark, I could hear Ginny breathing raggedly. She sounded like Haskell'd broken her skull.

When I tried to say her name, nothing came out.

Everything else was silent, muffled by snow and pain— the night outside the house, Haskell's movements downstairs, my internal bleeding—everything except the raw, faint rasp of air in and out of Ginny's lungs. I tried again.

But I didn't make a sound.

Dear God, what if he really broke her skull? Come on, Axbrewder, you bastard!

"Ginny."

Ginny Ginny Ginny, like an echo down into the bottom of an abyss.

No answer.

Ginny Ginny—

—stop. Forget the pain. So it hurts. So what? Push it out of the way. Try again.

"Ginny." For God's sake. "Wake up."

From so far away the distance wrenched my heart, I heard her breathing catch. She took in a muffled gasp, let out a groan. "God," she exhaled. "God damn that sonofabitch." A slurred murmur. "Who in hell—?"

Through the dark, I felt her stiffen. "What happened? Brew?" Her voice started to rise. "Brew?"

"Quiet," I sighed at her. I felt like I was whispering blood. "He'll hear you."

"Who? Where are you?" I heard her scuffling around,

and her head knocked against my shoulder. "Mick Axbrewder," she hissed furiously, "what in *hell* are you doing here?"

"Haskell's here." My voice was a wisp. It sounded even farther away than she did. "He's going to kill us."

She froze. I thought I could feel her listening to the dark. After a minute, she breathed carefully, "Why?"

Working at it practically one word at a time, I gave her all the explanation I had strength for. "He lied to us. He stole that twenty thousand. From a runner. He broke the kid's neck." My memory was playing tricks on me. I saw that parking lot attendant burning horribly in the Buick. I saw Señora Santiago cover her face with her apron. I thought I could hear Ginny hitting her stump against the wall of the den. "Pablo Santiago." I should've told her when I first read it in the paper. But I needed it for myself. To help me bear the grief of losing her. "That's why el Señor—"

"Why el Señor wants him dead," she finished for me. "Damn right." Then she faltered. "Pablo Santiago?" She'd known his parents as well as I had.

"Yes." I felt like I was weeping.

She sighed. "I wish I'd known. It might've made a difference."

Of course it would've made a difference. She would've understood what I was up to. But that wasn't the difference she had in mind. Her voice hardened.

"When I went to your room—when I saw you weren't there—I almost threw a fit. Maybe I would have, but I knew I didn't have the time. I had to catch you before you got out of the hospital.

"One of the ER nurses remembered seeing you walk out to the parking lot. And one of the security guards remembered seeing you picked up by a man in an old clunker. They didn't stop you because it never occurred to them you might be a patient. That left me with nothing. You were gone." She choked momentarily on the word. "I didn't have any idea what craziness you had in

mind. All I knew was, you had a bullet hole in your guts
and were probably bleeding like a stuck pig.

"So I went to see el Señor."

"What?" Somehow, she surprised me enough to get
through the pain. "You went—?"

"Sure. What else did you expect? I had to assume that
was where you were going. Either because of Muy Estobal, or to try to save Haskell's skin. Nothing else made
any sense. So I tried to get there ahead of you.

"I didn't see Estobal anywhere around El Machismo.
When I finally talked my way into el Señor's office, I told
him to call off his dogs. We'd turned Haskell over to the
cops, and that was the end of the case as far as we were
concerned. He didn't have any reason to go after us anymore. Besides, he was already ahead of the game. You
were the one who got hit—Estobal didn't have a scratch.
I told him to leave us alone."

I tried to imagine anybody in Puerta del Sol telling el
Señor what to do. But I couldn't.

"He just laughed at me. When he laughs at people—.
He told me that Haskell had already been released by the
cops—as I surely must have known, why else would I go
to el Señor with such a childish trick?—and that nothing
I could do or say was going to save his life. Or the life of
anybody who got in the way. Then I was escorted out of
El Machismo.

"I wanted to ask him how he knew what the cops were
doing with Haskell. But I didn't get the chance.

"After that, I had to move fast. First I went back to
the apartment, got the claw. I hate it, but it's better than
nothing. Then I came here."

Musing blood, I figured out the rest. Now I knew what
was going to happen. I knew what she was going to do.

I couldn't bear it. The simple thought made me want
to throw up. Nobody in their right mind would take that
kind of risk. But I didn't have any choice. Neither of us
had any choice. There wasn't any other way I could get
the woman I loved back.

"Haskell knows Estobal's coming," I said. "It's a trap. He's going to shoot Estobal with our guns. Frame all of us for killing each other."

For a few seconds, she went still. Then, grimly, she whispered, "Roll over, Brew. Give me your wrists."

The command in her voice was familiar, like an old friend. That was the only consolation I had.

It wasn't easy—the alcohol had turned my guts into jelly and anguish—but I did it. I rolled over. I was shrieking inside, but I didn't let it out.

Almost immediately, her hand and the claw grappled at my forearms. With her hand, she felt her way to the tape. Then—fumbling because she hadn't exactly had a lot of practice—she pushed one hook of the claw between my wrists under the tape.

Down at the base, the edges of the hooks were like a pair of shears. Bunching the muscles of her left forearm to make her artificial hand open and close, she cut the tape.

It was rough. For a couple of seconds, I thought she was going to tear the tendons in my wrists. But it worked. My hands twisted loose.

With my arms free, I was able to shift positions without quite as much pain.

For a minute, I lay there gasping while my head spun and my chest hurt. Now was the time for me to be a hero. Everything up to now was just preparation. This was the hero's big chance to do his stuff. The crucial point was to leave Ginny's wrists strapped so she couldn't try to stop me. After that, the rest was simple. Creep downstairs into that maze Haskell used for a house. Spring his trap on him. Take the guns away—tie him up. Then come back upstairs in time to catch whoever el Señor sent to do his dirty work. Simple. Just like in the movies. Then Ginny would realize how much I loved her. She'd go all soft and feminine, and I'd be big and strong, and we'd live happily ever after.

Neat, huh?

I didn't try it. Instead, I levered myself around until I could reach her wrists. It was too dark to see anything, and I didn't have a knife on me, so I had to find the end of the tape by touch and peel it back with my fingernails. At first, I couldn't do it. There wasn't enough sensation left in my fingers. In the back of my mind, I thought I heard myself sobbing. But when I tried again more gently, I found the rough line at the end of the tape. Once I'd scratched the end loose enough to get a grip on it, the tape came off pretty easily.

"All right," she breathed. "All right." She sounded hard and ready, like a stick of dynamite with a lit fuse. She was crouching beside me, her feet under her, her arms braced. "Now we're in business.

"I'm going after that bastard. Wait for me in the atrium. You can watch my back. If you see or hear anything, throw something down the stairs. I'll know what to do."

Even though she couldn't see it, I nodded.

When she left, I didn't hear her go. The carpet muffled every sound. But I felt her moving away, evaporating into the dark. Soon the house swallowed her.

It was Haskell's house. He knew his way around it better than both of us put together. And he was armed. And he was expecting somebody to come after him. What chance did she have?

Bleeding quietly to myself, I got up onto my hands and knees. The pain in my stomach was at least as big as the room, and as it expanded my life got thinner and thinner. I was fading. Without light, I couldn't get my bearings. But then I made out a faint glow reflecting from the streetlamps through the open window. I crawled in that direction.

When I reached the window, I found a snowdrift inside the sill, melting into the carpet. Snow was piled nearly three inches deep on the sill. Snow seemed to flow into my face, cooling the sting of my scratches—offering to cool the hot damage in my guts. Ginny needed me. I propped my hands on the sill, got my legs under me, and tumbled out through the window.

The impact when I hit the ground turned everything to the soft, thick, falling blankness of snow.

I didn't know how long I lay there, cradled by the cold. Probably not very long. If a significant amount of time had passed, I would've been beyond reach, my mind and my blood both oozing out of me and no way to get them back. I wouldn't've been able to hear the horn.

A car horn. Two quick blasts.

Somebody was coming.

That was why I was out here. In case somebody came. To take them by surprise instead of being trapped in the house. Like Ginny.

Ginny.

All I had to do was make myself move again.

For a while, I thought I might actually pull it off. I couldn't stand at all—when I tried, my feet seemed to spread out through the snow, and my knees refused to straighten—but I could still crawl. A few inches at a time. I worked toward the front of the house.

But the snow accumulated in front of me. It fell on my back and weighed me down. It was soft and kind, and it wanted me to rest—and it was too heavy to refuse. The cold made my bleeding hurt less. I got as far as the corner. If I'd looked around it, I could've seen the cedars guarding the entryway and Haskell's Continental. But I didn't look. I couldn't go any farther. Whoever the horn had tried to warn me about was already in the house by now. There was nothing I could do about it. Some things you just have to forgive yourself for.

Lying on my face in the snow, I let everything get away.

For a while, I was asleep. It was a good feeling. All my problems were gone, and I could feel peace coming. It was right around the corner. Coming this way. The only time in my life I'd ever had any peace was when I was stone drunk. And that never lasted. It was amber and bliss for a while, the pure blessing of alcohol—and then it changed into something else. Maybe anger. Maybe grief. Maybe nightmares and the howling spook of the d.t.'s.

Or maybe voices.

Two men rasping at each other.

I recognized Rudolfo Santiago, hissing curses and pain. Then I made out the other voice.

Muy Estobal.

"Silence, *pendejo*," he snarled in Spanish, "or I will crush your arms. You sought to warn the house of my approach. Now you will make recompense. You will shield me from bullets, serving as hostage, or I swear by the Mother of God I will leave you with no bone intact."

"Butcher," Santiago muttered. "Son of a whore." But he was no match for Estobal. I could hear him failing.

It was worth one last try. I'd been given another chance. If I waited, I'd be too late. And Ginny would be caught. Come on. Just once more.

I got my head up. I got my arms under me. I got my weight onto my legs.

Lumbering drunkenly, I rounded the corner and headed for the aisle of the entryway. The snow covered me. It was good as stealth. I didn't make a noise.

Past the cedar, I almost fell. But a few steps down the aisle, I crashed into Estobal from behind.

That saved me.

My momentum carried us a few more steps. He lost his grip on Santiago. My arms wrapped around him.

He spat a curse. When he got his balance, he tried to twist away from me.

I didn't have any strength like his. But I caught my right forearm under his chin and hung on.

His hands clawed at my arm. He yanked me from side to side as if I didn't weigh anything. Heaving himself backward, he slammed me against the wall. All his bulk seemed to sledgehammer my torn guts. As if he thought he could make me let him go kill Ginny.

Noises like shots went off in the distance.

I gripped my right wrist with my left hand so I could pull with both arms. My forearm ground into his throat. I held on.

Santiago crowded into the struggle. He was too close. He was going to get hurt.

A second later, he reeled away like he'd been kicked. He had Estobal's .38.

Estobal battered me around in the aisle like a ragdoll. Must've been an entertaining sight—Axbrewder being flapped in the breeze like so much wet laundry. With a little advance notice, you could've sold tickets. But I didn't feel any of it except the one sharp, absolute scream where my stomach used to be. And as long as that scream lasted I held on.

I didn't hear his larynx break. Sometime later, we lay down together on the cement. I didn't notice much difference. But when the light came on in the aisle, it snagged what was left of my mind. I turned my head in time to see the front door jerk open and Ginny appear, her .357 ready in her fist.

Quickly, she scanned the aisle. Seeing Santiago surprised her, but she didn't falter. As soon as he lowered the gun he was holding, she pointed her claw at Estobal. "Is he alone?" she demanded. "I've taken care of Haskell." The lines of her face were whetted, and her eyes burned with an alert, gray fire. "He's dead."

"Good for you," I croaked while I started to pass out. "Help me. I'm bleeding to death."

Chapter Twenty-one

Not being exactly what you might call on top of things at the time, I didn't get to see how the rest of the night turned out. But I heard about it later. Captain Cason showed up with about six squad cars and made a big deal out of storming the house. When he found there wasn't anybody left to shoot at, much less arrest, he tried to give Ginny bloody hell for ruining his case against el Señor. (That was why he let Haskell go— he said. To bait a trap. He wanted to catch Estobal in the act of trying to kill Haskell. I say he and his troops showed up a little late to be very convincing.) So she took his hide off for him in front of all his men. (She didn't tell me that part—Santiago did.) After that, the ambulance arrived.

At least now I didn't have to worry about el Señor sending anybody after me—not for a while. True, I'd killed his bodyguard. But there were too many cops involved now. And he was going to be too busy being hassled about why somebody who worked for him was so busy trying to shoot people. I might be safe for quite a while.

Three or four days later, I was conscious again. Another miracle of modern medicine. It's amazing what transfusions and antibiotics—not to mention a decent amount of sleep—can do for you. During visiting hours, Ginny and I got our first good look at each other in quite a while.

She stood beside my bed looking like she'd put on her best clothes just for me. There was a sheen to her hair, and she was wearing exactly the right amount of makeup. The only thing that kept her from being beautiful was the uncertainty in her eyes. Her broken nose didn't count. I always liked her nose. And her claw didn't bother me. It was necessary—nothing worse than that.

Feeling unshaven and grungy—the baths they give you in hospital beds aren't ever the same as being clean—I smiled up at her as well as I could. "Hi," I said. Another conversational masterstroke. My pleasure at seeing her was genuine. I just wasn't any more sure of myself than she was.

She gave me back a crooked smile. "Hi, yourself." Then she nodded at my IVs. "They wanted to tie you in bed this time. But I told them not to bother. Nobody pulls a stunt like that twice.

"On the other hand"—she shrugged, grimacing wryly—"most people don't even do it once. I wish I knew what in hell possessed you to be such a hero."

That was indirectly what she was uncertain about. She didn't want to come right out and say what worried her (that made sense to me—I was in the same position), so she was trying to sneak up on it.

I wasn't having any. Maybe I was still muzzy-headed with drugs and convalescence, but I knew better than to fall into the trap. "Me?" I protested, taking a stab at humorous sarcasm. "You're the one who had that talk with el Señor. When I tried that, it almost killed me. And you're the one who went after Haskell—in that house, in the dark, without even a gun." (Later, I got her to tell me how she did it. She made it sound simple. She went downstairs as quietly as she could, but when she got to the kitchen she made just enough noise to help him find her. Then she opened the refrigerator, helped herself to a carton of milk, and hid behind one of the counters, using the fridge light to watch the room. When Haskell finally came to investigate, she hit him in the face with the milk. That didn't keep him from shooting, but it unbalanced him enough to let her get close. Then she punched his throat out with her claw.) "You've got some nerve, accusing *me* of being a hero."

She smiled a little. But she wasn't deflected. "I mean it, Brew. I want to know. Why did you do it?"

She was dangerously close to what she really wanted from me. That made me nervous. On the other hand, it was an opportunity for me, too. "I'll trade you," I said with as much nonchalance as I had available. "You tell me why you finally decided to start using your claw."

Well, she was no dummy. It was funny the way we danced around each other, when both of us knew exactly what was going on and refused to say it. But it had to be that way. After a fashion, we were protecting each other.

She nodded, accepting the trade. "Talking to el Señor did it to me. I felt so helpless. You've been there—you know what he's like. I wasn't in the same league at all.

"But that changed the way I thought about"—she glanced down at her artificial hand—"about things. Until then, all I felt was that one hand and a claw was too much less than two hands. I was too crippled. But then I realized that a hand and a claw is still a hell of a lot more than a hand and a stump. And I needed all the help I could get."

That way, she avoided saying what she didn't want me to hear. *I did it for you.* As long as she didn't say it, I couldn't be sure it was true.

And as long as I could think she did it for herself, accepted the claw because she was willing to live with it, I had reason to hope.

So I said, "Mostly I think I was feeling useless. I wanted to work on Pablo's murder for myself to prove I was good for something. But I wasn't getting anywhere. I had to talk to the people who might know why he was killed, and that was my only chance. If I waited until I healed, the case'd be closed—or cold.

"Santiago must've told you the rest. When I found out Haskell killed Pablo, I had to go looking for evidence."

"He told me," she agreed. "Knowing you, it even makes a weird kind of sense. But after you'd done all that—after I finally got there, and we were free, and you didn't have to worry about it anymore—Brew, what in God's name made you think it was suddenly a good idea to climb out the window? You might've hemorrhaged to death out there in the snow."

I shook my head. "It's my turn." I was almost alert enough to enjoy what I was doing. "First you tell me what in God's name made you think it was suddenly a good idea to go after Haskell when you didn't even have a gun. You didn't have to do that. We could've both climbed out the window."

She let out a snort of disgust. "It wasn't a good idea. I was just too mad to do anything else. That bastard lied and lied to us until I couldn't stand to think he might get away with it. If I'd had any sense, I would've called the cops and let them handle it."

I wanted to applaud. This was getting to be fun. "You worry me, Fistoulari. Next to you, I'm a model of logic and sweet reason. Jumping out the window was the best idea I had all night. Haskell felt sure Estobal—or somebody—was coming after him, so I figured I could count on it. But as long as Estobal had the initiative—as long as he could come into the house whenever he wanted, however he wanted—I was a goner. My only chance was to get behind him."

It was working. The anxiety in her eyes was starting to fade. I hardly missed a beat. "Speaking of Rudolfo Santiago," I went on, cheerfully changing the subject, "what do you hear from him? How are he and Tatianna doing?"

That made her frown a little. She wasn't satisfied with my answers. But I put an I'm-an-invalid-you-ought-to-humor-me look on my face, and she relented. "I went to see them yesterday. They're still grieving, but I don't think it's as bitter for them as it used to be. He's secretly proud of himself. He believes he saved your life by taking Estobal's gun. And I got the impression she's relieved that it was an outsider who killed her son, an Anglo, not someone who's part of her community. All Anglos are crazy. That makes her feel better."

"Good." Since I couldn't get out of bed anyway, I was grateful for everything I didn't have to worry about. "I presume Canthorpe's off the hook?"

She nodded.

Good again. "I'd be surprised if there was anything we could do for Eunice Wint. What about Sara Haskell?"

Her frown narrowed into a black scowl. But it was a special scowl, one I fell in love with years ago. It said, I'm Ginny by God Fistoulari, and I'll be damned if I'm going to laugh at this. Her voice hard with control, she said, "I just got the papers this morning. Mrs. Reg Haskell is suing us for 'wrongful death.' She thinks we used excessive force on her husband. Also we were incompetent. My license is suspended until the board can schedule a hearing."

I would've laughed for her, but my stomach still hurt too much. "How long is that going to be?" We were safe on this one. Our board members get pretty snooty sometimes, but when they heard the evidence they were going to politely throw Mrs. Haskell's case out the window.

She shrugged. "Ten days. Maybe two weeks."

"That's okay. A little vacation won't hurt you. Besides, it'll be that long before I'm allowed on my feet again. You wouldn't want to do any work without me."

"Brew." I was doing my best, but she refused to give up what she wanted to ask. "Why did we take that case? What made it so important? What did we go through all that for?"

It was the same question she'd been asking all along. And she wanted an honest answer. But I didn't let the earnest gray of her gaze lure me into a mistake. Distinctly, I said, "Haskell wanted protection against el Señor. That time I went to see el Señor, I was desperate. And it wouldn't have cost him anything to help me. But he didn't. I knew this case was dangerous, Ginny. I just wanted revenge."

She understood. Both sides of it—what I said, and what I didn't. It seemed to make her face soft and sad and relieved all at the same time. "You know something, Axbrewder?" she murmured. "Sometimes you're almost a nice man."

Bending down, she rested a gentle kiss on my forehead.

My guts still hurt, and I had IVs plugged into both elbows, but I didn't care. I put my arms around her and welcomed her back.

ABOUT THE AUTHOR

Reed Stephens is a retired policeman who teaches "The Mystery Novel as Literature" and "Sociology of Crime" at Rocky Mountain University in Farmington, N.M. As a hobby, he studies the fantasy fiction of Tolkien and Donaldson. His true avocation, however, is bridge. He lives with his wife and young son in the Jemez Mountains, just outside of Farmington.

Attention Mystery and Suspense Fans

Do you want to complete your collection of mystery and suspense stories by some of your favorite authors? John D. MacDonald, Helen MacInnes, Dick Francis, Amanda Cross, Ruth Rendell, Alistar MacLean, Erle Stanley Gardner, Cornell Woolrich, among many others, are included in Ballantine/Fawcett's new Mystery Brochure.

For your FREE Mystery Brochure, fill in the coupon below and mail it to: